PREDATOR

STOPE PACKS
BOOK FOUR

REBECCA ZANETTI

To those who run with the wild heart of a wolf, who feel the pull of the moon, and who never back down from a fight.

To the ones who believe in fate, in pack bonds stronger than blood, and in love that howls through the night.

This book is for you.

May your instincts stay sharp, your loyalty unshaken, and your spirit forever untamed.

Current status of the Stope Packs coalition as of the beginning of this book

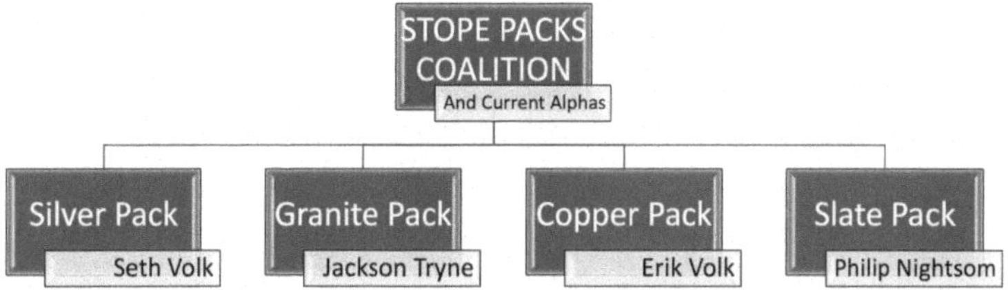

The Stope Packs coalition contracted years ago to protect each other against outside threats, although it's an uneasy alliance.

**A Stope is a dugout or tunnel in a mine.

CHAPTER 1

Her nerves jangling like a skeleton caught in a tumble dryer on high spin, Emily Nightsom clasped her hands in her lap and rocked on the rear veranda of the mansion, her chin up and no expression on her face. Anybody looking at her would see perfect composure and dignity. But anyone who truly sensed her energy would feel an eerie, skin-crawling unease. Thank goodness nobody had ever been on her wavelength.

Well, mostly nobody. Jackson Tryne didn't count. Ever.

Gentle lights shone down from chandeliers, edging out the darkness of night. The moon had risen, though only at half strength—which somewhat explained the weakness in her knees.

A storm edged closer, with thunder rolling across the sky. Lightning struck nearby with a crackle, and the smell of ozone filled the air. Then the skies opened, instantly releasing rain in sheets, filling the night with the scents of pine and fresh earth.

Sitting safely beneath the veranda's solid roof, Emily heard vehicles pull up in front of the home and looked toward the table laden with cold cuts, rolls, and cookies. Lovely etched glasses surrounded a full water pitcher, while wine bottles breathed to the side, stemmed glasses nearby. Swallowing, she stood and turned toward the double glass door, her mouth parchment-dry.

Her father emerged first, his gaze on the table and approval tilting his lips.

Well, at least she'd done something right. "Father."

"Hi, Honey." Philip Nightsom's smile and eyes were too wide. Shock?

"Where is she?" Emily angled her neck to see beyond him.

He straightened, and she took in his dashing gray suit and striped, green tie. For as long as she could remember, he'd always kept a three-piece suit in his town car in case he needed clothing. "She wouldn't, ah, ride with me."

Amusement surprised Emily as the sensation ran through her. "That's interesting."

He frowned and moved toward the table, pouring a glass of cabernet. "You might want to steel yourself."

"Why?"

The door opened again, and Miliki, her father's top Enforcer, strode out. At over a hundred years old, he had silver hair and sharp, brown eyes. "Miss Nightsom? I'd like for you to meet Nadia Hodge. Your, ah, half-sister." He stepped to the side, revealing a female.

Emily swallowed a gasp.

A female walked forward, her eyes a lighter black than Emily's. They both had platinum-blond hair and fine features.

"Hi." The female spoke first, her gaze on the wild storm beyond the veranda.

"Welcome to our home." Emily searched her sister's face for something. Anything. Man, they looked alike.

Nadia glanced at Emily's boot-covered feet and then her head. "Well. Guess you got all the height."

Amusement took over again. "Guess so." While Em was

around six feet tall, Nadia had to be…what? Five-foot-six, tops? "And you have a dimple in your left cheek. I don't."

Her father took a deep gulp of wine. "You both look just like my mother. It's fascinating, really."

The poor guy sounded like he was still in shock. Probably was, considering he'd discovered he had another daughter just a few hours ago.

Nadia slowly grinned. "You're truly beautiful, Emily."

Emily chuckled. "That's funny, considering we could be twins—minus the height difference."

"No." Nadia shook her head, her focus intense. "It's more than that. There's something about you. Beyond the bone structure and all of that. Real beauty."

"What a kind thing to say," Emily said smoothly.

Nadia snorted. "Kind isn't exactly one of my character traits. Telling the truth…is."

Likable. Her newly found sister was eminently likable. This might work out, after all.

A male strode through the door, his dark gaze taking in the entire veranda before he moved to the side, posting himself near Nadia in a position that ensured he could intercept anybody before they reached her. He stood to well over six feet tall and appeared muscled and strong.

Both Miliki and her father bristled.

"You brought your own Enforcer?" Emily asked. Or was there more to it?

Nadia nodded. "This is Caidrik. Our new, um, Alpha assigned him to my protection detail while I visited your territory."

Emily's eyebrow rose. Caidrik had some power. She could feel it. Was he an Alpha? Something was off here. "Your new Alpha? You mean Erik Volk?"

Nadia shifted her weight. She looked adorable in jeans and a pink sweater, with her blond hair up in a ponytail. "Yes. Erik

Volk. Our co-op joined the Copper Pack earlier today. We need farming land, and they need wolves. It worked out." She scrunched up her nose. "Although I'm not sure about having an Alpha, you know? My people have stayed out of wolf pack business."

Caidrik looked from Nadia to Emily and back, promised death with a hint of intrigue in his eyes. "Which is why we were almost taken out by a rogue pack. We'll be safer as members of the Copper Pack." He focused on Emily. "It's my understanding that you were engaged to Erik Volk, who is now mated to somebody else. Has that created bad blood?"

Miliki growled low.

Emily smiled, her shoulders relaxing. Apparently, her sister's guard dog had done his research. "Not in the slightest. I called off the engagement. Erik and I are good friends, and I adore Luna, his new mate. The Slate Pack and the Copper Pack are allies within the Stope Packs Coalition. Your people will be much safer now." Her legs trembled, so she turned toward the table to mask the weakness. "May I get you something to eat or drink? The wine is excellent."

Nadia's gaze narrowed. "I'd love wine. Thank you."

Had she seen the tremor? If so, it was kind of her to refrain from mentioning it. Or perhaps she was categorizing weaknesses to use against them later. "Caidrik?" Emily asked, pouring a glass of cabernet for her sister.

"No." At Nadia's quick look, he cleared his throat. "No, thank you," he said, his voice a low growl.

Emily handed Nadia the wineglass.

Their father finished his drink and then cleared his throat. "I didn't know that you existed until a few hours ago, Nadia."

"I know." Nadia sipped her wine. "By the time my mother realized she was pregnant, you had already mated Emily's mom. She chose not to tell you."

The female didn't sound like she cared much. "Where is your mother now?" Emily poured herself a glass of water.

"She passed away five years ago," Nadia said quietly.

Emily looked at her sister. "I'm sorry. My mother passed away, as well."

Nadia grimaced. "My mom had a very common wolf name, one that carries through all of the packs, so I often have folks say that they know her. But we pretty much kept to ourselves and our small co-op my entire life."

A clamor echoed from inside the house, and Emily sighed right before her cousin, Vic, strode outside. "Nadia, this is your cousin, Victor."

Vic looked from Emily to Nadia and then to Philip. "So, it's true? You have a bastard daughter?"

Caidrik launched from his post, and Nadia pivoted, putting her body between them.

Emily drew up to her full height. "You call my sister a name like that again, and you and I are hitting the grass, Vic. Last time we wrestled, you ended up crying for an hour." Of course, she'd been stronger then. Much. They'd been kids, really.

He whirled on her. "Oh, I'd like another chance at you, little girl."

Nadia shifted, somehow landing next to Emily. "I'd love to see you kick his ass, Emily."

Emily smiled, willing her left leg to stop trembling. The weakness was increasing, damn it. She couldn't even kick her *own* ass. "Father?"

Philip put down his glass. "Yes. I was stunned for a moment." He flashed his canines. "Victor? You might be my nephew, but Nadia is my daughter. You will treat her with respect. Understand?" Alpha power vibrated in his voice.

"Of course." Victor stood as tall as Caidrik, with green eyes and dark blond hair. The guy always wore gold: watch, necklace, even pinky ring. "I apologize, Nadia. This is just a…shock."

He rolled his neck. "I've been stressed lately, training to step in as the Alpha of this pack if and when it becomes necessary." He edged to the side, keeping Caidrik in his line of sight.

So, he *did* recognize the biggest threat—probably instinctively, because Vic rarely thought things out.

Nadia glanced sideways at Emily. "Why aren't you training to be the Alpha?"

Vic snorted. "Seriously? She's a female."

That was nowhere near why. If Emily wasn't dying, she'd take over as Alpha in an instant...until somebody good came along. She didn't want the position but couldn't let Vic take control. He lacked insight. "Nadia? Do you want the job?"

"God, no." Nadia took another drink of her wine.

Probably a good thing. While Nadia had Alpha blood, she wasn't big enough to fight off challengers. Emily had the size but not the strength—a fact she'd managed to hide from everyone. Her illness was getting worse, and she had to do something about it before Vic took over. Thank goodness her father was strong and healthy, even at his advanced age.

Nadia's chin lifted. "However, I do think a female could be the Alpha."

Philip sighed. "Maybe theoretically, but the challenges would come often, and she'd need to fight well." He paled. "Not that Emily can't fight, but her heart isn't in it, so..."

Emily cleared her throat. "I'll step up if needed, Father." Of course, she needed to be in top health, damn it.

Vic looked them both over. "We're fourth or fifth cousins, you know."

Nadia flicked her gaze to Emily. "So?"

Vic ignored her and faced Philip. "I understand you've promised Emily to Jackson Tryne. I'd like for you to reconsider."

Fire ripped through Emily, banishing the tremble. "Wait a minute—"

"Promised?" Nadia's voice rose, and she actually stepped in

front of Emily this time. "You've *promised* her to somebody?" Even her ponytail twitched in anger.

Emily easily stared at her father over Nadia's head. "No. Listen, little sister—"

"Big sister," Nadia corrected, placing her wine glass on the table. She put her hands on her hips. "I'm a year older than you. That makes me the *big* sister, and there's no way on this round ball of a planet I'm letting my little sister be promised to the Alpha of the damn Granite Pack."

Emily cocked her head. Her very petite sister had just called her the little sister. How adorable. "You've heard of Jackson?"

"Everybody has heard of him," Nadia said, her back visibly vibrating. "He's brutal in a fight."

Every Alpha was brutal in a fight. "He's not that scary," Emily said. "And don't worry, I'm not promised to anybody."

Philip poured more wine into his glass. "Actually, we could use the connection to his pack, Emily. That strength would be helpful since the Volk brothers now lead the other two packs in the coalition."

She understood his position. Their coalition was named after a stope—a tunnel in a mine—an apt moniker, as the four packs mined slate, granite, copper, and silver. With the Silver and Copper Packs now being ruled by blood brothers, it left her father feeling uneasy.

Even so, she shook her head. "I am not mating Jackson Tryne." She wouldn't mate for convenience, and besides, couldn't with her current illness—it wouldn't be fair to Jackson. She should probably tell her father the truth about how physically weak she felt, but she didn't want to worry him.

"What about me?" Vic puffed out his muscular chest.

Emily's mouth gaped, but she quickly pressed her lips together. "You want to mate Jackson?" she drawled.

Victor's face flushed red. "Funny, but no. I want one of you."

Nadia's head bobbed as if her chin had hit her chest.

Emily winced. "We're cousins, Vic. Don't be ridiculous."

Victor continued staring at Philip. "It would consolidate power, and we're all very distant relatives."

Nadia's ponytail jerked again. "Geez, Vic. Would you like to flip a coin for us?"

Sarcasm sounded good coming from the female. Emily sighed. "This is the dumbest conversation I've ever witnessed. The answer is no, Victor. Neither of us wants to mate you, so stop it. Right now."

He moved toward her, and Caidrik growled low. Lightning zapped near the tree line.

Vic stopped.

This was weird. "*Nobody* is getting mated, so everyone just calm the hell down," Emily said before any blows could land.

"Now, that just hurts my feelings." Jackson Tryne emerged from the darkness, the moon caressing his rock-hard form. The rain sluiced off him, molding his worn T-shirt to his impressive chest.

Emily stiffened, her body electrifying as her gaze slashed to her father's. While it didn't surprise her that she hadn't smelled him, as the Alpha, Philip should've known the second he entered their territory. Was Jackson that good at masking his scent and energy? Even with the help of the storm, somebody should've sensed the presence of an Alpha wolf. They emitted their own vibrations.

The Alpha strode across the back lawn and into the chandelier's light, his luminous blue eyes predatory. He glanced at Nadia and then back at Emily. "I heard the rumors. Appears true."

Victor moved closer to the table, his gaze hard. "Tell you what, Tryne, you can have the new sister. Nadia is all yours."

It was like he *wanted* Caidrik to rip out his throat.

Nadia bunched as if ready to attack, so Emily grasped her arm. "Take it easy, *big* sister." While Vic had no tact, the guy could fight. Emily doubted her new sister would stand a chance against him. "Nobody is going anywhere."

Jackson tucked his thumbs into the pockets of his ripped jeans, water dripping from his thick, black hair. "That's where you're wrong, baby. I'm done waiting."

Vic bristled. "Why are you fucking here, Jackson?"

Those blue eyes landed on Emily with a force stronger than the current storm. "I'm here for what's mine."

CHAPTER 2

Jackson hated that he had run into Slate territory the second he found out Emily might be in danger. His pack, the Granite Pack, held territory far north of this Slate Pack. But he had to make sure Emily was safe.

A quick glance at the smaller version of her clarified that if there *was* danger, it was *not* coming from this newfound sister. Jackson slowly lifted his gaze to the silent male standing close to the females. "Caidrik," he said.

"Jackson," Caidrik returned.

Emily glanced from one to the other, paling. "You two know each other?"

"No," they both said.

Jackson set his stance.

Emily's gaze narrowed. "Well, that's a lie."

"No shit," the female in front of her said.

"I'm Jackson," he murmured.

The female's eyes were a shade lighter than Emily's, framed by long lashes that gave her an ethereal look. Despite the delicate features, there was a sharpness in her gaze. "I'm Nadia. I know who you are."

"Good." Jackson tilted his head slightly. It was sometimes helpful when his reputation preceded him. Sometimes, it wasn't. Most people thought he was a party animal, when they truly had no idea how he spent his days. Or nights.

Philip Nightsom's gaze shifted between them. "Jackson, can I offer you a glass of wine?"

"I'd rather have a beer," Jackson murmured, his voice low as he took another step closer to Emily, feeling Caidrik's eyes tracking his every move.

Caidrik's shoulders went back, his muscles tensing subtly beneath his shirt.

"You're working for the Slate Pack now?" Jackson drawled, his focus narrowing.

"No," the Enforcer replied shortly. Caidrik was always a wolf of few words—a trait Jackson had appreciated in the past.

Emily's black eyes flashed with curiosity. "How do you two know each other?"

"We worked together once, but we don't really know each other," Jackson replied, although the truth was more complex. Now wasn't the time to go into any of that.

"Doing what?" Nadia asked, her curiosity obvious.

"Nothing," Jackson and Caidrik said in unison.

Philip moved to the barbecue area, where a small fridge sat tucked beneath the counter. The scent of grilled meat lingered in the air as he opened the fridge and pulled out a beer bottle. "Anybody else?" he asked, glancing around.

No one answered. Philip returned and handed the bottle to Jackson. The glass felt cool against Jackson's hand as he twisted off the top with a practiced motion. He took a long drink, the bitter tang of the beer grounding him.

"With the Copper Pack and the Silver Pack now solidly aligned, considering their Alphas are brothers, our packs need to create a similar alliance." Jackson shifted his gaze to Philip. "As you know, the Alpha of the Silver Pack is a distant cousin of mine, so I figured that might motivate you." The words hung between them, heavy with implication. He still hadn't decided whether Seth was an ally or an enemy, but blood ties often tipped the scales.

Philip nodded slowly. "I understand we need a stronger alliance." His expression hardened as if he were weighing the invisible pressures.

Victor stepped forward, his broader frame more imposing than Jackson remembered. The guy had clearly been hitting the gym. Hard. Gold winked from a pendant on his chest. "We would like to propose a new agreement."

Philip's eyes flashed with something unreadable. The tension in the air thickened.

Jackson didn't wait for Victor to say more. "You're not the Alpha here, Vic, and I doubt you ever will be. Why don't you go do something else? This is a meeting between Alphas." His tone left no room for argument, and he doubted Vic knew how desperate his pack was for access to the Embervault Mine. He had found veins of rare slate deep in its depths, the nature of which would take the Slate Pack out of the red.

Did Emily even know her pack needed money?

Vic's chin lowered. There was no doubt he had some Alpha blood in him, but Jackson didn't have time for this nonsense. The guy's eyes grew calculating. "I'm not kidding, Jackson. You can't have Emily. However, it appears we have an alternative."

Emily's mini-me gasped. "Listen, you fucktard—"

Jackson burst out laughing and caught a quick flash of amusement in Emily's eyes. "I like your sister," he drawled.

She tilted her head. "I like her, too."

Nadia frowned and blinked several times. Apparently, their approval wasn't something she had expected. "You all have to get rid of archaic customs, and I mean right now."

Emily placed a graceful hand on her sister's shoulder. "I could not agree more. Let's talk about this rationally."

Rational wasn't something Jackson felt in Emily's presence. He crossed his arms, still ready to attack or defend if necessary. "Philip, we came to an agreement."

Emily whirled, giving him her full attention. "I'm not something to be bartered, Jackson."

"I couldn't agree more." He wondered if her father had told her the full truth. "However, considering you were kidnapped months ago and the culprits still haven't been found and killed, you're not being properly protected here. As my future mate, that is unacceptable to me."

Victor stepped forward again, eyes hard with determination. "You can't seriously be considering this. Emily doesn't need—"

"Enough, Victor." Philip's voice cut through the air like a whip. "This is a conversation for Alphas, not you. Leave. Now."

Victor's jaw clenched, his hands tightening into fists at his sides, but Philip didn't waver. After a tense pause, Vic spun on his heel and stormed off, his footsteps heavy as he disappeared into the house. The front door soon slammed.

Emily watched him go.

Jackson shifted his stance, drawing her gaze back to him.

She lowered her chin and straightened her posture. "I am not your future mate." Her voice trembled with fury.

Jackson's breath hitched. God, she was glorious. She was truly the most gorgeous female he had ever seen in his entire life—probably the most stunning to ever exist, with her light-blond hair and black eyes. She was an avenging goddess. One he'd wanted for years. But it wasn't just her beauty. They had a connection that scared her and intrigued him. He wondered if she'd be brave enough to admit it. "Your father offered a mating, and I accepted."

Instead, her lips twisted into an almost sneer—she was too pretty to truly sneer. "We had one kiss when we were teenagers. You can't seriously consider that created anything between us."

It had been the best kiss of his life, and undoubtedly, hers, too. Yeah, they'd been fifteen, down by a river with a bunch of shifters, and he hadn't called her afterward. But he couldn't. His pack had fallen apart when his father died, leaving him to take over as Alpha far too young. "I wouldn't mind seeing how you kiss as an adult, sweetheart."

Pink bloomed across her high cheekbones. Satisfaction warmed him. He'd put color in her face. She'd been too pale for his liking when he arrived. No doubt from shock upon discovering the existence of her new sister. Still, Emily had always made it clear she didn't want to step up as the Alpha of her pack. Jackson needed a mate—more than Emily realized. So, what was the problem? Besides Victor.

Philip Nightsom sighed, scrubbing a hand down his face. "Jackson, I rescind the offer. Emily has decided to step up as Alpha of the Slate Pack when I decide to retire in about a century."

The guy didn't have a century. Jackson cocked his head, staring at the stunning blonde. "You've changed your mind?"

"I have," she said, meeting his gaze directly. "Duty binds us all, Jackson."

He smelled just a hint of lemon. Was she lying? If so, she was good at it. "I could enforce the agreement. We had it, and you know it."

"No," burst out of both Emily and Nadia at the same time.

Jackson smiled. Together, they were fricking adorable. The height difference made them even cuter.

Suddenly, the wind shifted. The hair on the back of Jackson's neck rose. In unison with Caidrik, he turned toward the opposite tree line as they both caught a scent.

Philip's head jerked up.

A crash exploded from the front of the mansion, and wolves barreled through the home and onto the veranda, glass shattering in every direction. More wolves bounded out of the forest. The storm had masked their scent, and they'd arrived from downwind.

"Fuck." Jackson shifted instantly, muscles bunching into his wolf form as he leapt into the air toward the threat. The Ravencall Pack. He could smell them. Emily shifted beside him, her silver-blond coat gleaming, even in the rain. The others shifted behind them.

Jackson reached the leader first and collided with him, teeth and claws tearing into flesh. Fury flowed through his veins. Blood splashed his muzzle, and the tang of copper filled his senses.

Caidrik ripped through two wolves on Jackson's left, jaws clamping down on their throats until they crunched. Philip lunged past them with his Enforcer on his heels, slamming into another attacker. The Enforcer snapped bones with brutal efficiency.

Emily fought beside them, swift and agile, her smooth coat flashing through the chaos. Nadia moved in tandem with her sister, fighting hard with no true tactics. Had the female never been trained? Caidrik stayed close to Nadia, guarding her flank with lethal precision.

The storm lashed around them, rain blurring the battlefield and turning it slick with mud and blood. Jackson locked jaws with another wolf, rolling and biting until the enemy went limp. Snarls and yelps echoed in the air as the fight raged on.

Emily took down a light gray wolf with a swift bite to its throat, then spun to help Nadia, who had two wolves circling her. Emily lunged, teeth flashing white in the dark, and dragged one of the wolves down, her claws raking its side.

Then Emily slowed. Her movements became less fluid, more sluggish. A wolf clipped her, and she stumbled, just enough to let another attacker slash her flank.

Jackson's wolf roared in fury.

She bared her teeth at the next enemy. Nadia leapt to her

sister's defense, biting and clawing until the wolf fled into the forest. Caidrik closed ranks beside Nadia, the massive black wolf tearing into another attacker as two more barreled out of the woods, aiming toward the sisters.

Jackson finished off the last of his opponents and charged toward Emily. The scent of her blood hit him like a punch to the chest. He lunged at the wolf attacking her, jaws locking around its throat as they crashed into the mud. The creature twisted and snarled, but Jackson clamped down harder, bones cracking between his teeth until it stilled.

He paused and looked around.

Fifteen wolves lay dead or dying in the rain-soaked clearing. The air reeked of blood, wet fur, and ozone.

He shifted back to human form, chest aching as he rushed to Emily's side. His hands found her shoulders as she shifted back, collapsing against him—pale, bleeding, and nude. Blood streaked her skin, the gashes along her ribs deeper than they should've been. Although the wounds did begin to heal in front of his eyes.

"Emily, what the hell happened? You shouldn't have taken those hits." His voice went hoarse.

"I—I don't know," she whispered, her eyes fluttering. "Didn't see him coming."

Nadia knelt beside them, breathless but unhurt. "She was fine at first. Fighting better than I've seen any female fight. But then she just slowed down."

Jackson scanned the clearing as rain dripped from his hair. Something felt wrong. Emily, strong and trained, shouldn't have faltered like that.

Philip stepped forward, wiping blood from his face. "Miliki? Call for reinforcements, and I want the entire territory searched for trespassers. Give the order to kill on sight."

"Got it." The Enforcer jogged through the rain and up the

porch steps, his bare feet kicking glass aside as he moved inside the demolished doorway.

Philip looked at his daughter. "We need to get her inside. Now."

Caidrik shifted back, standing silent and watchful as the rain continued to fall, soaking the battlefield of broken bodies and blood-soaked mud. "The one near the north tree line is still alive. I'll ask him a few questions." He looked down at Nadia. "Go inside and take care of your sister."

Jackson lifted Emily and turned toward the house, ignoring the wounds along his flanks and the glass cutting into the bottoms of his feet. He partially ducked to cover her from the rain, his mind absolutely spinning.

What was wrong with her?

CHAPTER 3

Emily protested with a strained breath. "I'm fine." Jackson carried her up the stairs to her bedroom. How did he know where it was? His grip was firm yet careful, the warmth of his bare chest pressing against her bruised arm sending tingles of awareness through her. At least the gashes in her side had almost healed.

Behind them, Nadia followed quickly, her footsteps light but hurried. "Are you all right? I didn't see you go down. I'm so sorry. I should've covered your six." Her voice sounded tight with guilt.

"My six was fine." Emily tried to keep her voice steady.

Jackson's breath warmed her temple as he spoke. "You must still be off from the kidnapping months ago. That kind of trauma can take a while to handle."

"I must be," she agreed quickly, wanting him off the subject.

His steps slowed slightly as if he considered her words, but he didn't respond. He carried her into her bedroom, his stride purposeful when he laid her on the bed as if staking a claim.

Nadia hurried behind them and grabbed the throw blanket from the foot of the bed to drape over her sister.

"There are clothes in the closet," Emily mumbled.

"Thanks," Nadia said, rushing inside. She returned moments later, pulling a T-shirt over her head and hopping into leggings that were capris on Emily but fell to the tops of Nadia's feet.

"You need clothing." Philip had already yanked on pressed pants and stepped inside to toss Jackson a pair of slacks.

Jackson caught them, frowning but gracefully stepping into them. The pants were too loose and stopped awkwardly above his ankles. Emily coughed out a laugh despite the ache in her ribs.

"This isn't funny," Jackson growled. "You're not safe here." He turned to face Philip, who stood in the doorway, arms crossed over his bare chest.

Irritation clocked through Emily. "I'm absolutely fine." The slight hoarseness in her voice belied her words.

"She's a good fighter," Philip snapped.

"What the fuck's going on here?" Jackson snapped. "Your daughter gets kidnapped mere months ago, and now the Ravencall Pack attacks you? They had no idea I'd be here. They came from downwind. I didn't smell or hear them." His eyes darkened with something lethal. "Who sent them?"

"The attacker died before I could question him." Caidrik stepped into the room, still naked with blood smeared across his chin and chest.

"Damn it, put on some pants," Philip muttered, storming into the hallway.

Emily kept her gaze resolutely trained above Caidrik's chest, but yeah, she'd snuck a peek at Jackson's strong body before he pulled on the ridiculous pants. The rumors were true. The Alpha was built...well.

Wolves were accustomed to nudity since shifting shredded their clothes, but there were limits. Philip returned with another pair of pants and tossed them to Caidrik. The male caught them with an easy motion, his blood-streaked chest still rising and falling from the aftermath of the fight.

"You should reach out to the new Alpha of the Ravencall Pack." Caidrik pulled on the pants, the fabric sticking to spots where blood had dried. "Either he sent these attackers, or they went rogue on their own."

Jackson wiped blood off his cheek. "Perhaps the pack isn't aligning with their new Alpha, although I understand why Erik Volk took out the previous one. I thought the pack just wanted to harvest and sell herbs and crap now?"

"I'll call the new Alpha," Philip replied grimly. "At the very least, they can come and collect their dead."

A tremble started in Emily's ankles, climbing up her legs like an icy current. The adrenaline crash was hitting hard. She gripped the blanket tighter, hoping no one noticed how her hands shook.

"Everybody needs to leave." Jackson's voice cut through the air like a whip. "Emily and I have to talk."

Caidrik hesitated, his sharp gaze sweeping over Emily as if assessing her condition. "Nadia? I'll be outside." Then, with a brief nod to Jackson, he headed out the door.

"We're leaving." Philip cut off Nadia's protest.

Emily twisted a loose thread from the blanket around her fingers. "Please set her up in the west wing. We'll talk later," she said to Nadia. "Sister to sister."

Nadia lingered for a moment longer. Her eyes met Emily's, and something unspoken passed between them. A flicker of concern? Loyalty, maybe? But when Jackson's gaze shifted toward her, she huffed a breath and marched after her bodyguard.

Something unfamiliar and warm bloomed inside Emily. This female, her sister, had tried to protect her. That mattered. It stirred something deeper than obligation within her. Maybe having a sibling wouldn't be so bad after all.

Jackson's lips twitched as Nadia disappeared, amusement dancing in his eyes. He masked it quickly, but Emily caught the faintest curve of his mouth before his expression shifted back to something more serious.

Philip lingered in the doorway, his gaze flicking between Emily and Jackson as if considering what to say. "I rarely go back on my word, Jackson, but I didn't have the right to promise my daughter to anybody. In addition, she has decided to lead this pack once I'm gone. So, she can't mate you." His gaze narrowed on Emily. "Unless she wants to. Because I'm young and healthy and don't need an heir right now." He gracefully exited the room and shut the door.

Silence thickened in the air around them. Jackson shifted his weight, the too-short dress pants doing little to diminish the air of authority he carried. His gaze found hers, steady and unflinching. Blood streaked his chest and chin—none of it his. His eyes gleamed with something primal, a reminder of what he'd done to keep her safe.

The room seemed to shrink around them, the air heavy with the weight of unspoken words. He stood at the foot of the bed, his broad shoulders casting long shadows against the wall, his gaze steady and unyielding as he took a step closer. Emily swallowed against the lump rising in her throat.

"You're not as fine as you claim," he murmured, gaze dropping briefly to the bruises peeking from under the blanket.

"I've had worse," she replied, lifting her chin.

"I don't like that. At all." The rough edge in his voice made her chest tighten.

The rain began falling again, tapping softly against the glass like a distant heartbeat. The smell of water hitting earth drifted through the slightly open window.

Jackson stepped back and dropped onto an antique chair next to a feminine vanity, the seat creaking beneath him. His gaze hadn't left her.

"I never agreed to mate you, so I haven't broken my word," she muttered. Of course, she was lying her ass off about stepping up as the Alpha for the pack. But they had to keep Victor from challenging her father until they figured out a better solution. "Unless you want to mate and take over *my* pack." She kept the teasing tone in her voice, but she was only half-joking.

"Funny, but no. I'm rather attached to leading my pack." His voice was low and steady. The antique chair groaned as he leaned back, his broad shoulders making it look too small.

Emily bit back a wince. If he broke that chair, she'd kill him. The beautiful antique had been her mother's. "Why are you looking for a mate, anyway? Won't that cut into your partying?"

"Not if you party with me." He flashed a grin that didn't quite reach his eyes. "I would mate you, you know."

"I'm not into partying."

"I do that a lot less than you think." His tone softened, the playfulness fading as honesty slipped in. "Truth be told, it would be a good alliance, and I'm fine with a contractual arrangement. Love is a myth. I don't know where Seth and I stand, but if there's ever a dispute between our packs and his or Erik's, they'll band together faster than wolves scenting blood. If that happens—"

Emily cut him off. "I'm friends with both Seth and Erik. They won't go to battle with us."

Jackson shook his head. "They might not have a choice. A weak pack can't be allowed to continue in the coalition. Plus, you and Erik were more than friends. You were engaged, and he's already mated to somebody else. That should be a declaration of war."

Emily's left arm felt numb. How badly had she been hit? "I called off the engagement, which we created to free his brother to mate the woman he loves. It was an arrangement. When I saw how Erik felt about Luna, I broke it off. I'm happy for them all."

It'd be nice to be happy for herself, but she didn't see that happening anytime soon.

Jackson held her gaze. "You really do seem fine that Erik mated Luna so soon after you ended the engagement."

"I'm thrilled for them." Her eyes drifted, almost against her will, to his bare chest. Even in a world of wolves, Jackson stood apart with cut muscles and impressive ridges that invited a female's gaze. She dragged her focus upward, locking onto his blue eyes. A myriad of shades swirled within them, from icy and pale to deep navy, intense yet unreadable. Seth Volk had similar eyes, but Jackson's held something darker, heavier. Something she couldn't quite name.

"Thrilled, huh? I guess that's better than war."

Emily didn't have the time or energy for war. Or for mating. "Your pack and mine can create a contract to protect each other even within the coalition. We don't have to mate." She probably didn't have that much time left, anyway.

Jackson waved a hand in the air. "Contracts mean jack shit to wolves, and you know it. Bloodlines matter. Matings matter. My council is on me about finding a mate and settling down, and an Alpha female is needed. There are now two in your family."

"Nadia? You'd mate her?" Emily questioned, the idea sending a sharp, unexpected pang through her chest. The sudden intensity of it shocked her. The idea of Jackson with her newly found sister made her want to puke.

"No. She's adorable," Jackson said with a slow smile, "but my eyes are on you, baby, and you know it."

Yeah, she did. Probably because she was the only female who'd ever turned him down. Oh, the kiss that summer had been spectacular, and he'd wanted to take it further, but she had said no.

He had rolled his eyes and made some flippant comment about her being cold to his buddies later. It wasn't the last time she'd been called that, but she blamed him for starting the rumors.

"What's that harsh look on your face?" he asked.

"When you called me cold," she said bluntly. "Years ago, at the summer get-together. The nickname stuck."

His eyes sobered. "If it stuck, I'm sorry. But you've rejected your fair share of males throughout the years. If it helps, I find nothing cold about you."

She didn't want it to help, but it did. He was appealing and dangerous. And she wanted him. She always had.

But right now, she was the only thing keeping her damn cousin Victor from challenging Philip, and she knew it. She would side with her father, and the pack would side with them both, thinking she would step up or mate somebody who would. They didn't know she was getting weaker every day from some odd illness that apparently the females in her lineage suffered from. That fact wasn't common knowledge, and she wanted it to stay that way.

If she left and became a member of Jackson's pack—her only option if she mated him—it would leave her father alone. Without her here to back him, Victor would attack immediately. Also, it wouldn't be fair to mate Jackson with her sickness. She'd been getting weaker for more than a month. While Nadia's arrival was amusing and welcome, she lacked fighting skills and wouldn't survive as the Alpha.

Victor would probably kill Philip. And Philip couldn't even see it. Or perhaps his ego was such that he didn't believe it. She loved her father and wanted to protect him. She was also short on time. If she mated Jackson, would his pack protect hers, even if she died?

It was a fucking conundrum.

A knock came at the door.

"Come in," Emily muttered.

Caidrik walked in and looked directly at Jackson. "Nightsom reached out to the Ravencall Alpha. Or at least he tried to."

Jackson stood. The chair protested with a loud creak, but it didn't break. Emily breathed out a relieved sigh.

"He's dead already," Jackson guessed.

"The Volk brothers probably don't even know that yet," Caidrik replied grimly. "But there's more. The Ravencall and Ghostwind Packs are in negotiations to combine forces."

"Oh, shit," Jackson muttered.

The two rogue packs had been making inroads with the Stope Packs Coalition for nearly a decade.

"It looks like they decided to attack the Nightsoms and the Slate Pack first," Jackson noted.

Caidrik nodded, his face grim. "Nightsom just took off to up the patrols and warn his soldiers. Should be back in a couple of hours."

Silence fell like a dropped stone. Emily crossed her arms tightly over her chest. Jackson ran a hand through his hair, his teeth clenched. When he met her eyes, something shifted in his expression. Maybe resignation. Perhaps resolve.

"Emily," he said, voice low but steady. "Your pack needs help and your father wants you safe. Mate me and you will be."

"What's in it for you?" Emily asked. Seriously. He was hot, dangerous, rich, and an Alpha. He surely didn't need an unwilling mate.

He took a step forward. "My pack's running low on Alpha blood. We've been holding strong, but the council's been breathing down my neck since I took over at fifteen. They've decreed that if I don't take a mate with Alpha lineage, they'll try to remove me. I'd win the fight, but I'd have to put down too many of the pack's elders."

Ouch. So much for the thought in the back of her mind that he wanted her. Like really cared for her. She was so dumb sometimes. "So, you need a political mating to keep from killing a bunch of old wolves?"

"Pretty much."

Emily let out a breath and rubbed the back of her neck. Her entire body felt like one long bruise, and her healing abilities had slowed. She had to hide that simple fact from him. "That's about as romantic as a tax audit."

Jackson's mouth twitched. "Not aiming for romance here. Just honesty."

She should've been mad. Should've been insulted. But instead, a laugh broke free before she could stop it. "God, I'm an idiot. I was actually pissed for a second that you weren't proposing because of my hot body."

"I mean, it doesn't hurt," Jackson said, deadpan.

She shook her head, laughter still bubbling under her ribs. The absurdity of it all hit like a slap. Politics, bloodlines, pack elders who were probably too old to even jump into the fight. And now, Jackson standing there like mating her was just another box on his to-do list.

But damn if some part of her didn't admire the honesty.

The other part? That one howled in protest. Damn bitch.

She would find a cure for her illness and protect her father. And the entire pack. Plus, Jackson was dangerous on a level the female inside her felt. "I appreciate the kind offer, but my answer is no."

Tension rolled from him, strong and sure. Then he smiled. "All right. Let's negotiate this. You come into my territory as part of our courting ritual, get my council off my back, fall in love with the town, and then mate me."

The words unfortunately sent a shock of thrill through her. "Counter-proposal." She'd never mate out of convenience, damn it. But she did want to get into his territory—sooner rather than later, if the rumors she'd heard about his doctors were true. "I'll come visit, get your council off your back, and find you a mate. I write romance and will put that to good use. In return, I have free rein while I'm there. You know, to see how modern you all are."

His eyelids dropped to half-mast. "Final proposal. You visit, get my council off my back, and *try* to find me a mate. Good luck, because we're really low in Alpha blood. If you fail, then *you* mate me. Either way, I'll then give your pack a ten year license to dig deep in my Embervault Mine."

She blinked. "Your what?"

Jackson snorted. "You didn't really think your father wanted to hand you over *just* for an alliance between our packs, did you?"

CHAPTER 4

A sharp knock rattled the front door, jolting Jackson from a deep sleep. Grunting, he swung his legs over the side of the bed and yanked on a pair of worn jeans. Barefoot, he padded down the hallway's hardwood floor, the chill of early morning brushing against his bare chest.

The smell of pine from last night's flight clung to his skin, a reminder that he'd pushed hard to get home. Helicopters beat running any day, especially when covering the entire length of Washington state. Five hours running flat-out—maybe seven at a normal pace—while the chopper made it in ninety minutes. He liked efficiency.

He opened the door, unsurprised to see three members of the council standing on his porch. Ancient wolves. Stubborn as stone and just as immovable. A glance to the side confirmed Thane Stormridge watched from the tree line, having patrolled through the night. Jackson nodded at his best friend.

Thane, tall and lean, smiled but didn't come closer. Jerk.

"Where is your mate?" Harland Whitaker demanded, his jowls quivering as he shifted his considerable weight.

"Don't have one yet," Jackson replied flatly. "Come in."

They didn't wait for further invitations. Moving with surprising grace for their ages, the trio swept into the formal sitting room. Heavy leather chairs flanked a stone fireplace, unlit but still carrying the scent of wood smoke. The hum of tension filled the air. Old expectations clashing against new realities.

Jackson raked a hand through his unruly dark hair as he followed them inside. He dropped into his father's old leather chair and stretched out, barefoot and shirtless, letting them feel the deliberate insolence in his posture.

The thin, wiry elder to Harland's right adjusted his stiff collar, his pale-blue eyes sharp as flint. Irving Carpenter had to be almost two hundred years old and probably had been underweight his entire life. The guy always wore an open-collared shirt with an amethyst pendant visible in his gray chest hair. "The council has been clear, Jackson. You're in your thirties. It's time to settle down. The pack needs more Alpha blood and a determined future."

"We had an agreement," Harland pressed. "You and Philip Nightsom—"

"We did," Jackson cut him off. "But his daughter didn't agree. I'm not about to mate an unwilling female. Especially not Emily Nightsom."

Emily. Fire and frost wrapped in one frustratingly tempting package. Stubborn enough to bite through steel and smart enough to make him regret underestimating her. The thought of waking up with her knife at his throat wasn't the worst part. It was knowing that she'd probably turn him on at the same time.

He yawned deliberately.

Oswald Brambleton adjusted his bow tie, his eyes narrowing with a steady calm that hinted at his decades upon more decades of experience. He always wore a damn bow tie with his silk suit, even when surveying the mines. "The council is united on this, Jackson," he said slowly. "You need to understand that if you don't show stability and an interest in continuing the Alpha line, we may turn to the Blount family."

Jackson kept his expression stoic. "Blount? There are only three of them. One very old guy and his two teenaged grandsons. Two more teenagers you can control for…what? Another decade? Are you that desperate to hold on to power?"

The air thickened with unspoken threats. Jackson could kill all three of them in moments if he wished. Oh, they were trained and experienced, but none of them had the Alpha blood coursing through his veins. Nor did they share his history—or his temper. Did they even realize that?

Harland settled his heavy bulk back into the sofa, eyes narrowing. "I know what's going through your head."

"Good." Jackson flashed his teeth.

Oswald tugged on his bow tie. "Killing us won't solve anything. Plus, the three of us might be tougher than you imagine. All at once."

Jackson doubted it. He'd been under their thumbs since he'd taken over as a teenager without a choice. Now, he had one. But they weren't wrong. If he wanted the pack to fall in line, he needed to at least appear like he was settling down, and he had to find the asshole who'd sabotaged his main mine last week. The explosion had torn through the granite face like a thunderclap from hell, scattering shards of stone and molten rock across the mine floor, halting production and putting three miners in the hospital.

Whoever was behind it wouldn't get a second chance.

The damage had cost them more than just time. Jackson had barely managed to smooth things over with their biggest client, Caldwell & Sons. They were a development company that worked all over the Pacific Northwest…and had no idea their contract was with wolf shifters.

But with the deadline for the newest Caldwell estate project exactly two weeks away, he needed the council out of his way until he fulfilled the order—which was why he needed Emily in town providing a distraction for that amount of time. Then he'd deal with pack internal matters. Any further delays would kill the contract and take the mine and his entire pack down financially. The Caldwell job wasn't just a paycheck; it was their ticket to pulling the entire community out of the red.

Jackson clenched his fists, his jaw tightening as he eyed the damn council. Someone wanted to see the Granite Pack fail. Maybe it was a rival outfit, looking to edge them out. Or perhaps it was someone closer to home. Either way, Jackson intended to drag them into the light before they struck again.

"Jackson?" Harland asked.

"I agree that it's time I found a mate and continued my Alpha line." Jackson leaned back in his chair. "I've never been one to plan for settling down, but a contractual arrangement works just fine for me. Emily Nightsom has agreed to serve as my matchmaker." Would they believe that nonsense?

Harland's gray eyebrows lifted. "Are you serious? The Nightsom heir, the one who writes romances, is going to matchmake for you?"

"Yes." Then when she failed, she'd mate Jackson and end up right where she belonged. "She'll be here for two weeks." Long enough for him to fulfill a granite contract that would take the holdings out of the red so he could get the fucking council off his back.

"Interesting." Irving rubbed his chin. "Perhaps you could also court her while she tries to help you?"

Jackson kept his face neutral, though his shoulders stiffened. Like he had one fucking clue about courting a princess like her. "That's a thought."

"From what I've heard, she writes romances that are very good," Harland added, tilting his head as if considering the idea of reading one himself. "You'll have to be romantic."

Jackson had read a few of her books. Hell, he'd practically devoured them. Each page had been soaked in heat and tension that left his blood thrumming. Emily had a knack for weaving desire and dominance into her stories, capturing raw emotion in a way that hit a little too close to home. Every time he read one, all he could think about was her. The curve of her lips, the fire in her eyes, the way her scent lingered in his memory. After the last book, he'd forced himself to stop. Stirring up feelings he couldn't afford to have was too dangerous.

Harland coughed. "Are you sure she isn't angling for the Alpha job with her pack? Philip is getting on in years."

"Writing is a full time job." Irving shook his head with a dismissive snort. "I mean, come on. A woman as the Alpha? She'd be challenged to fight constantly."

Jackson's jaw clenched, but he bit back the retort burning on his tongue. Irving's old-school views were well-known, but Jackson couldn't shake the image of Emily standing her ground the other night, so fierce, determined, and brave. Yet she'd been injured. There was a fragility to her he hadn't realized before.

She was vulnerable. Period.

The idea of her having to fight off challengers for the rest of her life set something inside him on fire.

The female needed protection.

Harland chuckled. "Last I saw her, she was healthy and tall and could probably fight, but we've never seen a female hold off attackers for long."

A low growl rumbled in Jackson's chest. He swallowed it back as the front door opened.

"I brought coffee," said Raya Ashthorne, stepping inside. She paused, taking in the three council members. "Looks like I'm not the only one here early. Where's your new mate?"

Jackson glanced at the woman who had served as the backbone of his entire organization for the last five years as its chief operating officer. "We hit a bit of a glitch there. But I'll get mated, and Emily is going to come and help me find the perfect mate."

Raya's eyebrows lifted. In her late-twenties, with sparkling brown eyes and curly black hair pulled into a loose bun, the wolf radiated confidence and a no-nonsense attitude. Her tailored blazer and dark jeans spoke of practicality, but there was a sharp intelligence in her gaze that no one dared underestimate. "Seriously? We're playing the dating game now? You need to stop watching old TV shows."

Jackson forced a smile. He was finished discussing mating, damn it. "This is business, not a game. A strong Alpha pair stabilizes the pack. It's about optics and strength. Perception matters."

"Sure," Raya muttered, shaking her head. "This is going to be fun. Maybe we should start a reality show. *Alpha Bachelor* has a nice ring to it."

"Very funny," Jackson replied dryly.

She ignored the jab and glanced toward the council members seated on the worn leather sofa, their faces etched with concern. "Anyway, I only brought coffee for the two of us since we need to review the mine projections. As you know, we're down two tunnels. Production's running at sixty percent capacity. If we don't get them cleared and reinforced within two weeks, we're looking at more than missed deadlines. We risk losing long-term contracts, including Caldwell's."

The weight of leadership settled heavily on Jackson's shoulders. "We'll get it handled. Failure's not an option."

"We know." Oswald tugged at his bow tie with a nervous twitch of his fingers. His usually calm demeanor seemed strained, betraying the pressure they all felt. "Find out who's trying to destroy our mines, Jackson. If you can't, we'll find somebody who can."

Jackson's gaze sharpened. "Is that a threat?" His voice dropped into a low, dangerous rumble that carried authority.

As if bound by the same unspoken command, the three council members stood as one, moving with the synchronized grace of seasoned wolves.

"It absolutely is," Irving replied smoothly, his eyes glinting with challenge. "Warren Blount is already whispering to scared pack members whose family members nearly died in the mine attack. Says the pack needs stronger leadership and someone with a legacy they can trust. His grandsons are circling like vultures, waiting for a chance to step in. Warren is too old and still limping from that mine collapse a century ago, but that doesn't stop him from scheming."

Raya's smile vanished. "Rumblings are spreading through town and the territory. You're in danger, Jackson. They'll force a challenge if you don't secure your position soon."

Jackson exhaled slowly through his nose, tension coiling in his chest. Not one ounce of him wanted to kill his own pack members during a challenge. The Blount kids were just teenagers, damn it. "Emily Nightsom will be here tomorrow morning to help."

Raya quirked a lip. "If she doesn't want to mate you, I don't understand why she'd travel here and play matchmaker."

Harland shrugged. "The female writes romances. Perhaps Jackson thinks she'll be good at the job."

Jackson was done talking about this. "Emily has agreed to assist me in exchange for my granting her pack a license to the Embervault Mine. They need the rare slate veins below the granite ones we've nearly depleted. In other words, I didn't give her a choice."

Raya lifted her chin. "I see."

Irving coughed. "See what?"

"Jackson just wanted to get Emily into our territory. You may have taken no for an answer, but you're not giving up on her." Raya's tone hinted at disapproval. Considering the female had been crucial in bringing the pack into current times, she no doubt had issues with contractual matings. Or extorted ones.

Harland straightened his shirt. "You have a plan?"

"I always have a plan," Jackson returned, his voice low and rough. While he had no intention of ever falling for a female, and he sure as shit didn't believe in love, Emily Nightsom set his blood on fire. Plus, she needed serious protection for some reason, and he didn't trust anybody else to cover her. The female wasn't mean enough to step up as an Alpha, and her father should get going on creating another heir. Philip wasn't that old. Maybe. At least Emily would stay safe while she visited Jackson's territory. "The three of you might want to remember that."

The threat hung in the air.

Raya's phone buzzed, and she lifted it to her ear, carefully balancing the coffee in her other hand. "Yes." As she listened, the color slowly leaked from her face, and her gaze slashed to Jackson's. "We'll be right there."

Awareness crackled down his back. "What happened?"

She clicked off the call. "That was Pency at the Hollow Mine. It looks like a tunnel collapse in the eastern extraction chamber near Shaft B. The rock face around the main drilling site caved in and took out the conveyor system, burying two loaders under several tons of granite and rubble."

Nausea rolled in Jackson's gut. "Injuries?"

"No. The crew went on an early break to celebrate a birthday—a total fluke. The structural braces along the ceiling were weakened like someone tampered with the bolts holding the steel beams in place. The inspection crew swears the supports passed the safety check last week. It doesn't add up."

Jackson's jaw clenched as he processed the implications. The crew taking an early break was just pure, dumb luck. Mining granite was already dangerous since the rock's density and unpredictable fault lines meant any weakness in the support system could turn lethal. The steel mesh and wooden beams lining the tunnels had been designed to prevent rockfalls, but if someone deliberately loosened the anchors, even a minor vibration from the drilling equipment could trigger a collapse.

"Drill lines were also compromised," Raya added. "Two of the pneumatic drills short-circuited because someone slashed their coolant hoses. That wasn't wear and tear. Pency said the cuts were clean, like they'd been made with a blade. And someone tampered with the ventilation system. The airflow was partially blocked, so carbon dioxide levels were rising by the time he pulled the crew out."

Jackson swore under his breath. A blocked ventilation system wasn't just sabotage. It was a death sentence. The mine relied on high-powered fans to pump fresh air into the tunnels and vent out the toxic gases. Without proper airflow, miners could suffocate before anyone realized what was happening.

"This wasn't random vandalism," Raya said, her voice tight. "Someone knew exactly what they were doing. They wanted to shut us down. Or worse, get someone killed."

Jackson's blood heated. "They nearly succeeded. But I'm going to find out who's responsible, and when I do, they'll wish they'd been buried under that rockfall. Let's go, and I want to see the camera feed on my phone. Now."

CHAPTER 5

Fresh from her shower, Emily walked carefully down the stairs to the expansive kitchen where a lovely breakfast had already been laid out.

Nadia stood up awkwardly, chewing on a piece of toast. "Sorry. I didn't know how long you were going to sleep since you were injured, and I got hungry."

"That's fine, of course." Emily poured herself a cup of coffee and sat, inhaling the rich aroma.

"Are you hungry?"

Emily shook her head. "Not really."

Nadia dug into an omelet like she hadn't eaten in years. "This is great food."

Smiling, Emily took a sip of coffee. Its warmth spilled down her throat and settled in her belly. "Yes. Our cook is one of the best." Setting her mug down, she leaned forward slightly. "So, I don't know much about you. Where did you live before joining Erik's pack?"

"We worked as a farming co-op," Nadia said cheerfully, reaching for her orange juice. "But rogue packs attacked, and we didn't have much choice but to join the Copper Pack. They gave us farming land, though."

Emily wanted to know more about this new sister. "So, you like to farm?"

Nadia paused, her fork hovering above her plate. "Not really." Her gaze—eyes as familiar as her own—met Emily's.

Emily chuckled. "You don't like to farm, but you're a farmer?"

Shrugging, Nadia stabbed a piece of her omelet. "Yeah. I like to organize. Anything, really. Drawers, houses, communities, farming equipment. You name it. If there's a spreadsheet around, I'm happy. Especially if it's color-coded."

Finding her new sister quite delightful, Emily leaned back in her chair. "We could use some help here. I finally talked my father into updating the computers for the mines a couple of years ago, but they still do most things old school and could certainly benefit from the organization."

Nadia's eyebrows rose. "Seriously?"

"Yes. My—I mean, *our*, father is a great Alpha when it comes to protection and strategy, but he's not so great with business."

Nadia munched on a piece of bacon. "What about you?"

Emily offered Nadia a small shrug. "I do some work for the mines, but to be honest, it's not my passion."

"Oh, yeah? What is your interest?"

"Writing," Emily said. "Romantic suspense, mainly."

Nadia's eyes lit. "That's cool."

"Yeah," Emily replied, swirling the coffee in her cup. "Aside from that, I help optimize mining operations with mainly logistics and safety. I review tunnel layouts and airflow systems, making sure everything runs smoothly. It keeps things efficient and helps prevent accidents." She liked the contrast of work with her creative side writing and her mechanical side keeping people safe.

Nadia watched her. "Sounds like you're a problem solver."

Emily smiled. "Something like that."

Nadia leaned forward, curiosity lighting her eyes. "Even though you told Philip you'd become the Alpha, I could tell you have no interest in the job."

Pausing, Emily took another sip of coffee, the warmth giving her a moment to gather her thoughts. "You read me correctly. Part of it is that you're constantly challenged by people who can take you down. While I can fight, it's not the life I want." Her fingers traced the rim of her mug. Trusting her new sister with the whole truth felt like a gamble. They didn't have enough history yet, but something about Nadia's open expression made her think that maybe, just maybe, she could tell the truth about her health.

Nadia nodded. "Fighting all of the time would suck."

That was true if Emily could even win a fight. That possibility seemed further away every single day, and she had no clue why. The only healer they had in the pack was Edra, a two-hundred-year-old female who still relied on herbs. Not that they weren't helpful sometimes, but she couldn't figure out what was wrong with Emily.

"What do you know about Jackson's pack?" Emily asked, her gaze steady.

"Nothing," Nadia replied. "I've heard of him and his Granite Pack, but you know what—?" She angled her head toward the doorway. "Caidrik," she bellowed.

The guard dog appeared almost instantly, his stance firm and gaze intense.

Nadia blinked. "That was fast. What do you know about Jackson? We both know you haven't told us everything about his pack."

Caidrik's chin dipped slightly. "I don't answer to you, little Nadia." His gaze shifted to Emily. "Or you, for that matter."

Emily drew in air. "Do you mind providing a little information?"

"Like what?" he asked.

"Geez," Nadia grumbled. "They've fed and clothed you. The least you could do is answer a couple of questions."

Caidrik's nostrils flared.

"Are you two together?" Emily asked, not wanting to cause a problem between the couple.

"God, no," they said at the same time.

Emily barely bit back a laugh as Nadia flushed a pretty shade of peach.

"Caidrik only joined our co-op a couple of weeks ago," Nadia explained. "He obviously has fighting experience. When our new Alpha asked if anyone would serve as my protector, he stood right up."

"I'm not much for farming," Caidrik said simply. "I was just looking for a place to belong."

Nadia's gaze softened. "The co-op's a good place. Or it was, I guess. Now, it's part of a pack." She frowned slightly. "I'm still not sure how I feel about that."

"You have a pack here," Emily said gently. "Your blood ties you to us. I'm hoping you might decide to stay." She looked at the obviously strong warrior leaning against the wall. "I'm sure you'd be welcome, as well, Caidrik. We always need soldiers. You worked with Jackson in the mine?"

Caidrik nodded. "Yeah. I worked with him. In the mine. For a bit."

That felt like a lie. Emily went on instinct, not missing that her sister listened raptly. "I can sense that you have Alpha blood in your veins. Right?"

"None of your damn business," Caidrik shot back, his tone flat.

"Be nice. We're guests," Nadia scolded him with a glare.

Emily patted her hand. "You're not a guest. You belong here." She had to convince Nadia to stay. Something deep inside told her this sibling might be more important than either of them realized.

Her feet were completely numb today, a chilling reminder that whatever this illness was, it was killing her. Her father figured she was still slightly off because of the kidnapping attempt months ago which had given her a heck of a concussion. She hadn't told him that she'd again visited Edra, the healer. Edra had no idea what was wrong but had said the sickness mimicked the illness that had killed Emily's mother...and grandmother. Most of the pack didn't know about that. The uncertainty gnawed at Emily. Every morning, she woke hoping the sensation would return to her feet. Yet every morning, it didn't. How could she even start to plan for a future if she didn't know if she even had one?

Clearing her throat, Emily turned to Caidrik. "I'm not asking for pack secrets, but you have spent some time with Jackson's pack, right? I've heard they have modern doctors or healers. Is this true?"

One of Caidrik's dark eyebrows rose. "Why?"

It was a good question. "We need to modernize a bit here like I've heard the Volk Alphas are doing with their packs. A medically trained doctor would be nice."

Caidrik didn't look like he believed her, yet he spoke anyway. "The Granite Pack has programs in place for younger wolves to attend universities."

Anticipation ran through Emily. "Really?"

"Yes. They've been sending younger pack members to study engineering, modern mining techniques, and medicine. I think they even have a wolf who's a licensed CPA. They had two doctors, fully trained in western and wolf medicine when I, ah, worked there. Jackson keeps it quiet, but the Granite Pack is much more modern than most. Even their mines use newer ventilation systems and automated drilling equipment. Safer and more efficient."

Emily's heart lifted slightly. So, they had a real doctor. The rumors were true. Perfect. "Well, good," she said casually. "I've agreed to help Jackson find a mate."

"Why?" Nadia burst out, her eyes wide with disbelief. "Why would you help him find some other mate? Especially since you turned him down."

"I had no idea they were so modern," Emily murmured. "I'd love to see how their pack operates. We're trying to modernize here, as well, and I could probably get some ideas during my visit. Their use of technology could help improve our mine safety and efficiency."

"Humph." Nadia eyed her suspiciously. "I think you have the hots for Jackson and just want to spend more time with him."

Emily's cheeks warmed slightly, but she ignored the teasing, already thinking of the possibilities that awaited her in Jackson's territory. "He's sexy and, yes, intriguing, but I don't want to be his mate. The guy's overbearing."

"That's for damn sure." Nadia poured more orange juice into her glass. "I'm glad you see it. Way too bossy."

From the corner of her eye, Emily noticed Caidrik cutting her a look before glancing away. "I'm going to check the perimeter." He strode out of the room with his usual gruff demeanor.

Nadia frowned. "He's always so grumpy."

"They all are," Emily replied, the memory of past encounters with Jackson's pack flashing in her mind.

Before Nadia could respond, polished shoes echoed against the wooden floor. Philip Nightsom entered the room, impeccably dressed in a three-piece suit like usual. He'd been out with his soldiers most of the night, and Emily hadn't gotten a chance to speak with him yet.

"Good morning, daughters." His voice carried warmth and hesitation, but his shoulders relaxed when Nadia offered him a smile.

She cleared her throat. "How could you offer Emily to Jackson Tryne to mate?"

So, going right for it, was she? Emily hid a smile.

Philip grimaced. "I panicked. When Erik took over the Copper Pack, with his brother Alpha of the Silver Pack, who's a distant cousin to Jackson, I just, well, panicked. But I fixed it last night, right? When I told Jackson that Emily will take her place as Alpha here? I just need everyone to believe that for the next thirty years or so, and I'll come up with a better plan during that timeframe."

Emily pushed her temper away. "That's not all, is it?"

"Hmm?" He adjusted the cuffs of his jacket, the lines around his eyes deepening with curiosity.

She kept her voice even. "I agreed to visit Jackson's territory to help him find a mate in exchange for a ten year license to the Embervault Mine."

Philip paused in mid-movement, his posture stiffening. "Jackson has a big mouth," he muttered, almost to himself.

"Tell me about it." Should it hurt that her father had tried to use her to barter for a darn mine?

Sighing, Philip lowered himself into a chair. "It's an old mine between our territory and theirs, about four hours away if traveling in wolf form. While it once produced high-quality granite for the Granite Pack, the real prize now is the slate found deeper within it. But it isn't ordinary slate. The deposits there contain a rare variant known as obsidian slate."

"Obsidian slate?" Nadia asked.

Philip poured himself a cup of coffee, his gaze distracted. "It's darker, denser, and has a natural sheen that makes it highly sought after for luxury flooring, high-end roofing, and architectural designs. Unlike standard slate, it's resistant to weathering and can be cut into thinner, more flexible sheets without compromising its strength."

Emily leaned forward, her pulse quickening. "So, if we could access that mine—"

Philip nodded. "It would change everything. Our slate mines are productive, but none of them yield obsidian slate. It's in high demand for custom homes, upscale commercial buildings, and even art installations. We've had architects and developers specifically request it, but without access to Embervault Mine, we've had to turn down those contracts. If we could secure mining rights, even partial ones, we could triple our profits and expand our influence across multiple regions to get ourselves out of debt. As you know, we're floundering."

True. They'd spent too much time gathering territory and scheming to take over the Copper Pack…which would've happened if Erik hadn't stepped up and agreed to be their Alpha. Subsequently, the mines had suffered. Terribly. "Why haven't we negotiated access before now?" Emily asked.

"Jackson's grandfather secured exclusive ownership before the obsidian slate deposits were discovered. When we approached him, he refused outright. Said his family was focused on granite, not slate, and that the quarry wasn't for sale. But he never reopened negotiations, not even after we offered a percentage of the profits. It's been locked down ever since."

Emily considered the implications. Access to that mine wouldn't just stabilize their finances. It could elevate their pack's status. "So I'll go help Jackson find a mate, and all will work out."

Her father met her gaze. "He doesn't want another mate. He wants you."

Emily sighed. "His ego wants me. I'll go, but his little plan won't work." She made the statement with full conviction but didn't miss the quick glance that took place between her father and sister. "He's not that charming," she protested.

Nadia appraised her. "He just wants you in his territory, and we all know it. I say you stay here. Forget him."

Like Emily could ever forget Jackson Tryne. "We need access to that mine."

"We do," Philip said. "Jackson texted earlier today that his final offer is you in his territory for two weeks in exchange for the mining license. I think he wants to court you and seems to be quite confident you'll end up wanting to stay."

"Is he, now?" While the pack needed that slate, she needed a doctor. Apparently, Jackson had at least two in his territory. "Don't worry. If Jackson makes any moves, I'll rip out his throat." If this illness didn't kill her first.

Emily hopped out of her pack's helicopter and ducked low, her backpack slung over her shoulder. The rush of wind from the rotor blades whipped her hair around her face, and she blinked against the sharp breeze. The air carried the bite of approaching winter. It was December now, but the first snow had yet to fall. Her boots crunched against the frosted grass as she jogged toward Jackson, who leaned casually against a silver work truck, looking long, lean, and more than a little dangerous.

As she approached, the wind picked up around her, tugging at her jacket. She adjusted her sunglasses, grateful she'd remembered them. His gaze dropped to hers as she stopped a few steps away. Even in the muted light, his eyes caught her attention. They were a stunning glacial blue that seemed to see through her.

"Is that all you brought?" he asked.

She laughed, the sound escaping before she could think better of it. "Of course not."

The pilot hopped down from the helicopter, circling the

aircraft to grab over-stuffed suitcases from the cargo hold. Embarrassment flushed through Emily at the sight.

"I got 'em." Jackson pushed off the truck and strode forward with effortless grace. His long legs ate up the distance, and he easily lifted the suitcases, muscles shifting beneath his dark jacket.

Emily waited as he tossed them into the truck bed, then walked around to open the passenger door. His courtesy threw her off balance. "Thank you," she murmured, accepting his hand as she stepped up into the cab. Sometimes, her height came in handy.

"No problem," he replied dryly, waiting until she was settled before shutting the door. Moments later, he slid into the driver's seat, and the space instantly filled with the wild scents of forest and wolf. The primal note in the aroma sent a nervous tremor down her arm, and she quickly covered the reaction by fastening her seat belt.

His door shut with a solid thunk, sealing her in the warm interior, alone with Jackson for the first time in ages. Her pulse jumped, and she swallowed hard.

What in the world was she doing?

Her father's pilot lifted the helicopter into the air, and the downdraft sent dried leaves and dead pine cones tumbling across the ground, clattering against the truck's side. Emily glanced toward Jackson, her pulse still unsteady.

"I can't believe you blackmailed my father into having me come to your territory," she murmured, her voice low and smooth.

"I think it's called extortion." Jackson steered the truck onto the dirt road. His hands gripped the wheel with a calm confidence that somehow made her nerves tingle. The flex of his fingers on the leather sent a surge of unexpected heat through her, and she shifted in her seat, annoyed by her body's reaction.

She arched a brow. "I think you're right."

"Hey. You agreed to come." He flicked a glance her way before returning his gaze to the narrow path cutting through the dense trees, the bare branches reaching toward the gray sky. The air smelled faintly of pine and distant snow, but she caught his scent beneath that. Wild, earthy, and undeniably male.

"I did, and I understand that my father needs access to the mine. He also wants me safe and thinks, deep down, that you're the key to that." Yet that would leave her father vulnerable. "I don't think so." Her gaze drifted to Jackson's jawline and the shadow of stubble on his skin.

"We'll see." He shifted gears as the truck bounced over a rut, drawing her attention to his muscled forearm. The air between them thickened. "Maybe you'll decide to stay."

She shook her head. "Not a chance. We had one kiss and that's all there'll ever be." That summer night at the lake when they'd met up as teenagers. Every once in a while, enterprising and rebellious teenaged wolves arranged a party outside of all pack territories where they all snuck out and had some fun mingling. There had been two such parties in her youth, and she'd only made it to one of them, where she'd met Jackson for the first time. He hadn't become the Alpha yet, so they were just two kids goofing off. They'd had a lot of beer.

Tons of it.

"You told me your secret wish to write romances."

She smiled. "You told me your secret wish to fly fighter jets." Then he'd kissed her. She'd fallen for him in a matter of hours. "Then your father died." Weeks later, really.

He turned onto a paved road, still blanketed by trees. "No fighter jets for me."

That must have been difficult. "I'm sorry."

"I've read your books."

She sat back, surprise stilling her. "You have?"

He lifted one shoulder. "Yeah. You're a great writer. I don't usually see the bad guy coming."

"Usually?"

He snorted, then looked at her and sobered. His gaze lingered on her lips before he turned back to the quiet road. "Yes. Usually. The sex is hot, too."

Silence settled between them, thick with tension. Emily pressed her lips together, her pulse quickening as the memory of his gaze lingered against her skin like a phantom touch. She had to change the subject. "Why is the council on you so hard to find a mate?"

Jackson glanced at her. "I've had two mines sabotaged the last month, and the council is noting that I'm not protecting everyone. I've had a contract I need to meet in two weeks for us to have enough funds to support the pack. Thus, I need to at least look like I'm settling down while I find the asshole and kill them."

What the heck? That's why he wanted her in town for two weeks? To provide a distraction? "Why didn't you just say so?"

"And let your father know I'm not protecting my people well enough? He attacked the second he caught wind that the Copper Pack was weakened. He'd own the entire pack if Erik Volk hadn't stepped up to be their Alpha." Jackson eyed the darkening clouds outside. "Please. While I'm sure he doesn't believe the story of my wanting you to matchmake for me, I think he wants me to seduce you. To mate you so we have that connection between the packs. The guy thinks he's going to live forever and isn't worried about a replacement Alpha."

"Right." She shifted uncomfortably, her pulse still uneven. Her father wasn't stupid, but like many Alphas, he failed to see his own mortality.

Jackson sighed. "I need to tell you something."

Dread trickled down her spine. "What?"

"Your father offered me another option—to mate you with the promise that in thirty years or so, when he needs someone else to take over, either you or one of our children do so."

She blinked. Rapidly. "Are you joking?"

"No."

Anger flushed through her, but she could see the rationale behind the offer. "Even if I thought that a good idea, which I do not, I would never send my child to fight to the death with Victor. Ever." Like Vic would wait that long, anyway.

"That's what I told your father," Jackson said quietly.

At least that was something. To everyone else, it appeared as if they'd all gone along with the idea of her helping Jackson find a mate. Now, she knew both her father's and Jackson's true motivations, but neither knew hers. She would find those doctors. Her chin lifted. She liked that.

The trees began to thin, and Jackson drove through a wide granite archway carved with elegant wolves in mid-howl and the name *Granite Hollow* etched into the stone. Multiple balloons in black and blue colors had been strewn along the arch with the words "Welcome Home, Emily," plastered onto a board in bright letters.

Jackson sighed.

Emily's mind went blank. "Um."

He drove beneath the arch. "My pack is looking forward to my mating." Beyond the arch lay a picturesque mining town that seemed untouched by time.

Stone buildings lined both sides of the main street, their façades crafted from granite in shades of silver-gray and charcoal. Ornate wrought-iron lanterns hung from lampposts, casting a warm glow as twilight approached. More blue and black balloons had been hung from several areas. "Blue and black?"

He nodded. "Best guess? Your eyes and mine."

Oh, for goodness' sakes. The street was cobblestone, slick

with a hint of frost, and the air smelled of wood smoke and freshly baked bread, even through the closed windows.

Hawthorne General Store sat to the left, its windows showcasing hand-knit scarves, local honey, and carved wooden wolves. Next to it, Ashwick Hardware displayed everything from mining equipment to antique tools. Across the street, Silver Moon Café bustled with life, the glow of its interior promising hot cocoa and pastries, and a weekly special of: Emily Frosted Cookies.

She gaped. "I have my own cookies."

His sigh sounded louder this time.

A few doors down, the amber lights of Ironclad Books & Bindery gleamed through frosted windows, as the silhouettes of patrons flipping through books or chatting over coffee were visible inside.

Emily breathed out. "Your town is adorable. Sweet, even."

"Thanks. We're off the main drag and rarely get tourists, but once in a while, we have a festival and sell wares to the humans. Maybe once or twice a year."

Sounded like fun. Emily's people rarely interacted with humans.

As they passed Granite Hollow City Hall, a grand building constructed from polished granite with carved columns and arched windows, Jackson slowed. Its clock tower, crowned with a copper wolf's head, stood sentinel over the town. Flags bearing the Granite Pack's sigil, a silver wolf against a dark stone backdrop, fluttered from the entrance.

On the sidewalk, a female in a long wool coat paused mid-stride, her eyes lighting up as she caught sight of the truck. She waved wildly, her smile widening as Emily waved weakly back.

Beside her on a bench, a male with a weathered face and a thick scarf around his neck lowered the newspaper he had been reading, his gaze tracking the vehicle with glee. He slapped his knee and then waved.

"My goodness." Emily waved back, gratified when his grin grew. "They do want you to mate."

"Yes." Jackson sighed. "Even though everyone's on edge from the mine attacks, romance rules around here, and folks like the thought of our packs being connected so closely. Many thought I'd come home with a mate, but I've put word out that you're here to assist me as an old friend."

She couldn't believe anybody would honestly fall for that. "They think you're going to seduce me." Just like her father did.

"Probably," he said carelessly. "But I do need you to provide a bit of distraction until I fulfill a big contract and also find the asshat messing with my mines, and in exchange, your pack can extract all the rare slate from my mine. Deal?"

Fair enough. "Yes."

Farther down the street, two female teenagers leaned against a lamppost, whispering and glancing toward the truck with quick, darting looks. They both had dark hair and lighter eyes. Waving, they ran toward the truck, reaching Emily's door.

Jackson stopped.

Emily rolled down her window. "Hi."

"Hi." The taller girl held out a button. "We made these for you." Giggling, she turned with her friend, and they ran across the road and into the Silver Moon Café.

Emily looked down at the button that had her picture next to Jackson's with a red heart drawn around it. "Wow."

He glanced at the button and started driving again. "It's nice to be wanted?"

She chuckled. It didn't suck.

"Now. How about you tell me why you insisted you have free rein in my territory." He almost phrased the statement as a question. "I understand your father's motivation, but I'm doubting yours."

She needed to see his doctor. "I wanted to see your town. You let so few wolf shifters from other packs visit."

"You're here to discover state secrets?"

She scanned the quaint storefronts again. "Exactly." Her gaze caught on a green-and-white sign that read *Family Medicine*. She made a mental note of its location. "I heard through the grapevine that your pack is more modern than most. You let younger members go off to school for a while."

"Grapevine?" Jackson pulled up beside the city hall. "You mean Caidrik?"

"Of course," she replied. "What did he do for you, anyway?"

Jackson cut the engine. "Worked as a miner. Of course."

Baloney. But that wasn't the mystery she needed to solve. "I'd like to know more about the programs that allow your young people to attend college. We need to modernize, and I really like the sound of that."

"You can speak with Raya," Jackson replied, his tone casual. "She handles all of that."

"Who is Raya?"

He sat back in his seat, looking at the granite building outside. "She's my chief operating officer. Runs the pack's logistics and business operations. You name it."

"Interesting," Emily murmured, glancing out the window, as well. The streets were quiet now, the lanterns' glow reflecting off the cobblestones damp from the earlier frost. Window boxes filled with evergreen branches and crimson berries hinted at the approaching holidays. Smoke drifted from chimneys, curling against the pale sky as dusk settled in. "I might have to get some ideas from her. If you don't mind, of course."

"I don't mind at all," Jackson said, his gaze steady.

Emily turned toward him and slowly smiled, her feet back under her. At least she understood why Jackson wanted her in town. "However, I'm also taking my other job quite seriously."

He turned to face her more fully. His presence seemed to expand in the enclosed space, the wild scent of wolf lingering between them. "What do you mean?"

Emily clasped her hands loosely in her lap, suppressing a grin. "I have made contact with several single female Alphas who are interested in settling down with a pack. They'll be arriving soon to meet you." She let her smile loose. "I fully intend to play matchmaker, Jackson."

CHAPTER 7

Jackson pressed his palm against Emily's lower back as he escorted her inside the building. The woman wore dark jeans, shiny brown boots, and a light green sweater beneath a leather jacket that made her look fresh and sexy as hell.

City Hall was spacious and impressive, with polished granite walls that gleamed beneath the warm glow of the wrought-iron chandeliers. The floor was a mosaic of dark slate and lighter granite tiles arranged in a pattern that echoed the mountains surrounding the town. Antique mining tools—pickaxes, lanterns, and rusted helmets—were displayed in glass cases along one wall, a tribute to the pack's history. Vintage photographs of miners at work lined the opposite wall, their sepia tones lending a sense of legacy to the space.

"My office is up here." Jackson steered her toward a broad staircase of granite steps that curved elegantly to the second floor. The wooden handrail had been worn smooth from years of use, and the hint of pine and stone lingered in the air.

"This is a nice building." Emily's fingers trailed lightly along the polished banister.

Jackson couldn't suppress the flicker of pride warming his chest. He also had the oddest urge to be a banister. "Thanks."

They reached the top landing, which opened to a wide hallway lined with three offices. Jackson led her to the middle one and knocked lightly before stepping inside. The smell of flowers assaulted him. "Raya, I'd like you to meet Emily Nightsom."

Raya pushed away from the bookshelf and Thane, her face flushed. "Um, Thane was just checking in on the, um, supplies for the south tunnel."

Thane grinned and leaned against the wall. Jackson's best friend had been dating Raya for months, although the female always seemed to deny it. "Seriously?"

Jackson shook his head, his gaze caught on the numerous bouquets behind Raya's desk on her credenza. "I couldn't care less if you two date, but if you break up, don't be assholes. I need you both." He looked down at Emily. "This is Raya Ashthorne, who runs the pack, and Thane Stormridge, who's in charge of schedules, security, and some of the finances." Plus, he was Jackson's oldest friend.

Thane gave a half bow. He was nearly seven feet tall and lean with an impressive brain. "It's nice to meet you, Emily." He strode toward the door. "I need to install new security cameras this morning since the older ones were hacked and melted. I'll see you later tonight after my patrol, Raya." Then he disappeared.

Raya stood behind her desk, smoothing her blouse before stepping forward with an extended hand. "All of these flowers behind me are for you from pack members." Her dark eyes reflected a mix of curiosity and disbelief. "It's very nice to meet you. I understand you're going to help Jackson find a mate?"

Emily's smile didn't waver. "That's the plan," she replied smoothly, her eyes flicking toward Jackson, who fought the urge to roll his shoulders. Had she been serious? He couldn't quite tell, and the uncertainty irritated him. "I'd love to speak with you about your university program and any other modernization initiatives. Our pack is a bit behind, and I'd appreciate your insight."

Raya's smile brightened. "That sounds wonderful. I'd be happy to discuss all of our programs."

Jackson interjected before Emily could answer. "Not tonight. It has been a long day."

"Okay. We'll find a time." Raya reached for her notepad. "For now, I've already arranged for you to stay in the hotel penthouse, and I can have all of these bouquets sent over."

Jackson winced. "It smells like a funeral home. There are too many of them."

"Thank you for the reservation." Emily smiled politely, though she shot Jackson a sideways glance. "The flowers are lovely, but they are a bit overwhelming. I don't want to hurt anybody's feelings."

Jackson shoved down an inexplicable pang of irritation. It wasn't as if he'd planned for Emily to stay at his place, but somehow, the thought of her alone at the hotel felt wrong. Shaking off the feeling, he gestured toward the door. "I'll take you and your luggage over once we're finished here."

Raya tapped her notepad. "If you want, I can have the bouquets taken to the closest hospital, about an hour away. Pack members will appreciate that you want to brighten the day of others, even humans."

"Thank you," Emily murmured.

As they stepped into the hallway, Emily's shoulder brushed his arm, a fleeting touch that sent a pulse of heat through him. He glanced at her, but she kept her gaze forward, the hint of a smile playing at her lips. Jackson swallowed hard, cursing the sudden tension that coiled low in his spine. "I'll show you my office."

"Sounds good," she said.

Jackson's stride slowed as he spotted Warren Blount and his eldest grandson standing outside his doorway. "Blount," Jackson said, his tone clipped. "I'm a little busy right now."

Warren Blount, a tough old man nearing two centuries, stood with his beaked nose and steel-gray eyes that seemed to pry into one's soul. His thin lips curled as he sniffed the air, nostrils flaring slightly before his gaze landed on Emily. "You must be Emily Nightsom."

"I must be," she replied smoothly, her smile polite but cool.

Jackson's hackles rose, heat prickling beneath his skin as he forced a tight smile. "What do you need, Warren?"

Warren inclined his head toward his grandson. "Zylas and I wanted to have a little discussion with you."

Zylas stepped forward, eyes locking on Emily. He was broad-shouldered for his age, around eighteen, with light blond hair and sharp blue eyes that seemed too intense for his years. "Hi, I'm Zylas." He held out a hand large enough to swallow hers.

Emily shook it, her lips curving into a smile. "Nice to meet you."

"I'm an Alpha."

"Are you, now?" she replied lightly. "That must be lovely for you." She glanced at Jackson.

How fucking irritating. "Again. What do you need, Warren?" Jackson didn't bother masking the edge in his tone.

"Someone is brazen enough to attack our mines more than once, and you haven't caught them," Warren said, his tone weighted with disapproval. "I think you should consider stepping down."

Jackson's gaze locked onto Warren's, unblinking until the older man glanced aside. "I'm not stepping anywhere. We'll find out who's responsible."

Zylas shifted his stance, a grin playing across his lips as he looked at Emily. "Ms. Nightsom, would you like to have a drink with me? Our local bar stocks rare whisky."

"You're not old enough to drink," Jackson interjected sharply. His pulse kicked harder than it should have as he cut the kid off. Everyone seemed to want a piece of Emily. He gently gripped her arm to remind himself—and anyone watching—that she was with him.

Warren sighed, filling the air with the smell of butterscotch. "Jackson, you're not doing the job we need as Alpha. You've been goofing off constantly with parties and females, and that's fine, but it's time for you to step down."

Jackson calmed. Completely. The old man had no clue how he'd been spending his damn nights, and it wasn't partying with females. At least, it hadn't been in years. "Or what?"

Warren gulped. "You'll be challenged. I mean, probably."

"Thank you for the warning." Jackson allowed his Alpha voice to deepen. "But I have things under control."

"No, you don't," Warren replied, his voice firm, his gaze still averted. "Things haven't been under control for a while now. Are you sure you want to lead this pack?"

"I really do," Jackson said dryly. "Now, if you'll excuse me." Without waiting for a response, he steered Emily into his office. The moment the door clicked shut behind them, he released her, but not before his fingers lingered just a beat too long against her skin, heat sparking between them.

The air seemed to hum with unsaid words, and Jackson stepped back, pulse drumming louder than it should have been.

Emily watched him with eyes that saw far too much, and the corner of her mouth lifted in the faintest of smiles. "That was interesting." She walked over to sit in one of the two leather chairs across from his desk. The dark-brown leather was worn soft from years of use, its brass nailhead trim gleaming in the light from the antique desk lamp.

"You have no idea." Jackson moved around the desk to settle

in his chair. The deep creak of the old leather accompanied his movements. The chair had belonged to his great-grandfather, and Jackson liked the continuity of it, the history of generations behind him.

"What's going on?" she asked, leaning forward slightly.

"I really don't know." He opened two manila files and laid them flat, sliding them toward her. Each contained photographs of recent mining incidents. "This one,"—he pointed to the first image—"was a collapse caused by someone weakening the support beams. The bolts were loosened just enough to fail when the pressure got too high. Nobody died, but workers were injured."

She studied the image of twisted steel and shattered rock. "And this one?"

"The second was near the mine's entrance. Someone jammed the ventilation system, cutting off the airflow and nearly suffocating a crew. The security cameras were disabled. It's an old system, easy to tamper with."

Emily tapped her finger against her lips, her gaze thoughtful. "Do you have suspects?"

He shrugged. "No idea. I can't believe anybody would do this."

"Well," she mused, her tone turning speculative, "if you want, I can wander around town a little. Talk to people. Gather information for our pack's modernization while I'm at it."

"Yeah, that'd be great. But stay within the pack boundaries," he said, his eyes locking on hers. "In fact, I'd prefer if you stayed in town."

She blinked. "Why's that, Jackson? Worried I'll find myself another Alpha?"

His low chuckle rumbled through the room. "Not even close, baby. I'm worried about that kidnapping attempt months ago."

"It wasn't an attempt. They kidnapped me." Her eyes darkened with irritation as she shook her head. "I was driving home after a meeting in town, and they ran me off the road. Three males dragged me out of the car and shoved a garlic-soaked burlap sack over my head so I couldn't smell them. I fought back hard and got bruised up pretty good."

Jackson's fingers curled against the edge of his desk. "How'd you get free?" he asked, voice low and tempered but taut with suppressed anger.

"They threw me in the back of the van and started driving." Emily's voice was steady, but Jackson caught the edge beneath her words. "I did what I had to do."

"You shifted in the back of a van?" His voice sharpened.

She clasped her hands in her lap. "I didn't have a choice. They didn't expect it."

"I wouldn't either," he muttered. "You're lucky you didn't break every bone in your body."

"No, I just bruised myself, hitting the sides. I jumped out the back and ran home. We still haven't figured out who they were or what they wanted."

That didn't make a bit of sense. "They didn't say anything?"

"Not a word. They were silent."

"Then you probably knew them," he murmured. "Or they would've spoken."

She swallowed, her gaze flickering toward the window. "That's my guess. I think maybe somebody wants to challenge my father."

"What about Victor?" The name tasted bitter.

"I don't think Vic would do something like that. Even though I couldn't smell anything, I think I'd sense if it was my cousin. Plus, why would he kidnap me? If Vic wanted me out of the way, he'd have killed me—or at least tried to."

Something low and fierce curled inside Jackson. The thought of anyone hurting her stirred a deep possessiveness he couldn't quite name. His fingers curled against the desk, the solid wood grounding him as a primal need to shield her burned beneath his skin. "You don't have one lead?"

"No. My father was in the middle of trying to take over the Copper Pack when it happened, and I've been healing at home since, so we haven't been out and about much." Determination hardened her pretty jaw. "When I get home, I will figure it out."

He didn't like the thought of her alone like that. "It's late. How about I take you to your hotel?"

"That sounds excellent," she said, her smile softening the tension between them. "By the way, you have a meeting at nine tomorrow morning with the first Alpha female I could find."

Jackson sat back, the leather chair creaking beneath him. His pulse kicked against his ribs. "You weren't joking about that?"

"No." She chuckled. "I really wasn't."

Irritation coiled through him. "How many am I supposed to meet with in this farce?"

She lifted one shoulder, delicate and maddening. "Only six, but I plan to find more."

"Emily," he snapped, the growl low in his throat.

"Sorry, Jackson." Her smile held challenge. "This is what you said you wanted."

He could not believe this. "How did you even find six Alpha females?"

"I used the Internet. I put out a coded message explaining the situation and instantly received six replies. I believe if I check my inbox, there will be more."

He held up a hand, the heat of frustration and something darker curling in his gut. "No. Absolutely not." Although, he did need a mate. But he only saw Emily's face when he thought about the future. Yet he understood her allegiance to her pack. If they mated, she'd be his. Not theirs.

She straightened. "Well, you have to meet with these six females. It would insult their packs otherwise."

"None of them belong to the Stope Packs Coalition, do they?"

"Of course not. Don't worry, Jackson." She leaned forward, her gaze catching his with an intensity that seemed to press against his skin. "By the time I'm done with you, you'll have the perfect mate."

Something about how she said the word *mate* made his blood heat for reasons that had nothing to do with matchmaking. The primal beast at his core raised its head, sensing a challenge.

He'd never lost one and didn't plan to start now.

CHAPTER 8

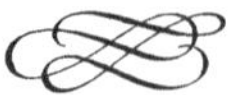

A little after eight in the morning, with the sun shining down on the frost-covered grass, Jackson pulled his truck up to his home and cut the engine. The scent of something sweet with a hint of spice drifted through the air. He stepped out of the truck, wiping grime from his face. His body ached from hours in the mine, but his mind was sharp.

The scent lingered. Emily.

Frowning, he strode to the front door and pushed it open. His home was a handcrafted log cabin, large and solid, built to house generations of Alphas. The entryway opened into a spacious living area with vaulted ceilings, exposed wooden beams, and floor-to-ceiling windows overlooking the forest beyond. A stone fireplace dominated one wall, and thick leather furniture sat atop a deep-brown rug. The crackle of the fireplace mixed with the soft hum of morning.

A delicious smell tickled his nose, pulling him down the long hallway toward the open kitchen. Stainless steel appliances gleamed on granite countertops, and rustic oak cabinets added warmth to the space. Emily stood at the stove, pulling a casserole from the oven.

Jackson blinked. He had imagined seeing her first thing in the morning more times than he cared to admit, though none of those fantasies had involved her wearing clothes. Today, she wore pressed black slacks, another pair of damn impressive boots, and a light-blue sweater that hugged her curves.

He just stared for a moment. "How did you get to my house?"

She blew out air. "Seriously. The second I stepped out of my room, I had ten escorts, male and female, all ages, who wanted to show me the town. I asked an elderly pack member named Atticus for a ride."

Jackson blanched. "Atticus had his license suspended. The guy can't see worth crap. No more rides from him."

"Oh." She slowly nodded. "That explains why everyone else protested." One of her slim shoulders rose. "Also why he hit your hydrangea bush right outside."

Jackson had liked that bush. "I'm glad you made it safely."

"Apparently, you were out all night." Her gaze flicked down his frame. "You're filthy."

Jackson glanced at himself. Even though he had changed his shirt after leaving the mine, dust and grit still coated his jeans. "I was working."

"Mining all night?" She took a step back. The movement only highlighted the contrast between her fresh, polished appearance and his rough, worn state.

Damn, she looked good. Too good.

"I like to take a shift now and then," he said, voice low. Make that every damn night, but she didn't need to know that. "Enjoy my time in a stope smashing for granite." The fact that she'd actually set up meetings for him with other females showed that she actually didn't want to become the Alpha female of his pack. Even if they formed an alliance, her loyalty would always be to her pack, and she obviously saw her father's mortality. Jackson understood that.

Respected it. But it meant she didn't need to know his secrets.

"Oh." A glimmer of approval crossed her eyes. "Well, take a quick shower. I made breakfast."

Jackson stood rooted to the spot, blinking once, slowly. "You thought I was out partying with other women, and you still made breakfast?"

Emily's lips quirked, but her gaze did not waver. "Yeah. I like breakfast." The air between them thickened, tension humming beneath the surface. Her pulse fluttered in her throat, and Jackson's wolf stirred, wanting to close the space between them. The smell of warm food mixed with her natural scent, making it hard to focus. He swallowed the urge to step forward and see how soft that sweater would feel in his hands. "Go shower."

Adorable. She was way too cute. "I'll, ah, go shower." Jackson forced himself to step back, his pulse thudding as he turned toward the hallway. The space between them might as well have been a thread pulled taut. Fragile and ready to snap.

Upstairs, he headed straight to the bathroom and stepped into the shower. The hot water hit his shoulders, easing some of the tension but doing nothing to cool the thoughts that had rooted themselves in his mind: Emily, standing in his kitchen like she belonged there. He dragged a hand down his face, exhaling as the water sluiced over him.

He hurriedly finished, wanting that delicious breakfast.

And the woman cooking it. Damn it.

Clean and dressed in worn jeans and a dark T-shirt, he stepped into the bedroom and caught his reflection in the mirror. Broad shoulders, lean muscles, a few scars. His hands were callused from years of labor. Not the kind of male Emily was used to. Her father practically lived in three-piece suits, and her home was a mansion. She probably preferred someone who wore Armani and carried a briefcase.

He wouldn't know Armani if it bit him on his ass.

He headed back downstairs, finding Emily already seated at the round log table by the wide window. The soft morning light streamed in, catching on the wood's natural knots and grains. His gaze snagged on the placemats, simple but neat. "Huh," he said. "Where did you find those?"

"In the drawer below the pots and pans. You must not use them often."

He gave a short nod. "I don't cook much."

"Yeah, I could tell from all the pre-made meals in your fridge and freezer." Her smile was faint but knowing. "The females in your pack must keep you stocked."

He chuckled. "Many do take pity on me. But to be honest, Gus from the diner takes care of most of it these days. He retired, but he still drops by with meals now and then. I try to go fishing with him when I can, though I've been meaning to take him ice fishing once the rivers freeze over."

"Sounds like he means a lot to you."

"Yeah, he does," Jackson admitted. The thought of Gus brought a tug of warmth to his chest, though it faded as his eyes drifted over the cabin's sparse decor.

"This place definitely needs a female's touch," Emily said, her tone light but her gaze lingering.

Jackson glanced around at the bare walls and unadorned shelves. "Yeah, I guess. I think there are pictures somewhere. Probably in a box up in the attic."

Emily tilted her head slightly, waiting.

"I packed everything away after my father died," he added. The words came out rougher than he intended. "Cleared the whole house when I took over as Alpha. Didn't think much about decorating after that."

Silence settled between them, heavy and tinged with tension. She didn't press him. Instead, she unfolded her linen napkin onto her lap, and Jackson did the same. The brush of fabric against his fingers felt strangely intimate. He had linen napkins? Who knew?

"So." She broke the quiet. "Who do you suspect for these mining attacks?"

He shook his head, frustration tightening his shoulders. "I really don't know. Did you call and tell your father about my troubles last night?"

Hurt slid in and then out of her expression. "No. Figured it was your secret."

There was that sweet side of hers. "I didn't mean to hurt your feelings. I'm sorry." Jackson took a bite of the egg casserole, the warm, savory flavors hitting his tongue. It had been a long time since someone had cooked for him in this house. Too long.

Across the table, Emily tucked a strand of hair behind her ear, the curve of her neck drawing his gaze before he forced himself to focus on his plate. While he didn't want to take advantage of her, the safest course of action for her was to mate him. Yet that left her father and pack in a bind. She mattered more, as far as he was concerned.

The food was delicious. Before speaking, Jackson took several more bites, savoring the warmth of the dish. "This is amazing," he mumbled.

Emily laughed, the sound light but warm. "I like to bake and cook. It's not a big deal."

"Yeah, it is." He spooned another helping from the casserole dish.

"I'm glad you like it." She took a small bite, her movements neat and precise. Reaching over, she poured coffee from a carafe decorated with little tulips.

Jackson blinked. "Where the hell did you find a carafe?"

"In one of the upper cabinets."

Where the heck did that come from? "I didn't know you had a domestic side."

She rolled her eyes. "Shut up. Now tell me about the Blounts and why Warren wants you gone."

Ah. On to safe subjects. Fine by him. He leaned back in his chair, the tension coiling low in his torso. "Twenty years ago, when I was fifteen and stepping up, Warren wanted the job. The council outvoted him. He was already too old, and his grandsons were too young. He's hated my guts since. Really didn't like when I started modernizing things."

"You mean letting pack members leave to live in the human world for a while?"

"Yeah." Jackson took a sip of coffee. A hint of cinnamon hit his tongue. It was rich and smooth, better than anything he'd had in months. "The old ways weren't working. As a kid, I wanted nothing more than to go out and explore the world."

"But you didn't get to," she said softly.

He shook his head. "Nope. Started training harder than ever. Worked every aspect of the mines. Figured if I was going to own all three, I should know everything about them."

She sat back, studying him with something unreadable in her eyes. "That was smart. Especially at fifteen."

"There wasn't much else to do," he admitted. "The council handled disputes, protection, all of that. I learned as I went."

She sipped her coffee. "Do they still run things?"

"No," Jackson said shortly. "They want to, but I took over years ago. They were against modernization, too."

"So, you won that one."

He set the coffee mug down, the sound loud in the quiet space. "I did. But I have a bad feeling the council might try to align with Blount and then drag in other pack members." Not that he couldn't take them all out. But that would make him a shitty leader, wouldn't it?

The air between them shifted. Jackson's pulse kicked, the warmth of her presence making it harder to focus on pack politics. He wouldn't force her to stay—probably. But he'd love to explore this attraction between them.

"They wouldn't go so far as to sabotage your mines, would they?" Emily asked.

Jackson slowed down now that his belly was warm and content. "I can't imagine they'd want to hurt anyone in the pack. We need every available body working the mines or on protection detail." It was as much as he was willing to admit to her.

"How many members are in your pack?" she asked.

"Plenty," he answered smoothly, taking another drink of coffee. "I appreciate you cooking me breakfast."

She glanced at her phone. "Anytime. Hey, we've got about half an hour before you meet your first possible mate." She sounded way too delighted about putting him in this position. Brat.

"You know, you could still have the job," Jackson said, meaning every word. He would love to come home to her every morning. Sure, he didn't believe in love, but lust? He had that in abundance for her.

"Thanks, but I can't desert my father. If I leave, Vic will challenge him. With me in place, our pack will continue to support my dad. For as long as they can."

Perhaps she'd consider a relationship outside of mating. No. He knew, without a doubt, that one taste of her, and he wouldn't let her go. Then he'd be at war with the Slate Pack. Maybe the other two Stope Packs, as well. "What's your plan at that point? Actually becoming the Alpha?"

She paled. "Yes." Was that a lie? It felt like a lie. Interesting. Perhaps Em had no clue what she'd do next.

Their territories were located on opposite sides of the state and couldn't be combined, so Jackson couldn't even offer that possibility. "Maybe next lifetime for us, huh?"

"As if we get more than one," she replied.

"Perhaps." He swirled the last of his coffee in the mug. "Never really gave it much thought."

She glanced outside the wide windows to the dark trees. "I visited your study earlier."

He lifted an eyebrow. "Snooping?"

"Oh, most definitely," she replied, her smile softening something inside him.

Jackson studied her. For the life of him, he couldn't figure out why anyone would call her an ice queen. Sure, she was tall with striking, white-blond hair, but there was nothing cold about Emily Nightsom. Heat lived in her gaze, and sharp intelligence behind her teasing smile.

"I saw all the miniature fighter jets and planes you've put together," she added.

His mouth curved slightly. "Did you, now?"

"Mm-hmm. Didn't take you for the model-building type."

"Gotta keep my hands busy somehow."

Her eyes flicked to his hands, where they rested against the coffee mug. Jackson swore the air thickened between them. He cleared his throat and set the mug down with a thunk. Damn woman was going to drive him insane.

He shifted in his chair, not wanting to feel exposed. "Everybody needs a hobby."

"It's a good one, Jackson," Emily said, her voice softening. "Takes precision, and it looks like you had fun."

He shrugged. "Something to do when I can't sleep. Started worrying about this pack when I was fifteen and haven't stopped since."

She chuckled lightly. "Yeah, that's the job, isn't it?"

"And you? Hobbies?" he asked, curious.

"Well, I like to shop," she admitted, her smile tilting toward playful. "Writing started as a hobby, but once I submitted a couple of books, I started making money from it. I don't do signings or anything, so I'm a bit of a recluse as an author. It's kind of fun."

He leaned back in his chair. "I'm glad one of your dreams came true."

Her cheeks colored slightly, though her eyes stayed steady. "Thanks. Enough small talk. You need to go change so you can meet your future mate."

He glanced down at his jeans and T-shirt. "This is what I wear."

She raised an eyebrow. "You should dress up a little."

"Absolutely not." He stood and stretched. "Whoever mates me needs to know exactly what she's getting."

Emily's gaze flicked over him, and the air between them tightened for a moment. He held her eyes for longer than he should have before taking his dishes to the sink. Was she actually going through with introducing him to other Alpha females?

It was going to be a fucking fascinating day.

CHAPTER 9

Emily settled into one of the guest chairs in Jackson's office, crossing her legs and smoothing the front of her sweater. He could have at least dressed up a little, but she had to admit he had a point. His usual jeans and dark T-shirt suited him more than any suit ever would.

A knock sounded on the door.

"Come in," Jackson said from behind his desk, where several ledgers lay open. He had been working for the past hour on mining business while Emily typed out a chapter on her phone. She preferred her laptop, but she could write this way when necessary. The tension between her and Jackson still hummed beneath the surface, a constant thrum she tried to ignore.

Raya poked her head inside, looking pretty and competent, her dark eyes sharp with unspoken thoughts. "Do you have a minute?"

Jackson glanced up and then gestured for her to enter. "Yeah, come in. What's on your mind?"

Raya stepped fully into the office and closed the door behind her. She wore a smart black silk suit and lovely Louboutin heels today. Her gaze flicked to Emily, lingering for a beat too long before returning to Jackson and handing over a stack of papers.

"What's this?" Jackson read the top page and then burst out laughing.

Raya wrung her hands together.

Emily looked between them. "What?"

Raya cleared her throat. "It's, ah, well a petition for you and Jackson to be formally married this Christmas in a celebration for the entire town. The Lady's Craft Crew needs that much time to decorate and plan."

A petition?

"You signed it?" Jackson snapped, flipping over a page.

Pink climbed into Raya's face. "The matchmaking scheme isn't a good idea, you know. Bringing in a potential Alpha female without fully vetting her pack is reckless. And this whole setup—" Raya's eyes shifted toward Emily again, her expression guarded. "It's asking for trouble."

"I appreciate your input," Jackson said, his voice even. "But I know what I'm doing."

"Do you?" Raya's smile was tight. "Because the pack has decided on Emily. We like her."

Jackson handed back the papers. "You don't even know her."

Raya's chin lifted. "We've all been reading her books, and we feel like we do. The Lady's Craft Crew loves her, and they hold weight." She turned on her heel and quietly left the office.

The door clicked shut, leaving the air between Emily and Jackson thick.

Emily blanched. "We've given everybody the wrong idea."

Jackson just growled and returned to his work.

They worked in silence for another fifteen minutes until Raya reopened the door, all efficient. "You have a Ms. Abilene Ironclaw here to meet you."

"Send her in," Jackson replied, his jaw tightening slightly. His gaze flicked toward Emily, who tried to hide her amusement.

The door swung open, and Abilene swept in with a grace that seemed more choreographed than natural. Emily blinked several times. The woman had to be at least six feet tall, with long, cascading curls as black as night and amber eyes that seemed to glow against her golden skin. Her bone structure was delicate, her waist impossibly narrow, and her curves perfectly placed.

Jackson stood. Emily did, as well, though far more reluctantly.

"Ms. Ironclaw," Jackson greeted, stepping around his desk and holding out a hand.

"Alpha Tryne," Abilene replied, her voice smooth and cultured as she placed her hand in his. Jackson gave it a brief, firm shake, and Abilene blushed slightly as their hands parted.

"Let's sit over here." Jackson gestured toward the sitting area near the wide window. The space was furnished with an old leather couch and two matching chairs that had probably been there since his grandfather's time. The coffee table in front of them bore scratches as though marked by restless hands over the years.

Jackson seated Abilene on the couch with care, which made Emily want to roll her eyes. For Pete's sake. Still, she followed and took one of the chairs across from them.

"Hi. I'm Emily Nightsom." She kept her tone pleasant. She might as well introduce herself before Jackson forgot she existed.

"Nice to meet you in person," Abilene replied, her smile revealing perfect white teeth and a single dimple that added an infuriating touch of charm. "Um, a couple of younger wolves stopped me on the way into the building and said you two had decided to mate each other?"

Heat flushed through Emily's torso. "No. Not at all. I'm facilitating this process for Jackson."

Abilene snorted. "All right. This is an interesting situation. I didn't know there was a matchmaking service for wolf shifters."

The joke didn't seem so funny now. "I'm new at this. It's a brand-new enterprise," Emily replied with a smile she hoped looked more professional than forced.

"It's kind of fun," Abilene said with a soft laugh, her gaze flicking between Jackson and Emily.

Jackson lowered himself into the chair beside Abilene and leaned back, all casual confidence. "Can I get you anything? Coffee, water…bourbon?"

Abilene's amber eyes warmed. "No, I'm fine. But thank you."

Emily forced her smile to stay in place, though her fingers curled slightly. She hated her already. Of course, she wasn't to blame for the stomach ache that plagued Emily daily.

Abilene glanced over, her amber eyes curious. "You're the matchmaker. What happens next?"

"Well, we just wanted to meet you," Emily said quickly.

Abilene turned back to Jackson, studying him with open interest. "Why are you having the Alpha female of the Slate Pack find you a mate? I'd think you could manage that without any help."

"I'm rather busy," Jackson replied, his tone easy. "So, why are you here?"

"Possibly to become the Alpha female of this pack." Abilene smiled.

Jackson's gaze flicked over her, assessing. "I'd imagine you could find any mate you wanted."

Oh, for goodness' sake. Emily caught the glimmer of amusement in Jackson's eyes—and interest, too. Not that she could blame him. Abilene was gorgeous.

"Finding a mate is not as easy as you'd think," Abilene shrugged delicately. "Most packs keep to themselves, and I'm related to many of the eligible wolves in mine."

"Which pack are you from?" Jackson asked.

Abilene perked up. "We're the Redridge Pack. From southern Utah," she replied. "We're more into snow and painting than politics."

"Painting?" Emily asked, surprised.

"Yes. We're pretty much a pack of painters." Humor lit Abilene's eyes. "We attend festivals and sell our work worldwide. We don't mingle much with other packs. We're too free-spirited, I suppose."

Jackson frowned slightly. "If you mated an Alpha, that freedom would end."

"I don't see why it should," Abilene replied smoothly. "I'd still paint, and I'd probably travel occasionally. Once I had children, I'd stay closer to home, but painting is part of who I am."

"I understand that," Emily said. "I write romantic suspense and thrillers. I sell them from home."

Abilene leaned toward her. "Do you ever go to signings?"

"No. I'm not interested in that. I suppose I could if I wanted to, though."

Abilene nodded. "You should think about it. I love traveling to showings."

"Traveling would be off the table, and I want you to know that up front," Jackson said, his voice firm. "If you became the Alpha female of this pack, the role would keep you here, and your safety would be our top priority."

Abilene lifted her chin. "How so?" she asked, her tone smooth but her eyes sharper now.

"An Alpha and his family have many duties," Jackson said. "We're involved in everything within the pack, which takes a lot of time. Although we do let our younger members go off to college and learn skills they then bring back to the pack," he added, his tone carrying a subtle emphasis.

"I understand," Abilene replied.

Emily tilted her head slightly. "As a free spirit and a painter, I assume you're a romantic. A contractual mating might be uncomfortable for you."

Abilene shrugged, her gaze sweeping Jackson's frame with an appraising slowness that tightened Emily's chest. "I admit it would be different, but again, I'm related to everyone in my pack. I'd like to have children someday. I'm in my early thirties, so I have time, but I think I could do well as the Alpha female of a pack. I'd like to see the packs become creative with painting, sculpting, and learning more about the world around us. It's time some of your packs stop warring with each other and start exploring the outside world."

"I agree," Jackson said. "But the pack has to come first. Always."

Abilene's smile didn't quite reach her eyes. "I agree," she replied, but something in her tone rang hollow.

Emily went with her instincts. "What are you hiding, Abilene?"

Abilene's shoulders stiffened slightly. "Excuse me?"

"That's not the only reason you're here." Emily kept her voice calm. "What is it?"

Jackson shot her a sharp glance but stayed silent as Abilene's gaze shifted toward the window. The pause stretched just long enough to confirm Emily's suspicions.

"We're low on males," Abilene admitted finally. "To be honest, we need protection. Other packs have tried to take us over, and while we value our freedom, we need the security of a much larger and stronger pack. If I mated Jackson and we reached such an agreement, I'd want my entire pack brought into yours."

Jackson's gaze narrowed slightly. "Who's in charge of your pack?"

"We have an Alpha," she replied. "His name is Glenden. But he's more than two hundred years old and has no direct descendants. I'm a distant cousin, and I do have Alpha blood in me."

"How many members are in your pack?" Emily asked, curious.

Abilene shifted, her posture still graceful, but a tightness appeared around her mouth. "About fifty," she said finally.

"Do you have any skills besides painting?" Emily asked.

Abilene's smile sharpened slightly. "I can negotiate. I've helped secure trade agreements with human communities near our territory, and I know how to lead when necessary. Being creative doesn't mean being weak."

Emily laughed, though the sound came out weaker than she intended. Her head throbbed with a hollow ache that seemed to pulse behind her eyes, and her arms felt weak. She rolled her shoulders back to hide the tremor, but the sensation clung stubbornly. "I totally agree with you."

Abilene visibly relaxed. "We're a good group, and we're hard workers."

"All right." Jackson stood, his movements smooth and certain. "Thank you for meeting with me today. Why don't you set up a meeting between Glenden and me? We'll talk about bringing your pack in."

Abilene rose gracefully, but her eyes widened slightly. "So, you do want to mate?"

"You don't have to mate me to join the pack," Jackson replied evenly. "If I like your Alpha, we have room. A lot of it, actually. We own a good portion of this area of the entire state. But I would require an oath of allegiance from every member, and I'd need to meet with each of them first."

Emily pushed to her feet, her legs heavier than they should be. Her pulse fluttered oddly in her neck. "You're taking in new members?"

"Sure." Jackson shrugged as if it was the simplest thing in the world. "I've got three mines. We could use more workers, and new blood wouldn't hurt."

Emily's stomach turned, her headache pulsing harder. Had

she already found a mate for him? Part of this had started as a joke, but now that thought twisted in her chest. What had she been thinking?

Jackson stepped forward and took Abilene's hand to shake. "So, arrange that meeting, and I'll meet with your Alpha. Then maybe you and I can go on a date and see if we actually like each other. But you don't have to mate me to protect your pack."

Abilene's smile softened, and Emily swore she saw the exact moment the female fell in love.

"I'd really like to go on a date with you," Abilene said.

"Excellent." Jackson glanced at Emily, dare and more than a hint of challenge in his too-blue eyes. "I'm sure Emily can set that up since she's taken over as my matchmaker. I greatly look forward to it."

Emily forced a smile, though her head throbbed harder. How in the hell was she supposed to sabotage this when she could barely stay upright?

CHAPTER 10

Emily thanked the five older male wolves who'd insisted upon walking the hotel stairs with her up to her floor.

"Sure." Obel Johnson handed over her purse. He'd gallantly secured it at the bottom of the stairs before his friends could. All five of them wore pressed slacks with button down shirts–probably their best. Their hair was coiffed and they were neatly shaved. "We left you some presents in your hotel room as well as our phone numbers."

Robert Montague, his white hair slicked back, hitched up his pants. "We'll keep our hearing aids in just in case."

"No, please don't. Get some sleep." She opened her door and backed into the room, offering a gentle smile. "Have a nice night."

They all bowed.

She shut the door. Wow. Just wow. It was kind of nice to be wanted, though. She tossed her purse onto the hand-carved desk in the hotel suite, her head ringing from her illness and the day spent with Jackson. The penthouse was undeniably charming, with large windows overlooking the quaint granite town. Exposed stone walls framed the space, blending rustic character with modern luxury. The bedroom held a king-sized bed with a dark wooden frame that sat against the far wall, dressed in crisp white linens and a plush navy throw with the embroidered outline of a howling wolf.

Someone had started the fire for her in the stone fireplace across from the bed, the flicker of low flames casting amber shadows against the smooth wooden walls. The smell of pine and fresh linen drifted in the air.

A myriad of gift baskets, new ones, had been placed on the desk and dresser holding all sorts of candies, cookies, and bath goodies. There had been just as many the night before.

Still, the comfort did nothing to settle the storm in her body, which ached more than usual. She felt two thousand years old.

What was wrong with her body?

She had met with two more prospective mates for Jackson, and frankly, all three females wanted him. What had she been thinking? Of course, they wanted him. He was seriously hot and an Alpha who ran an entire pack. Part of her had set out on this whole matchmaking journey to mess with him, but she hadn't quite considered how appealing the damn male would be to everyone else.

Of course, she couldn't mate him and abandon her father and pack. So, it made sense to help him. Except now she wanted to claw out the eyes of all three females.

After Abilene, she'd met with Bianca and Freya, who were from packs scattered across the States, both looking for protection. It made sense they would seek Jackson out. He was known to be a fierce fighter, and his pack was strong.

Still, she had to admit she was impressed he worked the mine at night. The rumors of him partying every evening had clearly been exaggerated, or maybe he'd just grown out of that behavior after his teenage years. Either way, it was yet another intriguing fact about the badass fighter.

Her phone buzzed. She glanced at the screen and answered without thinking. "Nightsom."

"Hi. It's Nadia." The female sounded unsure.

Emily sat on the bed, her headache still lingering. "Hi. Is everything okay?"

"Everything is weird. I keep meeting people who say I look exactly like you, except without the impressive height. If one more person calls me short, I'm going to lose my mind."

Emily chuckled. "Sorry about that. I'll be home as soon as I can."

"About that… I think I'm going to head back to my pack. Well, my new pack."

Panic tightened Emily's chest. "Please, stay. We need a show of force from the family, especially against Victor. Just your existence strengthens our father's position."

Nadia sighed, the sound more resigned than annoyed. "Fine. So, how's it going pretending to be a matchmaker for the hottie Jackson Tryne?"

Emily rolled her eyes, though a smile tugged at her lips. "I'm not pretending."

"Please. I saw the air combust between you two."

"Maybe," Emily admitted. "But it can't happen. I can't leave our pack, and there's no way two Alpha mates can live apart." Her stomach twisted as she spoke.

Nadia was silent for a moment. "I've always thought love trumps everything."

Emily coughed. "Love? Come on. The guy turns me on. That's all."

"Right," Nadia drawled. "Keep telling yourself that. For now, did you find out anything about Caidrik and his work with Jackson?"

Emily raised an eyebrow. "Why do you ask? You interested in him?"

"Of course not," Nadia shot back too quickly. "He's my

sudden and very intense bodyguard, and I don't even know the guy. I feel like I should at least understand his background."

"Uh-huh." Emily settled into the whole sister thing. "He's not a bad-looking guy, you know. Big, broody, all protective. I see the appeal."

"Seriously, stop." Nadia groaned. "I was just curious since you're there."

Emily chuckled. "I haven't found out much yet. Jackson's pretty tight-lipped about his pack, but I'll see what I can find out." Maybe she should take this matchmaking gig international.

"Thanks. Get some sleep, and we'll talk soon. 'Night."

"'Night." Emily ended the call, staring at the phone for a long moment before setting it aside. She needed time to get to know Nadia, so hopefully, the female would remain in town.

Standing, she headed into the opulent bathroom that also held several more gift baskets from pack members and took a shower, leaving her hair damp and loose as she changed into silk pajamas. The soft fabric clung to her skin, offering a hint of comfort, but her heart still ached. The undeniable pull between her and Jackson wouldn't let her rest. Yet every female they'd met today wanted him. Badly.

He'd been amused, kind, and gracious with each candidate in a way he'd never been with her. Not once had he needled them or flashed that infuriating smirk. And none of them had seemed to mind his torn jeans or worn T-shirt. One of the women had even called him charming.

Worse yet, he'd acted charming. Jerk.

Emily snuggled into the bed and opened her laptop, fingers punching the keys as she dove into writing a murder scene. A gruesome, visceral one that let her vent her frustration. Each keystroke helped chip away at the tension coiled inside her. Blood splattered, bones snapped, and by the time her fictional detective found the body, she felt marginally better.

Her eyes grew heavy. Tomorrow, she'd have to meet with three more females eager to claim Jackson. This time, instead of groaning about it, Jackson said he looked forward to it. It must be nice having females fawn over him all day.

Still, she understood his need to focus on discovering who had been sabotaging the mines. By the end of her chapter, her thoughts blurred. She brushed her teeth, slid back into bed, and exhaled as the mattress cradled her. The suite's rustic charm felt unexpectedly cozy, and the soft hum of the distant town sounds drifted through the window. Sleep claimed her swiftly, though the ache in her solar plexus lingered just beneath the surface.

The sharp, acrid stench of garlic sliced through her dreams. Adrenaline flooded her veins the second before her eyelids popped open. Before she could react, rough hands grabbed her arms, yanking her upright. Coarse fabric scraped across her face as a burlap sack was shoved over her head, muffling her gasp.

The whole damn thing smelled like garlic. Damn it. She couldn't smell the wolves at all.

Panic surged, white-hot and instinctive. Emily twisted violently, her muscles surging with the power of her wolf side as she drove her elbow back into someone's ribs. The solid impact made the male grunt in pain—it sounded male, anyway. Seizing the moment, she lashed out with her legs, kicking wildly. Her foot connected with another body, earning a sharp curse.

"Hold her still!" a voice barked, rough and breathless.

She didn't recognize the voice. Who was it? Were these the same guys as last time? The garlic clogged her senses, making her eyes water.

She jerked her head, trying to dislodge the sack as she threw her weight sideways, driving her captors toward the nightstand. The lamp crashed to the floor, the glass shattering and pinging across the wood.

There were two of them. She knew that much.

One cursed as she scraped her nails against exposed skin. She twisted again, managing to wrench one arm free.

She drove her fist hard into the nearest chest, but a pair of hands seized her from behind, pulling her off balance. She snarled, her instincts flaring to life as she used her body's momentum to twist sideways. Her knee shot up, aiming for what she hoped was someone's groin. She connected hard, and the satisfying groan of pain spurred her onward.

Another figure lunged, but she ducked beneath their grasping hands, lurching toward the door. Her pulse pounded in her ears as she sprinted forward, only to be yanked back as fingers twisted in her top.

"Not so fast, sweetheart." The same voice. Who the hell was that?

She gritted her teeth and threw her head back, smashing her skull into the attacker's face. Bone cracked, and the hand in her pajama top loosened.

Screaming, she lunged toward where she thought the door might be, her hands scrabbling for the stupid bag. Her spine stiffened, and she began to shift into a wolf.

Suddenly, a sharp blow landed on the back of her head. Pain burst behind her skull, white-hot and disorienting. Her legs buckled beneath her, and her vision blurred as she hit the floor. Rough hands seized her again, dragging her backward as her consciousness slipped toward darkness.

When she slowly came to, she held perfectly still as the uneven motion of a vehicle jostled her body.

Blinking against the darkness, she shifted and felt the rough texture of the carpet beneath her hands. Her wrists were bound tightly in front of her, and her pulse quickened as she assessed her surroundings. The space was tight. Way too tight to shift. Attempting to change forms would break every bone in her body.

Gritting her teeth, she yanked the garlic-scented bag from her head, wincing as the odor still clung to her hair and skin. Her head throbbed, a dull ache pounding just behind her right eye. The blow they'd delivered had left her disoriented, but adrenaline surged through her veins now. Her feet, blessedly free, pressed against what she guessed were the vehicle's taillights. She kicked hard with her bare feet.

Nothing happened.

She kicked again, harder this time, but the trunk's metal shell held firm. Pain clocked through her feet. The vehicle was probably an older model, as the taillights on a newer one would have shattered by now. Frustration coiled tight in her chest. How long had she been out? Minutes? Hours? She had no way of knowing.

Breathing through her nose to steady her pulse, she raised her bound wrists and tested the ropes, feeling their rough fibers bite into her skin. With deliberate focus, she let her canines elongate. The sharp points pressed against the ropes as she began gnawing, grinding through each strand with slow, steady determination. The fibers resisted at first, but her wolf's teeth were made for tearing through flesh and bone. Ropes were nothing.

The hum of the engine vibrated through the trunk. Sweat dampened her brow as she moved, changing her angle to bite through the last stubborn strands. Her wrists strained against the bonds until, with a final snap, the ropes gave way. The freedom sent a burst of energy through her limbs.

Yet her body still felt so damn weak. She had to figure out what was wrong with her. After she got out of this mess. If they'd wanted her dead, they would've tried already.

Probably.

She flexed her hands, feeling the blood rush back into her fingers. Her head still throbbed, but the pulse of determination overrode the pain. Curling her legs beneath her, she tensed, ready to strike the moment the trunk opened.

Whoever had taken her was about to regret it.

CHAPTER 11

J ackson was halfway into breaking through a stubborn vein of granite deep within his largest mine. The air was thick with the scent of earth and traces of mineral dust, and sweat clung to his back beneath his shirt. He gripped the handle of a pickaxe, enjoying the old-fashioned way of beating into the solid rock.

If nothing else, it helped him ease some pressure in his fucking body.

Pressure from one Miss Emily Nightsom.

He swung the axe, muscles straining as the rock face fought him. Each strike echoed through the narrow tunnel, sharp and rhythmic, as shards of stone broke loose and clattered to the ground.

The sense of granite lived in his blood. The material was dense here, and extracting it required precision. Oh, he had a jackhammer and a hydraulic splitter off to the side, but he wanted to feel the fight tonight.

Too much force and the slabs would fracture into useless fragments. Not enough, and the rock wouldn't yield at all.

"What the hell are you beating out of your system?" Leroy

Lakeland strode up, sweat pouring down his round face. He'd served as the mine foreman for longer than Jackson had been alive, and the wolf was as wide as he was tall—which was very.

"Everything." Jackson angled the pick just right before driving it into a natural seam. A thin crack appeared in the granite, and he set the tool aside. "It was a long day."

Leroy snorted, shoving the yellow hard hat back on his head. "I heard. You really picking a mate from an Internet search by the Slate chick?"

Chick? Emily wouldn't like that. "I have no fucking clue what I'm doing." Jackson leaned back against the battered rock, the rough surface biting into his shoulders.

Leroy wiped some dirty sweat off his chin. "I've seen a picture of Nightsom. You should enforce the agreement you had with her father."

Right. Forcing Emily to mate would lead to death. Probably for them both. Plus, he genuinely liked her. Always had. She was so proper and composed that he wanted nothing more than to shake her up a little. Catch her off balance. To catch her, period. "Politics makes our mating impossible."

"Fuck politics."

If only it were that simple.

"You haven't told her father about the attacks here, right? Or the fact that we're down workers…and soldiers?"

"Of course not," Jackson growled. He refused to show weakness to any other pack. "Emily knows about the attacks, but that's not a concern. She has no idea we lost so many pack members to the poisoning five years ago."

It turned out the Ravencall Pack had also poisoned some of Erik's pack five years ago, as well as more recently. They'd tried a similar attack against Jackson's, and the Granite Pack had lost members. Too many. At least the bastards specifically responsible were now dead. Jackson owed Erik Volk for that.

Now, Jackson just had to rebuild.

Adding new members to the pack would strengthen their numbers. Hell, this ridiculous speed-dating circus might actually serve a purpose. The three females he'd met that day had all been sweet, intelligent, and intriguing in their own ways. Any of them would make a suitable Alpha female. They were logical choices that would help secure the pack's future.

But none of them unsettled him the way Emily did.

The damn woman drove him crazy.

Part of him liked it, the other part wanted to tame her. Just a bit. The best path for her, the safest, was to mate him. But how could she turn her back on the Slate Pack?

Regardless, he might add one or two of his prospective mates' packs to his. It would give them numbers and strength, as well as new blood. They needed that.

Even now, surrounded by rock and silence, he could still hear the sharp edge of Emily's voice, see the spark in her eyes when she challenged him. It wasn't just her beauty, though that alone was enough to distract any male. It was her fire and refusal to back down. She stood her ground like a true Alpha, even when she had every reason to walk away.

"You got something there." Leroy nodded to the rock, grabbing a pry bar and tossing it to him.

Jackson caught the heavy steel instrument and wedged the tapered end into a narrow fissure in the granite. The colors tempted him. Good thing he had wolf sight. Leaning his weight into the battle, his muscles burned with the effort as the dense stone resisted.

Sweat trickled down his back, the heat from the surrounding rock pressing against him. The crack widened with a low groan, the vibrations traveling up the bar and into his arms. Fighting nature, he shoved. The slab shifted and came free with a sharp crack that echoed through the tunnel.

"Excellent," Leroy noted.

Jackson staggered back a step, his boots scraping against the rough stone floor as the slab tumbled to the ground, sending up a cloud of dust.

The foreman crouched and ran a gloved hand over the granite's rough, speckled surface. "Nice job, Jackson," Leroy said.

Jackson studied the slab. The mineral flecks caught the dim light of the overhead lamps, a mixture of quartz, feldspar, and mica gleaming beneath the dust. The quality was excellent. Dense, clean, and with minimal fractures. This load would fetch a good price, especially for construction and monument work.

Wiping the sweat from his brow with the back of his arm, Jackson straightened and glanced toward the tunnel's distant entrance. The hum of machinery echoed from somewhere above, the heartbeat of the mine pulsing around him. It was easy to focus on the work down there, surrounded by stone and darkness. But no amount of labor could erase the lingering heat that Emily stirred in him.

Leroy stepped beside him. "You know, Jackson, the council's been in serious talks with Blount. They're eyeing his grandsons."

"I know." Jackson's jaw tightened.

"They want to keep control, same as always. But you've got support. More than you think." Leroy patted some dust from his gloves and glanced sideways. "You need to secure that support, though. Mating Emily...it'd lock things down solid."

Jackson shook his head. "For our pack. Not hers."

"We'd become her pack. Want to, in fact. I signed the petition, you know." Leroy's radio dinged from his belt, and he lifted it, pressing the side button. "Lakeland."

"It's Dickie up in the office. There's a problem."

Of course, there was a problem. "Another attack?" Jackson asked.

Dickie sneezed. "No. I just got a call from the hotel."

Every nerve in Jackson's body went taut. "Excuse me?"

"Yeah. Frederick just called. Somebody knocked him out, and Emily's gone."

Jackson froze, the words slamming into him like a physical blow. Frederick Wallington had owned the hotel for years and was also a hell of a soldier in his day. Now, he was long retired. "Somebody knocked out Fred?"

"Yeah. He said he was up making warm milk because he couldn't sleep, and two males came through the back door and jumped him," Dickie said.

"Who were they?" Jackson's voice went low and sharp.

"Fred barely saw them. Said their faces were covered, and they reeked of garlic."

"Damn it." Jackson dropped his pry bar with a clatter and bolted down the tunnel toward the elevator shaft. Panic clawed at his chest, rising fast and hot, but he shoved it aside. Emily was in danger. He had to find her.

Leroy jumped into the elevator beside him as Jackson slammed the control panel.

"This is bad, Jackson. If we let the female Alpha from the Slate Pack get kidnapped—"

"Fuck that," Jackson growled. "We'll get her back. I want everybody in the vicinity of the hotel interviewed. Every single person. I want to know what everybody saw or heard. Got me?"

"Yes, sir. I'll get on it." Leroy swallowed hard as the elevator began rising slowly. Dust drifted from the walls as gears clanked above, the echoes bouncing off the tunnel walls.

"A few businesses are open late around the hotel," Leroy added. "Maybe someone saw something."

"They'd better have." Jackson's pulse hammered in his ears. His fists were clenched so tight his nails bit into his palms. His heart pounded with a force that made it hard to breathe. Anger burned through him like wildfire. Beneath it, sharp and undeniable, was fear. Real, gut-deep fear. And something darker. Possessiveness.

The primal, territorial urge to tear through anyone who dared to touch Emily gripped him so hard it almost doubled him over. The intensity of it shocked him and made his pulse stutter for half a second. She wasn't his. Didn't seem to want to be. But right now, none of that mattered.

The elevator shuddered as it reached the surface. Before the gate had fully opened, Jackson was moving, sprinting across the gravel lot toward his truck. The cold night air slapped against his overheated skin, but he barely noticed. Keys jingled in his hand as he yanked open the driver's side door.

Leroy scrambled in beside him, slamming the door shut. Jackson turned the key, the engine rumbling to life beneath the hood. His fingers flexed and curled around the steering wheel, knuckles white with tension.

"They can't have gotten far. We'll find her." Leroy's voice was steady, but Jackson could hear the uncertainty beneath it.

"We have to." Jackson shifted into gear and gunned the truck onto the main road, tires spitting gravel behind them. Streetlights flashed as they rushed past. He gripped the wheel tighter, like holding on to it could somehow pull her back to him. His mind raced, calculating possible routes the kidnappers might have taken, but underneath all the logic and planning, raw fury coiled in his chest.

The thought of Emily in someone else's hands, frightened and vulnerable, unleashed a fierce, uncontrollable force within him. It wasn't just the duty of an Alpha protecting his territory. This was personal. Bone-deep. No one would take her from him. No one.

Nothing could happen to Emily Nightsom.

He wouldn't let it.

CHAPTER 12

The vehicle hit a series of bumps, and Emily groaned as her body slammed against the roof and then the floor of the trunk. The scratchy carpet scraped her bare arms, and she bit back a curse. Her head throbbed worse than usual, and when she reached back to touch her scalp, she winced at the swollen bump beneath her fingers. Bastards.

Why would anyone kidnap her from Jackson's territory? None of this made sense. Curling onto her side, she tucked into a ball to minimize the impact of the rough ride. The vehicle rattled and bounced on what had to be a dirt road. The car slowed and she braced herself to attack.

Voices filtered through the thin metal.

"All right, you take her shirt that way to spread her scent, and you take these socks the other direction. I'll meet you at the rendezvous spot tomorrow at noon. Get out of this territory as soon as possible."

Emily pressed her ear against the side of the trunk, straining to hear. So there were three of them? They'd taken some of her clothing? Bastards. Her stomach clenched.

A percussion thudded through the air. Someone had shifted.

Then another wave. So two out of the three had shifted. Good. That left only one—the driver.

The vehicle rocked and a car door slammed shut. The vehicle picked up speed again, bouncing hard over what felt like potholes. She moved out of her attack position and flattened herself on the floor, clutching the ledge inside the trunk, trying not to slam against the walls. The driver didn't give a damn if she got bruised. She inhaled through her nose, but the lingering garlic clung to her senses, masking any scents of the trees or terrain. She ground her teeth. The minute she got out of there, she would shove that garlic-soaked sack down the bastard's throat.

A tremor started in her ankles and crept up her legs. Not now. Not when she needed to be at full strength. Her arms started to shake, and panic clawed at her chest. What the hell was wrong with her?

The vehicle traveled for what felt like forever before finally jerking to a stop. The sudden halt sent her tumbling forward, slamming her shoulder against the hard metal. Groaning, she rolled onto her hands and knees again, her muscles tensed to spring.

A heavy fist pounded against the trunk lid above her.

"Hey. I've got a gun loaded with silver bullets, and I'll use it if you try anything. Don't test me."

Emily froze. The trunk latch clicked, and the lid sprang open. Fresh air and the scents of damp earth and pine rushed in. Squinting against the sudden light, Emily's gaze locked onto the male standing several feet away, gun raised and aimed directly at her.

He held the weapon steady, eyes cold with a warning. He'd have more than enough time to fire if she lunged now.

"Get out," he ordered.

Swallowing back a curse, Emily grabbed the trunk's ledge and eased herself onto the muddy ground. Her white silk pajamas clung to her damp skin, offering little protection against the cool air. Vulnerability crept through her, but she shoved it aside. She just needed one opening to take him down.

She squinted through the darkness at the kidnapper standing several feet away. He had removed his mask, revealing a rugged face with sharp angles and dark eyes that reflected the dim moonlight. Long, blond hair, tied neatly at the nape of his neck, framed his face. Broad shoulders stretched his worn jacket, and he stood with the confidence of someone who knew how to handle himself.

"Who are you?" she asked.

"Doesn't matter." He gestured with the gun—some kind of semi-automatic pistol that could fire multiple rounds without pause. "Walk over there."

Emily's eyes flicked to the rocky path ahead, the jagged stones and rough dirt patches promising to punish her bare feet. She calculated the distance between them. Even if she shifted, he'd have time to get off at least one shot, if not several. The odds weren't in her favor.

"Fine," she muttered, turning and walking with measured steps, ignoring the sting in her feet. She wouldn't give this bastard the satisfaction of seeing her stumble.

The path led to a dark, crumbling cabin crouched against overgrown trees. Splintered wood clung to the weather-beaten frame, and two broken stairs creaked beneath her weight as she climbed them and pushed open the warped door. Inside, the air smelled of dust and damp wood.

Cracks showed in the walls, but no moonlight meant no illumination. Thankfully, her wolf sight still worked, even if her feet didn't. The place was a dump with bare wooden floorboards, a few mismatched lawn chairs, and a folding table cluttered with scattered papers. The chairs were the cheap, collapsible kind sold at gas stations, faded from sun exposure and fraying at the seams. Dust clung to every surface, and the air carried a chill that seeped into her skin.

"Nice place," she muttered.

"Sit," he ordered, gesturing with the pistol.

Emily lowered herself into one of the chairs, biting back a sigh as she took the pressure off her legs. Weakness continued to pulse beneath her skin, a reminder that this illness wanted to kill her. Or at least slow her down enough that she couldn't fight.

The male moved with slow precision, lighting several lanterns placed around the cabin. The soft yellow glow cast long shadows across the walls, and the crackle of a match followed as he tossed the flame into a wide stone fireplace already stacked with kindling. Firelight danced against the stone, offering a small reprieve from the cold air seeping through the walls.

"Who are you?" Emily asked again.

"I was just hired to obtain you alive," he replied, his voice carrying a bored edge that matched the dull gleam in his eyes.

Great. *Alive* didn't mean unharmed. "Why?"

"Don't know. Don't care."

She studied him, her pulse steady despite the tension tightening her muscles. "We've never met, have we?"

"Nope." His smile was slow, deliberate. "Unfortunately. I love the silk PJs, by the way."

"Gee, thanks," she drawled, though her mind spun with possibilities. "You work with two others, I take it? They took my clothing in opposite directions."

"So, you heard that, did you?" He dragged another lawn chair closer. The metal frame scraped against the floor, the faded fabric sagging slightly as he settled into the seat. His gun remained steady, aimed directly at her.

She kept her tone cool despite the panic starting to flood her veins. "How much were you paid to kidnap me?"

"A million," he replied, his aim never wavering.

Emily scoffed. "I'm only worth a million dollars?" How insulting.

He laughed, low and rough. "I have to admit, you're a pretty one. And one hell of a fighter. You nearly took out one of my guys."

"I did my best. I'd like another shot."

"Afraid this is the end of our relationship," he replied with a smirk.

Her brain felt sluggish, but she needed answers. "So, you're just some hired gun who kidnaps people?"

"I take jobs now and then, yeah. Don't work for anyone in particular. I'm more of a contract-basis kind of guy."

She had to keep him talking. "How do people find you?"

"If you don't know, you can't." He flashed a grin. "That's the beauty of it."

Emily eyed the gun, then his steady posture.

"You won't make it if you try to charge. I'll get off at least two shots," he replied easily.

"Might be worth it." Except she didn't have the strength. He didn't need to know that, though. "I don't understand why you won't tell me who hired you. I'm going to meet them anyway."

He checked his watch. "Yeah, but they're a ways off."

"Any idea why someone would want me alive at this point?"

"No clue." He stretched his legs, dark jeans and a black shirt blending into the shadows despite his blond hair.

"Do they plan to kill me?"

He glanced at her breasts beneath the thin silk. "Don't know. Don't care. My job's to deliver you. That's it."

"So it didn't matter that you took me from Jackson Tryne's territory?"

"Not to me." His shoulders lifted in a lazy shrug.

She coughed, trying to concentrate. "I take it you were in charge of the first kidnapping attempt on me?"

"Nope." He shrugged. "Found out all about it and loved the

garlic over the head idea, but you got away, didn't you? If I had kidnapped you, let's just say that you would've remained kidnapped."

Fantastic. Someone really wanted her out of the way. "Who were the other kidnappers?"

"Can't reveal names. Honor among thieves and all of that." He chuckled. "I doubled the industry standard fee to come into Tryne's territory to take you, because they would've just failed again."

She could mess with his head. "There's a reason for that, you know?"

"Meaning what?" His voice rose just a bit.

"Jackson will tear you apart for taking someone from his territory. Anybody, really. But you took me. I'm his friend and his current guest."

The guy's chin lifted. "So?"

"So?" Yeah, he was afraid of Jackson. Who wouldn't be? "Have you ever met him?"

"No."

That sounded truthful. Clearly, Jackson's reputation had this male on alert. She could play with that. "The rumors you've heard about him are true. He has no mercy and is the best hunter and tracker alive." She slowly shook her head as if in pity. "He'll tear you apart just for fun."

Her kidnapper swallowed. Loudly. "He'll never find me. I'm turning you over in a couple of hours, and then I'm out of here. Think I'll go far this time."

"Nowhere will be far enough." Her smile felt mocking. "However, there might be a way out of this for you. I can help. I have more money than whoever hired you. How about I pay you to let me go?"

He tilted his head, considering. "Tempting. But my reputation's my reputation, you know?"

Her pulse kicked up a notch. "How about this? I pay you to

let me go, and then I hire you to take out whoever hired you? That way, nobody knows you broke the contract."

His eyes glinted with amusement. "I like how you think."

"I do my best. What do you say to a fresh two million dollars?"

He rubbed his chin, his gaze calculating. "Three million."

"Two and a half," she countered without hesitation. "All in."

He pulled out a phone and tapped the screen. "You have the money?"

"You know I do. I'm Emily Nightsom. I have access to more than you can imagine."

"Do you, now?" His gaze sharpened slightly. "If I'm going to break a contract, I'll do it right. Just how much do you think your father would pay to get you back?"

CHAPTER 13

Jackson surveyed the demolished hotel room, his chest tightening at the signs of struggle. Emily had put up one hell of a fight. Shattered furniture, overturned lamps, and scattered belongings painted a chaotic picture of her last moments there. His gaze fell on her open suitcase near the bed. Stepping forward, he crouched and picked up the sweater she'd worn earlier, holding it to his nose. Her scent clung to the soft fabric—a delicate mix of wild berries and honeysuckle, warm and fresh with an undertone of something wilder, distinctly wolf.

Thane searched the bathroom and returned, shaking his head. "She fought hard."

Leroy ran into the room. "Okay," he panted, hands braced on his knees. "Doc Gwen was working late. She saw an old, dark-blue sedan, maybe late seventies or early eighties. Boxy frame and chrome bumpers. She didn't think much of it because of the interstate detour five miles back. Tons of different cars have been coming through."

"You need to start some cardio," Jackson muttered, tossing the sweater aside.

"I've been telling you for years that you need an Enforcer," Leroy shot back.

Thane nodded. "I've said the same."

Jackson had always handled his own problems. "I've never needed one before, and I don't need one now." Except somebody had just taken Emily Nightsom right out of his territory.

Zylas Blount stepped into the room, his face pale as he surveyed the destruction. He wore his high school football jersey and dark jeans.

"What the hell are you doing here?" Jackson asked.

"I found him outside," Leroy said, still catching his breath.

Zylas rocked back on his tennis shoes. "A bunch of us were at the movie theater when Leroy asked around. I know you don't have an Enforcer. I might only be eighteen, but I'm one of the best trackers we've got. Being an Alpha, I've got a sensitive nose. Probably better than yours."

"It's not better than mine," Jackson muttered. He was at his peak, and he knew it. Still, the kid had a point. "Do you want to help?"

Zylas squared his shoulders. "I want to help."

Jackson knew of the kid's skills. "Good. We're shifting and tracking her scent. You with me?"

"Absolutely," Zylas said, his jaw firming. "I like Emily a lot. I, uh, asked her out once."

"Yeah, I was there," Jackson replied, voice dry.

Zylas flushed, looking younger than his eighteen years for a moment. "Well, she's really pretty."

Jackson ignored the twinge of possessiveness that sparked in him. They didn't have time for this. "Let's move."

Leroy frowned. "Rumor has it you want to take out Jackson and be the Alpha?"

The kid didn't have a chance against Jackson, even if the council backed him. "Now isn't the time," Jackson growled.

Zylas rolled his eyes. "At the moment, all I want is to play football." Still, he stood a little taller. "But I'll step up for the good of the pack if that's what's needed. I'd never let Emily be kidnapped."

"We'll talk about that later. Right now, we've got to move." Jackson strode out of the room and down the stairs, his pulse hammering in his temple. The instant his boots hit the wet ground outside, he leapt into the air, shifting in mid-motion. Pain and then freedom shot through him as his muscles stretched and bones cracked, reshaping into his powerful wolf form. Rain slicked his thick coat as he landed, paws digging into the cold earth. Behind him, the air stirred as Thane and Zylas shifted, their scents sharp with anticipation.

Jackson lowered his nose to the ground and inhaled. Emily. His head filled with her scent, awakening something primal inside him. His blood pounded with rage and fear. They had hurt her. He'd seen the blood in the hotel room. He'd smelled her. Whoever had made her bleed would pay, and she'd better still be alive.

She had to be.

He surged forward, paws pounding dirt and mud as the rain fought him. The frigid rain promised snow before morning, but he didn't slow. Trees blurred past as he led the others beyond the edge of town, their breathing steady behind him. He pushed faster, driven by an urgency that burned through muscle and bone. Emily needed him.

After miles of relentless running, they reached a three-pronged fork in the road. Jackson skidded to a halt, rain dripping from his muzzle as he sniffed the air. Her scent branched in three directions.

Smart. That meant there were at least three of them.

Shifting back to human form, he let the icy rain cool his overheated skin. The other two did the same, their breath fogging the air as they waited for orders.

"All right. You follow the roads. Zylas, you go west. Thane, east. I'll continue north."

Zylas squared his shoulders. "We'll find her."

Thane nodded. "Got it." Without hesitation, he shifted back into his wolf form and bounded down the eastern road.

Zylas met Jackson's eyes, determination hardening his young face. "Don't worry. We'll get her back."

Jackson almost smiled. He was starting to like the kid. "Stay safe," he ordered before shifting once more. His paws struck the ground, propelling him forward with the speed of a creature born to run. Faster than any true wolf could dream of moving, he raced through the rain-soaked night, clinging to the faint trail of Emily's scent.

His thoughts churned with every step. Why the hell had he let her stay at the hotel? He'd known about the previous kidnapping attempt, yet he'd assumed she'd be safe within his territory. Now, she was paying the price for his misjudgment.

His heart pounded harder, his breath sharp with determination.

He had to find her.

* * *

Emily's feet had gone completely numb. They were bare, so that shouldn't alarm her too much, except she was a wolf. She should feel fine. The illness was progressing faster than she'd anticipated. It was time to stop ignoring the truth and seek medical help. Her mother had died from a mysterious sickness that seemed to target the females in their family. Emily had hidden her symptoms from her father to spare him the worry, but maybe she'd waited too long.

She shifted slightly, feeling the ache in her legs and the hollow weakness in her stomach. "What's your name, anyway?" she asked, her voice steady despite the tension in the air.

"You can call me Bob," he said.

"Bob?"

He shrugged, the motion lazy. "Sure."

"So, what's your next move, Bob?"

He leaned back in the chair, the gun resting on his thigh. "I think I'm gonna call your father. Might as well get more money out of this. Then I'll kill the guy who hired me."

"Who hired you?"

Bob tilted his head as if considering. "Don't know. It was anonymous. I deliver you, I get paid. But if the price is right, I could track them down."

Emily narrowed her eyes. "Double-crossing everyone? So much for honor."

He rolled his eyes. "Honor doesn't pay the bills."

"My father will pay to get me back." She redistributed her weight subtly, testing her balance. If she could regain enough strength, she'd make her move.

Bob's gaze flicked over her, assessing. "Yeah, I figured. Your family's loaded."

"So, who were the other two guys?"

"Just a couple of hired guns. I'll pay them off once this is over."

Good. That meant fewer threats to deal with. She just needed an opening. Her muscles coiled in anticipation, her illness forgotten beneath the sharp pulse of adrenaline that coursed through her veins. "Go for the bigger payout from my father." She kept her tone even, eyes locked on his. She would strike the second he dropped his guard. If only she could get her damn feet to cooperate. Her toes tingled, but the numbness still clung to her calves like a weight.

Bob's gaze drifted lazily over her, head tilting as if considering his options. "I guess if I'm not going to deliver you to whoever hired me, you and I might as well have some fun."

Fun. The word made her stomach twist. Fun for her would

be sinking her teeth into his jugular and holding on until he stopped moving. She forced a tight smile, tilting her head. "Oh, yeah? What did you have in mind?"

He shifted forward, elbows resting on his knees, gun still solid in his grip. The air in the room thickened as he leaned closer, eyes running over her as if seeing her for the first time.

A metallic scent clung to the air. Her blood mixed with the tang of gun oil and the rain-soaked earth from his boots. Emily swallowed against the weakness dragging at her limbs. Just a little longer. She could wait. She could strike when it counted.

She purposefully did not look at the gun.

He winked. "You are pretty."

"Gee, thanks. I think you're a colossal dickhead." There was no reason to be nice. Not anymore.

He stood, eyes gleaming with something dark. "That's just rude. Do I have to shoot you?"

"I'd prefer if you didn't," she replied evenly.

"Take off the pajamas."

"No." Emily ignored the throb of pain echoing through her kidneys. Her muscles coiled. Her pulse hammered.

He tilted his head and tapped the gun against his thigh. "I could shoot you in the leg. You don't need that."

"Yeah, but blood would get everywhere."

His grin widened as if the thought amused him. "I kind of like blood."

Emily clenched her jaw and braced herself. The moment he lowered that weapon, she would strike. Her breath hitched in her lungs, muscles preparing to spring.

The front door exploded inward with a deafening crack. Wood shards burst into the room, scattering across the dusty floor. A massive black wolf lunged through the splinters, eyes wild, teeth bared. It collided with Bob, driving him backward with bone-rattling force.

Jackson had found her.

Bob squeezed the trigger. The gun fired, the sound sharp and violent in the small space. Pain tore through Emily's arm, hot and searing, sending her sprawling.

Her head struck the floor, stars bursting behind her eyes. Dazed, she turned her head just in time to see the wolf clamp its jaws around Bob's throat, a vicious growl reverberating through the air. Blood sprayed across the room, dark and metallic.

Bob's body hit the floor with a hollow thud.

"I wanted to do that," she mumbled, her vision fading as darkness pulled her under again.

CHAPTER 14

Emily came to with a bright light shining in her eyes. She winced, lifting her hand. "Hey."

"Sorry," a soft voice said as the light disappeared. Light-green eyes in a heart-shaped face leaned closer. "How are you feeling?"

Emily blinked and looked around. She lay on a soft bed with the smell of bleach all around her. Bleach and a whiff of berries. "My head hurts," she murmured.

"Oh, I bet." The voice held a bit of humor. "You got clocked pretty good."

Emily pushed herself into a sitting position, the room swimming around her. She steadied herself, focusing on the woman standing nearby. Did doctors use words like *clocked*? "You're the doctor?"

"I'm one of them," the woman replied. "Dr. Gwen Irondock. Everyone calls me Dr. Gwen. Nice to meet you."

"Nice to meet you, too." Emily glanced down at her arm and saw the bandage wrapped snugly around her upper arm. The memory of the gunshot returned in a rush. "I was shot."

"Sure were. Silver bullet, too." The doctor winced. "Nasty stuff, but I got it out. You're lucky."

Emily studied Gwen more closely. The doctor stood around five-eight, shorter than most in the pack, with sharp, green eyes and straight brown hair cut bluntly at her chin. Her movements were quick and confident.

"You'll be fine," Gwen added. "I've got you on antibiotics and a few herbal remedies I've whipped up. The herbs should help with the healing process."

Emily exhaled slowly. Her body still ached, but the pain in her arm had dulled to a manageable throb. "How long until I'm back on my feet?"

"Give it a few days, and take it easy." Gwen's gaze sharpened. "And no shifting for at least seventy-two hours. Your body needs time to recover from the silver."

Emily swallowed a retort. She didn't have days to rest, not with everything happening, but arguing wouldn't help. For now, she'd have to focus on getting out of there and figuring out what the hell came next. "Anything else wrong with me?"

"Besides the lump on your head and the wound in your arm?" The doctor's eyebrows lifted slightly. "Not that I know of."

"Is she going to be okay?" a deep voice growled from the doorway.

Emily startled and turned her head, her heart stumbling behind her ribcage. Jackson leaned against the doorjamb, arms crossed over his bare chest, faded jeans riding low on his hips. The jeans looked a little too big. His gaze locked onto her, intense and unwavering.

"You took off that guy's head," she muttered.

"I did," Jackson replied, his voice gravelly. "He shot you. I didn't have much choice. What was his name? Who hired him?"

"Whoa," Gwen interrupted, raising her hands. "Back off, Alpha. She just woke up."

Emily's head swam. "Yeah." She swallowed, trying not to gag as bile rose in her throat. The room tilted slightly, and she pressed her palms against the mattress to steady herself.

Jackson took a step forward, but Gwen held up a hand. "Let her breathe. You can interrogate her after she's had a chance to recover."

Emily exhaled slowly and closed her eyes for a moment. When she opened them again, Jackson's gaze was still locked on her, unreadable and fierce.

"Tell me what happened," he said softly, his tone leaving no room for argument. His anger swelled through the air, heating it. There was nothing in life like a pissed-off Alpha.

Emily exhaled, gathering her thoughts as the dull throb in her skull pulsed harder. "The guy said his name was Bob. He wouldn't tell me who hired him, and also said he didn't kidnap me last time, although he knew about the garlic bag." She shrugged, wincing at the motion. "I think I turned him. He planned to ransom me to my father and then kill whoever hired him in the first place."

Jackson studied her, his gaze sharp. "Remember anything else?"

Emily rolled her eyes and instantly regretted it as pain stabbed through her skull. "Bob had two partners."

"We're looking for them now." Jackson's voice darkened. "I've got everyone who can scout the area out in each direction, but so far, all we've found is the dead guy."

Emily couldn't concentrate. "Did you find a phone on him? Maybe in the car?"

"Yes," Jackson said.

"Can you trace it?"

"Working on it, but the thing was a burner. I'm not holding my breath. I also don't have anyone really skilled with computers, except Thane. He'll do what he can."

Emily nodded, the room spinning slightly with the motion. "Hopefully, he finds something. Otherwise, we're blind."

"If it's a burner, we probably won't find much." Jackson's gaze softened. "Any idea who'd want to kidnap you?"

"No. Bob was just a hired thug." She should've tried harder to gain information from him. "No clue who wanted me kidnapped. Maybe they wanted to kill me themselves, or maybe even ransom me off to my dad after Bob turned me over."

"Seems logical," Jackson murmured. "But I'm more interested in who has an alibi right now. Maybe we should go talk to your cousin. Victor. What do you think?"

Emily just wanted to sleep for a month right now. "I spoke to him after the last kidnapping and didn't get any hint that he was involved. He's not exactly a genius, but yeah, I wouldn't mind talking to him again." She could read a liar.

"I'll speak with him."

Right. Sounded like Jackson would torture her cousin. She'd worry about that later. "You didn't call my father, did you?"

"No," Jackson replied. "Didn't want anyone knowing you were taken."

"Good. Let's leave it that way." She understood Jackson's desire to keep things quiet. His pack didn't need to appear vulnerable. Plus, she didn't want to worry her father. He deserved better than that.

"All right, good." Jackson's posture eased slightly. "I can take you home now."

Emily held up a hand. "Mind if I talk to the doctor alone for a moment? Girl stuff."

Jackson's eyes narrowed. "Wait a minute. That asshole didn't touch you, did he?"

"No," Emily said firmly. "Not at all. He hit me in the back of the head, but other than that, no. I rolled around a lot in the trunk, though, and I've got some bruises. I wouldn't mind having the doc check them out. Plus, I have a few…female type questions."

Jackson stepped back, hands raised. "Got it. I'll go check in with the scouting parties and see if anyone's found the other two who attacked you." His gaze sharpened. "Are you sure there were only three?"

"As sure as I can be," Emily replied, meeting his eyes. His concern settled somewhere low in her abdomen, but she shoved it aside. She needed to focus on healing and figuring out who wanted her taken.

"That's all right." Jackson's voice softened slightly. "I'll be back in a minute." He stepped out, shutting the door behind him with a faint click. His footsteps echoed softly down the hallway, fading into the distance.

"Whose pants is he wearing?" Emily asked.

"Oh. My partner's. Dr. Moore. They're about the same size," replied Dr. Gwen, stepping closer with a small, reassuring smile. The overhead light cast a soft glow across her light purple scrubs, her stethoscope gleaming against her chest. "Okay. So, where else are you hurt?"

Emily met her gaze. "We're covered by doctor-patient privilege, correct?"

Dr. Gwen lifted her brows slightly. "Of course. Anything we discuss stays between us."

"And you know what you're doing?"

"Yes." The doctor's gaze remained calm but steady. "I've trained at some of the best universities and medical schools in the world, as well as with several wolf packs that share their medical knowledge. I've seen a wide range of conditions, both human and shifter. Is there a reason you're asking?"

Emily exhaled slowly, her fingers curling into the blanket. Her senses told her she could trust the doctor. "Any idea who's been sabotaging the mines?" Perhaps someone had confided in their doctor.

"No."

Truth. The female was honest.

Okay. Time for Emily to be just as truthful. "There's something wrong with me."

The doctor's expression remained calm and reassuring. "Can you go into more detail?"

"Just over a month ago, I started getting weak in the knees. The feeling comes and goes, but now it is getting much worse. I'm not as strong as I used to be, and I need more sleep than before. It's not exhaustion. It feels like my body's slowing down." Her voice dropped. "My mother and her mother both died from strange illnesses no one could diagnose. I'm younger than they were when it hit them, but it's not getting better."

"That quickly of a progression?" Dr. Gwen asked, her expression growing more serious as she jotted notes on a tablet. "You're sure the illness is getting worse?"

Emily nodded. "Yes. Sometimes, I feel like my legs are going to give out entirely."

"Any other symptoms? Difficulty breathing? Changes in appetite?"

"Nothing like that. Just weakness, numbness, and wanting to sleep all of the time." Emily's throat tightened. "My healer doesn't know what's causing it, but she doesn't have the kind of training you do."

The doctor set the tablet aside and offered a reassuring smile. "I'll do everything I can to help, Emily. We'll run some tests and see what we can find."

"Sure. If you can help me, I'd appreciate it."

The doctor quickly drew several vials of blood and returned to her tablet, typing swiftly. "I need you to describe every symptom, no matter how minor. If there's a way to figure this out, we will. I promise."

"You can't tell Jackson or anyone else."

"I won't say a word," the doctor assured her. "But if you're planning on mating him, I think you should tell him the truth."

Heat flushed through Emily. "I'm not going to mate him."

"Are you sure?" The doctor's eyes softened. "You didn't see him pacing and growling while you were unconscious. I've never seen Jackson like that."

Emily swallowed hard. "We're friends. But there are too many reasons we can't mate, and this illness is only one of them. If you can figure out what's wrong, maybe I can step up as Alpha of my pack for now. They don't have anyone else."

The doctor nodded. "I'll do my best. I may need to consult with some outside specialists, but I promise I'll keep your identity confidential."

"Thank you." Emily pushed herself off the bed. The room tilted and spun, and she staggered. Strong hands caught her arms, holding her stable.

"Whoa. All right, breathe deeply." Dr. Gwen's grip felt firm and steady. "You'll be okay."

Emily inhaled slowly, her pulse evening out as the world centered again.

"You good?" the doctor asked.

"Yes." Emily released a shaky breath, her legs still wobbly.

A sharp knock sounded at the door. "Are you about done?" Jackson's low voice carried through the wood, rough and gravelly.

Dr. Gwen glanced at Emily, who gave a slight nod. "Come in."

The door swung open, and Jackson stepped inside, apparently having secured a blue T-shirt with Emily's face on it over a symbol of letters: GAE.

Her chin dropped. "GAE?"

"Granite Alpha Emily." He shrugged. "They all love you and want you to stay." His gaze swept over both females before locking onto Emily.

The doctor released her and stepped back. "I might have, um, well, signed the petition as well."

One of Jackson's dark eyebrows rose and he took a beat before speaking. "Is she okay?" he asked, his tone still edged with tension.

"She's got a bump on her head and an aching arm, but she's stable and can go home." The doctor picked up her tablet, tapping a few notes. "Emily, I'd like to see you in a day or so just as a follow-up."

"Of course. I'll be back." Emily managed a small smile, gratitude filtering through her. That was enough time to conduct a few tests. Hopefully, the doctor would have answers soon. "It looks like I'll need another room at the hotel," she added.

"Not a chance in hell, baby." Jackson's voice dropped an octave, rough and possessive. "You're coming home with me."

CHAPTER 15

J ackson drove slower than usual on the country lane, not wanting to jostle Emily too much. Sure, the road was asphalted, but the wind had thrown pine cones, rocks, and even branches in his way.

The clock on the dashboard read just past two in the morning. Thick clouds obscured the moon, yet Jackson could still feel the pulse of its power thrumming in his bones.

The sensation gave him peace since his strength waxed and waned in tune with the cyclical pull. Scientists among the packs theorized that their connection had nothing to do with ocean tides, as human scientists believed, but rather electromagnetic fields that fluctuated during different lunar phases. Jackson didn't much care about the science, only that the moon made him faster, stronger, and sharper when he needed it.

Emily stared at the starless night outside, her body stiff, pain emanating from her. The hum of the truck's engine and the rhythmic thump of tires against asphalt seemed to lull her into a fragile rest. Even so, Jackson's focus never wavered from the road. His grip on the steering wheel was firm, his senses heightened with the lingering adrenaline of the night. Every shadow along the roadside kept his pulse elevated.

She was safe. For now. But until he found the hired thugs who had helped kidnap her, that restless hum of tension wouldn't leave his veins. Not until she was truly out of danger. Not until he knew she was home and under his roof, where no one could touch her.

The soft vibrations of hurt from Emily hit Jackson harder than he'd expected. Her height made her stand out, but up close, her small-boned frame seemed more fragile than usual. Someone had bruised her.

That fact heated his throat with a rage so fierce it made him want to roar. He'd killed that bastard too quickly. Should've made him suffer. But the guy had pointed a gun at Emily, and Jackson hadn't had the luxury of dragging it out.

He cleared his throat, keeping perfect control of his emotions, especially his temper. "So…did the doc find any other injuries?"

Emily startled slightly as if yanked from her thoughts. Her gaze shifted to him, eyes focusing after a moment. "Huh?"

Awareness prickled down his spine at the haziness in her eyes. "You said you had bruises and…female questions."

"Oh, that." Emily waved a hand dismissively, but the movement exposed the scratches on her wrist where she'd been bound. His chest tightened, and a low growl rumbled from deep in his throat before he could stop it.

"The bruises are fine," she said quickly. "I just had some female-related questions. None of your business."

"Fair enough." He had no desire to discuss female issues, whatever the hell those were.

Emily shifted in her seat. "We don't have a doctor. Well, we have a healer, but some of her knowledge is out-of-date. Kind female, though," she added hastily.

"Good," Jackson replied. His pulse beat harder than it should.

Maybe it was relief. Maybe something else entirely. The air between them thickened, charged with a heat he didn't have the luxury of acknowledging. His grip tightened on the wheel as awareness of her—her scent, the warmth of her presence—sank into his bones. The truck cab suddenly felt too small.

Her hand flattened on the too-short, light-green scrubs she had borrowed. "I asked the doctor if she knew who was sabotaging your mines, thinking maybe a patient had confided in her. She had no clue, and I believed her."

He appreciated Emily trying to help him. "Thanks, but I've decided you should just snoop around for yourself and not try to help me. I'll figure out who's messing with us. You've been in enough danger already." He meant every word.

She shrugged. "Okay, but I wanted to tell you that I'm really impressed with how you've modernized your pack. I absolutely love the idea of wolves exploring the world to bring new skills back to the pack."

Pride swelled in his chest. He'd fought hard against the council to make that program a reality. "It's not just young people," he said, a slow smile tugging at the corner of his mouth. "Anybody can leave for a period of time as long as they bring back useful skills. We offer scholarships—or grants, I guess you'd call them. Raya oversees all that, making sure pack members have enough money to live while they're training. Right now, we've got two alternating families out learning more about sustainable farming."

"Oh, yeah?" Emily tilted her head, interest lighting her eyes. "The Copper Pack just brought in a group of farmers."

So, he wasn't the only Alpha adding ranks to his forces. Good to know. "It's smart. If we can grow our own food and raise livestock, we'll be ready for the next pandemic."

"Isn't that the truth?" Emily murmured.

Even wolves hadn't been immune to the last one, though none had died from it.

"And bringing in new members strengthens us, too," Jackson added. His fingers flexed on the steering wheel as the urge to reach over and hold her hand crept in. But what excuse did he have? Other than the simple fact that he wanted to touch her.

Her presence beside him felt too right, her scent weaving through the air like a thread tying them together. But she'd made her position clear. She couldn't mate him. Her pack needed her, just as the Granite Pack needed him.

Still, the heat in his body wouldn't fade. Not when she was this close, not when the night pressed around them and every instinct inside him bellowed for him to keep her safe and with him.

He tried to lighten the mood. "Not sure what I'm going to do with a bunch of artists, though."

Emily laughed softly. "It was kind of you to bring the painters in. You mentioned your pack holds an annual festival where you sell wares. Maybe they can help fill the coffers. Besides, I'm sure a few of them might end up working in the mines. We always need people, too."

"Yeah, we do." Jackson slowed the truck as they reached his home, gravel scattering beneath the tires. The house's dark silhouette stood tall against the night sky, faint light spilling from the porch lantern. Cutting the engine, he shifted toward her. "I'm sorry you were kidnapped in my territory. It never should've happened."

Surprise lifted her eyebrows. "That wasn't your fault."

"The hell it wasn't," he growled. "This is my territory. Somebody dared to come in here and take you. I will find out who hired that bastard."

"Yeah, well, I gave it a good shot, but he wasn't giving anything up."

He would most certainly be more persuasive than she'd been once he got his hands on the others who'd helped kidnap her. "Let's get some sleep and then head into the office. This afternoon, I'd like to fly into Slate territory and speak with your father and Victor. We'll take the helicopter."

"I didn't want to worry my father, but we should speak with him about the kidnapping attempt. You're going to pilot the craft, right?"

"Hell, yeah, I am." He grinned. "Didn't go on to fly fighter jets, but I can handle just about anything else."

Emily chuckled as she opened her door and stepped out, wearing boots borrowed from Dr. Gwen. The careful way she moved didn't sit right with him. She was still hurting. His chest tightened at the reminder. He couldn't believe she'd been injured on his watch. The air between them buzzed with unspoken tension, but he could only focus on ensuring she stayed safe from here on out.

He hopped out and met her near the steps to his wide veranda.

"We'll have to fly out late afternoon," she said as he approached. "You have meetings with the three other prospective Alpha females first, remember?"

Jackson groaned. "I don't like this modern dating."

"Oh, I know," she murmured, amusement in her tone. She turned to take in the wide expanse of his home. "It's much easier when the father just hands the female over, right?"

He noted the amusement in her sweet voice. "You're having fun with this whole matchmaking scheme, aren't you?"

"Yes," she replied, eyes twinkling.

"You enjoy being a pain in my ass."

Her soft chuckle loosened something inside him. "Maybe I do." The breeze picked up, carrying the crisp bite of winter. She tilted her face toward the sky, inhaling deeply. "Snow's coming," she murmured.

"I know. That's why we're flying today and not tomorrow. A good storm is on the way."

"I'm glad the snow is finally coming. Autumn's pretty with

the leaves and all, but then they die, and everything turns gray. It's time for snow."

Her unexpected burst of romanticism threw him. Without overthinking, he reached over and took her hand. Her fingers were cool from the night air, but her warmth seeped into his skin.

"I'm not sleeping with you, Jackson," she said without pulling away.

"I've got a guest room, sweetheart. Three of 'em, in fact."

Her gaze moved to the house, studying the grand log home with its wide front porch and tall windows reflecting the mysterious moonlight. "Your house is bigger than I expected. It surprised me when I came over to make breakfast."

"You thought I lived in a shack in the woods?"

"Yes. Ramshackle with tons of booze and lube. The ultimate bachelor pad," she mused.

He chuckled, adjusting his grip on her hand as they approached the stairs. It had been much too long since he'd been a free spirit, although he hadn't minded giving that impression to the other packs.

Being underestimated was always a good thing.

Yet he'd also had to fight battles, so his reputation had quickly darkened. That also kept his pack safe.

Her hand, small and delicate in his, contrasted sharply with the strength he knew she possessed. They climbed the steps, boots clunking against the wood, and he pushed open the heavy front door, the hinges creaking slightly. Warmth spilled out from inside, chasing away the chill of the night as he led her across the threshold.

She smiled, looking around. "Earlier I noticed how lovely your home is."

"It was my father's." Jackson guided her inside. "Feels like a good home."

"When did your mother die?" she asked.

The personal question caught him off guard, but he quickly recovered. "When I was just a baby. There was an attack from a rogue pack. During one of the rough patches the Stope Packs Coalition went through, I believe."

Her sigh held sadness. "That's happened a few times, hasn't it?"

"Yeah, but we've always had each other's backs. Or at least that's what I was told. After the attack, the coalition banded together and wiped out that rogue pack. It doesn't exist anymore."

Emily swallowed and pressed her free hand against her rib cage. Was she bruised there, as well? "I miss my mother so much. I knew her until I was ten."

Silence stretched between them as their footsteps echoed across the hardwood floor. They had that in common—being raised by Alpha fathers without a mother's touch. Yet, where Jackson carried a rough edge, a product of stepping into leadership too young, Emily wore her grace like armor.

"Your father did a good job," Jackson said.

She snorted softly and nudged him with her hip. "So did yours."

Jackson's lips quirked as he guided her into the main gathering room. The fire inside the massive fireplace crackled warmly, casting shadows over the worn leather furniture arranged around a low coffee table. He'd had Thane stop by earlier to make sure all the fires were lit, especially the one in the guest bedroom he planned for Emily.

The scent of pine and woodsmoke lingered in the air, grounding the space in earth and tradition.

Emily paused as if soaking in the warmth radiating from both the fire and the walls. Her light hair glowed in the firelight, and her eyes had darkened to an unfathomable midnight.

He turned her to face him and released her hand to cup her face. "Are you sure you're all right?"

Her gaze dropped to his mouth.

His groin hardened instantly.

Then, shock of all shocks, dignified and graceful Emily Nightsom levered up on her toes and pressed her sweet lips against his.

CHAPTER 16

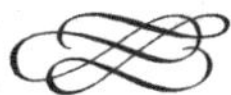

Shock trilled through Emily. What in the world was she doing? The image of Jackson bursting into that cabin earlier in his wolf form, fierce and unyielding, wouldn't leave her mind.

He'd come for her.

Her skin tingled, and her pulse thrummed, yet her mouth was on his. He had stilled as if her touch had stunned him. Oh, God. This was about to become the most embarrassing moment of her life.

She started to pull away, but his hand pressed against her lower back. The heat of his fingers spread through the thin scrub shirt, his touch spanning her waist as if he could hold her there through sheer will alone.

He slowly tilted his head and moved his mouth against hers. A rumble vibrated from his chest, low and deep, traveling through her lips and down her spine. Her knees weakened, but this time, it wasn't from her illness. With a growl that seemed torn from somewhere deep inside his hard-packed body, he pulled her closer. The kiss shifted from soft to claiming, his mouth firm, hot, and demanding as he tilted her head back.

The world outside ceased to exist. Fire streaked through her veins, settling low in her belly, heating her from the inside. Her heart pounded so hard she could feel it in her throat, her pulse a wild rhythm that matched the need suddenly coursing through her.

Her fingers slid up the back of his neck, nails scraping lightly as if she could tether herself to him. His groan rumbled through their joined mouths, sending a pulse of awareness straight to her core.

He lifted her effortlessly, and she wrapped her legs around his waist. The solid strength of his body against hers sent a new shock of desire through her system.

Heat rolled off him, his breath ragged as he held her tightly against his chest. The pressure of his hand splayed across her lower back kept her anchored, even as she clung to his shoulders.

Her world spun, and her control shattered. She kissed him harder, her body surging with a strength she hadn't felt in months. A warning flickered somewhere in the back of her mind, but she shoved it aside, lost in the storm of Jackson's heat and strength.

This was so wrong.

She didn't care.

Both of his hands dropped to cup her ass, fingers flexing as he moved with purpose. She had no idea where they were headed, and she didn't care. His kiss consumed her, fierce and unrelenting, as if she were the only thing that mattered in his world. For this moment, she knew she was.

Her back hit a wall, the impact stealing a gasp from her lips as she arched into him. Her legs still clung tightly to his waist, her body instinctively seeking the heat and strength of his.

He broke the kiss, his breath ragged as his forehead rested against hers. "Did I hurt you?"

"No," she panted, her lungs fighting for air, her pulse thundering in her ears. When he leaned back, she could only stare at him.

His eyes blazed a deep, enigmatic blue. Not the color of a river, lake, or ocean, but something darker and more intense. A color she couldn't even name.

His gaze locked onto hers, hunger carving harsh lines into his face, his nostrils flaring like a wolf that had just caught a scent.

He was the ultimate predator.

"Emily," he growled, her name rough like a warning.

Her legs trembled, her strength faltering as the adrenaline started to wane.

He adjusted his grip, holding her firmly with absolute strength. Easy strength. All Jackson.

The heat of his palms seared her through the thin fabric of her borrowed scrubs, each touch igniting a pulse of need low in her belly. The scent of pine and earth clung to his skin, grounding her even as her heartbeats quickened.

"You're hurt," he said, though the words sounded more like a reminder than a statement.

"I'm fine," she whispered, breathless and aching.

His grin was slow and knowing, a dangerous curve that sent a fresh wave of heat through her blood. The firelight flickered across his features, casting shadows that emphasized the hard lines of his jaw and the intensity in his eyes. The air between them thickened, heavy with need and hunger.

"I wondered," he murmured.

"I wondered, too," she admitted, her gaze falling to his mouth. It was just as talented as before. Even more so, really. How many dreams had she had throughout the years about that simple kiss at the lake?

He'd only been a boy then.

The adult wolf holding her now had shed any semblance of boyhood. The memory of its heat lingered on her lips. His breath was warm, brushing her skin as if teasing her to close the distance.

She wanted to do just that and get lost in him. To forget reality for a short time. "That kiss was just as good as I remembered."

"Ditto." His hands flexed against her, the possessive squeeze making her pulse stutter. The rough calluses on his fingertips sent sparks of sensation through her, even through the cotton blend of the scrubs.

The warmth from the fireplace mixed with the heat of his body, enveloping her in a cocoon of safety. Temptation. Her fingers curled into the fabric of his shirt, feeling the taut muscle beneath, and her breath hitched when he leaned in just enough that his lips hovered near hers, their breaths mingling.

Her body craved him, but that mistake couldn't be made. Her heart pounded, urging her forward, but her mind whispered about the consequences.

She'd fail to protect her pack if she made a move like that. No one besides her doctors could know the truth. Not only was she growing weaker, but any children she might have could face the same fate. The future of her bloodline was uncertain, fragile in a way she would have to admit to him, just to be fair.

Her father should have had more children. At least there was Nadia now, though the female wasn't a fighter. But that didn't erase the weight of Emily's responsibility, pressing against her chest like a stone.

If she went any further with Jackson, she owed him the truth. While she doubted her illness was contagious, considering only the females in her ancestry had caught it, she wouldn't keep a secret like that from him. Not from someone who wanted to mate her.

But revealing it would expose the weakness in her pack. Duty always came first. Didn't it?

She leaned back, breaking the magnetic pull between them.

The loss of his touch was immediate and sharp, but she forced herself to breathe, steadying the tremble in her legs. The crackle of the fire seemed louder now, filling the silence between them as if waiting for someone to break it.

"I can tell there are a lot of thoughts going through your head," Jackson said, smiling. "Yes or no, baby?"

He was the only soul on the planet who could get away with calling her *baby*. "We're meeting with your prospective mates in a few hours, Jackson. It would be seriously wrong for us to take this further. You get that, right?"

"I do, and I don't care."

Okay. So, he'd laid it on the line.

"I do care." But she wanted him. Badly. "I'm sorry."

He stepped away from the wall, allowing her to unclasp her ankles and let her legs slide to the floor.

She wavered but then regained her balance.

"Come on, Em." He took her hand again and led her down a long hallway, the walls lined with Western oil paintings depicting sweeping landscapes, wild horses, and rugged mountains. Their footsteps echoed softly against the hardwood floor until they stopped at a bedroom door.

Jackson opened it, and Emily gasped. The room was stunning. Soft and inviting. Pale cream walls reflected the golden glow of a roaring fire in a fireplace framed in polished stone. A thick, woven, earth-toned rug covered most of the floor, and the bed—a grand four-poster with carved wooden posts—was dressed in layers of plush white blankets and soft pillows. Lace curtains framed the tall windows, their edges drifting from a heat vent in the floor. Across the room, a vanity with an antique mirror and delicate floral carvings sat beneath a chandelier with crystal drops that caught the firelight.

"The bathroom is through there." Jackson nodded toward a door on the far wall.

She barely heard him as he stepped closer and tucked a stray strand of her hair behind her ear. The brush of his fingers sent tingles across her cheek and down to her breasts, making them ache with a need she had no business feeling. If she leaned just a little closer, she could taste him again.

"If you change your mind, my room's at the end of the hall," he murmured, leaning down to kiss the tip of her nose. Her breath caught as he straightened. "Your belongings are being brought from the hotel. I'll leave them outside the door. Get some sleep, Emily."

The last words were firm, as if he could command her body to rest. Then he was gone, the door clicking shut behind him.

Her knees buckled, and she sank to the floor, gripping the edge of the bed to steady herself. She was so tempted to chase after him that her hands trembled. Or maybe that was the illness. She pressed a hand to her chest, feeling the rapid beat of her heart and trying to slow her breathing, knowing sleep would not come easily tonight.

It was long past time she told someone the truth. Emily picked up her phone and started to text her father but hesitated, glancing at the clock. It was too late for a conversation like this. She would tell him everything in person later. The thought made her chest feel both lighter and heavier all at once.

For now, she needed to focus. Three more meetings loomed on her schedule this coming morning. Three more encounters with undoubtedly stunning, appealing, and brilliant Alpha females, all of whom she was supposed to pair with the man who had just kissed her into oblivion.

Good Lord. What had she been thinking?

She pushed herself up from the floor, her toes in borrowed socks curling into the soft rug beneath her. The hint of pine from the burning fire mixed with the lingering trace of Jackson's scent in the air. It wrapped around her, making it impossible to push him from her mind.

She ran her fingers over the smooth, white comforter, the

fabric cool beneath her fingertips. The crackle of the fire was the only sound, filling the room with a soft hum of warmth and solitude. Yet the silence seemed to amplify the ache low in her belly, the memory of Jackson's hands and mouth still too vivid.

She inhaled sharply and sat on the mattress. The springs gave way beneath her, and she rested her elbows on her knees, head bowed. Tomorrow, she would face her duties. Tomorrow, she would be composed, efficient, and focused.

After she finally got some sleep, she would help Jackson find a mate.

CHAPTER 17

Just after lunch, Jackson started on his third coffee of the day, seated in one of the leather chairs in the sitting area of his office. Emily sat across from him, scrolling on her phone, her fingers moving with quick efficiency. Her scent, soft and warm with a hint of something wild, wrapped around him, making it hard to focus. His wolf stirred beneath the surface, restless and craving her.

After leaving her room after that kiss, he shifted and ran hard through the woods, trying to burn off the tension coiled inside him. The ground had been damp from the night's rain, pine needles clinging to his paws as he tore through the underbrush. He'd met up with Thane, and they'd run together for a while. Still, the physical exertion hadn't cleared his mind as much as he'd hoped.

Returning just in time to change for work, he had thrown on a worn T-shirt and torn jeans, ignoring Emily's raised eyebrow when she took in his appearance. He'd simply shrugged.

Her smile had lingered longer than it should have, making it hard for him to remember why she couldn't be his.

The leather creaked as he shifted in his seat, stretching out his legs. The fire in the hearth crackled, casting an amber glow over the room's paneled walls. Rain pattered softly against the tall windows, blurring his view of the distant mountains. The methodic tick of the antique clock on the mantel marked the slow drag of the afternoon.

There had been a multitude of balloon basket gifts waiting for her in his office that morning, and they'd hidden them all in a supply closet. Yet the place still smelled like latex a bit.

The entire situation was awkward as hell. He needed to find a mate. Someone who could stand beside him and help lead the pack. Emily had made it clear that person wouldn't be her. As much as he wanted her with every cell in his body, he understood her reasons. She had her pack. Her responsibilities.

But that didn't make it any easier. He also wasn't sure it mattered. She was safer with him, and the wolf inside him knew it.

He scrubbed a hand through his hair and downed the last of his coffee, the bitter heat sliding down his throat. It had been a long-ass day, and he was ready for it to be over.

They had already met with two prospective mates, and neither had sparked even an ounce of interest in Jackson. The first had arrived with a long list of expectations, including everything from a grand home to private schooling for future children. Her mood had swung from enthusiastic to indifferent within minutes.

The second female had been so timid she barely made eye contact, her nervous energy palpable. Jackson had assured her that he'd welcome her entire pack if they joined his, and though relief had softened her features, it was clear that she had no real interest in him. The entire process was growing more bizarre by the hour.

A quick knock sounded on the door, and Raya entered without waiting for an invitation, several trays in her hands. "Cookies for Emily. All baked by different members." Was that a bit of chocolate at the side of her mouth? She placed several plates on his desk and then a couple on the table by the sofa. Then she handed Jackson a notebook with three checks clipped to the front.

"For my trip to Vegas," she said matter-of-factly.

Emily glanced up from her phone, curiosity sparking in her eyes. "You're going to Vegas?"

"Yes," Raya replied, excitement dancing in her eyes. "They host an annual mining convention. Humans occasionally develop innovative machinery, and it's worth seeing what's available. Efficiency is key if we want to stay ahead."

Jackson signed the checks swiftly, then glanced up at her with a raised brow. "You're not planning to stay an extra week this time, are you?"

Raya rolled her eyes. "No. Last time was a fluke."

Emily chuckled softly. "Must have been a good trip."

"Let's just say I made enough to buy a brand-new kitchen set," Raya replied, her smile widening as she tucked the checks into her notebook. The air shifted with a hum of amusement, though Jackson caught the sharp glint of disapproval in Raya's gaze. She really didn't like his method of finding a mate.

Was the efficiency expert a closet romantic?

The clock on the mantel ticked steadily, marking the minutes until his next—and hopefully final—meeting of the day.

"What did you play in Vegas?" Emily asked, tilting her head.

Raya's eyes lit up. "Craps."

"Just for the conference, Raya," Jackson said sternly.

"I know, I know. Efficiency first," Raya shot back with a smirk. "The house usually wins, and I don't have time to test the theory. Plus, if it's okay, Thane wants to come with me. Maybe we can catch a show."

Jackson leaned back. "Fine by me. Sounds like fun."

Raya nodded. "But next year? I get the week to gamble." She

turned on her heel and exited the room, shutting the door quietly behind her.

"I like her," Emily said with a smile. "But she really does want to stay and gamble after the convention."

"No kidding," Jackson muttered. "But she doesn't need another vacation. She already had one earlier this year."

Emily glanced at the fire. "You're a tough employer. She's the one making sure everything runs smoothly. How long has she worked for you?"

"About five years," Jackson replied. "She took over as my chief operator when her father died."

"Oh, I'm sorry to hear that." Emily's voice softened. "How did he die?"

Jackson glanced at his watch. Raya's father had been one of the victims of the poisoning attack—something he had never admitted to any of the packs. He didn't intend to start now. Before he could respond, another knock at the door spared him.

Raya stepped back inside. "I'd like to introduce Ms. Xandra Millstone and her Enforcer, Traxon."

A female stepped into the room with the grace of someone used to commanding attention. Her raven-black hair framed strikingly blue eyes that seemed to assess the room at a glance. She stood about five-foot-ten, with a fit, athletic build that hinted at both strength and discipline. Her green silk skirt suit was perfectly tailored and paired with understated jewelry that added a touch of elegance.

Her Enforcer was built like one. Tall and broad with a threat in his brown eyes.

Jackson stood immediately. "It's nice to meet you." He extended his hand to Xandra.

Xandra's smile was warm yet composed as she stepped forward to shake with him. "It's a pleasure to meet you, Alpha Tryne."

Emily rose, and Jackson introduced them.

"Ms. Millstone seems to be an expert in computers. She was the first to answer my rather covert call to the wild," Emily said.

"Call me Xandra," she replied, her gaze sweeping the room before she settled onto the sofa, crossing her long legs with effortless grace. "I like computers and a bit of hacking, but I'm nowhere near an expert."

Jackson and Emily both sat.

Staring at them, Traxon settled his bulk against the wall by the door.

"Hello," Jackson said.

"Hi." Traxon's gaze moved to Emily and warmed. A lot.

Raya still stood in the doorway. "Would either of you like coffee?" Did her eyelashes just flutter when she looked at the Enforcer?

"No, thank you." Traxon smiled at her.

She blushed a light damask. "Well, if you want anything, I'm right outside." She backed away and shut the door.

Xandra looked at the closed door. "I'm fine, as well. No coffee for me." Amusement thickened her voice. She glanced at Traxon. "Maybe we should stay in town, Brother."

Traxon rolled his eyes and then seemed to catch himself, sobering.

So, she'd brought her brother? Jackson liked that. "Do you have a large family?"

"No." Xandra focused her gaze on him. "Just the two of us and no pack. So, you need a mate?"

Amusement ticked through him. "Apparently."

"Why?" she asked directly.

Emily leaned back slightly, watching the interplay, her gaze interested.

"I took over as Alpha when I was fifteen," Jackson explained. "A council helped guide me, but they're still involved. They'll only step back if I find a mate. Besides, it's time. I'd like to have children."

Emily jolted just enough that he noticed, though he kept his gaze steady.

Her scent surrounded him again, making it hard to focus. He reminded himself they had agreed to remain friends, although the kiss from earlier still lingered on his lips. Would he always taste Emily Nightsom?

Xandra nodded thoughtfully. "I understand."

"Why are you interested in mating?" Emily asked.

Xandra glanced at her before returning her focus to Jackson. "I like the idea of the position. Of being the Alpha female of a pack. Our parents were wanderers, moving from pack to pack. It was exciting, but Traxon and I want to settle somewhere and put down roots. Financial security and comfort are important to me, as well."

Her answer was honest and practical. Since Jackson was approaching this as a business-like relationship, he could understand her perspective. It made sense, even if something in his chest tightened at the thought.

His wolf howled in rejection of the idea. Yeah, he was a romantic bastard, no matter how hard Jackson tried to beat it out of him.

"I am available now," Xandra said. "I'd like time to get to know you before we mate, but I am willing to stay in town as we court. If I join the pack, so does my brother." Her gaze flicked toward Emily again, something unreadable flashing in her eyes. Emily didn't so much as twitch, but Jackson could feel the hum of irritation coming from her. He liked that. Not that he would ever admit it.

"Sounds like a good plan." Jackson stood. "I'll leave directions for rooms to be readied for you at our little hotel. It's our only one, but it's comfortable."

"That sounds lovely." Xandra rose gracefully. "We have some matters to attend to, but we can return late tomorrow night.

How about we start with breakfast the next day? Spend the day together?" Her smile turned flirty.

"I'd like that," Jackson replied, though the words tasted like gravel in his mouth.

"Good. Thank you." Xandra offered her hand. He shook it, her fingers cool against his palm. She turned and extended the same courtesy to Emily before striding out of the office with her brother on her heels.

Emily flopped back into her chair, exhaling through her nose. "She's one cold fish."

Jackson chuckled, settling back into his seat. "I agree. But this is a business arrangement."

"Oh." Emily sounded somewhat surprised. "Well, you've met all six females with Alpha blood that I found. I can look for more if you want."

"No, that's okay. I've narrowed it down to Abilene Ironclaw and Xandra Millstone. That is—if you approve?"

Emily's mouth opened slightly, then she shut it again, her eyes shadowed. Was he needling her, or did he mean it? Even he wasn't sure. But he needed a mate, and those were the two best prospects—after Emily, of course.

"I do approve," she murmured.

Good. "All right."

"So, you're telling me that out of all six of them, you're choosing between the free-spirited painter and the female who sees you as a business transaction?" Emily asked, her voice dry.

"Yes." He met her gaze. "I felt a connection to them more than anyone else, and I understand where they're coming from. I figure I'll date them both and then see." God, he hated the sound of that. The whole situation lacked romance. But he needed to be practical and step up with his pack.

"Well," Emily said, her voice neutral but her gaze a little too steady, "I'm glad I was helpful."

His eyes held hers for a long moment, tempted to push her

right into his bedroom, pack politics be damned. "You certainly have been. And I owe you one." Silence settled between them before he shifted, stretching out his legs. "We need to get going before the storm strengthens. It's a bit of a flight."

She sighed. "I wish our territories weren't located at opposite ends of the damn state."

"Ditto." Both the Silver and Copper Packs lived between them in mountainous territory. "However, the Embervault Mine is to the east of any claimed territory, so we could create some sort of route between our lands that skirts everybody else." How, he had no clue. They both lacked the necessary pack members to sufficiently patrol such an area.

"If only we had more members." She bit her bottom lip and then released it, her tone softening. "I would like to ask you to be, well, polite when you speak with Victor in a few hours. I don't believe he was behind my kidnapping."

"He's the most likely suspect, considering he wants to take over your pack, but I don't know why he'd have you kidnapped."

"I agree," she murmured, frowning. "If Victor is behind the kidnappings, he should've just had me killed to get me out of the way."

Jackson's gut twisted at the thought. His wolf growled low in his chest, rejecting the very idea. "No one's killing you, Emily." His voice was rougher than he intended. "I'll take out even the remote threats. I promise."

CHAPTER 18

With late afternoon snow falling, Emily waited patiently in Jackson's truck, keeping the chill outside. She was tired but hadn't slept much earlier. Sometimes she wondered how much time she had left on this planet. Even now, her hands and feet tingled with numbness. Hopefully Dr. Gwen would have a treatment plan soon.

Outside, Jackson circled the helicopter, inspecting it with the focus of a male who knew every inch of his machine. Snow fell lightly around him, drifting lazily from the overcast sky. Emily watched as he ran a hand along a rotor blade, his movements precise and sure. His broad shoulders filled out a black jacket, the worn leather molding to his frame. The wind caught strands of his hair, tousling it against his forehead. His jeans, faded and snug in all the right places, clung to powerful legs that moved with the easy grace of a predator.

Heat curled low in her belly, unbidden and distracting.

Her phone buzzed, jerking her back to reality. She lifted it to her ear. "Nightsom."

"Hi, Emily. It's Dr. Gwen. Do you have a moment?"

"I do." Emily's pulse quickened. She watched Jackson test the fuel cap, completely unaware of the effect he had on her. "Do you have an answer?"

"I have a couple of ideas, but I need more blood samples."

Emily winced. "I don't really have time to head into your clinic right now. We're flying into my territory to meet with some of my family."

"No, I don't need any of your blood. You're going into Slate Pack territory? That's fantastic, actually. I need your father's blood and that of any other relatives you can find. If there's any way you can get those, it would help. A lot."

Not an easy ask by any means. "I might be able to get my father's and my sister's. Well, half-sister's," Emily amended.

"You have a half-sister? I didn't know that."

"Yeah. It was news to all of us. I think they'd be willing, but other than that, the only other family member I know of is a cousin who doesn't like me."

Gwen sighed. "I'd love to test his blood to compare to yours. What in the world would I do with it that would concern him?"

"Nothing I can think of, but he won't want to help me," Emily admitted. As a wolf shifter, Gwen wouldn't want the truth about their packs getting out, either.

Gwen snorted. "Wolves have avoided science for far too long. Don't ask me why."

"I couldn't agree more." Emily's gaze shifted back to Jackson. The snow clung to his hair and shoulders, highlighting his rugged features against the wintry backdrop. Her stomach dipped as he glanced her way, eyes locking with hers for a heartbeat before he turned back to the helicopter. "I'll see what I can do," Emily added softly.

"Great. I don't have a way to get vials to you, so why don't you share the contact information for your healer? That way we can coordinate our efforts."

That made sense. "Sure. I'll text Edra's contact info to you. Please remember patient-doctor confidentiality."

"Of course." Dr. Gwen clicked off.

Emily forwarded the contact information and then shifted in her seat, searching for the best way to approach her family. Did she consider Nadia family? Definitely. Although the illness seemed to run in Emily's mother's family, perhaps Nadia's blood could provide some insight into a cure. Maybe Em's blood was missing something.

Her father would be hurt that she hadn't confided in him, but he'd still want to help. Hopefully. Giving up blood wasn't in an Alpha's nature. Victor wouldn't want to assist her. Period.

Jackson stepped away from the helicopter, a sleek black Bell 407 with polished rotor blades gleaming against the snow-dusted sky. Its streamlined body reflected the light of the overcast afternoon, and the hum of the idling engine vibrated. He gestured her over.

Taking a deep breath, Emily pushed open the truck door and stepped into the cold air. Snowflakes clung to her hair and the shoulders of her coat as she crossed the distance, refusing to let the weakness in her legs slow her stride. "Flying again," she muttered. Being off the ground so far didn't appeal to her wolf side.

"I'll get you there fast and safe." He flashed a grin, all confidence and ease.

Before she could react, he grasped her waist and effortlessly lifted her into the passenger seat. She yelped, startled by the unexpected motion, but his hands were gentle despite their strength. Her pulse kicked hard, warmth chasing through her as her body registered his heat and closeness. "Manhandle much?" she quipped breathlessly.

His smile held a trace of something darker. "Only when necessary." He helped her secure her shoulder harness and belt, his fingers brushing against her hip with heat. Emily swallowed, staring straight ahead as he stepped back, shutting the door with a solid click. Snowflakes tapped lightly against the windshield, melting as they landed.

Jackson crossed around the front of the helicopter, his movements fluid and sure as he slid into the pilot's seat beside her. He handed her a headset, their fingers grazing briefly before she slid it on. The hum of the engine vibrated beneath her as Jackson adjusted a few controls, his gaze sharp and focused.

Was he trying to drive her crazy? Or was her body betraying her yet again?

Within seconds, they lifted into the air, snow swirling in their wake. The interior remained warm, but the sight of the snow-covered trees and distant mountain peaks sent a chill down Emily's spine.

"Do you have a fear of flying?" Jackson's voice rumbled through the headset, low and clear.

"Not really." She glanced down at the town laid out beneath them, the polished granite buildings glinting under the thin layer of snow. "Oh, for Pete's sakes."

Jackson leaned and looked out the window. "That took some time."

On top of what appeared to be the school, somebody had created a heart out of something red with *Jackson + Emily* in the center. "What is that?"

"Red ribbons?" Jackson guessed, banking hard to the left.

Emily yelped, then laughed as adrenaline surged through her veins. "Just keep me alive, all right?"

"Oh, that's fully my plan." The grin in his voice sent warmth curling low in her belly. He flew southeast, skimming the dense forests and snow-dusted hills until he descended the aircraft toward an area below, where fences marked a wide swath of land.

She leaned closer to the glass, studying the network of

equipment and dirt roads below at the Embervault Mine. "Do any of the smaller packs claim the area around the mine?"

"Not really. The Ravencall and Ghostwind Packs patrol here, but the territory doesn't belong to anyone. There are a few rogue groups scattered around, but we have this mine pretty well secured from trespassers and nobody has really tried to infiltrate it."

She couldn't blame them. Not if they had any sense. She had no doubt Jackson would go after them with a vengeance, making a statement as he did. His reputation for swift retribution preceded him. Silence settled between them as the helicopter sliced through the sky, the rhythmic hum of the rotors filling the space. Below, the snow-dusted landscape rolled past, dark patches of forest and gleaming rivers breaking up the white. The tension in her chest tightened the closer they flew to Slate Pack territory.

Jackson set the aircraft down in a clearing near a small runway, where the two Slate Pack helicopters gleamed in the pale light by the tree line. As the engine slowly died, Emily spotted Miliki standing yards away beside a sleek black town car.

"Stay here." Jackson released his belt and jumped out. He strode quickly around the front of the craft, opened her door, and unbuckled her harness before lifting her out. The strength in his hands sent a jolt through her system, but she failed to hide a wince as his thumb brushed a bruise on her ribs.

"Are you still bruised, or were you able to heal yourself?" His tone was soft, but his gaze was sharp as he scanned her face.

"I healed myself." She lied without hesitation. The bruises still clung to her skin, stubborn and slow to fade, her body too preoccupied with fighting the illness to mend as quickly as it should have.

"All right." His hand slid down to her elbow as he guided her toward Miliki. The gravel crunched softly beneath their steps, and the snowflakes continued drifting down, melting as they touched her skin.

The Enforcer's eyes swept over her, assessing. "Emily, how are you?"

"Absolutely fine." She kept her voice light and steady. "Anything happen while I was gone?"

"Nope. All good."

Jackson opened the car door for her, his hand brushing her back as she slid into the plush leather seat. The scent of leather and pine surrounded her, warm and faintly familiar. Seconds later, he joined her inside, and the door clicked shut.

"Your father's looking forward to seeing you. He's missed you," Miliki said as he entered the vehicle and started the engine, his broad frame fitting snugly behind the wheel.

"How's Nadia?" Emily folded her hands tightly in her lap.

Miliki's gaze caught hers briefly in the rearview mirror. "As well as can be expected."

"Are people being kind to her?"

The Enforcer shrugged. "I don't know. I haven't asked. *I'm* kind to her."

Emily almost smiled. Miliki was kind to everyone until he wasn't. Then throats tended to get ripped out. "She's settling in nicely?"

"I guess, although that bodyguard of hers is a little intense."

Considering Miliki could be terrifyingly intense, that was a statement. "His job is to protect her," Emily murmured. She looked at Jackson. "You never did tell me what he did for you. Not really."

"He worked in my mine for a while and then helped me root out a couple of rogue packs that kept stealing from us." Jackson shrugged. "Caidrik is a hell of a tracker and fighter. If his goal is to keep your sister safe, then she will be."

Miliki's gaze flicked to Jackson in the mirror. "Did you find a mate or what?"

"Still working on it," Jackson replied easily.

"Hmph," Miliki grunted, his expression skeptical as the car rolled smoothly down the drive toward the heart of Slate Pack territory. Snow dusted the towering pines that lined the road, their branches weighed down as if bowing in respect to the passing vehicle. The air outside was crisp and still, the dusk breaking through the thick clouds.

Emily stared out at the landscape, the beauty of her homeland offering little comfort against the knot tightening in her belly.

CHAPTER 19

Jackson soon found himself in the Nightsom mansion's opulent living room with a glass of aged scotch in his hand. Actual doilies decorated each polished table. He resisted the urge to snort as he glanced sideways at Emily beneath his lashes. Did she like doilies?

"They were my mother's," she said softly.

Made sense. If Philip took Jackson up on his newest offer, would he have to take doilies back with him? He'd do it if it made Emily happy. One kiss had nearly set them both on fire, and he wanted her in his bed. He also wanted her fucking safe.

Philip Nightsom sat across from him in an ornate, floral-patterned armchair, his posture straight and gaze steady. Victor lounged on the matching sofa beside him, his green eyes assessing. Emily sat beside Jackson on the loveseat, the warmth of her leg a temptation he shouldn't have noticed.

The door opened and Nadia bustled inside, her cheeks flushed. "Sorry, I'm late." She clutched a clipboard against her chest as she moved toward Victor, sitting beside him with a quick smile. "I was meeting with a few people interested in starting a farm. We have enough territory for both crops and livestock. I think crops should go on the eastern side and livestock on the west. I'll draw up a proposal." Her smile widened. "Hi, Emily. How are you?"

"I'm good." Emily laughed, her eyes filled with mirth. "How about you?"

"Much better. Hi, Jackson," Nadia added, and he nodded in response. "I think I can help with the farming here. I've got some plans and sketches. They're efficient." She patted the clipboard as if it contained the key to their future.

"I'm sure." Emily's eyes warmed. "Where's your hulking bodyguard?"

Nadia blushed. "Outside working on his new truck. He avoids being inside as much as possible." She turned her attention to Jackson. "I don't suppose you know anything about him?"

"Nope." The resemblance between her and Emily still threw Jackson. It was fascinating, really. Nadia looked happier than the last time he had seen her, which gave him hope. One glance at her and he knew she wasn't a fighter, though deep down, he was starting to doubt if Emily was one, either. She presented as delicate, even with her height. It would tempt many to challenge her if she tried to serve as the pack's Alpha.

The safest course for Emily Nightsom's life was to mate him. The truth strengthened his resolve. It was the best thing for her. Plus, it was what he wanted. For now, he sat back and studied Victor, who looked insolent. "Somebody kidnapped Emily the other night. Did you hire them?"

Victor reared back. "What the fuck are you talking about?"

"I believe my words were clear." His voice dropped Alpha low.

Philip Nightsom set down his scotch and looked at his daughter with concern. "Are you all right?"

"I'm fine," Emily said. "But somebody hired three males to abduct me. The ringleader said someone hired him." She stared at her cousin as she spoke. "Vic, you're the only one I know with a motive."

"Motive?" Victor sneered. "What motive would I have?"

Nadia jerked her head toward him. "Duh. You want to be the Alpha of this pack someday, and right now, Emily's got the job if she wants it, right?"

"Exactly," Emily said smoothly.

Victor crossed his beefy arms. "I'm not worried about you being the Alpha, Emily Nightsom, and you should know that right now. I don't think you have a chance in hell. If you try to step up someday, I'll challenge you, and I'll win."

Silence thickened in the room, but Emily didn't flinch. "If you come at me, Vic, you'd better not miss."

Victor's eyes narrowed, a predatory gleam in their depths.

Jackson's wolf rumbled beneath his skin, itching to tear into the cocky male. "You should watch how you speak to her," Jackson warned.

"I don't answer to you," Victor shot back.

"Yet," Jackson replied, his smile cold. "But if you come after Emily again, you will."

Victor met Emily's stare, his chest puffing out as tension thickened the air.

Philip's gaze shifted between them, his mouth tightening. "I'm not going anywhere, but it's good to plan for the future."

"You're getting older." Victor's tone was flat, lacking any pretense of tact. "I could challenge you now and win."

A low growl rumbled from Philip's chest, vibrating through the room.

Jackson watched them closely. His gut told him Victor was right in that, as a younger wolf, he'd probably win. The only thing stopping him was the pack's devotion to Emily. But loyalty could only shield a leader for so long.

"I'm ready," Victor said, the muscles in his jaw tightening. "Ready to succeed at the trials."

"Trials?" Jackson asked, glancing at Emily.

She inhaled slowly. "I have no idea what he's talking about."

Yet another fucking secret. Fantastic.

Philip nodded. "Jackson, it's none of your concern."

"I see." Jackson's voice dropped, steel threading through the words. His pulse pounded hard in his head. "I'm going to ask you one more time. Did you come into my territory and kidnap Emily?"

Victor's eyes flared. "No. I don't need to kidnap anyone to take what's mine."

Emily studied him closely, finally settling back in her seat. "I believe him. Vic doesn't know anything about either kidnapping."

That's what Jackson's gut told him, as well. His gaze slid to Nadia. "How about you?"

Nadia's eyes widened. "Why would I kidnap my sister?"

"Answer the question," Jackson ordered.

The female paled. "I don't know anything about a kidnapping."

"Jackson, she's telling the truth." Emily slapped his jean-clad thigh in a warning. "Besides, neither of us knew we had a sister during the first kidnapping. There's no connection."

The thought of Emily being vulnerable under someone else's control made Jackson's wolf claw at him. It never should have happened. Not even once.

"That's not exactly true." Nadia's voice softened. "I've always known that Philip Nightsom was my father, but I never planned to come here until he invited me. When he did, I wanted to meet everyone." Her smile brightened as she glanced at Emily. "I have a sister."

Emily's smile was both sweet and unguarded. "You do have a sister," Emily said smoothly. "Also, you don't seem much like a kidnapper."

Nadia tapped a finger against her lips. "I bet I could think of a nice and efficient way to do it, but I see no reason to bother."

"Agreed," Victor said lowly. His gaze held a spark of something dark and unreadable. "Since we're having this little family get-together, why don't we talk about a transition of power?"

"No." Philip's voice cut through the room with the finality of a judge's gavel. "I'm not giving up my role as Alpha of this pack. So, back the fuck off."

Victor glared at him, muscles tightening in his arms as if ready to strike. His shoulders squared, and his nostrils flared, but something held him back.

Jackson studied the younger wolf. Perhaps Victor wasn't as confident in his ability to beat Philip as he pretended. That was interesting.

The tension in the room thickened, tightening like a rope about to snap. Emily's gaze flicked from her father to Victor, then to Jackson, her thoughts hidden behind her cool, composed mask. Snow tapped against the tall windows, soft and persistent, a reminder of the storm brewing beyond the walls. The fireplace crackled behind them, its warmth at odds with the chill running beneath the surface of the conversation.

"Well." Nadia broke the silence, her tone light. "This is cozy."

Nobody laughed.

Philip might last another thirty years in the role, but he did look older and slightly weaker than just the other day. Was the stress getting to him? Age was normal, and his progression was standard. Jackson wondered why Philip hadn't mated again to produce more heirs. Unless he had truly believed that Emily would take the reins. Why didn't everyone see the fragility in her that Jackson did? The thought tightened his chest in a way he didn't appreciate.

Emily took a deep breath. "Jackson, I hope you don't mind, but I'd really like to speak with my family alone."

He tilted his head slightly, his eyebrows lifting. "Why?"

She blinked, surprise flashing across her face at his bluntness. She should know by now that he was usually blunt.

"Pack business," she said simply as she stood. "And since we aren't—" She hesitated, her lips parting slightly before she continued. "Since we aren't mated, you don't belong in that conversation." She gestured him toward the door.

Irritation clocked through him, and he masked it. He stood. "That's fine, but after your meeting, Philip and I need to speak. Alone."

"Agreed." Philip leaned forward slightly, his sharp gaze locking with Jackson's.

Jackson followed Emily to the door, walking outside as she firmly shut it behind him. What did she need to discuss with her family that required his absence? Exactly what kinds of secrets did Emily Nightsom have? The question lodged in his chest, unwanted and persistent, as he forced himself to focus on the task at hand. If Philip agreed to his terms, there would be no more secrets between them.

Period.

* * *

Emily shut the front door as Jackson stepped onto the porch, irritation cascading off him. She rolled her eyes before returning to the living room.

Nadia flipped through her notes. "What are we discussing?"

"I like your idea of creating farming land." Emily offered her sister a small smile.

"Thanks."

Victor stood abruptly. "I'm done with this conversation."

"Wait." Emily's smile didn't waver, though heat simmered beneath her skin. "I wanted to say something about your threat to challenge my father."

Victor cocked his head. "Oh, yeah? What's that?"

Emily swung without hesitation, her fist connecting solidly with his nose.

Blood spurted as Victor staggered back, clutching his face. "What the fuck?"

Philip surged to his feet. "Emily! There will be no fighting in my house."

"Oh, my goodness." Emily snatched a linen doily from the nearest table. It was one of the replacements, not one her mother had made. "I'm sorry. I just lost my temper." She patted Victor's face awkwardly, dabbing at the blood.

"She hit me," Victor growled, voice muffled behind his hands.

"I said I was sorry." Emily shrugged. "Besides, you're an Alpha male, Victor. You'll heal within minutes. Probably."

Victor glared at her, eyes dark with fury, but he didn't say another word. He stormed toward the door, pausing just before stepping outside. "This isn't over, Emily Nightsom. We're going to come to blows one day."

The door slammed behind him, and his footsteps thudded down the stairs outside.

"What the hell was that about?" Philip rounded on her, eyes blazing.

Emily exhaled, placing the doily carefully on the piano and ensuring no blood touched the polished wood. "Sorry about that. I needed his blood."

Philip took a step back. "Excuse me?"

"I need to speak with both of you." Her voice softened slightly as she glanced toward her sister.

Nadia's eyes remained wide as she lowered herself onto the edge of the couch. "You just punched him right in the face."

"I did."

Nadia cleared her throat. "Were you really that angry?"

"No. Like I said, I needed his blood." Emily clasped her hands tightly, her fingers cold despite the warmth of the room. "I've been feeling off for the last month or so. It comes and goes, but it's gotten worse.

Her father sat heavily in his chair and reached for his scotch. "How bad?"

"Dizzy spells. Nausea. Weakness and numbness in my limbs —especially my legs."

The glass paused halfway to his lips, his eyes darkening. "Why didn't you say anything?"

"I didn't want to worry you. Our healer doesn't know what's wrong." She took a steadying breath, her pulse drumming in her ears. "But I think you know."

Philip's shoulders slumped. "I can't believe it's happening again."

Nadia leaned forward, her hands gripping her knees. "What's happening?"

Emily's gaze met hers, steady and unflinching. "The women in my family, on my mom's side anyway, die young. My mother. Her mother. I remember how Mom went from being fine to dying in a short timeframe, and she told me about the illness. We both hoped I'd be different."

Philip's hand trembled slightly as he set down his glass. "So did I."

"How far back does it go?" Nadia asked quietly.

Philip ground the heel of his palm against his eye. "We don't know for sure. But Emily's great-grandmother died young, as well. No one ever found out why."

Emily swallowed the lump rising in her throat. "I need everyone's blood. A doctor in Jackson's pack might be able to help. She's more advanced with scientific research."

Philip's jaw clenched, his eyes darting toward the window before returning to Emily. "Do you trust her?"

"I do." Emily stepped closer, her voice firm. "This is my chance, Dad. Maybe my only one."

Silence weighed heavily until Philip finally nodded. "All right. I'll do whatever I can to help."

"Me, too." Nadia placed her hand over Emily's. "But I don't see how my blood will assist you since the illness is on your maternal side."

Emily shrugged. "Who knows? Maybe your blood will show what mine's missing."

Nadia patted her hand. "Then you can have all you need."

Emily nodded. "Dr. Gwen is bound by doctor-patient confidentiality. She promised not to tell anyone, including Jackson." She stared at her father. "I'm sorry I didn't tell you before, but I didn't want to worry you."

His gaze darkened. "You can tell me anything, Em. I'm here to help."

Emily smiled. "Good. I trust the doctor. She's corresponding with our healer now, and she should be here shortly to draw blood." At least their healer had enough training to take blood samples.

Philip's gaze drifted to the window, then back. "I'm trusting you with this."

"And I'm trusting the doctors," Emily replied. "If there's a chance I can live longer, I'm taking it."

"Hey, if they fix this," Nadia murmured, "you can step up as the Alpha someday, right?"

"It's possible," Emily replied, glancing at her father. "But not for decades."

Philip chuckled, the tension in the room easing slightly.

Emily barely held on to her smile. "What was Victor talking about when he claimed he was ready for the trials?"

Philip looked down and then back up. "I can't tell you unless you declare your intention to become the Alpha. I've taken an oath in blood."

Just fantastic. Deep down, nothing inside her wanted to be the

Alpha of this pack. The responsibility, the constant weight of being challenged to the death, had never been part of the life she'd imagined for herself. But she knew if Victor ever got his hands on the pack, he would destroy everything her father had built.

The truth was simple. She only had two paths in life: either she died young, like her mother and grandmother before her, or she stepped up as Alpha and fought to survive for as long as she could—after going through some secret trials. Both futures weighed heavily on her, settling in her chest like anchors tied to her ribs.

And neither path led to Jackson Tryne.

CHAPTER 20

After a tense meeting with Philip, Jackson felt more settled than he'd been in weeks as he piloted the helicopter away from the Slate Pack territory. They'd reached an agreement, and Emily wasn't going to like it—which was why her father hadn't wanted to tell her. But Jackson would explain it to her later. "I'm sorry we couldn't stay longer, but the storm is coming in fast," he murmured through the headset. Thank goodness for the storm.

He banked left, noting the patrolling squads below them. He employed similar methods, but he needed more bodies. Sooner rather than later. For now, he was done with secrets from his soon-to-be mate. "Would you like to tell me now exactly why I had to leave the house? What are the trials? What else are you hiding from me, Em?"

She looked out at the snowcapped peaks jutting through the low-lying clouds and remained silent. "Let's talk later when we're safely on the ground."

He hated secrets. Like *really* hated them. But he'd give her a little time to gather her thoughts.

Turning the craft, he aimed once more to look at the Embervault Mine, lowering to make sure the fences remained secure. Snow dotted the windshield as the storm increased in force. The wind slammed into them, winter finally arriving.

Emily adjusted her harness, her gaze flicking between the instruments and the landscape beneath them.

"It's just a little storm, Emily. Trust me, you're fine."

She nodded and stared at the quiet mining area.

Maybe he could distract her. "Your father can move his miners into the Embervault Mine this week," Jackson said through the headset, his voice calm but focused as he scanned the airspace. He gripped the cyclic and collective with expert precision, the hum of the rotors steady above them.

Emily opened her mouth to respond when a sharp ping echoed through the cabin. The radar monitor flashed red.

What the holy fuck?

Jackson had to look twice. "Missile lock," he barked, yanking the controls and sending them into a steep bank.

Emily gasped and pointed out the window.

He looked to see a streak of smoke slicing through the air. Fast, deadly, and headed straight for them.

Damn it. He forced himself to remain calm and threw the craft into a hard dive. Trees blurred past the windows as alarms blared. "Hold on," he muttered.

Emily clutched the edge of her seat and let out a terrified yelp.

Another sharp ping. A second lock.

"Another one," she yelled, pointing frantically out the window.

Out of nowhere, the thought occurred to him that he'd never seen her frantic or even remotely out of control before.

The mountains echoed with the roar of the helicopter's engines as he twisted the craft through the valley, skimming dangerously close to the deadly cliffs. Snow and ice banged against the windshield as he maneuvered between narrow rock formations, using his wolf senses to keep them alive.

The first missile exploded behind them, shockwaves rattling the frame. Smoke and heat swirled through the air as he wrestled to maintain control.

Somebody had actually obtained fucking Stingers?

Before he could react, a second missile streaked. Too close. The tail rotor screamed as shrapnel sliced into it. Warning lights blazed on the console.

"Damn it." Jackson fought the controls as the helicopter spun wildly.

Emily went stiff and silent next to him. The damn horizon whirled past in a blur. Pine trees rushed toward them. The metal frame groaned as Jackson pulled hard on the collective, trying to slow their descent.

"Brace yourself," he ordered.

Emily curled forward, grabbing her knees as the craft dropped through the tree canopy.

Branches and ice shattered against the fuselage, ripping at the rotor blades. Metal shrieked as they clipped a ridge and skidded through the snow-covered ground. The world became a tumbling mass of gray, white, ice, and fire.

When they finally came to a stop, Emily gasped loudly for breath through the headset. The air reeked of burning pine and scorched metal. Gray, mutinous smoke unfurled from the twisted remains of the rotor blades above them.

"Emily," Jackson rasped, already unbuckling his harness. Blood trickled into his left eye. Was his head cut? "Are you all right?"

"No. Seriously." Her fingers shook as she fumbled with her harness. "We just got into a fucking crash."

They had to find shelter. Frigid air blasted into the cabin. Beyond the broken glass, snow pounded through the air, smothering the forest floor.

Jackson kicked open the mangled door and jumped into the snow, scanning the tree line. He calculated the distance between the mine and their crash point. A wolf could cover that in about an hour. "We need to move. Now." He reached in and pulled her out, careful of the glass. The snow was to his knees, so it reached her thighs. "Can you shift?"

She blinked snow out of her eyes, her backpack in her hand. "Of course."

He tightened his grip on her arms, forcing her to meet his gaze. "The doctor told you not to shift for a few days because of the silver bullet. You have to tell me the fucking truth. How do you feel?"

She faltered, looking away.

Shit. They were too far from either of their territories in unclaimed land. His best move was to head straight west into Copper territory and hope Erik was in a good mood. But in human form, they wouldn't make it before whoever shot them down reached them. They had to shift into wolf form. "Emily?"

Her chin firmed, and she looked up. "We don't really have a choice. I'll shift, and you can go on for help if I get too weak."

His hackles rose. "Sure. I'll just leave you in the snow and come back later after I've had a nice supper."

The cold turned her flawless skin a bright pink, and her eyes watered. "We don't have time for sarcasm, jackass." Her temper reassured him as nothing else could.

"All right. We shift and head due west. Should make Copper territory in about an hour."

She gulped and nodded. "All right. There's room in my backpack for our clothing, just in case."

He shook his head. "We'll be faster without it. We can find clothing when we arrive."

Her jaw firmed. "I'm not arguing." With that, she shrugged out of her jacket, already shivering as she shoved it into the pack.

Neither was he. Quicker than her, he shed his shirt and jeans, followed by the boots.

Snarling, she grabbed his clothes and shoved them in with hers. "Our boots and your jacket won't fit."

Did the female sound sad about that? "I'll buy you new ones. Leave the pack."

"No." She shivered almost violently, and now nude, he could see the bruises remaining on her ribs.

He willed himself not to look anywhere else and forced his gaze up to her face. "Emily? Why are you still bruised?"

She sighed. "I don't know, but I have blood in the pack that should tell me. All right?"

Blood? What the hell? Whose blood was she carrying across pack lines? In the distance, a wolf bayed.

Damn it. "We have to run. Now." Turning away, he shifted into his wolf form as she did the same. He engaged in a brief tug-of-war with her for the pack, finally ripping it free. Then he launched into a run, slowing to make sure she stayed on his six.

His instincts flared.

Their attackers were coming. Fast.

THE COLD RIPPED into Emily's paws as she struggled to keep up with Jackson. Their breath steamed in the icy air, vanishing before it could rise past their muzzles. Snow clung to her fur, weighing her down, and her pulse pounded in her ears as exhaustion gnawed at her muscles. She could hear the wolves behind them, their growls and panting breaths carried by the wind.

Lifting her head, she sniffed the air and could make out four different scents. She had a gift for smell, and it often came in handy.

Jackson cut a path for her, his powerful frame surging

through the snow with a relentless pace. His massive paws barely seemed to touch the ground.

Emily dug deeper for strength, trying to force her legs to move. The icy wind attacked her, freezing her ears as the jagged ground scraped her already frozen paws. Branches whipped past, and the sting of sleet bit into her face. Snow clumps dropped from branches high above, and one hit her on the head.

The impact knocked her sideways, her body rolling through the snow, pain echoing throughout her rib cage.

A growl tore through the air, and in an instant, Jackson stood in front of her. His jaw latched onto her scruff with a firm but careful grip, pulling her upright. Leaning in, his nose touched hers as he scanned her.

In his wolf form, he towered over her even more, with thick fur the color of onyx and those unmistakable blue eyes that glinted with fury and determination.

Emily yipped, shaking off the snow and signaling she could still run.

Jackson's gaze lingered for another moment before he spun, snatching the pack from where it had fallen. Muscles bunching, he broke into a run again, his paws tearing through the snow with barely restrained power.

She had to keep up with him. Taking a deep breath, she barreled herself forward, adrenaline dulling the ache in her legs.

Their pursuers' howls echoed through the trees, closer now. Too close.

Panicking, she pushed forward, each step harder than the last. Snow bit into her paws, and her breath came in ragged gasps. Desperation clawed at her chest, but she focused on Jackson's form ahead, muscles rippling beneath thick fur as he cut through the snow with relentless speed.

Her vision blurred.

The silver in her blood pumped sluggishly alongside the illness, both slowing her down. The wind sliced against her fur like needles, and branches above them creaked, dropping shards of ice that stung as they hit.

She followed Jackson, pushing beyond the exhaustion, but her limbs refused to obey. Each step felt heavier than the last until her body almost buckled beneath her.

They reached an outcropping of rocks offering a shallow shelter, the branches overhead catching most of the falling snow. She lurched into the space, her body trembling as it betrayed her, and she shifted back into her human form. Her knees hit the frozen ground, and she collapsed forward.

"Emily." Jackson shifted back in a heartbeat, catching her before her face hit. His arms closed around her, heat searing her frozen skin. "What the fuck?"

"I don't know." Her whisper trembled from her lips as her body shook violently.

"Damn it," he muttered, holding her tighter against his chest as if willing his warmth into her. "The silver…it's still in your blood. It's fighting you." His voice roughened, and his gaze swept the woods beyond their shelter.

The wind carried the sound of paws scratching over ice. The wolves were closing in.

"All right. Okay." He shifted his hold, pulling her fully onto his lap. "We need to get clothes on you."

He reached into the pack and yanked out her sweater, pulling it over her head in one swift motion before grabbing her jeans and jacket. "Put these on."

Her fingers fumbled with the fabric, stiff and clumsy from the cold, but she managed to tug them up over her trembling legs. He crouched and slid socks onto her feet. First hers, then his thicker pair, before zipping up her jacket and tugging the hood over her damp hair. Her breath puffed out in shaky clouds, and her teeth chattered uncontrollably.

His eyes narrowed. "Okay. If I shift, can you ride me?"

She tried to snort at the innuendo, but it came out as more

of a shaky exhale. Still, she managed a nod. Heat radiated off his body, even though he stood completely naked in the freezing air, snowflakes melting the second they touched his skin.

He brushed snow off her face. "Hold on tight. We're not far."

A crash echoed through the trees behind them. He took several steps away from her, and his body shimmered and shifted into his massive wolf form, fur bristling, eyes alert.

She swung the backpack over her shoulders, her fingers fumbling with the straps before she leaped onto his back. She clutched his thick ruff, leaning forward until her face pressed against the warmth of his neck.

He launched forward, paws pounding against snow-packed earth as the forest blurred past in streaks of white and gray. The wind slashed at her face, icy and sharp, but she clung tighter, tucking her fingers deeper into his fur. Beneath her body, his muscles moved with power as each of his long strides carried them closer to safety.

He ran gracefully between trees, with some branches snapping back and breaking off. She squeezed her eyes shut and went limp so he could move them both. His heart beat steadily beneath her palms, and she counted each one, trying to hold on.

Her arms shook, and her legs went numb.

All she had to do was *hold on*.

Something collided with Jackson, and they both flew through the air into the forest. Emily tumbled off his back, snow bursting around her as she smashed into a snowbank. She rolled wildly, gasping for breath, and clawed her way to her feet, waist-deep in snow.

Four wolves advanced.

Jackson skidded across the icy ground, hit a tree with a sickening thud, and dropped. Blood splattered against the white snow.

Her pulse pounded in her ears as he leapt back up in wolf form, snarling with lethal fury. He lunged at the closest wolf, claws slashing through fur and skin as he clamped his jaw on the attacker's throat. Bones crunched, and blood sprayed hot against the snow as Jackson wrenched his teeth from the wolf's neck, and the lifeless body dropped. The other three wolves attacked in unison.

"No!" Emily screamed. She flung the backpack aside, heart hammering as she sprinted forward. One of the wolves pivoted and leapt at her, jaws snapping. She kicked hard, connecting with its head, but the impact barely slowed it down. The snow clung to her legs, slowing her down as the wolf lunged again.

Jackson tore into the other two wolves. His claws raked through one's skull, and blood splattered in arcs across the snow. He spun to the last wolf, jaws clamping around its hind leg, bones snapping.

Emily ducked as the wolf attacking her surged again, its teeth grazing her shoulder. She dropped into a low stance, fingers curled into fists. The icy air burned her lungs as adrenaline surged through her veins.

Jackson roared.

She tried to scramble back as the wolf came at her, slowly herding her toward the rocks.

Her body froze, movements sluggish as the wolf advanced. She fell onto her back.

The wolf climbed her, yellow canines flashing, dripping saliva and blood. A sharp yelp echoed through the trees. Jackson? Was he hurt?

Fear surged through her veins as she tried to punch up. The wolf pressed its massive paws against her shoulders, pinning her as its hot breath blasted her face. Its dark eyes gleamed with malicious curiosity.

It sniffed and inhaled deeply as if committing her scent to memory. She coughed against the stench of the Ravencall member. She didn't know this wolf, but the scent marked it as one of them. A claw traced her cheek, deliberate and slow. Panic flared, and she shoved upward with both arms, striking its muzzle. The blow glanced off, barely registering. Its lips curled, almost like a smirk.

A blur of fur and fury crashed into the wolf, knocking it sideways. Jackson's growl vibrated through the air as he slammed the attacker into the trees with brutal force. Snow exploded in a spray of white. Branches cracked. Emily pushed herself up, shaking with cold, her vision swimming. She tried to stand, but her legs buckled beneath her.

She gasped Jackson's name, her voice thin and weak. The cold wrapped around her, dragging her down. The world tilted, narrowing to a pinpoint as warmth blossomed somewhere deep within, slow and steady like a heartbeat.

Then everything went wonderfully warm…and dark.

CHAPTER 21

Jackson clutched Emily tightly against his chest, shielding her as he sprinted through the forest. His bare feet had gone numb miles ago, but the pain didn't slow him down. It couldn't. He couldn't shift with her in his arms, and leaving her behind wasn't an option. So he'd yanked on his shirt and jeans, staying in human form. The air burned his lungs with each ragged breath as branches tore at his skin, slicing across his shoulders and thighs.

Four wolves lay dead behind them, but their pack wasn't done. He could feel their energy. Intense, predatory, and closing in fast. His pulse pounded in his ears as adrenaline surged through him, driving his legs forward even as exhaustion threatened to weaken them.

He crashed through the tree line and stumbled into Copper Pack territory. The moment his feet hit the border, six wolves appeared from the shadows, their eyes glowing amber in the moonlight.

Jackson halted, his chest heaving and his grip on Emily tightening. Blood slicked his skin, hot and thick, from wounds in his chest and thighs. His pulse weakened, but he planted his feet, his gaze sweeping over the wolves.

The largest shifted first. Oakley. Seventeen years old, tall and lean with agile muscles, he had a sharp jawline and intense eyes. Jackson had met him briefly. He was one of Erik's youngest Enforcers, already fierce and loyal.

"Jackson?" Oakley's gaze dropped to Emily's unconscious form, shock flickering across his face.

"We were attacked," Jackson said, his voice rough from cold and exertion. "She needs a doctor. Now."

Oakley's eyes widened. "Come on. I'll take you to Luna. She's a great healer. Do you want me to carry her?"

Jackson's snarl cut through the air. "No. I've got her."

Oakley didn't ask again. He turned and bolted through the trees.

Jackson followed, holding Emily close and whispering nonsense to her.

Oakley led them down a narrow path toward a snowy road where a battered green truck covered in snow waited. "We keep these scattered around in case we need them."

"Got it." Jackson climbed into the passenger seat, still holding Emily to his body in an effort to warm her. She felt like ice.

Oakley slipped behind the wheel and started the engine.

Heat blasted from the vents, searing Jackson's raw hands and dragging pain back into his consciousness as his nerves reawakened.

"Emily," he murmured, shaking her gently. She didn't stir. Breathing in her scent, he closed his eyes to listen for her heartbeat. It was sluggish and too faint. "Damn it. Wake up."

She didn't move.

Oakley glanced sideways, concern flashing in his eyes as he grabbed his phone and issued rapid orders to secure the border against the Ravencall wolves. Then he looked down at Jackson's feet before focusing on the icy road. "You warming up, man?" he asked, his voice steady despite the tension.

"Yes," Jackson said curtly. Why wasn't she waking up? Had her shift and run pushed more of the silver through her veins? To her heart or brain?

Oakley sped through the Copper Pack territory, weaving through snow-dusted roads until the lights of the main town glimmered ahead. He turned down a side lane leading to a small log cabin where Erik Volk and his mate, Luna, waited on the porch.

Jackson jumped out before the truck had fully stopped. "She was shot with silver yesterday, but she had to shift. Her body couldn't handle the cold," he said quickly, his gaze locking on Luna.

"Bring her inside," Luna said, her voice soft but firm. Her dark hair framed her delicate face, intelligent eyes gleaming with determination.

Jackson stepped past Erik and into the warmth of the cabin, hope battling with fear inside his chest.

Erik followed Luna into the warm living room, and Jackson gently placed Emily on the sofa.

"Stoke the fire hotter," Luna ordered her mate.

Erik Volk moved to the fireplace, tossing more logs onto the flames. He stood as tall as Jackson but had lighter blue eyes and dark-blond hair. He resembled his older brother, Seth, more and more with each passing year.

"I've got her." Luna knelt beside Emily and placed a blanket over her. "Get me some warm tea, please, Erik."

Erik glanced at Jackson. "There are socks in the bedroom," he muttered before heading into the kitchen.

Jackson hesitated, his gaze fixed on Emily.

"It's all right, Jackson. I've got her," Luna urged. "Your feet are blue."

Jackson exhaled slowly and made his way into the bedroom.

Finding a drawer, he pulled out socks to wear, then returned to the living room.

Emily stirred just as Erik entered with a steaming mug.

"Hey, Emily," Luna said softly. "I need you to take a couple of deep breaths, all right?"

Emily gasped, her eyes flying open as she bolted upright.

"Whoa." Luna gently patted her arm. "You're okay."

Emily's wild gaze darted around the room. "Jackson."

"I'm here." He circled the sofa, careful not to block the warmth of the fire.

"We were in a helicopter crash," she murmured as if trying to piece things together. Her gaze shifted to Luna.

"Seriously?" Luna glanced over her shoulder at Jackson.

"Yeah." He gave her a short nod before locking eyes with Erik. "Apparently, the Ravencall Pack got their hands on some Stinger missiles."

Erik's expression darkened. "How?"

"Hell if I know." Jackson's feet tingled as they warmed more.

It was true that many wolf shifter packs had decent underground sources for weapons and always had. But for the Ravencalls to not only afford but acquire Stinger missiles meant they were gearing up for war.

"Damn it," Erik muttered. "We need to have a meeting of the coalition."

"Agreed." Jackson glanced over at the couch.

Erik rubbed a hand down Luna's hair, his gaze beyond her. "Em? You doing okay?"

Emily nodded. "Yes. We appreciate the help."

Erik winked. "Well, I am your ex."

Jackson's chin lifted, and his chest heated.

Emily caught his gaze. "In name only."

Erik smirked. "Tryne? Let's step into the kitchen. We need to talk."

Luna smiled, her tone soothing as she touched Emily's shoulder. "I've got her. She's all right."

Emily pressed a hand to her temple. "I'm fine, Jackson. Just a little weak."

"We'll get some tea into you." Luna offered her the mug. "Sip it slowly, okay? Then I have some herbs I want you to take." Her voice softened with empathy. "So, you got shot with silver?"

"Yes. We need to figure out an antidote for that stuff." Emily's shoulders stiffened.

Jackson shook his head, guilt weighing heavily on his chest. Under his watch, she'd been kidnapped, shot with silver, and now caught in a helicopter crash. He clenched his fingers into a fist. He certainly wasn't taking decent care of her.

Luna adjusted the blanket over Emily with care, her soft voice filling the room. Emily's cheeks had regained some color, but she still looked too pale, fragile.

He had to force himself not to sit and drag her onto his lap. "Em? How are you really feeling?" he asked, not caring that the Alpha of the Copper Pack wanted to speak with him. Now.

Emily sipped more of the tea. "I'm fine, but I don't know when I'll be able to shift again. I feel…empty." Tears filled her eyes.

He took the tears like a punch to the gut. A hard one.

"You will," Luna said with quiet confidence, patting Emily's knee. "Believe me, you'll be just fine."

Jackson forced a breath into his lungs. "I'll be in the kitchen if you need me." His feet resisted the urge to move away from her, but he made himself turn to follow Erik.

"I know," Emily murmured.

"Now, let's get these wet clothes off you. You'll feel much better." Luna's kind voice filled the room. "I've never been in a helicopter crash before. Tell me all about it."

Jackson paused in the doorway, the sound of Emily's soft laughter tugging at something deep inside him. She'd been beyond brave and strong when she'd clung to his back as he ran through the icy forest.

No way in hell was he letting her go. Ever.

* * *

With Luna's help, Emily changed into one of Erik's extra-large, long-sleeve shirts, sweats, and thick socks since Luna's clothing was too small and way too short. Her muscles ached as she moved, her limbs still sluggish from the cold and the lingering effects of the silver. She shivered slightly as her body slowly warmed beneath the soft fabric.

"There you go," Luna said, her smile warm. "Feeling better?"

"I am. Thank you."

Luna helped her back to the living room and settled her onto the sofa, pulling a soft blanket over her. "Let the fire warm you even more."

The low murmur of male voices drifted from the kitchen, grounding Emily in the present. She tucked her legs beneath the blanket, holding her hands out toward the fire's heat. "How have you been?"

Luna chuckled, her eyes bright with humor. "A lot better than you have."

"No kidding." Emily glanced at the backpack resting near the hearth. Her pulse skipped. Jackson had brought it with them? "How long can blood stay out of refrigeration before it spoils?"

Luna's smile faded. "Depends on what you need it for. Twenty-four hours if you just need DNA. Much less for other tests. Why?"

Emily held her gaze, waiting.

Curiosity sparked in Luna's eyes. "You have blood in there?"

Emily nodded. "Yes. Will you refrigerate it for me?"

"Sure." Luna took the pack, her movements slow and deliberate. "I'll run it down to my lab."

"Thank you." Relief filtered through Emily.

Luna disappeared down the stairs and soon returned, her eyes glimmering. "Want to tell me why you're carrying blood and...what was that other thing? A bloody doily?"

Emily chuckled. "Yeah. I *do* want to tell you, and if you don't mind, I'd like you to correspond with my doctors."

Luna's smile faded into something softer. She placed a hand over Emily's knee. "Oh, Em...are you sick?"

"Yes." Emily told Luna the entire story, winding down with her current situation.

Luna's eyes kept widening the entire time. "Impressive. The fact that you got shifters to give up blood is shocking, though. I have to admit, I appreciate the punch to the nose and the doily trick. However, to be honest, we probably won't get a good sample from that. But the important blood is yours and your fathers, even Nadia's, so we're fine."

Emily had heard that Luna was pushing to modernize her pack's medical practices. Thankfully, Erik supported her, because Luna seemed like a force of nature. Emily's nose twitched, catching a scent in the air. Something a bit earthy yet sweet. Baby powder? "Luna," Emily said softly. "Congratulations."

"For getting mated? Thanks. You already sent me flowers, remember?"

"No." Emily met her gaze with a small smile. "For the baby."

Luna froze, her face going pale. "What?"

Emily covered her mouth, realizing she'd spoken too soon. "You didn't know yet?"

"No. What are you talking about?" Luna asked, her voice shaking.

Emily reached for her hand. "You're pregnant. I have an advanced sense of smell. I've always been able to tell. I could smell a baby just now."

Luna blinked several times. "Are you sure?"

"Yeah. I knew when Mia was pregnant, too." Mia had mated Seth Volk and was due sometime in the next few months.

Luna sat back, tears welling in her eyes. "I wasn't sure I could have children. I mean, I thought maybe once I mated with Erik, but I didn't know if it was possible. I can't believe this. How wonderful! Are you absolutely sure?"

Emily squeezed her hand. "I'm one hundred percent positive."

Joy transformed Luna's face, her smile radiant. "Oh, this is incredible. But don't tell Erik yet, okay?"

"I won't say a word."

"Good. I want to surprise him after I double-check. No offense."

How wonderful for the couple. "No offense taken. It's one of my gifts."

Luna's gaze brightened, and she inhaled sharply as if holding back a rush of emotions. "Let's focus on you now." Her voice turned brisk, her healer instincts apparently taking over. "I need you to tell me everything again, from the first symptom to the latest. Don't leave anything out."

Emily hesitated, her fingers knotting together on her lap as she lowered her voice. "This has to stay between us. Doctor-patient confidentiality and all that."

"Of course." Luna tilted her head, whispering back. "Does Jackson know?"

"No." Emily's voice dropped. "But I'm sure he has questions since he knows I was carrying blood."

Luna snorted. "Oh, I'm sure he has questions. You know, you can tell him the truth. Your packs are aligned, and besides, there's something between you two."

"There can't be," Emily said firmly.

Luna waved a hand through the air. "Oh, that's just silly."

"No, it isn't." Emily appreciated her friend's encouragement but held her ground.

"Well, I'm not done trying," Luna teased. "But tell me. Did I hear right that he's looking for a mate on the Internet?"

Sometimes, wolves gossiped worse than humans. "I've been using the Internet to find one for him. So, yes, that rumor is true."

"Girl, that's the dumbest thing I've ever heard." Luna shook her head.

"Maybe. Maybe not." Emily took a deep breath. "For now, can you help me?"

Luna's gaze sharpened. "Yes. I'll coordinate with the doctors and healers in all four packs. We'll figure this out, Emily."

For the first time since falling ill, Emily felt hope.

CHAPTER 22

Jackson carried Emily into the cozy guest cabin and looked around. The place had been furnished with hand-carved wooden furniture holding thick, blue leather cushions. A fire crackled in the hearth, flames reflecting off copper etchings of wolves encircling the stone mantel. A small kitchen lay beyond the gathering area, fitted with what appeared to be brand-new appliances. To the left, a hallway led to two bedrooms, their doors slightly ajar.

"You really don't need to carry me, Jackson," Emily said, though she seemed to cuddle closer against his chest.

He kicked the door shut with the heel of his boot and crossed the room, setting her gently on the sofa. Without hesitation, he grabbed a hand-knitted blanket in copper and blue from the armrest and draped it over her legs. The thick yarn still held the scent of the cabin's woodsmoke.

"I'm really okay," she added, her voice soft.

"You're pale and felt fragile in my arms," he muttered, crossing to the fire to add another log. Sparks flared as the flames licked the fresh bark. The cabin's clock ticked steadily above the mantel. Midnight had come and gone. Heavy and full, the moon outside pulled at his blood, sharpening his senses.

He returned to the chair beside her, sinking into the worn leather. His elbows rested on his knees as he studied her. Her platinum-blond hair framed her face in a wild halo, the tips still damp from their time outside. Her eyes, a deep black now, met his. He noted the absence of the worn backpack she'd guarded so fiercely earlier. His patience had thinned. No more secrets.

"What?" she asked, her shoulders tightening.

He held her gaze, unmoving. The fire popped softly. The air between them thickened until a flush spread across her cheekbones. She looked away first. Alphas knew how to stare down anyone, but this female carried Alpha blood of her own.

"Where's the backpack?" His voice came out low and steady.

Her hands twisted the blanket's edge. "With Luna."

"Why?"

Silence clung to the walls, broken only by the distant hum of the fridge. Emily's fingers stilled. When she finally spoke, her voice was quieter than before. "It's not your problem."

"Wrong," he replied. "It became my problem the minute you collapsed outside the border. Whatever you're hiding could get you killed. That makes it my concern."

Emily's eyes flicked to his. The firelight reflected in their dark depths, giving them a glint that hinted at secrets he hadn't begun to guess. The air thickened again. She seemed to weigh the cost of the words before she gave them.

"I'm not dragging you into this." A tremor ran through her voice.

"You already have," he replied. "Start talking." He kept his gaze steady. "Emily," he said, tone low and calm.

She sighed like a teenager caught sneaking out past curfew and turned back to him. "All right, fine. First, thanks for saving my life."

"Was that given grudgingly?" he asked, the corner of his

mouth threatening to twitch. Amusement stirred beneath his ribs, but now wasn't the time to ease the tension. Instead, he raised an eyebrow.

Her arms crossed over the blanket, drawing his gaze. The sight of her wrapped in Erik Volk's shirt stirred a low growl inside him. It was none of his business whose clothing she wore. Still, it sat wrong. He waited.

She rolled her eyes so hard he half-expected them to disappear into her skull. "Fine. You deserve the truth."

"I believe so."

"I…" She exhaled, her shoulders dropping. "The females in my maternal line have died young from an illness nobody's been able to identify."

Alarm spread through Jackson, though he kept his posture relaxed as he leaned back in the chair. Deceptively calm.

She tucked a wayward strand of hair behind her ear. "I haven't been feeling well for more than a month now, and I'm getting weaker. Our doctor doesn't know how to help me, so I talked to yours. And Luna. Well, you know she's kind of a mad scientist."

Jackson had heard the rumors. He just hadn't paid much attention. "They think they know what's wrong with you?"

She shook her head. "I don't know. I managed to get blood samples from my dad, Nadia, and…" She winced. "Victor."

His brows lifted. "Victor gave you blood to test?"

"Not exactly."

He waited.

Her hands twisted the blanket's edge. "I had to punch him in the nose."

Jackson barked out a laugh before he could stop it. "You punched him in the nose?"

"Yeah. And then I used one of those doilies to gather the blood."

His laughter echoed through the cabin. The tension in the

air cracked, if only slightly. But her confession still pressed between them, heavy and unspoken. His smile faded as quickly as it had come.

"Emily." His tone softened.

Her eyes found his again, shadows lingering there. He wanted to reach across the space between them, but not yet. First, he needed the whole truth. All of it.

Wait a minute. "Not your mom's doilies?"

"Oh, no. Definitely not one of hers."

Why had his mind even gone there? He really was losing it around this female. "You hit Vic, and he didn't hit you back?" If he had, Jackson would tear the bastard apart.

"No, he just kind of whined that I broke his nose." She shrugged as if it were nothing.

"Well, score one for Victor," Jackson muttered. He had to give the guy props for not retaliating, although Philip's presence had probably kept the situation from escalating. "If I have to take him out for you, I will."

"I don't like that idea." Emily turned back to the fire. Its steady crackle and warmth lent the cabin a sense of calm.

Jackson stretched out his legs, his shoulders sinking deeper into the chair. At least now he knew the truth. Or part of it. "Tell me more about this illness."

"Weakness in the legs, difficulty shifting, losing energy. She straightened the blanket.

"Your mother was older than you when it hit her, right?"

Emily nodded. The color drained from her face until even her lips looked pale. "Yes. And her mother was older still. But it seems to be hitting us younger with every generation."

"They both died from it?" Jackson asked, his voice rougher than intended.

"Yes." Her fingers stilled against the blanket. "There's not much I can do about it."

Finally, some of this made sense. "Is that why you didn't want to be Alpha? Because you can't be?"

"That's one of the reasons," she admitted. "Can you imagine the number of challengers I'd face?"

Jackson had stepped up at fifteen, and even with the council backing him, challenges had come fast and hard. He'd been brutal back then, taking down his first two challengers without hesitation or mercy. After that, nobody had dared to try again.

Looking at Emily now, he realized she wasn't built that way. Mercy lived deep in her bones. That classy kindness had always drawn him, even from a distance. But in an Alpha challenge, kindness wouldn't cut it.

"It's a good thing your father is still healthy," Jackson said. "Your father and I reached an agreement, but you do have a say."

Emily's lips pressed into a thin line. "Oh, do I? What agreement? I told you I'm not sending one of my kids to fight to the death."

"I know. The agreement is that when Philip needs to step down, if he doesn't have another heir, either one of our kids or *I* become the Alpha."

Her mouth dropped open. "You'd become the Alpha of the Slate Pack."

"Yeah." He didn't want to, but he would.

"What about your pack?"

It seemed obvious to him. "Then our kid could step up in our pack."

She shook her head. "That's great, but what if my dad doesn't have a few decades?"

Jackson exhaled. "Couldn't Victor lead for a short time?"

"No. Victor's as bad as you've heard. Worse, maybe."

Jackson's pulse ticked up a notch. "Define *worse*."

"He's put more than one female shifter in the hospital. I know of two." Her fingers twisted the blanket's edge. "We don't have domestic violence laws, but…we probably need them."

"So, nothing's happened to him?"

Emily's jaw tightened. "Oh, no. My father and his Enforcers beat the ever-living hell out of him. Both times."

"Both times?"

She nodded. "The last time, I think he barely survived."

"Good." Jackson's hands clenched against his knees. He forced himself to relax. "What about the females?"

"They stayed away from him. And he stayed away from them."

"Because of your father."

"Yeah. Dad made it clear that if Victor came within a hundred yards of either female, he'd kill him."

The fire popped softly, throwing shadows against the walls. Victor might have learned caution, but a temper like that never stayed buried for long.

Okay, so they did have some decent laws. However, the idea that somebody like that could step up as Alpha was unthinkable.

"I could offer to combine our packs, but—"

She was already shaking her head before he could finish the sentence.

"I know," he said. "That wouldn't work."

It was becoming common practice to fold smaller packs without full-blooded Alphas into larger ones. But for two powerful packs like theirs, merging would be chaos. Their different traditions, Alpha bloodlines, and pack dynamics would create internal war instantly. And outsiders would seize the chance to attack. Not to mention the fact that their territories were way too far apart.

"I can't believe the Ravencalls have actual missiles," Emily said.

Jackson allowed her to change the subject, needing time to think as well. "There are underground trafficking networks moving weapons around the world that human governments haven't caught up with. Plus, getting anything across the southern border has been easy in recent years."

Her gaze sharpened. "Do you have missiles?"

Since she'd been telling secrets, he would, too. "Of course, I have missiles. I'm sure your father does, too, Em. Every once in a while, you need to show that you can do more than bite to protect your pack."

"Oh," she murmured. "I'm feeling much better." Her gaze swept over him with a look that sent heat low in his gut.

"I'm glad." He meant it, though his muscles coiled with restless energy. The urge to shift and burn it off clawed at him, but her presence anchored him. Leaving her right now? Not happening.

She drew in a breath. "I made a decision tonight, Jackson."

His attention sharpened. "Is that a good thing or a bad thing?"

"I think it's a good thing," she said.

"What's that?"

"I've decided to live."

He blinked. "That's a good thing, sweetheart. I figured that was already the plan."

"No, not like that." She dropped the blanket and stood, each step deliberate as she closed the space between them. His heartbeat thudded faster with every inch she crossed.

"I'm tired of half living and waiting," she continued. "I don't know if I've got a week, a year, or a century left. I hope for centuries. But right now, I'm going to live each second like it might be my last. Because it could be."

Her words landed heavily between them. The air seemed to thicken.

"What does that mean?" His voice emerged as a guttural growl.

She moved close, her gaze steady as if daring him to look away. Slowly, she swung one knee over the outside of his thigh, then the other, settling her weight on him, straddling him. His brain misfired as heat shot through his veins.

Her hands found his shoulders, fingers curling into the worn fabric of his shirt. Leaning close, her breath brushed his cheek, warm and sweet with the scent of huckleberry tea and bourbon.

His pulse hammered against his ribs.

"I'm tired of wondering about this, Jackson. I'm not agreeing to mate you and still haven't figured out how that could even work. But we have right now. Do you really want to miss out on even one night together?"

Her lips found his, soft and warm and deliberate. No hesitation, no holding back.

Fire shot through him so fast his breath hitched, and he wrapped his arms around her before he could think better of it. Logic, reason, and hell, the whole world, ceased to exist the moment her mouth touched his.

CHAPTER 23

What was she doing? Emily Nightsom had never needed to make the first move with a male, not once in her entire life, and now she'd done it twice. She kissed Jackson as he sat there like he was trying to give her space, as if he thought she needed it. She didn't. She was done with space. Done with wondering. And she was beyond tired of worrying about dying.

They could've died earlier today when the helicopter went down. Again, when those four wolves attacked. Both times, Jackson had saved them with absolute focus and brutality. Each time, she'd come face-to-face with the reality that tomorrow wasn't guaranteed. And right now? She wanted him. She wanted to feel alive. To feel good. Maybe she didn't have a future. But *they* had this moment. Sometimes, that had to be enough.

Jackson's hands tunneled through her hair, warm fingers curling at her scalp. He tilted her head back, his gaze locking on hers. His eyes flashed a mystical blue—sharp, focused, and unmistakably hungry. "Are you thinking clearly?" His voice came out rough, the sound vibrating against her chest.

"I am, Jackson." She inhaled his wild, masculine scent, her

pulse kicking up. "We had one kiss eons ago and another the other day. I haven't stopped thinking about either of them."

"Ditto." His gaze dropped to her mouth. "But you were hurt and almost frozen," he murmured.

Maybe he could help banish the cold. "I may be fighting an illness, but I'm still an Alpha female," she shot back, strength sparking. "I'm healed as much as I can be. My brain's intact, Jackson. How about yours?"

His nostrils flared. "I'm not exactly the honorable type, sweetheart. I'm not gonna do the right thing and put you to bed in a room by yourself for your own good. You can worry all you want about the future, but I know what I want right now."

He was wrong. Everything about Jackson was honorable. Maybe he didn't want it to be. Maybe as a fifteen-year-old Alpha, he hadn't had the luxury. But now? Now, honor clung to him as tightly as the heat thrumming between them.

That side of him pulled her in like nothing else. She'd noticed the way his gaze flicked to Erik's shirt on her, the brief flash of distaste he hadn't quite hidden. He didn't like seeing her in another male's clothes. And the strangest part? She liked that. Possessiveness in a boyfriend had never appealed to her before. But with Jackson? Everything felt different.

If they'd been different people with different lives and loyalties, they probably would've ended up together without hesitation. But their packs defined their futures.

Duty would always come first.

If she regained her health, she could back up her father. But what then? What about Jackson? She owed her pack. But tonight? No more thinking. Tonight, she was taking this moment for herself. "If you don't want me, say so."

"You'd have to be three centuries dead for me not to want you." His voice was a rough murmur.

Yeah. That's what she'd thought. She slid higher onto his thighs, heat curling low in her belly as she felt the pulse of him through the thick, too-big sweats she wore. They'd fall right off if she tried to walk too far in them. Which, frankly, was part of the plan.

"You're sure?" he asked, the words brushing against her skin.

"Just this night," she replied.

He grinned. "That's my line."

Yet somehow...it wasn't.

Jackson aimed to build a family, and she knew it. She didn't see how she could be part of his future. Or was she just lying to herself? A shard of jealousy cut through her at the thought of the female he chose. That wolf would have a good life. But tonight? Tonight belonged to Emily.

She leaned in, her lips brushing his, teasing with soft, lingering kisses. The fire warmed her back, while Jackson's heat warmed her front. His fingers threaded through her hair, his palm cradling her head as his other hand slid down her spine, stopping at her waist to draw her closer.

"If anything hurts, tell me," he murmured against her mouth.

Instead of answering, she pressed harder into him. He captured her lips fully, deepening the kiss until her breath hitched. His grip tightened, locking her against him as sensation overwhelmed her. She fell into the wildness that spun between them, heat spiraling through her limbs and pooling low in her belly. Her breasts ached where they pressed to the solid plane of his chest, her body coming alive in ways she hadn't felt in years.

He growled low, the sound rough and primal, before kissing her deeper, both hands adjusting her hips into the perfect position to absorb the pleasure he fed her. Still holding her close, he stretched effortlessly to his feet, lifting her without breaking the kiss. The world tilted, and she clung to his shoulders, her heartbeat thundering against his. The air around them crackled with heat, both from the fire and the raw energy coiling tighter between their bodies.

She wrapped her arms around his neck and returned his

kiss, drawing in the taste of scotch. He and Erik must have had a drink in the kitchen while cleaning up after dinner—yet another side of Jackson she hadn't expected. Capable. Domestic. Protective.

He moved, carrying her down the hallway, but she didn't care where. Her fingers tangled in his thick hair, savoring the soft, springy strands that felt almost too silky for a male as tough as him. The contrast fascinated her. His whiskers scraped her chin, rough and teasing, sending another rush of heat through her.

She barely noticed when he lowered her onto a bed, his strength effortless as he moved, keeping her close. Then he sank to his knees in front of her, his hands sliding up her thighs, skimming to the oversized shirt she wore. He slowly lifted the fabric, watching her with an intensity that sent shivers through her. She helped him, pulling it over her head and letting the cool air wash over her skin just before his warmth replaced it.

His mouth found her breasts, pressing soft kisses before teasing, licking, and nipping. It was slow, unhurried worship that had pleasure winding deep inside her. She had expected something rough, fast, but this? His tenderness and patience made something inside her crack open. He wasn't just touching her body. He was reaching deeper and further into places she had long since locked away.

"Jackson," she breathed.

He looked up, eyes dark with hunger, then yanked off his shirt. Hard cut muscles now stretched before her, all raw strength and honed power. She ran her hands over his warm skin, trailing her fingertips over the deep ridges of his abs, feeling the way he trembled under her touch.

No belt stood in her way. Her fingers brushed the top of his jeans, then flicked the button open, sliding the zipper down with slow, deliberate ease.

He gently pushed her back onto the bed, and she laughed

when her head hit the soft comforter. His hands, rougher now, yanked the sweats down her legs. She kicked her feet, and he caught her ankle with a firm grip.

"Socks. Leave the socks on." His gaze locked on hers.

She blinked. "You have a sock fetish?"

His grin was boyish, almost charming. Well, as close as Jackson could get to boyish. Even in a playful mood, he radiated pure predator. "No sock fetish. But your feet were freezing. We're keeping them warm."

"You're kind of bossy."

"I'm trying to temper that this time." His tone softened, but something in his eyes made her breath catch.

This time. The words clanged through her like a warning. There could only be this time. She wasn't sure she would survive this and still walk away.

He pressed her down again, his hands sliding along her thighs, opening her. Then his mouth found her, and she jerked against him, her cry echoing off the walls.

"Jackson," she gasped.

He kissed her clit, slow and deliberately, thumbs pressing into the soft skin of her inner thighs. Heat flashed through her. Vulnerability brushed against her, but then he did it again. Hot, wild, and deep. Any trace of shyness vanished. Her world narrowed to the fire of his mouth and the pressure building inside her.

"You're beautiful, Em," he said against her skin.

She couldn't answer. Her body shattered beneath his touch, the first orgasm hitting so fast she forgot to breathe. She hadn't known she could come like that, and he did it again before she could gather herself. By the third time, her vision blurred, and her limbs were boneless, her breath ragged.

"Jackson," she whispered.

"Yeah?" He stood and shoved off his jeans in one swift motion. Firelight sculpted shadows across his body, highlighting muscle and strength. Dangerous. Deadly. Built like a warrior stepping from the flames. And tonight, he was hers.

He grasped her hips and lifted her higher onto the bed, following her down and covering her with his body. His heat surrounded her, and then he kissed her again.

Slow, deep, and all-consuming.

Every inch of her skin had felt his mouth, tongue, and teeth, yet he showed no signs of stopping. He nibbled along her jawline, found her ear, and bit gently. A shiver danced down her spine as she widened her legs, needing him more than she could explain. Not just physically. She wanted this connection with him and no one else.

"You sure?" His breath warmed her ear.

She dug her nails into the hard muscle of his ass, loving the solid feel of him. Then she smoothed her hands over the indents she'd left, silently telling him she wanted more.

"Fair enough," he murmured.

Sliding an arm beneath her leg, he lifted her, aligning their bodies. Slowly, he began to press inside her. She inhaled sharply. He was thick and hard, stretching her in ways that made her toes curl. He moved slowly, giving her time to adjust while nuzzling her neck, the rasp of his whiskers rough against her skin. She welcomed the burn, that raw scrape of sensation.

Her other leg widened, and she clamped her hands hard on his buttocks, urging him deeper.

"Please," she whispered, half plea, half demand.

His gaze lifted, and something feral ignited in his eyes. With a thrust, he powered all the way inside her, stealing her breath. Her body clenched, instinctive and tight, then softened around him as if recognizing exactly where he belonged. His mouth found hers in a kiss so tender it cracked something wide open inside her.

"Em," he whispered. Just her shortened name, one simple syllable that tunneled straight through her chest and into her heart. The moment held, suspended between them, before he drove into her again—hard, fast, and relentless. She clung to his shoulders, her nails digging in for purchase as he pushed her higher, faster, and toward the edge she both craved and feared.

He kept her wide and open for him, that arm hooked beneath her knee, holding her exactly where he wanted. Her breath hitched. The look in his eyes was wild, possessive, untamed, and sent another pulse of heat straight through her. He pushed her over the edge, and she shattered, crying out his name as pleasure crashed through her in rolling waves that left her boneless. Every limb felt weak, spent, but satisfaction hummed through her veins.

She murmured his name, still catching her breath, and realized he wasn't finished. His body kept moving against hers, slow and steady. She clutched his shoulders, fingers digging into hard muscle as she tried to ground herself, but the tension was already building again, too fast, too sharp.

"Now," she whispered, frustration lacing her voice when he slowed his pace.

His wicked grin sent heat pooling low in her belly. "Oh, we're taking our time," he murmured.

"Are we?" She scraped her nails down his back, then gripped the muscle of his thigh, determined to push him over the edge.

His breath hitched, his control slipping. His chin lifted slightly, and she saw it. The moment restraint shattered. He drove into her harder, deeper, every thrust sending sparks burning beneath her skin. Her body clenched around him, tightening as the pressure built impossibly high.

A riot started inside her. One of hunger and dark need. His name broke free on a gasp as pleasure detonated, white-hot and relentless. Her eyes squeezed shut as she climaxed, every nerve singing with sensation. He shuddered against her, his release following hers in rough, staggered bursts that made her cling tighter.

Their breaths mingled, harsh and uneven as the aftershocks slowly faded. His hand brushed her hair back from her face, and he kissed her softly, a lingering touch of lips that felt more like a promise.

"You okay?" he asked, voice rough with exertion.

"Better than okay," she admitted. "I've never felt this good in my life."

His smile was pure trouble. "Good. Because I'm not done."

Before she could reply, his mouth captured hers again, and he thrust deep, pulling her right back into the fire.

CHAPTER 24

Jackson finished his second cup of coffee that morning, eyes fixed on the fireplace as Emily slept quietly in the other room. Contentment and restlessness warred inside him, an odd mix he couldn't quite shake. His life had never been smooth sailing, but last night had settled something deep in his bones while stirring something else entirely.

A scent drifted from outside, pulling him from his thoughts. He stood and crossed the cabin, the floorboards cool beneath his bare feet. Opening the door, he stepped onto the wide front porch. Crisp air bit at his skin, but he welcomed the chill. Snow blanketed the ground, reflecting the pale morning light.

Erik Volk leaned against the porch railing, arms crossed, eyes sharp. His gaze swept over Jackson like a challenge. "I smell Emily all over you. What the hell are you doing?"

Jackson rolled his shoulders, the now dry jeans sitting low on his hips, his chest bare to the cold. He should've cared, but the warmth still lingering in his muscles kept the chill at bay. Walking across the smooth planks, he dropped to sit onto the top step, extending his legs down the other three until his feet touched snow. The bite of frost grounded him, steadying his pulse. "None of your business."

Erik's gaze flicked to the cabin, then back to him. "She's not at full strength yet."

Jackson met the Copper Pack leader's gaze without flinching. "Do you honestly think I'd take advantage of Emily? Your instincts are better than that."

Erik looked down at his boots, scuffing snow from the step, then exhaled and nodded. "Yeah, they are. She's a friend and has been for a long time. I don't like that someone's kidnapped her twice."

Jackson's gaze stayed steady. The first time, she'd been engaged to Erik. Even he hadn't found the kidnappers. "I'll get them," Jackson said, his voice low but confident. "Don't worry."

Erik studied him for a moment longer, then gave a single nod. The cold air swirled between them, but the tension had shifted. Not gone, just waiting.

Jackson had feelers out in every direction, ready to catch the smallest whisper of whoever wanted Emily and would dare to take her out of his territory. The hired thugs showed someone really didn't want to be identified.

Erik tilted his head slightly, his gaze sharp and unwavering. "You need to start traveling with an Enforcer, Jackson. Especially if Emily's with you."

Jackson winced. "I've always avoided taking one on. The council bossed me around for too long. I've got several good fighters I can call when needed but having one full-time doesn't work for me."

The suggestion hung in the air, a hint of concern beneath Erik's blunt tone. Jackson let the cold bite into his bare chest, grounding himself as the snow beneath his feet soaked into his skin. The pine-laced air filled his lungs, crisp and sharp, a reminder of everything that still needed to be done. "When I take a mate—I'll hire a couple of Enforcers."

Erik's light-blue eyes, clear in the morning light, studied him. His dark-blond hair, pulled back at the nape of his neck, had deepened to brown over the years. "Emily or not?"

"I have an agreement with Philip, but I want one from Emily. She's getting there."

Erik studied him. "It's too bad you can't just combine the packs, but you'd have a civil war in seconds."

"Yeah, our packs are too different and our mining operations don't mesh well." Jackson ran a hand down his face, the rough scrape of his whiskers grounding him in the moment. "You know, Philip could have more kids." That would let Emily off the hook.

"Wouldn't surprise me." Erik shrugged. "The guy's still strong and stubborn as hell."

Jackson huffed a laugh and shook his head. "Yeah." He should suggest it.

"We're calling a meeting of the Stope Packs Coalition. All leaders meet today at eleven. I figured you and I could go together," Erik said. "I assure you Emily will be safe while we're gone. Luna wants to meet with her anyway to draw more blood." His tone dropped, turning disgruntled.

Jackson fought a grin. "You don't know why?"

"No." Erik growled low. "Luna wouldn't tell me."

Jackson rolled his neck, trying to demolish a knot. "That's both amazing and adorable. Didn't you ask nicely?"

"Shut up."

"You shut up."

Erik tucked his thumbs in the pockets of his jeans, the tension in his shoulders easing slightly. "Luna takes the whole doctor-patient thing seriously. Even though she's not a doctor. More like a mad scientist."

"That's her reputation," Jackson replied. "But if Emily and Luna aren't telling you, neither am I."

Erik's gaze steadied on him, the humor fading from his eyes. "Is Emily okay?"

Oddly enough, Jackson didn't want to lie to someone he almost considered a friend, so he said nothing.

Erik's mouth tightened. "That's what I thought. Do you think she'll be okay?"

"Yes," Jackson answered without hesitation. "I do." She had to be.

The rumble of an approaching engine drew their attention. The same old, green truck from before rolled to a stop, tires grinding over snow-packed gravel. Oakley jumped out, his high school football jersey visible beneath an unzipped jacket. Jeans tucked into thick boots, he moved with the confidence of someone twice his age.

"Patrolled the eastern side. Guards are rotating." Oakley shook snow from his sleeves.

Jackson studied the kid. Young to be an Enforcer—too young by most standards—but Oakley carried himself with purpose. From what Jackson had seen, he handled his responsibilities well. "What are you planning after you graduate?"

Oakley smiled, looking like a teenager again. "My mom and sisters come first, but the pack can help with them. I'm thinking of training in warfare and military operations."

What a smart idea. Jackson gave a firm nod. "I like that you are finally modernizing." He'd done so for years but needed his allies to catch up.

"We're working on it," Erik said, his tone practical. "I think starting a farming community within the pack is a good start. You should do the same."

"I'm planning on it," Jackson replied. Wolves had always taken from the wild or bartered with humans, so creating a farm was modernizing for them. The logistics weighed on him already. Raya could probably handle organizing it, but she had enough on her plate. Emily's sister crossed his mind. She knew farming and would probably like to help, but her hands had to be full with joining the Slate Pack. Still, it might be worth asking.

"Training's about more than muscle these days," Erik added. "We need strategy and discipline. Tech, too. It's not enough to fight. We have to think ahead."

Jackson had sources everywhere and needed to check in with them. Unlike the other packs, he'd been thinking ahead since he turned sixteen. His gaze drifted toward the cabin. Emily's presence lingered like a steady heartbeat, grounding him even from a distance. "Yeah. We need to be ready for whatever's coming next."

"It's always coming." Erik's eyes met his. "Best we meet it head-on from every front, including owning cattle. Never thought I'd own cattle."

"I don't suppose we could combine farmland," Jackson murmured.

Erik huffed out a breath. "We've always had problems combining land. Even if you're letting Philip use the Embervault Mine, I'm sure you just granted him a license."

"Of course, I did."

Oakley snorted. "I've gotta get to school. Erik, don't forget that prom's Friday night, so I'm off duty."

"I won't forget," Erik said. "Did you get your tux?"

"Yeah. I had Mrs. Pompion change the cummerbund. Apparently, there's a difference between eggplant and purple." Oakley shook his head, muttering something before jumping into his truck. "Later."

Snow flew under the tires as the truck pulled away, leaving clouds of exhaust in the cold air.

Jackson watched the vehicle disappear down the road. "He's an odd choice for an Enforcer, but he fits."

Erik pushed away from his truck as snow began drifting down again. "He's good at the job. I've got a couple of older members backing him up, but that kid's gonna be valuable. I like him. He stepped up after his dad died. It's not easy, but he's doing it."

"Look at you, all domesticated and responsible," Jackson said, half-smiling. "Taking care of a whole pack."

Erik brushed snow off his shoulders. "I don't know how you did it starting at fifteen."

"I had the damn council breathing down my neck." It was time for all three of those males to find a hobby before he found one for them thousands of miles away from his territory.

"I can imagine that was a pain in the ass." Erik chuckled, shaking his head. "And they're still holding on, huh?"

"Unfortunately, but I'm about to take care of that problem." Jackson blew out a breath, watching it fog the air. He studied his ally. "When I was at Nightsom's the other day, Victor mentioned something about being ready for the trials to step up as the Alpha. You know anything about that?"

Erik frowned, the lines around his mouth deepening. "Trials?"

"Yeah."

Erik exhaled slowly. "I think my pack had a series of trials several centuries ago that Alphas had to endure before claiming leadership. Strength, endurance, strategy, and they had to survive them all. But we scrapped that stupidity generations ago. Too many good wolves died proving a useless point."

How dumb. "You think the Slate Pack still does that crap?"

"I don't know, but if Victor said it, maybe. Their pack leans more toward the traditional. Sometimes, old traditions die hard."

Jackson considered that, tension sliding along his spine. "I should ask Emily."

Erik's gaze sharpened with something unreadable. "You two seem pretty close these days. What's going on between you, anyway?"

"None of your damn business." Jackson pushed to his feet.

Erik chuckled, low and rough. "So you already said. I'll see you in about an hour."

"Looking forward to it."

Erik lifted two fingers in a mock salute. "Say hi to Emily for me."

Jackson didn't bother replying. He watched Erik move toward his truck, boots smashing packed snow. The engine rumbled to life, and as the vehicle pulled away, Jackson let out a slow breath, the air fogging white in front of him. Something about Victor's words stuck like a splinter beneath his skin. The Slate Pack couldn't be so backward that they still had physical trials, could they?

He wouldn't ever let one of his kids endure a stupid trial. So he'd have to become Alpha of another pack. Emily was worth it.

Jackson turned and walked back into the cabin, the warmth of Emily's presence still clinging to the air. One night with her, and the thought of moving forward without her wrapped a band around his chest. She belonged with him. He'd held back last night, kept control, made himself gentle when his instincts urged him to claim.

Footsteps shuffled across the floorboards. Emily stumbled out of the bedroom, her platinum hair tousled, the oversized shirt she wore falling to her knees. The sight of her so sleep-warmed and slightly rumpled stole the air from his lungs. His gaze snagged on the bare skin of her legs, and heat flared low in his gut.

Her eyes landed on his mug on the table. "Coffee?"

He crossed to her without hesitation, his body already awake, the hard press of his cock uncomfortably tight against his jeans. Lifting her as if she weighed nothing, he reveled in her surprised laugh, light and free and so damn perfect it cracked something inside him. He wanted her agreement, though.

"Jackson," she protested, wrapping her arms around his neck.

"Morning," he murmured against her hair, inhaling the scent of wild berries and sleep. He carried her back to the bedroom, sitting with her tucked against him. She tipped her head back, meeting his gaze with a smile that made his chest ache.

"I don't usually laugh before coffee," she teased.

"Guess I'm good for something."

Her smile softened, something unspoken passing between them. He wanted to hold her tighter, to tell her that last night had meant more than he could explain. Instead, he captured her gaze. "The night isn't over."

Her soft laugh right before he took her mouth broke something inside him, even as he let the flames retake them both.

He'd do what he had to do to gain her agreement. She might not be ready, but there was no turning back for either of them.

CHAPTER 25

Her body deliciously sore, Emily sat in the basement of Luna's cabin, her gaze flicking over the shelves of vials and potions lining the walls. Some glowed faintly, others sat dark and still. The air smelled of herbs and something metallic. "What is all this stuff?"

"Remedies." Luna walked swiftly from shelf to shelf. Her fingers moved with practiced ease, collecting items and setting them aside on a metal tray. The hum of a machine kicked on, vibrating low beneath the wooden floorboards. The sound blended with the soft click of keys as she adjusted the laptop.

Dr. Gwen's face popped up on the computer screen, her sharp eyes scanning the camera. "Hey, Emily. How are you feeling?"

"Much better," Emily replied.

"I bet," Luna muttered, her back to the screen.

Dr. Gwen leaned closer to the screen. She wore light pink scrubs today, making her appear young and fresh. "What was that?"

"Nothing," Emily said quickly.

Luna stepped closer to the laptop, hands on her hips. "I've

got all the blood stored and started running basic genetic tests, but my equipment's limited. I'm using an old centrifuge and an IEC HN-SII, to separate plasma and red cells, but it's slow and only holds a few samples at a time. I've got a manual ABO blood-typing kit with glass slides, anti-A, anti-B, and anti-D serums, but it's outdated. And my microscope is an old Olympus BH-2. It works, but the resolution isn't great."

"I have top-of-the-line equipment," Gwen interrupted smoothly.

Luna jerked. "You do?"

"Jackson invested in modern equipment. I've got a Beckman Coulter Allegra X-30R centrifuge. This little baby can process more samples faster and at higher speeds. And I managed to get an Ortho Vision Analyzer for blood typing."

"Wow," Luna breathed. "That lovely thing is automated, precise, and faster than manual methods. What else do you have?"

Dr. Gwen preened a little. "My microscope's a Nikon Eclipse E400 with phase contrast, which makes spotting abnormalities easier."

Luna exhaled, rubbing her forehead. "I'm jealous and might hate you a little. I can't tell you how many hours I've spent staring through that old scope or waiting on the centrifuge."

"Well, pack those samples up," Gwen said. "Send them my way. We'll get faster results, and I'll run advanced genetic sequencing while I'm at it."

Luna glanced at Emily, her shoulders relaxing slightly. "We are totally going to discover what's wrong with you."

Dr. Gwen chuckled. "Jackson's been investing in upgrades. Convincing wolves to donate DNA is still tough, but I'm getting enough to work with. There are too many illnesses running through the packs that we need to eliminate."

"Ditto," Luna said. "I've been meaning to loop in Dr. Sharon.

She's the doctor for the Silver Pack, and we correspond often. She's very sharp. You'll like her."

"Good," Gwen said. "More coordination between packs would help. Medicine shouldn't be bound by territorial lines."

Luna adjusted the screen, her gaze flicking to Emily. "Totally agree."

"Yes." Emily traced her finger along the table's edge. "We're all adding farming to our mining operations. Feels like something that could bring us closer together. We'll trade crops and resources, which will only strengthen the coalition."

"Agreed," Luna said. "Erik talked to his brother about farming the other day, so now even Seth and his Silver pack are thinking about growing crops."

"How's Mia?" Emily asked. The other female was pregnant, and from what Emily had heard, she and Seth had likely conceived before they'd mated. The situation wasn't unheard of, but the risks increased when a human became pregnant by a wolf outside of a mating bond. Legends warned of babies being born feral, their instincts too wild to control.

"She's wonderful," Luna replied, sliding a tray of vials into the fridge with a soft click. "Not worried about the baby at all. I mean, the kid is Seth's, so wild is a given."

"True." Emily was so happy for her friends. Hopefully the packs would spend more time together now that everyone seemed to be getting along. "But Mia's pretty grounded, so who knows? Either way, I can't wait to meet the little one."

Luna read over her tablet. "Me neither. I'm going to have a niece or nephew, which is pretty cool. And if I'm pregnant, I mean, if your nose is correct, then our kids can grow up together. Isn't that fantastic?"

"I believe so." Surprising happiness flowed through Emily. Her nose was never wrong...Luna was definitely with child. "Hey, I have a sister now, so someday I'll have a niece or nephew, too."

Luna laughed. "That's definitely exciting." She crossed to the computer and tapped a few keys. "I'm preparing my results and will send these along with the blood samples when you take off."

Emily leaned closer to the screen, focusing on Gwen's face. "You mentioned having a couple of thoughts about my illness."

"Just ideas with nothing to back them up," Gwen replied, her tone measured. "I'll know a lot more when I start my tests. No matter what I find, I'll tell you the full truth."

"No matter how bad?" Emily asked, her voice quieter.

Gwen's eyes softened. "No matter how bad," she confirmed. "But I'm not stopping until I find a solution."

"And neither am I," Luna added firmly from beside her. "We'll figure this out."

"It has to be genetic," Emily said. "Or it wouldn't pass from mother to daughter. Even humans with advanced genetic research haven't cracked a lot of hereditary diseases."

"Yeah, but we're wolves," Luna shot back with a quick smile. "We adapt faster."

Gwen chuckled. "True. All right, Emily. I'll see you tomorrow?"

Emily's stomach dipped. "Actually, we'll be back today," she said. "Jackson has a meeting, then he wants to head home to his territory. And, well...he's got a date tomorrow night." The growl at the end slipped out before she could swallow it down.

Gwen's smile flickered but didn't fade. "Understood. I'll see you when you get in."

The screen went dark with a click, leaving Emily staring at her reflection.

Luna coughed. "Give me a break. Are you really going to let him go on a date with another shifter?"

"Jackson and I took one night away from reality. That's all it was." Emily's voice was steady, but something inside her twisted.

"Come on. Isn't there a solution? I mean, I don't know your

cousin Victor, but he can't be that bad. Let him be the Alpha if your dad wants a break."

Emily couldn't do that to her pack. "He's beaten the crap out of former girlfriends. And last time, my dad nearly killed him."

Luna blanched. "Okay, that's bad."

"Yeah. My dad should've kicked him out of the pack, but Vic's a good fighter, and we all need those around these days."

Luna rolled her eyes so hard it looked like they might get stuck. "Seriously, why are the packs always so focused on fighting?"

"Well, if the Ravencall and Ghostwind packs weren't attacking us, we wouldn't have to be."

"Yeah, about that…" Luna's voice dropped, and she winced. "What do you think the Alphas are planning?"

Emily's fingers tapped against the edge of the table. "What do I think the four leaders of the Stope Packs Coalition are planning right now?" She exhaled. "I imagine they're preparing for an attack." That's what she'd be doing. She needed to discuss the matter with both her father and Jackson.

Luna paled, her hands tightening on the edge of the counter. "I'm so tired of the fighting."

"So am I." Emily's stomach clenched. But tired or not, she knew the truth. The best way to stop the fighting was to eliminate the strongest fighters from the rogue packs. Brutal, but necessary. It was how things worked. How they'd always worked. And whether she liked it or not, she was part of that world.

She wasn't sure anyone's fighting skills were truly up to par. The four packs were strong together, but their territories were stretched wide and separated. Hers and Jackson's were the farthest, which complicated everything. Even if she wanted to figure out a way to combine their packs—which was impossible —the distance alone made it unrealistic.

"Don't be sad." Luna leaned over to pat her knee.

"I'm not sad," Emily replied. Not really. But for one brief, wonderful moment, she'd imagined a future with Jackson. He'd been kind and gentle, a side of him she hadn't expected. Someday, some lucky female would get to see that side of him every single day. "Sometimes, life sucks."

"Yeah, but we usually figure it out," Luna said with a small smile, flipping open her notepad. "I think you might be underestimating Jackson. What if his mind is already made up?"

Emily's chest tightened. "There's nobody else like Jackson."

Luna raised an eyebrow, the corner of her mouth quirking upward. "Well, that sounds suspiciously like someone already halfway in love."

"Stop." Emily shook her head, but the warmth in her cheeks wouldn't abate.

"Fine, fine." Luna tapped her pen against the page. "Let's get back to your illness. I need to know more about your ancestors." She paused, her eyes gleaming with mischief. "Unless you'd rather tell me about your night with Jackson. Now that, I'd love to hear."

* * *

BACK IN THE guest cabin that still carried the scent of Jackson, Emily sat at the round kitchen table, scribbling notes for her next book. The notepad, borrowed from Luna, rested under her hand. When Luna started muttering intensely about blood tests and medical theories, and the air in that basement lab had begun to feel too heavy, Emily had excused herself and returned to the cabin.

What in the world was she going to do about Jackson? How was she supposed to help arrange dates for him with other females? The thought twisted her stomach into knots, especially since she put herself in this situation. On purpose.

Her phone buzzed against the tabletop. She picked it up and pressed it to her ear. "Nightsom."

"Hey, it's Nadia," her sister's voice came through.

She relaxed in the kitchen chair, her legs extended, and her feet resting on another seat. "Hey. What's going on?"

"I just wanted to know…what are my rights here?"

Emily tapped her pen against the notepad. "What do you mean?"

"Philip left the territory for some meeting today, and Vic's here at the house acting like he owns the place."

Emily's feet dropped to the floor. "What?"

"Yeah," Nadia said, frustration lacing her words. "I kind of want to kick him out, but…it doesn't feel like my place."

"It is your place," Emily said firmly. "You have every right to kick him out."

"Are you sure?"

Unbelievable. Who did Victor think he was? He just wanted to intimidate Nadia. "Yes. Vic has his own house. He doesn't need to be there."

"Well, he's not measuring windows for new drapes or anything, but he's sitting in the dining room having the cook make him a late lunch. Is that normal?"

"No," Emily replied, her tone sharpening. "It isn't."

Nadia's voice dropped. "He mentioned once again about being ready for the trials. What does that mean?"

Emily's fingers tightened around the phone as she glanced toward the window. Snow clung to the tree branches outside, but the calm didn't touch the knot forming in her gut. "Dad wouldn't tell me. For now, try not to worry about it, okay?"

"How can I not worry? Victor is in here barking orders like he owns the place. My overbearing bodyguard is about two seconds from throwing him out."

Who could provide backup? "Did Miliki go with Dad?"

"No. He headed into town. Philip wanted to go alone in some show of strength or power, I guess."

That figured. "Yeah, I'm sure the other Alphas did the same." Emily exhaled slowly, the tension pressing against her ribs. "Listen, kick Vic out if you want. Or I can call him right now and make it clear."

"No, that's okay." Nadia's tone brightened, a hint of mischief slipping in. "I'll have Caidrik do it. They don't like each other anyway."

That didn't surprise Emily in the slightest. "Good. You have every right to be there, same as me. It's your home, too."

"Thanks," Nadia said softly.

"Hey, since I have you," Emily added, shifting her notepad aside, "Jackson's thinking about adding farming and ranching to his property. You interested in consulting? For an exorbitant consultant fee?" Hopefully Jackson's pack had money.

"Of course." Nadia laughed. "I'd love that. Never had a job that paid a lot of money before."

Emily twirled the pen. She should consider handing over half of her trust fund to Nadia. She'd have to figure that out when she returned home. "Real quick, is there anything going on with you and Caidrik?"

"God, no. He's big, growly, and grumpy. I didn't even know him before I got here. What about you and Jackson?"

"Nothing long-lasting," Emily said, the ache curling low in her chest. "I'll see him happy and mated someday, and then I'll come home."

Silence stretched for a beat too long.

"What?" Emily asked.

"I'm new to this whole sister thing, but I feel like I should tell you that you're being a total dumbass."

CHAPTER 26

"Thanks for the boots." Jackson sprawled out in the passenger seat of Erik's truck.

"I want them back," Erik replied, his hands steady on the wheel as they drove miles away from his territory. The farther Jackson got from Emily, the stronger the pull to return to her became. An ache bloomed low in his chest.

The three-hour trip was mostly silent until Erik pulled up to a stone structure nestled against the mountainside. Equidistant from all four packs, only the Alphas knew the location. Erik's tires slid as he parked beside Seth Volk's black truck, which sat silent beside a sleek, dark town car.

Jackson hopped out and crossed the uneven snow, borrowed boots biting into the icy ground as he ascended the stone steps and pushed the heavy front door open. The air inside carried the smell of leather and…history.

Philip Nightsom already sat on the far side of the round table, its surface a stunning mosaic of silver, granite, slate, and copper crafted by their ancestors, forged from the mountains that divided their lands. Four hand-carved chairs surrounded it, each worn smooth from centuries of use.

It was the only piece of furniture, except for a long counter with a sink beneath the lone window. Glasses and two alcohol bottles sat on the counter. Once, somebody had brought food, but Jackson couldn't remember who.

Seth stood at the bar near the sink, pouring amber liquid into crystal glasses. The clink echoed as he turned, his gaze sweeping over Erik. "How's Luna?"

"She's great. Working in her lab right now." Erik pulled out a chair to sit. "How's Mia?"

"Good. A little dizzy, but that's normal." Seth's smile softened.

"I can't wait to meet my nephew," Erik murmured.

Seth lifted one shoulder as he approached the table, balancing four glasses and the bottle. "Mia's convinced it's a girl."

"That'd be fun, too." Erik took a glass.

Seth's gaze shifted to Jackson. "Good to see you."

Jackson met his cousin's eyes. They were distant cousins, but the resemblance was undeniable. The same layered shades of blue in their eyes, the same broad, solid build. Yet Seth carried himself with a polished air these days, dressed in black slacks and a crisp white button-down shirt, open at the collar.

Jackson suppressed a grin as he drew out a chair and sat. He didn't remember Seth dressing this well before mating Mia. As for him, he had no plans to trade in his worn jeans and T-shirts for anyone. Whoever ended up with him would have to take him as he was.

Jackson figured if he ever took Emily out somewhere nice, he might need to get a decent outfit. That thought hit hard, halting his mind for a beat. She hadn't quite agreed yet, damn it. Yet her warmth and the feel of her against him lingered in his senses.

"Cheers." Seth sat and lifted his glass.

Jackson clinked his against Seth's and downed half the

expensive brew. Smooth. He made a mental note to bring alcohol next time. It would be his turn. He'd have to find something good.

"How's Emily?" Philip asked directly.

"She's good. Having fun with Luna right now," Jackson replied smoothly. Emily had asked him not to mention her illness, and he wasn't about to betray that trust.

Seth's gaze flicked toward Erik before settling back on Jackson. "We need to talk about the helicopter crash."

"Totally agree." Jackson kept his fury at bay. Emily could've been killed, damn it.

Erik swirled his scotch. "If the Ravencalls have Stinger missiles, we all need to know."

Philip slammed his now-empty glass onto the table. "My daughter was in a helicopter crash?"

"Yes." Jackson leaned forward. "We were shot down with Stingers, but I landed the chopper safely. We made it to Copper territory. Your daughter's unharmed."

"She's perfectly fine," Erik added, his voice steady.

Good. At least the Copper Alpha backed him up. Philip didn't need to worry, which would just cause Emily to worry.

"Are you sure it was the Ravencalls?" Philip asked.

"Yeah," Jackson said. "Four of them attacked us on the way to Copper territory. We took care of them."

Philip's eyes widened. "Emily fought?"

"Yes. And she fought well." Jackson kept his tone even. If he was already lying, he might as well stick to it. No need to worry Philip more than necessary. He only hoped Erik hadn't shared the full story with his brother, though he doubted it. The good news was that both Volk brothers generally liked Emily, and Jackson didn't see either of them wanting control of Nightsom's pack.

Clearing his throat, he leaned back in his chair. "So...we haven't all met in a while. Should we talk about the fact that

Philip tried to take over the Copper Pack?" His voice stayed deliberately bored.

Erik's eyes gleamed with interest as he leaned forward. "Yeah. Should we talk about that, Philip?"

Philip pounded a fist on the table. His gray hair, neatly trimmed, framed a face etched with age and authority. Intense black eyes, the same shade as Emily's, locked onto Erik. Despite the lines on his face, the power beneath his skin was undeniable. "You were engaged to my daughter and are now mated to someone else."

"Your daughter called it off," Erik replied calmly. "And you know it."

Philip's jaw flexed. "Yes, all right. But you weren't the Alpha of the Copper Pack when I attacked them, were you?"

"No," Erik admitted. "But I am now. Still want to challenge me?"

Philip's mouth curved slightly. "Not in the slightest."

Seth, seated beside Jackson, shifted forward with a glint of amusement in his gaze. "Still...I think compensation is in order."

"Excuse me?" Philip reached for the bottle of scotch. He tipped the bottle toward Jackson, who held out his glass for a refill.

"Compensation is due," Erik said. "You attacked my pack. You've got to pay."

Philip scoffed. "I'm not paying you."

"Yeah, you are," Erik shot back without hesitation. "I want a quarter of the profits from the Embervault Mine you're leasing from Jackson."

Philip's gaze stayed steady, the look of a man who'd negotiated more times than anyone at the table. "Five percent, and that's it."

"Fifteen," Erik countered.

"Ten," Philip replied, extending his hand across the table.

"Deal." Erik clasped his hand, the shake brief and firm.

"Well, wasn't that nice and easy?" Jackson leaned back in his chair and swirled the amber liquid in his glass.

Philip set his glass down and straightened. "Now, we need to discuss the fact that the Ravencall and Ghostwind packs might combine. Are you sure it was only the Ravencalls that attacked you?"

"Yeah. Four of them," Jackson replied.

Seth looked around, appearing healthy and dangerous. "Anybody have intel on either pack?"

"Modern for my new pack is an updated Internet browser," Erik admitted, shaking his head.

"Come on, Seth. You must have something," Jackson said.

Seth sipped his drink. "I've got a little. We believe they moved their headquarters and are now about a hundred miles outside Granite Pack territory, which puts them roughly a hundred miles from mine."

Jackson pulled out his phone and pressed it to his ear. "Thane, I need the most up-to-date intel you've got on the Ravencall and Ghostwind Packs." He clicked the speaker button and placed the phone on the table.

"Of course," Thane replied without hesitation, his voice sure through the phone. "Satellite feed shows Ravencall's headquarters near Chelan. Ghostwind's base is closer to Lincoln. There's been some movement in Douglas County, but so far, it's been all Ravencall wolves."

Erik slowly turned his head to stare at Jackson. "You have satellites?"

"No, I don't have satellites," Jackson replied, a slow smile tugging at his mouth. "We just know how to hack into them." He took a sip of his scotch, the burn sharp and familiar. "While you brothers were worried about who'd step up and who had to die," he added, glancing between Erik and Seth before turning to Philip, "and you were focused on who's taking over, I've been building my structure. Advanced weapons, surveillance. You should all get on board."

"Fine, Mr. Surveillance." Seth crossed his arms. "So, what else do you know?"

"Thane?" Erik prompted.

Thane cleared his throat, the hum of static from the speakerphone filling the room. "Right. Based on the latest intel, the Ravencall Pack is about three hundred members deep, while Ghostwind has been gathering members like a tumbleweed rolling down a hill. They've got at least a hundred—all fighters. The Ravencalls are being led by an Alpha named Burke Creed," Thane said. "Based on the lineages we've pieced together, he's a distant cousin to the former Alpha."

"You have lineages?" Erik asked, his voice low with surprise.

Jackson met his gaze evenly. "We try to keep track."

"Creed is brutal," Thane continued. "Used to be their Enforcer and killed Forrest just a few hours after the poor guy stepped up as Alpha."

"After I killed his brother," Erik muttered. "I only exchanged a couple of words with Forrest but he seemed likable. I take it Creed is not."

"Nope," Thane said through the speaker. "And his reputation's well-earned. He likes to kill. I mean, *really* likes to kill."

"Where is he now?" Jackson asked.

The sound of keys clacking came through the speaker. "Right now, Creed and his two top Enforcers are still at their main headquarters. I'll send the coordinates."

"Great." Jackson could use a good fight.

Philip leaned forward. "What's their security like?"

"Standard patrols," Thane said. "Wolves run in pairs on a regular schedule. Shouldn't be hard to slip through once we map the pattern."

Jackson needed to give his friend a raise. "Good. What do you have on the Ghostwinds?"

"Their Alpha's a guy named Feren Voss. Intel says he spent years working as a mercenary before forming the pack. They've mostly kept to themselves, living off raids by targeting both humans and other packs," Thane said.

Seth's gaze narrowed. "Does Voss have a solid base of power?"

"He's been in power for ten years, so maybe. Both packs own several smaller mines in the region. I think that's part of why they're targeting our territories. They want to expand their mining operations."

Jackson could understand the reasoning, but they were going to die. "Anything else?"

"Nope," Thane replied. "See you when you're home."

Jackson clicked off the call.

Seth eyed him, calculation in his blue eyes. "That's good intel."

Silence settled over the table until Philip muttered, "Status."

Jackson leaned back. "Mine's strong. The pack's thriving. The granite mines are doing well, and I need the council off my damn back. Once I mate, they're gone." Of course, he had to fulfill the deal for Caldwell and Sons as well as find the asshole sabotaging his mines.

"You haven't listened to your council for years." Seth smirked.

They had more power than Jackson liked, but he wasn't about to share that. Nor had he ever mentioned that, five years ago, the Ravencall Pack poisoned a quarter of his soldiers. The loss still sat heavy in him, but dwelling on it wouldn't change anything. "Next?" he muttered.

Erik nodded. "I'm assimilating well as the Alpha of the Copper Pack. The farming community we brought in is thriving, and I'm solid in terms of soldiers, miners, and farmers. Everyone's recovered from the poisoning attack by the Ravencalls, and I don't expect another one. We won't let anyone get that close again."

"Good," Jackson said, his fingers tapping lightly against the glass in his hand.

Philip turned to Seth. "Silver Pack?"

"Strong and steady," Seth replied. "Aside from those grandfathered in, I've pushed most humans out of the territory. I want the town wolf-only." His gaze hardened slightly. "Good ole Brother Jeremiah and his environmental group are still nosing around, but since I restricted human access, they've been less of a problem. I may need to deal with him at some point, but so far, everything's fine."

"The business?" Philip asked.

Seth took a measured sip of his drink. "The mine's operating well. Mia's healthy, and the pack's strong. If the Ravencall wolves come knocking, we're ready for them."

Jackson glanced toward Philip, reading the lines etched deeper into the older Alpha's face.

Philip nodded. "The Slate Pack's holding steady. The coffers are fine, but once I secure the slate from the Embervault Mine, we'll be flush." He took another sip of scotch. "Everything's just normal. In addition, Jackson and I have an agreement that is beneficial to both of our packs. We're solid."

"It's private," Jackson said smoothly at the Volk brothers' inquisitive expressions. "However, Philip, for the record, you're still walking and breathing. Why don't you find a mate and create a few more heirs?"

Philip's gray eyebrows rose. "I'm too old. Well…maybe." He quirked his lip.

Seth glanced between Philip, Erik, and Jackson. "What do you all want to do about the Ravencalls?"

Jackson straightened, shoulders squared. "Considering they shot down my chopper and came after Emily and me, I want their Alpha and his Enforcers taken out. Brutally. A statement needs to be made."

Erik's eyebrows lifted. "That's pretty much declaring war."

Jackson growled. "No. Shooting me down was declaring war. We're already *at* war."

Seth leaned forward and rested his forearms on the table. "I agree. And I think we handle this ourselves. No Enforcers."

Philip gave a sharp nod. "I'm in. We need to send a message."

"Good," Jackson said. "Tonight. Midnight. We meet here, and we take care of it. I'll have the latest satellite images of the Ravencall camp. Let's hit them hard enough that the Ghost-winds will run the other way." He stood, tipped back the last of his scotch, and placed the glass on the table. "Philip?"

Philip looked up.

"It's your turn to do the dishes."

Philip snorted but didn't argue as Jackson walked toward the door, wanting to get back to Emily.

She would agree to be his. Soon.

CHAPTER 27

Emily clutched the seat belt in the helicopter, fingers tightening every time the craft hit a gust of wind. Jackson piloted them from Copper territory to Granite, the hum of the rotors vibrating through her bones. It was already well after dinner time, and darkness pressed in from the snowy night.

Thane sat in the back, flipping through ledgers with an ease that made her stomach twist. He had flown the older craft to pick them up, but Jackson had insisted on taking them back. The cabin smelled like fuel and metal.

"Take a deep breath," Jackson said beside her, his voice low and steady.

"I'm fine," she muttered, though her pulse told a different story. The slight sting of whisker burn still warmed her skin. "We got shot down last time we flew, you know."

His hands appeared more than capable as he maneuvered the small craft with a swirling snowstorm battering them. "I know. But I had my security team review satellite feeds from the past year. I don't think the Ravencalls have any more missiles. It would've been hard enough for them to get their hands on two."

Her gaze slid toward him, her voice tinny through the headset speakers. "They must've really wanted you dead."

"Most people do."

Thane snorted from the back seat. "We're fine now, but in about thirty minutes, the storm is going to be too strong to fly. So, your timing is perfect."

The first huge winter storm seemed intent on taking down the helicopter.

Emily tried to calm, inhaling slowly through her nose. The hum of the rotors and Jackson's steady presence beside her helped, but her grip on the seat belt didn't loosen.

"Emily," Jackson ordered.

She nodded and inhaled, her face still pale. He closed his hand over hers, warm and solid against her thigh. He must not care if Thane saw from the back seat. "I'm not going to let anything happen to you. All right?"

Her gaze briefly met his, and the truth she saw there relaxed her. A little. "I know," she whispered.

The helicopter touched down smoothly on the landing pad where the other bird had once sat. Jackson powered it down, and the craft went dark. "I need a new helicopter."

"Already on it," Thane said. "I have several available options, and all are newer and faster. I'll email you a complete report."

They jumped out, the wind from the rotors kicking up snow around their boots as they crossed through the night to a nearby work truck. Jackson slid behind the wheel, Emily settled beside him, and Thane took the back seat, his eyes already back on his ledgers. He used the flashlight on his phone to illuminate the stack.

Emily glanced over her shoulder. "What are you always looking at?"

"Printouts from our online accounts. I'm just tracking the money," Thane replied without glancing up. "That's what I do on Tuesdays."

Amusement sparked through Emily, and she shared a smile with Jackson. "What do you do on Wednesdays?"

"Security and satellites, as well as scouting the territory for threats." He looked up and his eyes focused.

Absolutely fascinating. Jackson's best friend was a happy nerd. "And Thursdays?"

Thane smiled, showing even white teeth. "Special projects, like maybe this farming community you've been talking about."

"I see." Emily studied him briefly. He had to be a few years older than Jackson but not by much. The man seemed to live with one foot in a ledger and the other watching the world from above. "So, you've been working with Jackson his entire time as Alpha?"

"I have," Thane replied. The wolf was tall with horn-rimmed glasses that seemed at odds with his predatory nature. Emily had rarely seen a wolf wear glasses before.

She could use some of his skills. "It's nice that you're so organized."

"Well, almost organized," Thane said with a half-smile. "Compared to Raya, nobody is."

Probably, true, but still, the guy seemed shockingly efficient. Emily had to admit that Jackson surrounded himself with people who knew their jobs inside and out. "Are you a decent fighter?" she asked.

"I am. Thought I might be an Enforcer someday, but efficiency called." Thane shrugged. "Still, I'll step up if Jackson needs me to protect and defend."

Jackson drove around a downed tree as the snow flew sideways at them through the darkness. "You've defended my ass more than once." He slowed down to cross over more branches. "When I get mated, I'll need Enforcers. If you're not interested, I should probably start putting out some feelers."

"Sure." Thane made a quick note on a yellow legal pad.

Emily's mind drifted to her pack's structure. They had a

pack administrator, but Mrs. Flowergate wasn't anywhere near as efficient as Thane and Raya.

"When you talk about satellites and surveillance, what exactly do you mean?" she asked, curiosity sparking through her.

Jackson groaned. "Why? Why would you ask him that?"

Emily blinked. "What?"

Thane leaned forward, his eyes lighting up. "Okay, so when it comes to satellites, here's what we've found and how we can hack into them—"

He launched into a detailed explanation that lasted a solid fifteen minutes. Emily tuned out somewhere around the five-minute mark. Half of what he said sounded like a different language, but Thane didn't seem to mind what had to be her glazed expression.

Jackson barely hid a smile.

She wondered why her father had never considered updating their pack's technology. Wolves seemed to get stuck in the past sometimes. Jackson was different. Maybe stepping up as Alpha so young had made him more open to modernization.

Her stomach growled as the hour stretched even later. Jackson glanced at her. "I need to swing by the office for a few minutes, then we'll grab something to eat. You're staying at my place tonight."

Emily should argue. She should remind him that, according to Thane, two of his potential mates were already in town at the hotel. But the idea of one more night with him was too tempting to resist. "I know it's late, but our healer often works odd hours. Is there a chance one of your doctors is around?"

He took his phone from his pocket and shot off a quick text. An answering ding came almost immediately. He looked down to read, his hand sure on the steering wheel. "Yep. Doc Gwen is there tonight."

Hope ticked through Emily. "Could you drop me by the doctor's office? I'd like to speak with her."

"Absolutely. I'll drop you off, then swing back to pick you up to get a very late dinner."

She wanted to spend more time with him before she left for good. "Sounds like a plan."

"What's up with the doctor?" Thane asked, leaning forward again.

She glanced back at him. "Nothing important. Just…female stuff."

Thane blanched and immediately leaned back in his seat. "Got it. Sorry. Didn't mean to pry."

Jackson sped up. "Thane, you patrolling tonight?"

"Depends. Do you need me? I was hoping to look at some of our investments in Japan."

Jackson clicked the heater on higher. "I also need you on patrol."

"Okay," Thane replied cheerfully. "It's been a while since we've had a good fight."

"You don't think the Ravencall wolves are going to attack, do you?" Emily asked.

"I do," Jackson said. "I just don't know when." He glanced at her, then back to the road, where snow drifted slowly down, barely covering the ice.

Awareness had her instincts humming. "What?" Emily pressed.

"Nothing."

"Jackson," she said, her tone sharper. "I can usually tell when someone's lying to me. What aren't you saying?"

He hesitated, then said, "If the Ravencalls attack anyone, it'll be the Slate Pack. I think your people are in danger. Your father says you've got enough resources, soldiers, and patrol squads, but I'm not sure I believe him."

"We do," she said, though doubt scratched at the back of her mind. "I don't know if we're as well-trained as some of the other packs, but we've got the numbers. And while Victor's an ass, the guy can fight. He's trained many of our younger members."

"Any unrest?" Jackson asked. "Word's got to be out that other packs let their young wolves leave to experience the world."

A very good point. Was there unrest? "Not that I know of," she said thoughtfully. "But it's something we should look into. It would make sense."

"You know," Jackson said with a glance her way, "you could let them have a life."

They passed beneath the granite archway marking the town's entrance.

She glanced around. "Everyone has decorated for the holidays." Sparkling lights were everywhere, as were placards of Jackson and her in the middle of a wreath. "Wow. That picture must be off the Internet?" She was dressed in a white gown. Where had she worn that?

Jackson stopped near the doctor's office where a light glowed beyond the reception area. A tree sparkled happily, framed perfectly in the windows. "Need me to come in?" he asked.

"No, I probably only need fifteen minutes, maybe half an hour."

"Great. I'll be back." He nodded, and she hopped out, boots scuffing on snow as she crossed the sidewalk. The door swung open with a soft chime, revealing a vacant waiting room and the hum of a heater kicking on in the back.

Emily looked up as footsteps echoed down the hallway. A shorter male appeared, looking to be around fifty, with salt-and-pepper hair and sharp green eyes that hinted at a quick mind. "You must be Emily Nightsom."

"I must be," she replied with a grin. "And you must be Dr. Moore."

"I am." His smile was warm but brief. "What can I do for you?"

She clutched her backpack. "I was hoping to see Dr. Gwen."

"She's on the phone, but I'll let her know you're here." He glanced toward the door. "Jackson with you?"

Why would he be? "He went to the office."

"Okay. Thanks." With a nod, Dr. Moore disappeared back down the hallway.

Emily wandered over to a chair, flipping through a magazine about mining, until she heard approaching footsteps and a familiar voice.

"Hey, Emily. Come on back." Dr. Gwen still wore light pink scrubs and had a stethoscope draped around her neck.

"Thanks." Emily adjusted her backpack as she followed the doctor into a different lab room from the last time. This one had shelves of labeled vials, cabinets with neatly arranged medical tools, and equipment she couldn't name aside from a few microscopes.

"Nice lab," Emily said.

"Thanks." Gwen back slightly on her tennis shoes. "What do you have for me?"

Emily handed over Luna's blood samples and test results.

"Interesting." Gwen studied the papers, her brow furrowing slightly. "I think I may have a hypothesis." She glanced up. "I need an hour or so."

Anticipation with an edge of hope licked through Emily. "Yeah, that works. I'm grabbing a late dinner with Jackson. Will you be working that late?"

"Yeah, come back after you eat. I often work well past midnight, so I'll be here." Gwen had already turned away, her mind clearly elsewhere.

Emily shrugged and returned to the waiting area, where Dr. Moore was tidying the stack of magazines.

"All good?" he asked.

"Yes, thank you," Emily replied.

He glanced at her, a smile tugging at his lips. "Rumor has it you're trying to find a mate for Jackson."

"I am." The admission twisted in her stomach.

He straightened to his full height. "The pack is hoping you'll stay. Is there any chance?"

"I don't see how." She forced a smile. "Did you sign the petition?"

"Everybody I know signed the petition for you to make a home here." He winked before disappearing down the hallway.

For some reason, the gesture lightened her mood. It was comforting to be wanted. She stepped outside, spotting Jackson already waiting at the curb, his truck running and snow dancing across the headlights. His gaze flicked to her, lingering for just a second too long before he hopped out of the truck and opened her door.

Several teenaged boys came running up, and Jackson pivoted to put his body slightly between them.

The tallest, a kid with green eyes and black hair, handed her a high school Letterman's jacket.

She accepted the leather coat, glancing at the back, which read *Tryne*.

Jackson sighed. "You're giving her my jacket?"

"Yeah. We took it down from the wall at the high school. She should have it, man." The kid nodded, turned, and ran off with his buddies.

Emily smiled, touched. "It is nice to be liked."

"I would think so." Jackson's hand grazed her waist as he helped her inside, the warmth of his touch sparking awareness across her skin.

"I didn't know you were waiting for me out here. Sorry." Her pulse kicked up.

"It's fine." His voice rumbled awareness beneath her skin. He shut her door and circled the truck before sliding into the driver's seat. As they drove past the hotel, tension hung heavy between them.

Part of her wanted to jump him right in the truck.

The other part wanted to savor the moment and attack him later back at his place. So she smoothed the dark blue jacket over her legs.

"Tonight was the fried chicken special," he said, the shift to casual conversation not quite masking the heat still thrumming in the air. "I'm hoping there's some left—even this late."

"Sounds good."

When Jackson parked at the curb by the diner, Emily hopped out, and he followed suit, meeting up with her at the front of the restaurant. His fingers brushed the small of her back as he held the door open, and she had to fight the shiver that chased down her spine. The warm scent of fried food and fresh bread wrapped around them as they entered. The clatter of plates and the hum of conversation faded slightly as her gaze landed on Abilene Ironclaw and Xandra Millstone seated together at a nearby table.

"Well, hey there," called a woman with white hair tucked into a bun as she bustled toward them. "You must be Emily Nightsom."

"I must be," Emily replied with a smile. "This place is packed. It's so late."

The woman wiped her brow. "The miners have been working double shifts, so we have a late dinner offering every night. I'm Laura. Gus and I own the place." Her gaze flicked toward the two females at the table. "Well, your competition's here. I think they waited for an invitation around the normal dinner time and just showed up here a couple of minutes ago, giving up on Jackson for the time being. Why don't I sit you with them? Other than that, the wait's about an hour."

The restaurant truly was bustling with every table taken, and

Emily's pulse stuttered as she glanced toward the two women, both watching her with interest.

"Oh." Jackson glanced at her, and panic flickered in his eyes, quick and sharp.

"Of course," Emily said, her stomach sinking as heat crept up her neck. The two females had already spotted them, and leaving now would only seem awkward. For better or worse, there was no easy escape. "We would love to join the ladies for a late dinner," she added, her voice steadier than she felt.

Her gaze caught on Thane and Raya sitting at a two-top against the wall. They both seemed to be trying very hard not to laugh.

She couldn't be entirely sure, but she thought she heard Jackson mutter, "Fuck," under his breath.

CHAPTER 28

Jackson was in hell. He could not believe he was having a late dinner with two potential mates and Emily Nightsom, the female he fully planned to mate. The women cast each other sideways glances like they were sizing up competition at a county fair, but everyone seemed determined to play nice. For now.

Still, Emily had paled even more, and the urge to scoop her up and haul her home pressed against Jackson's chest like an itch he couldn't scratch. The clink of silverware and the hum of conversation filled the diner, but every second stretched painfully long.

Abilene smiled brightly, her fork spearing a crispy piece of fried chicken. "This is excellent," she said. "I spoke with my Alpha, and no matter what happens, Jackson, we'd love to join your pack and start a painting community."

"That's great," Jackson replied, genuinely meaning it since they needed more bodies. "Do you have any decent fighters?"

"Maybe about ten," she said. "Some younger fighters, if you need them. A few guys are interested in mining, but most of us just want to paint. We can contribute by selling our work."

Xandra, seated beside her, arched a brow. "You paint for a living?"

"Yep." Abilene nodded happily. "We do shows and sell our paintings. It's a good life. Do you like to paint?"

"God, no," Xandra chuckled. "But I shop. I shop well."

Abilene's grin didn't waver. "Cool. I've never been much of a shopper, but I imagine it takes skill."

"I like to decorate, too. But shopping's my thing."

Jackson resisted the urge to rub the back of his neck. He glanced at Emily, who had barely touched her chicken, her fingers toying with the napkin on her lap.

"What about you, Emily?" Abilene asked, tilting her head.

Emily straightened slightly. "I write romantic suspense novels and work on safety schematics for the mines. Both are gifts, and I enjoy them."

"That's interesting," Abilene said, sounding sincere.

Xandra's gaze shifted between Emily and Jackson. "You two spend a lot of time together. Why are you helping him find a mate, Emily?"

It was a fair question. Jackson glanced sideways, curious about how Emily would answer. At least now he knew she'd wanted into his territory to meet with his doctor, and not for any nefarious reasons.

Before she could respond, his phone dinged. The timing felt like a lifeline thrown to a drowning man, and for once, Jackson considered kissing whoever had sent the text.

"Saved by the bell," Emily muttered, her lips quirking as she picked up her fork and finally took a bite of chicken. Jackson nearly choked on his drink, trying not to laugh, and the tension in his limbs loosened. Just a little.

"Excuse me." Jackson read a 911 text from Thane to meet outside right now. Why hadn't the guy just walked across the restaurant? More than eager to escape the table of females, Jackson stood and stepped away, striding outside to meet his friend, who was waiting in the snow. "Yeah, Thane. What's up? And take your time," he muttered.

Thane brushed snow off his shoulders. "I thought I should tell you first. Philip Nightsom was attacked leaving the meeting earlier. I just got word from contacts we have in his pack."

"Ah, shit." Jackson glanced back at the table, his gaze lingering on the back of Emily's head. "How bad? Is he dead?"

"No. He made it back to his territory, but a couple of our sources there say it's bad. I don't know how bad yet."

Shit. What now? "Damn it. All right, thanks."

Raya stepped outside, wrapping a scarf around her neck. "I paid the bill."

Thane zipped up his jacket. "Thanks. I'll head back to the office to keep an ear on things, Jackson."

Jackson wiped snow off his chin. "Call me with any news."

"No problem." Thane slipped an arm over Raya's shoulders. "I'll escort you to your car."

Jackson walked back inside and returned to the table, surprised Emily's pack hadn't contacted her. "Hey, Em. Where's your phone?"

She blinked and looked around, quickly standing. "Oh, crap. I must've left it in the truck. Why?"

He placed cash on the table. "Ladies, you'll have to excuse us."

Xandra glanced at the money. "Are we meeting tomorrow?"

"I'll give you a call." He didn't mean a word of it.

"What's going on?" Emily pressed as he guided her toward the door with a hand at the small of her back.

He waited until they'd walked outside into the blasting snowstorm to speak. "I don't know all the details yet, but your father was attacked on the way back from our meeting."

"What?" Her face drained of color. She bolted toward the truck, yanking open the front door. Her phone sat on the passenger seat. "Oh no. I missed five calls." She clutched the phone tightly, her breath coming quicker as she scrolled through the missed calls, fingers trembling as she tapped the screen.

She quickly dialed Nadia, who answered immediately. "I just heard," Emily said rapidly.

"Hi." Nadia's voice came through clearly on speaker, sharp with worry. "Philip was attacked. He said it was by Ravencall wolves, but he got away. It's not good, Emily. The doctor said one of the wounds almost reached his heart."

Emily drew in a deep breath, steadying herself as snowflakes swirled through the air, clinging to her hair and jacket. "He can heal since he's an Alpha."

"I know, but Victor's making noises, and I don't know what to do." Nadia's voice wavered with panic.

Emily glanced at Jackson, who kept his gaze steady on her. "It's okay. Just hang in there. I'll be home in a few hours."

"No, you won't," Jackson interrupted, his gaze shifting toward the swirling snowstorm. The wind howled against the truck, rattling the side mirrors. Snow fell thick and fast, already blanketing the road in icy layers. Visibility had shrunk to mere feet. "I can't fly in this, Emily. Driving is too dangerous, as well."

Emily shuddered as she looked around at the storm, her breath fogging the air. Snowflakes spun wildly through gusts of wind, clinging to the windshield like frozen lace. "Nadia, just hold it together until I get back. As soon as I can fly out, I'll be there. Trust me."

"Okay. Just keep your phone on. I'll call if anything changes," Nadia said.

Emily steeled her shoulders. "Can he talk?"

"Yes, but the doctor sedated him so his body could heal. He's stable right now." Tears trembled in Nadia's voice.

"We'll handle this, I promise. Just sit tight." Emily ended the call and leaned against the side of the truck, snowflakes melting on her cheeks.

"He'll be okay." Jackson stepped closer to brush snow from Emily's brow. Her skin felt chilled beneath his fingers, but her eyes stayed distant. He opened the truck door. "Get in."

She slid into the seat without a word. Jackson crossed around the front, then started the engine and steered onto the snow-covered road. The tires cracked the ice as he pulled away from the restaurant.

His phone buzzed and Jackson hit the button on the dash. "Thane?"

"Yeah. Just got off the phone. Sources on the ground say Ravencall wolves attacked Philip."

"I just heard the same thing. Emily's at my house tonight. I now want *double* patrols around the perimeter at all times."

"You got it. You want me personally on-site instead of in the office?" Thane asked.

Jackson's grip tightened on the wheel. It was impressive how well Thane knew him, down to predicting his next move. He'd planned to let his friend have a night off, but apparently the Ravencalls were making a move. Now. "Yeah. I want you covering her."

"Understood. I'll be there in half an hour."

"Excellent." Jackson ended the call, glancing at Emily. She stared straight ahead, lost somewhere in her thoughts.

"Your dad's tough," he said, though it sounded hollow even to him. Letting the silence settle, he dialed Erik next. The call went to voicemail, so Jackson left a brief message before phoning Seth.

"Jackson," Seth answered. "You hear?"

Anger roared through Jackson, and he shoved it down. "Yeah. Sounds bad."

"I know. But I don't think we should change our plans tonight." Seth said.

Good. They were on the same page. "I agree. They won't expect us in a storm like this. Let Erik know. We move forward."

"Got it. Meet you at midnight." Seth sounded as if he was already moving.

"Midnight," Jackson confirmed, clicking off and pulling into his driveway. His gaze swept the property for threats before he exited the truck, circled to Emily's side, and lifted her into his arms. Her breath hitched, but she didn't resist as he carried her inside, holding her close.

"What are you doing?" she asked, sounding lost.

"I'm carrying you." Jackson saw no reason not to state the obvious. "Sorry about dinner tonight."

"Oh, that?" She shook her head. "That just felt bizarre."

"Your father's going to be okay." He knew he had no right to promise that, but the words came anyway. The clock on the wall ticked the hour, and he had to get moving.

Emily's fingers slid through his hair, grounding him in the moment. "As soon as it's safe to travel, I need to get home."

"I know." His voice roughened slightly.

Her gaze dropped to his lips, the air between them heating despite the chill that clung to their clothes. "But we do have tonight," she whispered.

"I have a job to do tonight, but I'll awaken you when I return," he replied, placing her gently on her feet near the fireplace. He quickly lit the fire, its warmth chasing away the cold in the main room.

She blinked at him, looking lost. "What are you planning to do tonight?"

Jackson held her gaze, the crackle of the flames filling the silence. "Make a statement."

* * *

EMILY PACED NEAR THE FIREPLACE, her steps restless against the rug. Out the window, she could see Thane making another pass around the cabin. She'd asked him to come in, but he'd refused, focused on his patrol. Her phone buzzed, breaking the quiet.

She pressed the speaker. "Nightsom."

"Hi, Emily, it's Dr. Gwen."

Oh, crap. She'd forgotten about the doctor. "I'm so sorry I didn't come by after dinner. It's well past midnight. Please don't tell me you've been waiting for me."

"This is normal for me, but I actually lost track of time."

Emily sat on the sofa and stared at the fire. "Did you find something?"

"Yes. My hunch was correct. I went over the test results two times just to make sure."

Emily's pulse quickened. "Tell me."

"You have a genetic disease tied to inbreeding."

What the heck? Like cattle? Hadn't she seen something on television about that? "What does that mean?"

"It means your pack has a limited gene pool, which has caused a recessive mutation to show up in your family line. Both parents need to carry the gene for it to affect their children. But since Alphas usually only mate with other Alphas, the mutation is seriously strong in your lineage."

"Oh," Emily murmured. Her stomach twisted. Victor's offer of mating seemed more repulsive than ever. The packs had stayed too isolated for too long, and it was clear that letting in new blood was essential, even if it meant fighting her father at every turn. They had no choice. She clutched the phone tighter. "So, this can stop?"

"Yes. Expanding the gene pool would prevent future cases."

Emily ran through scenarios. "You're telling me that if I mate somebody outside of my pack, my children should be all right?"

"Yes."

Emily's breath shuddered out of her. She knew enough about genetics to understand the dark truth. "But it's still going to kill me."

"Not necessarily," Gwen replied, her tone cautious. "I have a theory that if you mate with an Alpha, such a connection could help suppress the progression of your illness."

"But both my parents were Alphas," Emily protested.

"From the same pack," Gwen pointed out. "That's the difference. They both carried the recessive mutation, which is why it manifested in you."

Just great. This was headed somewhere she couldn't face. "Dr. Gwen. Seriously?"

"Yes. If you mate with an Alpha from outside your gene pool, I think there's a chance his DNA could introduce stronger, non-mutated alleles that may offset the effects of the mutation. Essentially, the dominant genetic traits from his chromosomes could override the faulty ones, which might help your cells function more efficiently. It could slow or even halt the progression of your illness."

"Or I'd be mating someone just to die on them not too long after."

Dr. Gwen fell silent for a moment. "Yes."

Emily appreciated the truth. "So, you just have a theory. That's all."

"Well, yes," Gwen confirmed. "I'm hoping your genetic code isn't beyond repair. There's a chance it just needs a new combination of traits to stabilize."

Emily's head ached. "That sounds like a long shot."

Gwen sighed. "Maybe. I'm just spit-balling here. The last thing is that timing is crucial. The longer the mutation affects your system, the harder it will be to reverse the damage."

Well, of course, timing was crucial. Why wouldn't it be?

"But, Emily, I will tell you it's your only chance."

Emily barked out a laugh, though she didn't feel an inch of humor. This was unbelievable. She could mate Jackson and maybe live or die on him the next week, leaving him alone once again. She couldn't do that to him.

And what about her pack? Either way, it was screwed. "There has to be another way," she insisted.

"I'm sorry," Dr. Gwen replied quietly. "But you and Jackson seem to have an attachment, and he's a perfect candidate."

Perfect as a guinea pig? What if they mated and she died? Oh, she knew without a doubt that he'd mate her to save her life. He cared about her. She could feel it, and someday, she'd take that strong sensation to her death. But if they mated and she died, what then? One more family member would've died on him. Could she even consider putting him through another loss?

She concentrated on the phone still in her hand. "Thanks, Doc. I appreciate you staying up so late."

"Goodnight, Emily."

"Goodnight." Emily clicked off, but it rang again before she could set the phone down. Heart pounding, she answered. "Hello?"

"Hey, it's Nadia. Philip's taken a turn for the worse." Nadia's voice cracked. "I don't know if he's going to make it. Victor's already trying to take over the house. I don't know what to do."

Emily stood, pulse thudding in her ears. "Okay. I can be there in three hours." She wasn't sure she had the strength to run the whole way in wolf form, but she could drive. Fast. "I'm coming. I promise."

She ended the call, grabbed her bag, and dashed outside. The storm had worsened. Snow swirled violently through the air, branches whipping against the wind. Ice splintered beneath her boots as she crossed to the truck. The air smelled of pine and frost, sharp and biting in her lungs. But she was a wolf, and she was a mountain girl. She could get home in time.

She had to.

CHAPTER 29

In human form, stark naked in the blistering storm, Jackson dragged four dead wolves behind him by the legs. Snow clung to his skin, melting against the heat radiating from his body. Seth and Erik flanked him, each pulling four more wolves, their breath steaming in the icy air. Their footsteps crunched over frozen ground as they moved into the heart of the new Ravencall territory.

The camp sprawled in a rough circle around a massive bonfire, its flames twisting against the dark sky. Thick clouds blotted out the moon, yet Jackson could still feel her pull beneath his skin. Around the fire, tents of dark canvas and hastily built wooden cabins stood haphazardly, their rough edges still raw from recent construction.

Why the hell had they chosen to move away from their last headquarters? The place had been well planned and would've made a good permanent territory.

The air felt heavy and thick with the smoke from cooking fires and burning wood. Snow covered the canvas flaps of tents and the hastily built structures, casting the entire area in shades of gray with orange from the fires.

Faces appeared in doorways, eyes wide as wolves and humans alike stepped out into the cold to watch. Low murmurs rippled through the camp as Jackson and his companions approached the fire. He dropped the bodies with a dull thud, Seth and Erik doing the same. Blood soaked the snow in dark patches, steam rising where it touched the heat of the fire.

Jackson stood tall, unflinching against the cold, uncaring that he was naked and bloodied. Red streaks flowed from gashes across his chest and ribs, and a deep wound on his right thigh oozed sluggishly, but he ignored the pain. His breath fogged the air, and his gaze swept the gathered crowd with a fierce, unyielding challenge.

"Here's your current Alpha and eleven of his enforcers or soldiers," Jackson called out, his voice rising above the crackling bonfire and whispering wind. "It only took three Alphas from the Stope Pack Coalition to take them down."

His gaze swept the gathered crowd—sharp, unyielding. Snowflakes clung to his bare shoulders, melting against the heat of his skin. "I suggest you end your association with the Ghostwind Pack immediately. Find yourselves a decent Alpha and go back to peddling your spices."

Murmurs rippled through the crowd. The Ravencall Pack had built a surprisingly lucrative operation growing, blending, and selling exotic spices. It was an enterprise that should have kept them thriving without resorting to violence.

Seth stepped forward, shoulders squared. "I'm Seth Volk, Alpha of the Silver Pack."

Next to him, Erik added, "Erik Volk, Alpha of the Copper Pack."

Jackson stood straighter, his chest rising with a slow breath as he stepped forward. Apparently he should've introduced himself. All right. He'd play nice. "Jackson Tryne, Alpha of the Granite Pack. Your pack attacked the Alpha of the Slate Pack, who now lies wounded. We make no promises that the entire Slate Pack won't retaliate and kill you all after he recovers."

The flickering light cast shadows across the gathered wolves, their breath visible in the frozen air as tension crackled like the fire itself.

A female stepped forward from the crowd, her dark eyes searching Jackson's face, defiant yet uncertain. She stood with squared shoulders, brawny and strong, her silk cloak clinging to broad shoulders. Deep lines etched her face, placing her somewhere in her sixties, and her eyes burned with sharp intelligence. "We didn't want to align with the Ghostwind Pack," she said, voice rough from the cold air. "And we didn't want war. The Alpha and his ilk took over. They didn't represent us." Her gaze swept over the bodies on the snow-packed ground, and her mouth pressed thin. "But they were strong."

A younger man stepped forward beside her, barely eighteen by the look of him. His breath fogged the air as he glanced between the dead Alpha and the three Alphas standing before him. "We just want to focus on our spices and stay out of wars. But..." His gaze lingered on the fallen wolves. "We don't have the soldiers to defend ourselves against another takeover."

Jackson scanned the crowd, seeing a few able-bodied adults and quite a few teenagers. "Do you have any protection?"

Silence answered him.

All right. Well, he wanted to diversify, and these folks wouldn't last without protection. For the first time in his life, he considered offering something that went against every rule of his pack that would extend protection beyond their borders. But he needed numbers, and these wolves needed to belong somewhere.

That, he could provide. "I am willing to let you all interview to be members of the Granite Pack if you're interested."

The kid's eyes lit up. "Seriously?"

"Yes. We are expanding our mining operations as well as

beginning to farm and ranch. Growing and selling spices cannot be that different. However, I will need to speak with each one of you personally." Well, after Raya interviewed each wolf. Jackson paused, already imagining her reaction when she found out she would have to skip the mining conference in Vegas this year. She wasn't going to like it.

The Ravencall female hesitated, her gaze shifting to the others before returning to Jackson. "My name is Janet, and I guess I'm the de facto leader for now." She squared her shoulders, determination hardening her features. "What do you want us to do?"

"First, get everyone together. Make sure they understand this is an opportunity, not a guarantee. I need to know what skills each of you brings to the table. Farming and ranching require discipline. Mining is dangerous and physically demanding. There is no room for anyone unwilling to put in the work."

Janet nodded. "We understand. We just need a chance."

That seemed fair. "You'll get one."

The young man beside her stepped forward. "I'll be there. I know how to work."

Jackson met his gaze. "Good. We will see if that is true."

Seth and Erik stood silent on either side of Jackson, their faces unreadable. The snow beneath Jackson's bare feet had begun to seep through his skin, sending a dull ache through his legs. Still, he kept his posture straight. "Bury or burn your dead. Decide who wants to join my pack and understand that it means full allegiance. If we're attacked, you fight. If not, you contribute through your spices, mining, or farming. Everyone will be trained to defend themselves, and some of you will be assigned to work where the pack needs you most."

Janet clasped her hands together, shoulders sagging slightly with what looked like relief. "That's fine with us. We've been searching for a place for so long. This could really work."

"It could," Jackson agreed. "Dawn will arrive in a few hours, so do what you need to do here and then head north. You may enter through the southern border of Granite Pack territory. You will be met there, and each one of you will be interviewed. No one is forced to come, but if you take the pack oath, you are in for life."

Janet's chin lifted, a hint of hope softening her eyes. "We'll be there. I promise."

Jackson focused on her. "Good. Prepare for harsh winters and long workdays. Loyalty and discipline are non-negotiable. I need people who are willing to build something stronger than what we have now."

"We're ready," the young man beside Janet said. His gaze met Jackson's, steady and unflinching.

Jackson held his stare for a moment longer. The kid might make a decent Enforcer. "I'll see you when you arrive."

The fight was over, and the adrenaline had drained from Jackson's veins, leaving behind a bone-deep ache that settled into every muscle. Snowflakes clung to his skin, melting in rivulets that traced down his chest. The metallic tang of blood still clung to the air, sharp against the crisp winter wind. He turned in sync with Seth and Erik, their movements silent and purposeful as they walked past the dying fire and into the swirling snow beyond the camp.

He shifted into wolf form through the air, needing to heal himself. He could repair all injuries better in wolf form—except when silver was involved. Snow whipped sideways across their path, blurring the outlines of distant trees. The wind howled and tried to kill him, shooting through his fur to his bones. His paws tore through the ice on the ground, and he ignored the shadows all around them. They'd killed the enemy, and they were the most dangerous animals in the forest.

The transition brought a brief surge of warmth, fur shielding them from the worst of the weather as they ran through the snow-laden woods. Branches scraped their sides, and ice cracked beneath their paws as they sped toward the hidden stone building tucked deep within the forest.

Frost clung to the building's rough-hewn walls, its heavy wooden door half-buried in snowdrifts. The trucks parked out front sat coated in a thick layer of snow, their windshields frosted over. Jackson shifted back into his human form, breath steaming as he tugged open his truck door. Reaching inside, he grabbed a worn, long-sleeved T-shirt with frayed cuffs and pulled it on. The jeans he found were torn at the knees, but they would do. He quickly laced up his boots, fingers stiff from the cold, then glanced back toward Seth and Erik as they dressed beside their vehicles.

"You guys good?" Jackson asked, adjusting his shirt as the wind bit through the fabric.

"Yeah," Seth growled, wiping blood from the gash above his brow. The wound still dripped a slow streak of red down his skin. "I think we made an impression killing the Alpha and his Enforcers."

"Me, too." Erik pulled on his coat. His breath fogged in the air as he fastened the buttons. "Rumors will spread far and wide. Maybe the Ghostwind Pack will back off. They're outnumbered."

"They know it, too," Jackson agreed.

Seth glanced sideways at him. "You sure about bringing more pack members in?"

"I am. We need to expand, and having people who know the spice trade could turn profitable fast. Plus, the numbers will help with defense," Jackson said.

Erik gave a curt nod. "Tell Emily I hope Philip recovers soon. I need to get back to my mate. Also, I want my boots back at some point." He climbed into his truck without waiting for a response.

"He's always been particular about his footwear," Seth said as he stepped toward his vehicle. Ice crackled beneath his boots as he paused and looked back at Jackson. "Cousin."

"Cousin," Jackson returned, shaking his head.

Seth grinned and then slid into his truck.

Jackson climbed into his, the seat stiff and cold under him as he started the engine. Heat slowly seeped from the vents, but it was enough to thaw his hands. He glanced at his phone. No signal. Even now, years after their ancestors had built the stone building, the place cut them off from the world. Cell phones didn't work in the vicinity and probably never would.

Snow thickened against the windshield as he backed up and eased onto the narrow road, leaving the site behind him.

He drove for several miles, the snow pelting the vehicle, as the wipers scraped across the glass. The phone on the dashboard lit up, catching his attention. Five missed calls. A chill that had nothing to do with the weather trickled down his spine. Both Raya and Thane had called. He tapped the screen and dialed Thane first. Straight to voicemail. Damn it.

He hit the button to call Raya. The line barely rang before she answered. "Jackson," she said, her voice rushed and tight.

"What's going on?" He gripped the steering wheel.

"Thane is out looking for her now, but apparently, Emily took one of your trucks and headed out into this storm."

Jackson's pulse pounded at his temples. "What the fuck?"

"My guess is that her father took a turn for the worse? She just left while Thane was out patrolling," Raya said quickly. "He shifted to wolf form to track her in case she needed help and asked me to keep trying to get ahold of you."

Jackson exhaled, the frost of his breath mingling with the warmth inside the cab. "Thanks for telling me," he said. "Stay put. It's too dangerous in this blizzard. No scouts." He calculated the route between the territories via vehicle. "When did she leave?"

"After midnight, but I don't know the exact time," Raya said, panic threading her words.

He pressed the gas pedal down. Hard. "Okay. It's all right. I'm far enough away. I might be able to cut her off."

"Let me know when you find her."

"Will do." Jackson clicked off and tossed the phone onto the passenger seat. His fingers tightened around the steering wheel, muscles coiled with tension. Fury licked through his veins, hot and fast, burning through the last trace of cold in his chest.

He drove even faster, the truck jolting forward as snow swirled against the headlights. Trees loomed on either side of the narrow road, branches weighed down with ice. The engine growled as he pushed it faster, ignoring the ache in his muscles and the exhaustion dragging at his bones. All that mattered now was finding Emily.

He soon reached the main interstate, which was blissfully vacant. Only his reckless female dared be out there. Jumping out of the vehicle, he let the storm batter him, lifting his face to the wind.

He caught her scent. Barely.

Growling, he jumped back into the truck and turned south toward the Slate Pack territory, which was still hours away.

The stubborn female had better fucking be alive.

CHAPTER 30

Snow and ice whipped against the windshield, the wipers scraping rhythmically as Emily hunched forward, straining to see through the storm. Visibility was near zero, and her wolf senses weren't as strong as usual.

Not even close.

This might've been a colossal mistake.

The interstate stretched dark and empty in both directions, no lights showing as far as she could see. At least she didn't have to worry about hitting another car, though sliding into a snowbank remained a real possibility.

Her limbs felt heavy, her fingers stiff from gripping the steering wheel so tightly. Her shoulders trembled, muscles locked from tension and cold. She adjusted the heater dial, but the truck's vents blew only lukewarm air against her frozen hands. Her breath kept fogging the windshield, and she had to wipe at the glass with her sleeve to clear her view.

The engine's low hum filled the cab, the sound swallowed by the wind roaring past the windows. Snow swirled and tumbled across the hood, collecting in uneven piles along the windshield wipers.

Her left foot had gone numb against the floorboard, and she shook it, trying to restore circulation. Dizziness threatened to pull her under, her vision blurring at the edges.

Maybe she should have waited out the storm. This had probably been a mistake. But she had to check on her father and also keep Victor from taking over. She gritted her teeth and tightened her grip on the wheel. She was an Alpha female, heir to the Slate Pack. One storm could not stop her. She refused to let it.

She couldn't believe her illness stemmed from inbreeding. For goodness' sake, she sounded like a backwoods cliché. The thought made her stomach twist, but she shook her head and forced herself to focus. Her mind kept drifting, which was dangerous, considering she could barely see the road ahead. Snowflakes smashed against the windshield while the headlights failed to cut through the white haze outside.

A dark shape came out of nowhere and darted across the road. Her pulse spiked. An elk? She hissed in panic as she slammed on the brakes. The truck skidded sideways, tires scraping against ice before catching traction just long enough to fishtail violently. Her breath caught as the guardrail loomed closer and she hit. The impact jarred her teeth as metal shrieked and gave way. The truck lurched, teetered, and then flipped.

Over and over, she rolled, the world spinning in a blur of whiteness. The airbag exploded, burning her face and chest as she braced against the seat belt digging into her collarbone.

Then, only the sound of the wind through the trees echoed in the world.

Her ragged breaths fogged the windshield even more. She hung upside down, heart hammering as she fumbled with the seat belt. Her fingers trembled as she released the buckle and dropped, tucking so her shoulders took the impact of landing instead of her head. Pain ripped down her spine.

"Crap," she gasped, her voice hoarse.

She shoved the crumpled door open and crawled into the

snow, icy flakes stinging her cheeks as she staggered to her feet. Wind whipped her hair across her face as she scanned the area. Nothing. No elk. No headlights. Just endless white swallowing the road and the woods beyond.

Taking a deep breath, she tried to shift. Her bones stretched and popped, but nothing happened. Panic hit hard and fast. The truck sat upside down, silent except for the ticking of cooling metal. One tire still spun, throwing shadows in the snow. Her wolf sight allowed her to see better than a human, but there was nothing to see. Just snow and darkness.

She crawled back inside the cab, knees denting the roof, which now lay on the ground. The air smelled like burned rubber and gasoline. Her fingers scraped over broken glass and twisted metal as she searched for her phone. She finally found it and clutched it tightly before hitting the screen. No service. Of course.

Her pulse pounded in her ears. Focus. She needed to shift, get warm, and get out of there. She gritted her teeth, forcing her body to respond, but her muscles locked up, and her skin burned from the cold.

Her breaths came faster. She was getting worse. Her illness was catching up with her. Each second out there dropped her chances of survival. The snow piled against the vehicle, and the wind cut through the shattered windows. She pressed her hands to her chest, willing herself to shift, but the wolf inside her remained silent. If she couldn't shift soon, she'd freeze to death.

A flicker in the darkness caught her attention. Headlights? Some other idiot was out in this storm?

Panicking, she coughed and scrambled out of the truck, her boots slipping on the ice. She steadied herself, her heart hammering against her rib cage.

She hesitated. If she moved into the road, she'd get hit. How could she get the driver to see her without risking her life? Her breath puffed out of her, forming clouds in the cold air. How would she explain to a human why she was stranded out here? And why would a human be out in this mess anyway?

Her entire body shook as she leaned back into the cab, fumbling with the dashboard until she managed to re-engage the headlights. They flickered weakly against the storm. She tried again, slamming her hand against the switch. The lights sputtered and then held, casting faint beams into the snow. The approaching vehicle slowed.

Wind whipped against her, carrying a familiar scent. Her breath caught. Jackson. Relief mixed with the adrenaline still pounding through her veins. His truck slid to a stop. His door flew open, and he was across the snowy road instantly, scanning the wreckage.

Blood trickled from a cut on his jaw.

His gaze locked on her. "Are you hurt?"

"No," she whispered. "I think I'm okay." Even though her legs had gone numb again.

He crossed the distance in two strides and lifted her away from the wreckage.

She wanted to hold on, but her body shook too hard for her to control her arms.

Snow whipped around them as he jogged back to his truck, his breath harsh and quick.

The heat inside the cab hit her. She slid into the seat, gasping as warmth seeped through her clothes. She pressed her shaking hands to the vents, trying to feel her fingers again. Her pulse still thudded in her ears as she tried to catch her breath. The smell of the forest and leather mixed with the trace of Jackson's scent and grounded her as she fought to stop trembling.

Jackson was back inside the vehicle in seconds, flipping it around with sharp efficiency. Snow pelted the windshield, and the engine growled as the tires gripped the icy road.

"What are you doing out here?" she asked.

He whipped his head toward her. Fire burned in his eyes,

intense and unyielding. "Me? What am *I* doing out here?" he ground out.

Her pulse hammered. She was face-to-face with one furious Alpha male.

"Do you want to tell me what *you* were doing out here, Emily?" His tone was calm—far *too* calm.

A tremor ran through her that had nothing to do with the cold. "I was trying to get home through the storm."

"In your condition?"

She spun toward him, heat rising beneath her skin. "Condition? I don't have a *condition.*"

"Except that you're sick. Why didn't you shift into your wolf form? It is freezing out there."

She dropped her gaze to her hands, her breaths shallow.

"Emily," he said sharply.

"I couldn't," she whispered, the words tasting like defeat.

His eyes flicked toward her again, and something shifted in his expression. The hard edges softened slightly but not enough to ease the weight pressing against her chest.

"So, you're telling me," he said slowly, his voice still too calm, "that you drove into a blizzard in one of my trucks, knowing you couldn't shift?"

Her shoulders tightened as she squirmed on the seat. The heat from the vents brushed against her face but did nothing to slow her racing pulse. "I might not have been thinking clearly." She fell back on a defense mechanism, and her voice turned haughty. Not consciously. It was just instinct, a shield against the frustration radiating from him.

His jaw tightened more as he steered the truck off the main road. Snow compressed beneath the tires, muffled by the storm's relentless howl.

Emily frowned, her fingers tightening on her coat. They were about the same distance from his territory as they were from Copper territory, but he headed in that direction. "Where are we going?"

Jackson glanced her way, but his eyes immediately flicked back to the road. Tension filled the cab, thick and unyielding. The heat from the vents did little to ease the chill coiling down her spine.

"How ill are you?" he asked finally. His voice was steady, but the strain beneath it was unmistakable.

She hesitated, her gaze shifting to the snow-laden forest flashing past the windows. The trees stood tall and dark against the storm, their outlines blurred by wind-driven snow. The route made no sense.

"I don't know," she admitted quietly.

"Did the doctor talk to you?"

"Yes."

Jackson's hands tightened on the wheel. "What did she say?"

Her pulse jumped. "It's…a little embarrassing."

One eyebrow lifted, sharp and impatient. "Embarrassing is fine. Deadly is not."

She leaned closer to the heat, rubbing her hands together as if that could chase away the tension clamping her ribs. "It's kind of both," she muttered.

"Explain. Now." There was no mistaking the iron in his voice. His patience had worn thin, and she doubted there was much holding it together.

She drew in a deep breath, steadying herself as the truck's tires hummed against the snow-covered road. "Fine," she said. The words scraped her throat as she launched into the story.

He stayed silent the entire time she spoke, his expression unreadable.

Finally, she wound down.

"So mating will save you?" he finally asked.

She gulped. "There's no guarantee."

The tires gripped the icy road until he stopped outside a

barely visible stone building, partially hidden by the surrounding trees.

Emily craned her neck, taking in the structure's rough-hewn walls and heavy wooden door. "Where are we?"

"This is a secret," Jackson said. Snow whipped past his shoulders as he opened his door. "Only the Alphas of the Stope Packs Coalition know it exists. We'll wait out the storm here."

Before she could protest, he reached across and hauled her out of the truck by her arms, muscles flexing beneath his coat as he tossed her over his shoulder. Wind and snow hit her as he strode toward the entrance.

"Still mad, huh?" she muttered, holding on to the back of his coat.

He kicked the door open, stepped inside, then set her on her feet. The warmth from the room hit her instantly. The air smelled faintly of wood smoke and pine.

Jackson crouched by the fireplace, expertly stacking wood before striking a match. Flames roared to life, throwing golden light across the stone walls and the dark wood floor.

Emily rubbed her hands together and glanced around. Her gaze snagged on the massive table to the side. Copper, slate, granite, and silver swirled in an intricate design across the polished surface. She stepped closer, tracing the cool metal with her fingers. "This is incredible," she murmured.

"It's centuries old," Jackson said without looking up. When he did, the firelight highlighted the hard planes of his face.

"I'm sorry about your truck," she offered.

"You think I care about my truck?" He stood and closed the distance between them in two steps. Heat radiated from his body, his eyes locked on hers.

"Well…maybe it was a little foolish," she muttered, shifting her weight. The small space didn't seem to have a bedroom or even a sofa. "What now?" she murmured.

His gaze dropped to her mouth. "Now, we mate."

CHAPTER 31

Fury churned through Jackson, hot and sharp, as he stared at the graceful wolf. What the hell had she been thinking, putting herself in danger like that? His pulse pounded in his ears. He could finally take what he wanted. What he'd needed since the first time he laid eyes on her. "You want to live?" he asked, his voice rough.

Emily squared her shoulders, her hands settling on her hips. At least she had enough sense to dress for the weather in jeans, a thick sweater, and a coat that clung to her frame. Her boots were lined with fur—thanks to Raya, no doubt.

"Of course, I want to live," Em said evenly. "But I'm not going to mate you just to survive."

"Oh, yeah?" Her scent permeated the air, close enough to fill him. "Baby, I'm not giving you a choice."

"Of course, you are." Her eyes flashed with defiance. "I know you better than that, Jackson. You're not the type of male who forces anyone into anything."

The fact that she was right just pissed him off. "Were you running from me?" he asked mildly.

She blinked. "No."

His chin lowered. "What did you think would happen once I learned the truth? That mating me might save you?"

She put her hands on her hips, all defiant female. "I won't use you like that."

Something dark and primal ran through him. "Use me?"

"Yes. I'm not into some pity mating, either."

She was scared. He could sense it. Taste it. Of him? Or of herself?

"Em," he said, his voice low, rough. "You could've died in that wreck out there. Or frozen to death. What the hell was going through your head?"

Her breath hitched, but she held her ground. The wind howled against the stone walls outside, but inside, the world narrowed to just the two of them, the fire crackling behind him with its own energy.

She shoved her hands into her coat pockets, but Jackson had already noticed the slight tremor in her fingers. She wasn't healthy. He could fix that. He had to.

"Nothing. I'm not going to discuss it." Her voice wavered, but her chin lifted with pure stubbornness.

"That's not going to work." Before she could react, he grasped her waist and lifted her, setting her on the ancient table and stepping between her legs. He moved deliberately, unzipping her coat and sliding it off her shoulders, his fingers brushing against the soft wool of her sweater. The air inside the stone cabin had already begun to warm, but the heat between them burned hotter. "What is going through your head, Em?" His voice dropped lower, rough with something that had nothing to do with anger.

"Nothing," she said quickly, though her breath hitched. "I just want to go home, keep Vic from taking over, and make sure my dad is healing all right."

"I get that." Jackson's hands rested lightly on her thighs, holding her still. "But to live, you need to mate. Right?"

She shook that smooth mane of spun gold hair. "It's just a theory," she whispered.

"Just a theory?" His gaze locked onto hers. "Don't you understand? This makes sense. We make sense." They always had. He'd always known it, even if he couldn't figure out how to make it work.

Her pulse thudded against her ribs. The air between them thickened, heavy with hunger…and need.

"It's not a good idea," she whispered.

"Why not?" His voice dropped even lower. He wasn't about to let Emily Nightsom die when there was a chance, no matter how slim, he could save her.

"Because it probably won't work, Jackson," she said softly, her eyes searching his. "You don't get it. If we mate, there's a good chance I'll still die. Maybe next week, maybe in six months. But don't you see? If we're together, it'll break you if I die. I've always known that."

"So have I," he replied, his voice rough with emotion. "But I'm taking that chance."

She shook her head, her breath hitching. "I can't leave you alone. I won't do that to you."

Realization hit him, heavy and sweet all at once. She was trying to protect him. He brushed snow from her hair, his thumb lingering just above her cheek. "You're worried about me," he said, more statement than question.

"Yeah," she admitted. "You're big, strong, and mean when you need to be, but I remember the kid you were when your dad died. I know what that loss feels like. I miss my mom every day. I can't mate you and then leave you. I won't."

"Then don't." His hands planted firmly on either side of her hips as he leaned closer. "Between the two of us, we have the strongest bloodline there is. If there's any way to fix this, I'm it. And I'm not giving you a choice."

His gaze locked onto hers, fierce and unyielding. He could

force her hand, but he didn't want that. He needed her to choose him.

Her breath quickened, eyes wide with something she couldn't mask. Desire flared hard and fast, too obvious to hide. But she tried. She looked away. "I can mate another Alpha."

"Not in this lifetime." Fire churned inside his chest. "I'll kill anyone you let close enough to try."

Her gaze slashed back to his, and he let her see the truth in his. Not one bit of him was lying. He would rip apart anybody who tried to take her. It was too late for either of them. Not just because of her illness and the chance to save her but because it had been too late the second he kissed her all those years ago.

"There's only one path for either of us, and you know it," Jackson murmured, his pulse pounding in his ears. "We both know if I kiss you, the discussion is over. We'll combust. You know it. I know it."

"Then don't kiss me," she shot back, her chin tilting in a challenge so clear it almost made him smile.

"Emily." His voice dropped lower. "You told me you wanted to live. That you were tired of holding back. Tired of not feeling everything."

"I know," she whispered. "But I won't risk—"

He was done talking. "The fuck, you won't." His hand tangled in her hair, tilting her head back as he took her mouth in a hard, claiming kiss. Her moan vibrated against his lips, desire flaring hotly between them, sharp enough to steal his breath. He kissed her deeper, pouring every ounce of his wildness into her.

Her hands gripped his shirt, fingers twisting in the fabric before she yanked it upward. He broke the kiss just long enough for her to drag it over his head, the air cool against his heated skin. Then his mouth was back on hers. Rough, unrelenting, and desperate. His hands gripped her waist, sliding under her sweater to feel the heat of her skin. There was no space for hesitation. The time for thinking was over.

* * *

For the first time in her entire life, the wolf and Emily merged into one. Thought faded, leaving only sensation. She accepted Jackson's kiss as if she had a choice, then kissed him back just as fiercely, her nails scraping down the hard planes of his chest. Bruises and nearly healed cuts marred his skin, evidence of recent battles.

"Why are you wounded?" she asked, her breath ragged.

"Killed a bunch of wolves," he muttered against her mouth, his voice rough as he pressed her back onto the table. The cool stone chilled her skin, and the ancient metals whispered beneath her.

He stripped off her boots and pants with swift efficiency.

"Ravencall?" she guessed.

"Yeah. Don't say that word again when I have you naked."

"I'm not naked."

He paused, gaze dropping to her feet.

"No socks this time," she said, her voice steadier than she felt. She was totally on board for sex. For mating? She couldn't do that to him.

His grin was wicked, slow, and deliberate as he bent down. Sliding both socks off with deliberate care, he palmed her feet, his thumbs brushing the arches.

"You don't have a foot thing, do you?" she asked, her breath hitching.

"No," he murmured. "I have a my-mate-almost-froze-to-death thing. Your feet aren't too chilly."

Without warning, he leaned in and bit the arch of one. Heat shot up her leg, fast and sharp, arrowing straight to her core.

Her gasp echoed in the space between them, and his smile only deepened as he moved upward.

"You'll be warm enough in a minute," he promised, gripping her thighs and yanking her toward him. She yelped, sliding across the cool metal and stone of the table. His mouth found her ankle, licking and nipping his way up the inside of her leg, leaving heat in his wake.

"I'm not sure we should do this on a piece of art," she managed, her breath hitching.

"Oh, this is exactly where we should," he murmured, right before his lips closed over her clit.

The orgasm hit so fast it stole her breath, her body arching as pleasure crashed through her. Every thought of holiness and centuries-old tables vanished as she shattered against him. Beneath her, the table seemed to hum with heat, or maybe that was just Jackson. She couldn't tell.

He moved to her other thigh, his teeth grazing her skin, leaving marks that burned with sensation. His palms slid up the backs of her calves, thumbs pressing just enough to make her shiver.

Then his mouth enclosed her clit again before moving lower. This time, he lingered, teasing her, bringing her to the edge, only to pull back. She squirmed, arching toward him, but he held her firmly in place. Her hands tangled in his hair, pulling as if she could guide him back to where she needed him the most.

"Jackson," she moaned, her voice rough with need. His answer was a sharp nip to her clit and the sudden thrust of two fingers inside her. Her gasp echoed in the room as sensation shot through her, sharp and deep. She arched off the surface, crying out his name as wave after wave of pure ecstasy tore through her, sharp and unrelenting. "Oh, God, this might kill me," she whimpered, breathless and trembling. She came down somehow, impossibly wanting more.

He stood, muscled and fierce, his hands flattening against

her abdomen before sliding upward, fingers curling around her rib cage as he caressed her heated skin. His touch lingered, deliberate, until his palms cupped her breasts. He hummed low, a rough sound that vibrated against her bones. Leaning down, his hair brushed her first, soft and fleeting, before his whiskers grazed her skin with a commanding burn. Then his mouth closed over her nipple, hot and demanding.

He licked, kissed, and nipped, his teeth tugging just enough to send sharp bursts of pleasure through her. The contrast of roughness and control unraveled her, her hips shifting against nothing as need clawed through her veins. He chuckled against her breast, the sound dark and wicked.

Sliding his hand between her thighs, he pressed two fingers inside her again, curling them just enough to stroke that spot that made her entire body tighten. His thumb found her clit and rubbed with slow, devastating pressure. Her breath hitched, then broke as the orgasm seized her, intense and all-consuming. She gasped, arching against him, every nerve sparking with sensation until she collapsed against the table, completely wrung out.

Before she could catch her breath, his mouth found hers. The kiss was hard, raw, and possessive, stealing what little air she had left. He pinned her beneath him, chest to chest, skin to skin, his heat sinking deep into her bones. Power radiated off him in waves, thick and unyielding. His eyes went beyond mere blue, shifting into something primal, a color without a name. Sharp, focused, and predatory. His gaze locked onto hers with an intensity that sent a shiver straight down her spine. He leaned in, their breaths mingling as he kissed her. Deep, demanding, and dangerous.

"Say yes." His voice was rough and edged with something wild. "I could push you there and we both know it. Say it now."

This felt right. It shouldn't, but she was tired of fighting.

She'd deal with reality later. "Yes." The word fell from her lips without hesitation. There was no other answer.

Something in him shifted. Something subtle but undeniable. His hands gripped her waist, and he lifted her effortlessly, flipping her onto her hands and knees atop the ancient table. The metal burned against her knees and palms, but she didn't care. Anticipation coiled hot and heavy in her core.

He pulled her back toward him without preamble, no more waiting, no more holding back. His hips drove forward, and he impaled her in one fierce thrust. Air rushed from her lungs as pain sliced through her, sharp and blinding, only to melt into a liquid warmth that spread through her veins. She gasped, clutching at the table, but he gave her no time to adjust. He pounded into her, each thrust harder, faster, and more relentless.

Her head dropped forward, hair falling into her face, but his hand pressed firmly between her shoulder blades, holding her down and opening her to take every inch of him. He didn't slow, didn't ease up. He took what he wanted, his control stripped away, leaving only raw, untamed need. Her pulse pounded in her ears, drowning out everything except the sound of their bodies colliding, the ragged breaths, and the helpless moans torn from her throat.

Pleasure built fast and sharp, climbing higher with every thrust until she thought she might break apart. Her body vibrated with tension, each nerve stretched to the brink until the heat inside her burned white-hot. Then he leaned over her, his breath hot against her shoulder, rough stubble scraping her skin. His teeth grazed her flesh and then sank deep. Pain and pleasure fused in a shockwave that shattered her world, and she screamed as her climax ripped through her, raw and unrestrained.

Her body convulsed with the force of her release, every nerve burning white-hot. Somewhere deep inside her, something shifted as if locking into place. The world narrowed to the heat between them and the sound of her ragged breaths.

As her eyes fluttered open, the metal beneath her seemed to ripple and shift like molten and melding metals, though it remained solid beneath her.

Jackson kept moving, driving her through the aftershocks until she gasped, her cries soft and breathless. When the tremors finally slowed, he withdrew his fangs and flipped her over to sit on her butt with effortless strength, lifting her hips and plunging inside her again.

"Your turn," he growled, his voice rough and primal.

Instinct overrode thought. Her wolf surged forward, and she leaned up, sinking her fangs into the skin directly above his heart. The taste of his blood hit her tongue instantly. Coppery and powerful, filling her senses with raw energy.

His body shuddered against hers as he thrust deeper, muscles tightening with brutal force. His growl rumbled through his chest as he came, his release surging deep inside her.

She slowly retracted her fangs, licking the wound she knew would mark him forever.

He lowered her onto the table again, his hands brushing her hair away from her face before capturing her mouth in a kiss. Hard, fierce, and possessive, he left no doubt that she was now his.

Forever.

CHAPTER 32

Mid-morning, the storm finally cleared enough for Jackson to drive, though the interstate remained mostly empty. Snow was piled high on the shoulders, and the wind swept drifts across the lanes. His hands stayed steady on the wheel, but his gaze drifted toward Emily.

She lay curled against the door, her head resting on the glass, sound asleep. Each breath fogged the window faintly, her body still and soft in the warm cab. He adjusted the heat to make sure she stayed comfortable.

They hadn't slept the night before. He couldn't get enough of her. Finally having her settled something deep inside him—a place that had been waiting just for her.

Her face, pale and delicate, appeared peaceful in her slumber.

Good. He wanted to give her peace. He had been without family for far too long, and he would hold on to her—his new family—with every ounce of Alpha power he possessed.

Her platinum hair had slipped from its braid, the strands curling around her neck and shoulders. Even in sleep, her body seemed to hold the remnants of their connection, something both fierce and fragile.

Mating had taken its toll on her, which he'd expected. Hopefully, in a good way, that would heal her chromosomes or DNA or whatever the fuck was ailing her.

No way in hell would he lose her now.

He exhaled slowly, tightening his grip on the wheel as snow-covered trees blurred past. Every instinct in his body, tightened and strengthened naturally from their mating, wanted to secure her safely within the territory of his pack. Driving away from that and into Slate Pack territory made the wolf inside him buck and growl in anger.

But she had every right to see her father. Even though they'd just mated, Jackson could feel the worry and deep concern living inside her.

He felt her beneath his skin, through every part of his body, embedded deep in his heart. He had wanted her for as long as he could remember, and now she was his. Nobody would harm her, but protecting her from Philip's injuries was beyond his control. They should reach Slate Pack territory soon. Then Jackson could assess for himself how much time Philip might have left. The odds didn't sound great.

His phone buzzed. He tapped a button on the dash and lowered his voice. "Yeah?"

"Why are you whispering?" Thane asked softly.

Jackson glanced at his mate. "I'm driving, and Emily's asleep in the passenger seat."

"Ah." Thane's voice dropped further. "I can call later if—"

"No. I'm on the way to Slate Pack territory, so talk now."

Thane's exhale crackled through the speaker. "All right. Somebody trashed my cameras last night. Brand-new ones, too. Wires ripped clean out of the ground. No tracks, no clues. Can you believe that?"

Jackson's pulse ticked up. Damn it. Who was fucking with him? He needed to bring in more pack members sooner rather than later. His force was good, but he needed bodies. "Any suspects?"

"No. Good news is that the saboteur didn't have time to do any other damage. Zylas Blount found the demolished cameras and called it in right away."

Jackson tapped his fingers on the steering wheel. "You think it was him?"

"No. The kid's solid. He was patrolling when he spotted my mangled devices. If it was him, he would've done a lot more damage before calling it in. But whoever did it knew what they were doing. Hit the exact spots to blind us, used the storm as cover, and they were quick about it."

Jackson's grip tightened on the wheel. Snow swirled past the windshield, but his mind was already racing ahead. The kid could've been injured or worse. "I know our numbers aren't great, but I want squads of two at all times. Make that three wolves if one of them is younger than twenty-one." He had to protect the pack's future.

"Good idea, although a few of us like to patrol on our own. Like me."

Jackson watched a branch skate across the snowy road. "Me, too. Set parameters for that. Base it on experience and age, so older members can patrol solo if they want. But I want everyone, including you, to check in with a central location before and after patrolling."

"Got it. A couple older members of the pack would probably love such a job. I'll call it something catchy like Wolf Dispatch Coordinator and send out an invitation to apply for the position," Thane said.

Jackson considered his current resources. "Now that you mention it, we do have many older pack members who aren't contributing. They have every right to retire and fish all the time, but I'm wondering if we shouldn't at least offer job opportunities that don't involve mining or protection. Something that isn't physically taxing."

"I can ask Raya to come up with a plan for that."

Jackson's eyebrow rose. "You finally admitting there's something going on?"

"Whatever. You and I have never talked about females."

True. They both kept that close to the vest. Plus, the only female Jackson had ever wanted to spend time thinking about was currently sleeping in his truck—right where he could keep an eye on her—and now wore his teeth marks. He rubbed his chest. He wore hers, too. It was more than he'd ever hoped to have. "Thane? Thanks for the hard work on this. I want a full report about the destruction by the time I get back, and I want the cameras reinstalled instantly."

"I'm already on it," Thane said, his voice clipped. The guy really didn't like anybody messing with his equipment. Ever.

Jackson rested a hand on Emily's thigh, needing to touch her. She didn't stir. The last thing Jackson needed right now was to look weak within his pack, and the fact that he hadn't found whoever had been sabotaging his mines, and now his damn cameras, didn't look good.

"Speaking of Zylas Blount, do you think the kid will challenge me?" Jackson asked. He'd hate to have to hurt the kid.

Thane coughed. "No, not really. I don't think he wants the job."

Smart kid. He seemed to be doing a good job with the patrolling. "Good. Tell him I want him to step up as Enforcer since I just took a mate."

Silence reigned over the line for a moment.

"Jackson? Please repeat your last," Thane rumbled.

"I mated Emily Nightsom. I need Enforcers."

Thane was silent for several more moments, then finally bellowed, "Raya!"

The sound of footsteps echoed through the phone. "What?"

she muttered. "I'm trying to go through the camera feeds to see who took them out. So far, nothing. The storm certainly isn't helping. What do you want?"

"I'm on the phone with Jackson."

"Oh, hey, Jackson," Raya said. "Where the heck are you? We've got issues. When will you be home?"

Jackson turned off the interstate. "As soon as I can. I'm going into Slate territory right now."

"Why?" she asked.

He glanced at his sleeping mate. "I'm taking Emily."

"Jesus," Thane muttered. "That's not the news."

"What's the news?" Raya asked.

"He mated her," Thane said.

More silence.

"You mated her?" Hope and what sounded like excitement filled Raya's voice. "Yes," she said. "I knew those other females weren't right for you. That whole dating game was just stupid."

Jackson couldn't agree more.

Raya rushed on. "Do you want me to make an announcement? We should have a shower."

"A shower?" Jackson asked.

"Yeah, like they have bridal showers. I think it'd be fun. It'd be a good way for the entire pack to get to know her."

Jackson thought about it. "Yeah, okay. That's a good idea."

Emily hadn't been at full strength for quite a while. Would their mating help her, or was he going to lose her? His shoulders tensed as fire lanced through him. There was no way in hell he would lose her. This mating bond would hold, and they'd live to be hundreds of years old with a pack full of kids. Their kids would probably be tall, too. He grinned.

"Jackson, you still there?" Thane asked.

He jerked back to the moment. "Yeah, sorry. I was just dreading another party," he lied.

"I'll put it together," Raya said. "After I finish with the camera feeds. But you do need to get back here. We need a show of strength."

"I understand." His responsibilities and duties pulled him in two different directions. "I'll check in later," he said. "Find out who destroyed the cameras."

He clicked off and kept his hand on Emily's thigh. Her warmth seeped through his skin. His chest tightened as determination flooded his veins. He'd figure this out. No matter what, she would be safe.

He drove through the main town area for the Slate Pack, noting the gleaming storefronts all with slate accents. The place was quaint, like his town. Smoke curled from several chimneys, and the golden lights from within reflected off the snow outside.

Somebody had shoveled each sidewalk and plowed the road, making it much easier for him to drive. Turning after the main drag, he drove along a freezing-looking river, noting that the road had been freshly plowed.

He turned down the Nightsom driveway with trees spinning by on each side. As he parked in front of the mansion, he noted wolves in human form, many of them, congregated on the driveway, porch, and along the trees on each side.

What the hell was going on?

Emily stretched awake as if feeling his tension. She blinked several times, looking around with blurry eyes. "What are all these people doing here?" Her voice rose on the last, and she fumbled for her door.

"Stop." He grasped her arm. "You stay in here until I figure out what's happening."

"They're my people."

Maybe not. He tightened his grip. "I need to know before we go out. How are you feeling?"

She paused. "The same. My legs are weak."

Was that from the mating, the illness, or the silver that might still be in her system? "All right. Then I want you to stay here. Got it?"

She glanced at him and then set her jaw. For what would probably be the first of a million times during their mating, she disobeyed him completely. She pressed the button, and her window rolled down.

CHAPTER 33

Emily looked for a familiar face and spotted Bussy near the porch. "Bussy? What's happening?" she called out.

The older woman, wrapped in a bright purple knit scarf with several shades of the color woven through it, ambled forward, her breath puffing white in the cold air. Snow clung to her boots as she stepped onto the shoveled path. "We're waiting on news about Philip. Nobody's heard anything yet." Her eyes, sharp despite her age, darted toward the house. "It's been too long."

Emily's shoulders slowly relaxed. "Oh. Thank goodness. I thought…" She shook her head. "I thought it was worse." She opened the door. This time, Jackson let her.

He was out of the truck in an instant and around to move with her, his posture loose but ready, scanning the crowd as they approached the porch.

"Hello, everyone." Emily tucked her hands into her coat pockets.

"Hey, Em," called an older male near the steps, his white beard dusted with snow. His flannel shirt stretched over broad shoulders, but his posture sagged slightly with age. "We're all here for the same reason. Still no word from the doctor. It's not looking good."

Emily pressed her lips together as she climbed the steps and then turned to face the crowd. "My father is strong. He'll pull through."

Movement from the tree line snapped her attention toward the forest. The air thickened as Victor stepped into view. His heavy boots crunched through the snow, and the slight smirk on his face sent a low hum of warning through her bones.

"It's over, Emily," Victor announced, his voice carrying easily over the quiet crowd. "No Alpha should be down for three days. It's time."

Her breath misted in the air as she turned to face him fully. "He's not gone yet."

Victor climbed the stairs two at a time. Jackson moved instantly, placing his body between them. He squared his shoulders and kept his eyes steady, watching Victor without blinking.

"There's nobody else," Victor said, scanning the group. "You all know it. I can lead this pack."

"I can do it," Emily replied. "I'm prepared to endure the trials."

Jackson didn't move, but his muscles visibly locked. His expression stayed carefully blank, but he met Victor's gaze without wavering.

Emily kept her composure, knowing the thoughts running through his mind. They had no idea if the mating would cure her, and if it did, how long it would take. Basically, they had no clue. Plus, she had to figure out what these trials entailed. Now that she'd declared her intention, she had a right to know.

Victor widened his stance. "No. I'll challenge you now, and then one of us will go through the trials."

Jackson turned toward him. "We haven't even seen Philip yet. This is nonsense. Knock it off."

"Yes," Emily said, her voice breaking on a gasp. Her left foot had gone numb, and the trembling she'd grown accustomed to snaked through her legs to crawl up her spine. What was happening? She blinked hard, trying to focus, but the faces around her blurred. She had to stay upright. She needed to be strong.

"Let's go check on my father," she said, but her voice emerged weak and strained.

Jackson murmured her name, grasping her arms.

The world spun faster than the snow. She fought to hold on, but the darkness clawed at her, dragging her down. Her legs buckled. Strong arms caught her before she hit the ground, Jackson's warmth pressing against her.

"See?" Victor's voice rang out, clear and cold. "I don't know what's wrong with Emily, but we all know she hasn't been herself for a while. She's not strong enough to lead this pack. The Ravencalls have regrouped, and the Ghostwind Pack wants to take us out. We need a strong leader, and it's going to be me."

"No," Emily whispered weakly. The idiot didn't even know that the Ravencalls had agreed to join Jackson's pack.

"We're going inside," Jackson barked. "Everybody go home. You'll get an update soon from your Alpha, Philip Nightsom." He stressed the last words.

Emily stirred weakly in his arms, but Jackson held her firm and strode toward the house.

His boots clomped loudly against the porch, the hollow sound echoing against the tense air. He pushed open the heavy oak door, and warmth instantly wrapped around her. She blinked, her lashes heavy as her vision blurred. She clung tighter to Jackson, feeling his steady heartbeat against her shoulder, grounding her as the heat from inside pulled her back from the brink of fainting.

"Emily?" Her father's voice came from across the room, thinner than she'd ever heard it.

Sucking in a breath, she opened her eyes, willing her vision to clear. It did. Jackson cradled her in the center of the opulent living room. A fire crackled in the stone hearth, the scent of pine logs mixing with traces of antiseptic and whiskey. Rich leather furniture and dark wood-paneled walls surrounded them, familiar yet somehow foreign in the tension-laced air.

Nadia sprang up from a chair near the fireplace. "Emily, you're as white as the snow outside. What's wrong?"

"I think I just nearly passed out in front of half the pack," Emily muttered, embarrassment curling through her already raw nerves.

"Shit," her father rasped from the sofa.

Aptly put. "I'm okay now, Jackson," Emily said quietly.

He lowered her to her feet and turned her to face her father, bracketing her from behind and wrapping an arm around her waist. His body heat seeped into her, solid and unyielding, whether to hold her upright or mark her as his, she wasn't sure.

She patted his hand. "I can stand."

He slowly removed his arm. Steadying herself, she stepped toward her father and dropped to her knees beside the sofa. Up close, the change in him was undeniable. His skin, once tan and weathered from years of leading, now looked ashen. A blue vein stood out sharply at his temple, and his face seemed hollow as if the attack had drained the strength from his bones. His frame, once solid, had withered beneath the blanket, the loose folds of fabric revealing how much weight he had lost.

"How bad is it?" Her voice cracked.

"It isn't good," Philip said, running a hand down her hair with a gentleness that clashed with the harsh lines of pain bracketing his eyes.

Nadia paced near the window, arms crossed tightly over her chest. "Victor's outside, giving some kind of speech," she said, her voice clipped.

Fear scraped through Emily, sharp and cold. She glanced toward the doorway where Caidrik and Miliki stood, both

Enforcers rigid with tension. Their eyes met hers, grim and unflinching.

Miliki shook his head. "I can challenge him, but I don't have Alpha blood. I might win, but then what?" His gaze dropped to her, assessing. "You just passed out. What's wrong with you?"

She sighed and shook her head. "I've been ill for a while with genetic problems."

"Ill? With the same sickness that killed your mother?" Miliki's eyes softened. "Oh, Em, I'm sorry to hear that." The Enforcer looked stricken. He'd been in her life since she was a baby and felt like a grandfather to her.

"I might be okay," she said, her knees still weak. "I mated Jackson last night."

Philip tried to surge from the sofa and then fell back weakly. "You did what?"

"It'll save her," Jackson said shortly. "Something about chromosomes and mutated and recessive genes. I don't know. You could call my doctors if you'd like a better explanation. Just know that my blood and mating me is the only thing that will save her. You want her alive, don't you?"

Philip reached a gnarled hand out and brushed Emily's hair away from her face. "Of course, I want her alive," he said softly. "More than anything else."

Nadia finally stopped pacing and strode over to them, grabbing a monstrous book with slate-colored binding. The pack's grimoire looked dusty. "Caidrik and I've been going through this."

"You have?" Emily asked, cutting her a look. She had tried to go through the pack's ancient book of laws as a teenager and had fallen asleep within minutes. In fact, she'd forgotten the book even existed since they didn't really use it any longer.

"Yeah, we're looking at some old English in here," Nadia grumbled. "He actually likes reading it more than I do."

Caidrik shrugged one massive shoulder. "I like puzzles."

Nadia nodded. "We've been searching for anything that can help."

Emily held her breath. "Any luck?"

"No. I haven't found anything yet. Victor, as an Alpha of the pack, has every right to challenge our current Alpha." She looked at Philip. "I am sorry, Philip. I'll keep looking."

Philip pushed himself up to more of a seated position, keeping the blanket on his legs. "Would you please call me Dad?" he asked, his eyes lighting as if the request surprised him.

Nadia shifted on her feet. "Okay." She looked at Emily. "I don't suppose you could be the Alpha of this pack while Jackson remains the Alpha of his?"

Emily sucked in air, her temples aching. "It might've been possible had I not just passed out in front of everybody. I'm not strong yet, Nadia. I have no idea when I will be, and Victor is ready to go through the trials right now." Whatever the hell those were.

"What the fuck are the trials?" Jackson asked shortly.

Philip looked at him, then at Emily, and his shoulders sagged. "We still follow the old laws. There are three trials a new Alpha has to endure and survive to become the Alpha of this pack, and that's after any possible challenges."

"What are they?" Jackson looked at Emily this time.

She shrugged. "I have no clue."

Philip's jaw tightened, his lips pressing together. "The trials are none of your business, Jackson. I'm sorry, but you're the Alpha of another pack. You don't get to know this information unless and until you decide to become the Alpha of our pack." His gaze moved to his daughter. "Emily, since you declared her your intention, I could tell you, but Victor is just going to challenge you first. You can't beat him right now."

No kidding. She couldn't feel her feet right now.

Nadia pushed her hair away from her face. "What about me?"

Philip's gaze softened even more. "You're not a fighter, Nadia."

"Who says a fighter has to survive the trials?" She shook her head. "I haven't even gotten to what they are yet. They must be explained in the grimoire."

"I know what they are. I survived them," Philip murmured. "You need to be a fighter. Trust me." His chin lowered. "I'm healing, but not quickly. It could take weeks."

Emily's temples pounded. "Victor won't wait weeks."

"No," Philip said, his voice rough with fatigue. "I don't see much of an option. I can try to hold Victor off, but I don't know how long it'll take for me to regain my strength. They used silver in the attack."

Emily gasped, leaning back. "Nobody told me that."

Nadia's eyes widened, so much like hers that it was like looking in a mirror. "He didn't tell me either, or I would've shared."

"I didn't tell anybody," Philip admitted. "They stabbed me in the thigh, so I can't shift to heal myself."

"I wondered about that," Nadia said. "I thought you might be too weak, but I didn't want to say anything."

Philip nodded, his gray hair looking thinner than it had just a week before. "Yeah, it could take months to heal from this. In my current state, I probably won't be able to shift for at least a month."

"That will be too late," Emily said, frustration crawling through her.

A heavy knock sounded on the door before Victor strode inside and took in the occupants.

Jackson bristled, stepping forward instinctively, but Emily shook her head. If he attacked, Miliki and Caidrik would likely back Jackson up, but the pack members outside would not.

Victor scanned the room, his gaze steady. "I'm sorry about the current situation, but this is over." His eyes flicked to Jackson. "Get out of my territory. I don't want members of any other pack here while I prepare to undertake the trials." His gaze locked onto Emily. "You mated him."

She blinked. "How did you know that?"

"I can smell it," Victor said simply. "Can't you?"

Truth be told, all she could smell was Jackson, but she didn't know if she was giving off the vibrations of mating. Her pulse pounded in her ears as Victor's words hung in the air.

"You just passed out, Em. You're done." His cold gaze flicked to Jackson. "You have half an hour to leave my territory with your mate." Then he looked at Nadia. "I'll give you two more weeks to get to know your father, but then you need to return to your farming community with your guard dog. We are not adding additional members to this pack. Ever." Finally, his eyes settled on Philip. "I expect you to be ready in two weeks for the ceremony that will make me the Alpha. Don't make me kill you."

With that, he turned on his boot and exited the house, shutting the door quietly behind him. The silence that followed pressed against Emily's chest.

Her head dropped as her father patted her shoulder.

"Sometimes, things happen that we don't want," he said softly. "There's a good chance Victor will mate somebody strong and with good lineage. One of his progeny might step up as Alpha. Or...maybe when I feel better, I'll challenge him. Or, even in the far future, thirty years from now, either Jackson or your child will become the Alpha. That's the agreement."

Emily swallowed the lump in her throat. There was no guarantee her father would ever recover. She lifted her gaze to Jackson, searching for an answer, but none came. Victor, her dumbass, brutal cousin, was about to become the Alpha of the Slate Pack for the foreseeable future, and there wasn't a damn thing she could do about it.

CHAPTER 34

"Thanks for flying in to get us," Jackson said, stepping out of the truck with Emily already in his arms, considering she'd ridden on his lap from the landing area. Thane had flown the helicopter to pick them up, and Jackson had piloted it back, needing to get the hell away from Slate territory before Emily challenged Victor.

Oh, Jackson would've stepped in, but then they would've fought to the death. No matter who won—and it would've been him—their packs would've ended up in a war neither could afford.

"Any time." Thane flipped the switch to turn down the heat. "Want a ride to the office?"

Jackson shook his head. "No. I'll take one of my other rigs after I get Em settled in." Nothing in him wanted to leave Emily alone right now, but he had to put measures in place to protect his pack. Plus, her eyelids kept closing. The female needed a nap.

Thane rolled his neck. "Great. I left everything you need on your desk as well as tons of cookie platters and holiday cakes for Emily from pack members. They really want her to join the quilting, knitting, Mah Jong, bridge, golf, soccer, book, and gin rummy clubs. If you have questions, give me a call. For now, I plan on getting some sleep."

Jackson shut the door and moved through the snow and up his porch.

"You don't always have to carry me." Emily had an arm over his shoulder and felt exactly right against his chest.

He clomped across the porch and reached down to twist the doorknob. "You're exactly where I want you." True statement. Completely.

She looked over his shoulder as Thane no doubt drove away. "How are you going to get your truck back?"

"Dunno. I'll figure it out later." A truck was the least of his worries. His new mate had been entirely too quiet for the trip home. He opened the door and walked inside, placing her gently on the sofa before lighting a fire. Warmth flickered through the room, casting light over the walls and catching on the worn fishing gear that had once belonged to his father. Rods and reels, polished and maintained, hung neatly along one wall, reminders of summers that felt a lifetime away.

In the corner sat the single armchair that had belonged to his mother, its dark leather soft from age. It was the only thing of hers he'd ever known since she'd passed when he was a baby.

Jackson glanced at Emily, her face pale in the firelight. "Would you like something grander?" he asked.

Her gaze shifted toward him, distant as if she'd forgotten he was there. After a moment, she blinked. "Grander than this place?"

While he loved the home, he'd give her whatever she wanted. "We could build something else."

"No," she murmured, her voice soft. "I like your home."

"Our home," he corrected, crossing over to sit next to her. Her unique scent, all female and wild berries, calmed him. Completely. "I'm sorry about your pack."

She swallowed and looked at him, composed as usual. He could feel her unshed tears since they'd mated, but he doubted Emily Nightsom cried very often. "I've been thinking," she murmured. "There has to be a way to combine the packs under you."

He'd tried to reason out the possibilities as he flew them home through the light storm. It wasn't nearly as bad as the one from the day before, but it was enough to force him to focus. "We don't have the numbers to defend more territory yet," he admitted. "One-fourth of my soldiers were poisoned by the Ravencall pack five years ago."

She sat back, her eyes widening. "What the hell? You never said a word."

"Of course, I didn't." His voice remained smooth. He didn't blame her for being irritated. "The second your father discovered the Copper Pack was vulnerable, he attacked. It was only because Erik Volk took over that they survived."

Her head dropped. "Yeah, you're right. I know. So, wait," she said, her brow furrowing. "You're down members. Is that why you work the mine?"

"It's one of the reasons," he replied. "I actually like getting my hands dirty. But yeah, we're waiting for the next generation to come back. We'll be better off once they return from college and other training programs. Until then, we make do with who we have, and we keep building." His fingers brushed hers, grounding them in the moment. "We'll figure this out, Em. Together."

"That's why you're also bringing in new packs and new wolves," she murmured, the firelight casting shadows across her face.

"Affirmative," he said. "I'm glad I am, especially after learning the cause of your illness. All the packs need new blood."

Damn, she was pretty. Tall and classy with that unreal hair. He'd thought of it before as spun gold, but that wasn't right. The strands were like moonlight on frost, cold and luminous. Shit. He'd only been mated a day, and he was already waxing poetic. He wasn't a guy who believed in love, not really, but he believed in family. In this connection between them.

Sorrow darkened her eyes. "It sounds like Victor is going to stop any programs to bring newcomers into the Slate Pack. We need new people. All the other packs are bringing in outsiders."

Jackson wasn't entirely sure about the Silver Pack, since Seth Volk was one stubborn bastard, but with his brother succeeding in the Copper Pack, maybe Seth would come around. Jackson didn't give a shit about that right now. What mattered was Emily's pack.

"I can't reason with Victor," Jackson said. "I could reason with your father and find an agreement, but Victor will challenge him. Your father won't win. We could go to war, but we'd both lose too many soldiers. Neither pack can afford that. It would leave us vulnerable."

Emily dropped her gaze to her hands. "I've been trying to think of a way to combine the other three packs to take him out, but the territories are too spread out."

Jackson had already done the math. "If my pack was twice its size, or better yet, three or four times larger, we could combine our territory outside the other two packs with the Embervault Mine dead center."

"It would be perfect," she breathed.

Jackson shook his head. "We don't have the numbers, Em. I'm willing to consider it, will even go to war, but you have to understand how many wolves would die."

Her shoulders slumped. "That's not what I want."

He had to fix this for her now and not in thirty years. "We'll figure it out."

She swallowed hard. "Are you hungry?"

"No." His eyes darkened. "Not for food, at least."

Before she could respond, he pulled her onto his lap, his

hands threading into her hair as he kissed her. Her heart stuttered against his chest.

"Tell me you're feeling better," he whispered against her lips.

"I'm feeling better."

His brow lifted slightly. "Are you lying?"

"Yes," she admitted, laughing softly. "I'll call the doctor tomorrow and see if there's any way to—"

He silenced her with another kiss, slow and consuming as if he could chase the sickness from her body through sheer will. Finally, he slowed down, knowing she needed rest. "I want you to call the doctor first thing tomorrow."

Emily ran her palm across his jaw, no doubt scratching her tender skin. "My guess is she'll probably want to wait a week or two before testing my blood."

"I would think so." He enjoyed the heat of her body against his lap. Her warmth seeped into his skin, stirring something low and insistent inside him. "We'll figure this thing out with your pack, but it may be that Victor steps up as the Alpha for the time being."

She sighed, her fingers curling slightly against his shoulders. "I don't completely trust him not to kill my father. Just to make sure the threat is gone."

"I don't think he's that stupid," Jackson replied, voice rough. "The pack would turn on him whether he liked it or not."

She nodded, her eyes clearing. "That's true."

He could at least give her that peace. "I'll speak with Seth and Erik. Even though none of us interferes with the business of each other's packs, I think I can get them to agree to protect your father. We can tell Victor we'll all go to war if he hurts Philip." It was a long shot, but he'd give it a try.

She swallowed. "Okay. That would go against tradition, but why not ask?" Her hands slid down his chest. "What now?"

His breath hitched. "Now, you figure out what you want to do with my pack," he said. "And I expect you to keep writing because you enjoy it. We could use your help with the safety procedures for the mines, like you've done for your father."

"I'd like that," she said, though the lost tone in her voice hadn't disappeared. She barely concealed a yawn.

He stood, lifting her effortlessly. She yelped, smiling as he laid her back down on the sofa. The smile lingered on her lips as he grabbed a blanket somebody had given him at some point from the nearby chair and draped it over her, smoothing it into place and lingering on the good parts. "I want you to take a nap." He let the Alpha show in his voice. "Your body needs to heal, and sleep is the best way. I have to run into town with Thane and look over schematics."

Her eyes met his, heat flickering there. "Hurry back."

"I will," he promised, brushing a kiss across her forehead and stepping away before the temptation to stay overruled everything else. "I'll have patrols on the house the whole time." The place felt like home with her in it. He crossed the room, his boots scuffing softly against the wooden floor, and paused near the wall beside the fireplace. Reaching up, he removed a small painting, revealing a sleek security panel embedded in the wall.

Emily sat up, surprise widening her eyes. "What is that?"

"A security system." Given the price of the damn thing, it'd better be as good as Thane promised.

She blinked. "You have an actual security system? Like a human one?"

He snorted. "Yeah. We're all modern, remember? Thane insisted upon installing it when he updated City Hall awhile back. To be honest, I've never used it before, but now, your safety is all that matters." He booted it up. Hopefully, it still worked. Relief flitted through him when the green light blinked and then glowed. "The code is 0802, just in case you need it."

Her lips curved slightly. "0802?"

"August second." He felt warmth rise in his chest despite himself. Would she remember the date?

"The day we kissed at the lake so long ago?" she murmured, her smile softening the tension in the air.

Jackson's pulse kicked up. "Yeah. That was one hell of a kiss." The memory still stirred something primal inside him. He'd waited so long to feel her mouth beneath his again, her hands gripping his shoulders.

Silence thickened between them, charged with something that had always simmered beneath the surface. Her gaze dipped to his mouth, and for a moment, he considered crossing the room and showing her just how much he still remembered that kiss.

Instead, he exhaled roughly and adjusted the panel. "Okay, that's good. I'll be back in about an hour. Take a nap."

"You're bossy."

"You have no idea," he muttered, hoping she understood him. "You're gonna need your rest, baby." With that, he engaged the alarm, opened the door, and jogged out into the swirling snowfall, his mind already focused on finding whoever the hell was trying to sabotage his mines so he could return and spend the night with Emily.

His mate.

Finally.

CHAPTER 35

Emily couldn't sleep. She spent about half an hour curled up on the sofa, watching the fire. Her mind spun, but no answers came to her. She hated even considering the possibility that Victor would become Alpha of her pack. Not once had she truly believed he could manage the feat. But then again, she hadn't expected her father to be attacked with silver, either.

Reaching for her phone, she hit the speed dial for Nadia.

"Hello?" Her father's voice sounded groggy.

"Oh, crap. Hi, Dad. I'm sorry. I didn't mean to wake you up. I was calling Nadia."

Philip sounded like he fumbled for something. "Oh. This is her phone. It was by the sofa."

"Where is she?" Emily asked.

"I don't know," Philip murmured. "I fell asleep. The house sounds quiet. Maybe she went to get dinner."

Emily didn't like her father being left alone. Hopefully, Miliki stood somewhere near, but she didn't want to insult her dad by asking. It was one thing to be ill from silver, and quite another to need a babysitter. "I was basically calling to see how you were feeling."

"About the same." His voice softened. "Em, you need to stop worrying. Take care of yourself."

"I am," she said. "I'm feeling better already."

But was she? Her lips still tingled from Jackson's kiss, and she wished he'd hurry home, but did she feel stronger? Not really.

"It's only been hours, not even a full day yet," Philip said gently. "Give yourself time. Maybe when the moon is full next time, you'll sense a difference."

"Dad, you guys really need to bring in new members to the pack. My illness should teach us that, if nothing else."

Philip sighed. "I know, sweetheart. But Victor's adamant against it. In a couple of weeks, if he survives the trials, his word will be law."

She gulped. "What are these trials, and is there any way we can make them more difficult?"

"Emily." Her dad barked out a laugh, sounding more like himself. "You're not really trying to become the Alpha, so I can't tell you about the trials. Unfortunately, we can't make them more difficult. Though I appreciate the thought. That little bloodthirsty side of you has always reassured me."

She watched the fire. "Reassured you? How so?"

"You're smart and strong. I always want you to be safe," he said, then yawned loudly.

She bit back a yawn of her own. "I'll let you get back to sleep," she said. "Have Nadia call me when she gets home, okay?"

"All right," Philip said. "I'll leave her a note. Love you."

"Love you, too." She set the phone down on the table. Man, she was thirsty. Standing, she walked through the hallway to the wide kitchen, searching the cupboards until she found a mismatched hodgepodge of glasses. She poured herself water from a pitcher in the fridge.

Jackson at least needed matching glasses.

Curious now, she opened the other cupboards and found that nothing matched anywhere. The contents weren't antiques, either. It looked like he'd just picked up a bowl, plate, or cup during his wanderings and tossed it in the cupboard. Wait a minute. She recognized the plate with small violets around the edge. And the platter with little wolves. She'd been given cookies on each. So pack members had brought Jackson meals on different plates, and he'd kept them. Her heart warmed. There was something charming about the idea that his cupboard held patterns from many of his pack members.

A small ding echoed from the other room, and her heart started to race. That had been the alarm deactivating.

Jackson had returned much faster than she'd anticipated.

Finishing her water, she set the glass down and walked as slowly and as dignified as possible out of the kitchen and down the hall to the gathering room. Once there, she paused, blinking, trying to understand.

The front door was wide open, snow blowing inside.

She looked around. Nobody was there.

Her heart pounded harder—and not from excitement this time. Shock zapped through her. She had to get out of there. A hood instantly slammed over her head, the smell of garlic permeating her senses.

"Damn it!" she yelled, swinging as hard as she could with a closed fist. She hadn't smelled anybody. The illness even took that away. A muffled "oof" sounded, and then pain flashed through her skull.

She saw lights and explosions of color, then dropped to the floor, her knees hitting hard enough for pain to ricochet up her hips.

Jackson's face filtered through her mind.

Where was he?

The wolf inside her tried to awaken, and she focused everything she had on shifting. Her bones stretched, her tendons gathered, and then—

Her energy sputtered out.

She still couldn't shift.

And right now, she couldn't even see.

The back of her head ached, and she could feel blood sliding down her neck.

Darkness claimed her.

She awoke as something rumbled beneath her. Cold seeped into her bones, but all she could smell was garlic. She tried to move her hands but found them tightly bound behind her back. Fury burned through her veins, but the ache in her head was too much. Her stomach rolled as she slid sideways.

Oh, God.

This wasn't a car trunk. Not this time.

She was in a helicopter.

Her knees ached. She tried to say something, anything, but no sound emerged. It was like her mouth had been stuffed with cotton. Pain flashed through her head, stealing her focus.

If she shifted in the craft, she'd probably knock out the pilot with the energy she released. Right now, she didn't care. She tried again, focusing all of her remaining energy—and then nothing. Sparks flashed behind her eyes.

This time, when unconsciousness took her, she stayed under.

* * *

Jackson drove slowly through yet another storm, snowflakes splattering against the windshield as he made his way back from the office. A catalog for wedding dresses sat on the seat beside him. The owner of the clothing shop, Mrs. Plankton, had marked several pages that she said Emily would love, and the female wouldn't let him leave until he agreed to take it with him.

Next to the catalog sat a softly rustling bag holding three different kinds of ice cream.

How odd that he'd mated a female he'd dreamed about for years and still had no clue what kind of ice cream she preferred. He doubted Emily Nightsom would consider ice cream a decent dinner, but it was one he'd had often enough. A smile tugged at the corners of his mouth at the thought of her waiting for him at home. His home. Their home. The word settled deep inside him with a sense of rightness.

Did she want to get married? A lot of modern wolves did these days, though the idea had never crossed his mind until now. His fingers tightened slightly around the steering wheel. He had his great-grandmother's ring, which had been a present to her from his great-grandfather when they'd opened the Embervault Mine. The ring was tucked away in one of the safes back at the house, waiting for the right moment. The right female.

The band was platinum, sleek and simple, with a deep black onyx stone set in the center, flanked by two smaller diamonds. Elegant, timeless, and fitting for Emily. With her platinum-blond hair and eyes so dark they nearly matched the stone, it was as if the ring had been waiting for her.

He wasn't a romantic guy. Never had been.

But Emily made him think of things like that. Considering she'd kept her mother's doilies all these years, he figured she might appreciate a family heirloom.

The truck slid over the fresh snow as he turned onto the long drive leading home, anticipation humming through his veins. Turning onto the long drive, his pulse quickened when his headlights swept across the front of the house—and the open door.

What the fuck?

Ice cream forgotten, he threw the truck into park and launched into the snowdrifts, boots pounding up the porch steps. The front door banged against the frame as he rushed inside.

"Emily!" His bellow echoed through the room, swallowed only by the crackle of the fire and the whistle of the wind through the open doorway. His breath came fast and hard as his gaze swept over the room.

The table near the fireplace had been knocked over, and one of the heavy iron fire pokers lay abandoned on the floor. Dropping into a crouch, Jackson picked it up and froze.

Blood.

His vision sharpened, going both predator-clear and tunnel-dark with fury. The familiar scent of berries lingered in the air. His muscles locked, so close to shifting that his claws burned beneath his skin. For the first time in decades, his control nearly slipped.

He inhaled again and then staggered back.

Garlic.

Rage surged through him, fierce and hot enough to tear through bone. How the hell had they gotten inside? His head whipped toward the keypad near the front door. The small red light blinked, signaling that the system had been disengaged.

"Damn it." His voice was a snarl as he bolted back outside, snow crunching hard beneath his boots.

The bitter air sliced through his lungs as he sniffed again. Faint. Too faint. But it was there.

Emily.

Shifting mid-stride, he hit the ground as a massive wolf and tore through the snowdrifts. His paws hammered the ground, heart slamming against his rib cage. He followed her trail through the forest, trees whipping past in a blur until the path stopped abruptly in a small clearing a mile away.

Jackson slid to a halt, panting hard as he scanned the area.

Snow swirled in the air, masking the scents, but he could still smell it. The burn of fuel. The churn of blades against the air.

A helicopter.

A growl rumbled from his chest as he shifted back into his human form, barefoot in the snow as he scouted the clearing. She'd been there. And then someone had taken her.

His hands clenched into fists so tight that his nails bit into his palms, but he forced himself to breathe. To think. Fear clawed at his throat, primal and savage, but he shoved it down.

He had to focus.

Shifting again, he ran full-out as a wolf, snow flying beneath his paws as he raced back to the house. His mind was already moving faster than his legs when he morphed back to human form.

He grabbed his phone from the truck, snatched his shredded jeans off the porch, yanked them on, and then stepped inside, his heart hammering against his ribs. The cold bit into his bare chest, but he barely registered it. Thumbing through his contacts, he pressed Thane's number.

The call rang. No answer.

"Shit," he growled. Thane always said he was going to sleep but ended up patrolling through the night half the time.

The voicemail beeped. "Hey, it's Jackson. Somebody took Emily. They flew her out of here. I need to know where. Call me." His voice vibrated with barely leashed fury as he clicked off and tossed the phone onto the counter.

He dragged air deep into his lungs and forced his mind to focus. Panic wouldn't help her.

Stepping back onto the porch, he scanned the dark tree line, eyes narrowed. The wind carried traces of her scent, but the storm had churned everything into chaos. His pulse pounded harder as adrenaline spiked, his wolf clawing at his skin, but he pushed the urge down. He needed information.

He bolted across the yard, legs pumping hard until he

reached the nearest tree. He scaled it quickly, muscles flexing with smooth efficiency as he hoisted himself onto a branch. His breath misted in the air as he balanced against the trunk and scanned the property.

When Thane had insisted upon installing the security system, Jackson had mounted hidden cameras in several trees around the perimeter, figuring that someday he'd have a family and want a little security. Until now, the system was never used since his presence alone was usually enough to deter threats.

Had the cameras engaged when he armed the system? He was the only person who knew he'd planted cameras out there.

Damn it, he should have thought this through.

Clenching his jaw, he scanned the area, searching for any flicker of movement beyond the trees. Snowflakes drifted past his vision, catching glimmers from the porch lights, but nothing stirred in the darkness.

How the hell had the enemy gotten into his territory again?

Or worse—was it someone he knew?

He ripped the memory card from the camera nearest the front porch and dropped from the tree, landing hard with a spray of snow beneath his feet. His breath came fast, fogging the air in short, sharp bursts as his mind churned with thoughts he couldn't control. Fear, cold and suffocating, clawed through him, unlike anything he'd ever experienced. He crushed it down with pure rage and sprinted toward the house, ice biting into the soles of his bare feet as he tore across the clearing.

He hit the porch at full speed and barreled inside without slowing, sliding across the floorboards. The scent of her blood in the air nearly had him shifting into wolf form again. A snarl ripped from his throat.

Charging into his office, he slammed the door shut behind him and shoved the memory card into his computer. The machine took too long to boot up, the seconds dragging like nails against his nerves as update prompts flashed across the screen.

"Come on," he growled, fingers twitching against the desk. His pulse pounded in his temples. Every wasted second burned through him like fire.

Where the hell was she? Was she hurt? Had they harmed her?

The questions hammered through his skull as another program began to update. His patience snapped. His hand shot out, fingers curling against the edge of the monitor, ready to rip the entire system apart. He forced himself to still, white-knuckling the desk as his chest heaved with ragged breaths. He was so close to seeing who had taken her.

When he found them, he was going to rip out their throats.

CHAPTER 36

Emily came to with a sharp intake of breath, the world around her still and cold. She felt solid rock under her, rough and unyielding. Her arms, now bound in front, ached from the strain.

Ducking her chin, she lifted her hands and heard the rattle of a chain. Grunting, she fumbled with her fingers until she managed to yank the rough hood from her head. The smell of garlic clung thickly to her nose and throat, coating her breath with its acrid sting. Her eyes watered, and the dull throb at the back of her skull reminded her they'd hit her in a different spot this time. Fantastic. She bit down a slightly hysterical laugh and forced herself to focus.

Dust swirled in the air, thick and stale, carrying the metallic tang of iron mixed with the earthy scent of damp stone. Beneath the dust and age, she caught the faint whiff of oil—old machinery oil—and something sulfuric.

The place felt unused for years, maybe decades, but the smell of coal, rusty tools, and old wood still clung to the air. She blinked rapidly, her eyes adjusting to the dim lighting.

The room was bare, the walls hewn from jagged rock and patches of decayed timber beams reinforcing the ceiling. Rusted metal brackets jutted from the stone, once used to hold lanterns or equipment. Opposite her, a set of old block windows lined the middle of the wall, the kind divided into squares like industrial glass bricks, dirty with age and grime. Beyond them, she glimpsed a narrow hallway carved from the rock, lit by a single dim bulb that buzzed in the silence.

She pressed her back against the wall, extending her legs and trying to warm them by kicking out. The chill from the stone had seeped deep into her bones, and her teeth chattered.

Metal hurt her wrists. She looked down to see shackles over each one, secured by a chain that attached to the wall above her head. The heavy links rested on her shoulder. At least there was enough slack to rest her hands in her lap.

Tugging, she tested the strength. The chain appeared new. Fucking great.

Movement flickered beyond the window. Her breath hitched. She went utterly still, holding herself motionless as a figure crossed the narrow hallway. The echo of footsteps on gravel and the rustle of fabric carried through the air.

A fluorescent light flickered to life overhead, casting harsh shadows against the stone. Blinking rapidly, Emily willed her vision to clear, heart pounding as she strained to make out the figures through the grimy glass.

Her breath caught. "Nadia," she whispered.

Her sister's profile came into view through the block windows, clear even in the dim light.

Betrayal cut so deep and sharp that Emily gasped, her breath hitching in her throat. Oh, God. Was her father okay? Had Nadia hurt him? How had Emily not sensed this? Her illness had been worse than she'd thought if she hadn't known her sister was dangerous. She had thought what? That because Nadia was shorter, she was somehow adorable? Cute? Loving?

Everything hurt, from Emily's toes to the top of her head, and the pulse hammering at the back of her skull promised a painful lump. Dried blood itched along her shoulders, but she could still feel fresh droplets trickling down her neck. Through the murky glass, she watched as Nadia walked along the corridor, a male whose head rose above the glass shadowing her. Broad shoulders. Wide frame.

Caidrik. It had to be.

Her breath caught as her pulse stuttered. The bulb above the window barely illuminated the hallway beyond, and the damn garlic still clogged her senses, muddling everything.

The door creaked as Nadia pushed it open, fumbling for the light switch. A fluorescent glare flooded the room, stark against the rock walls, making Emily squint as pain shot through her skull.

"Emily?" Nadia murmured, eyes wide with something Emily couldn't read.

"What are you doing?" Emily rasped, her throat dry and raw. She shook her head, instantly regretting it as pain crashed from her skull down her neck. Bile surged in her throat, hot and sharp, and she doubled over with a retch, barely managing to hold back the vomit that threatened to choke her.

Footsteps clomped on the hard floor as the male stepped in behind Nadia. Blinking through the haze, Emily tried to focus.

Not Caidrik, but somebody just as large.

"Who the hell are you?" she slurred. Damn it, why was her voice so thick?

The male smiled, slow and easy, like someone at peace with the moment. His shoulders filled the doorway, and thick, brown hair framed a square jaw, his eyes a dark shade of brown that nearly blended into the shadows. "I'm just here for the money."

Emily lifted her head, trying to smell him and pinpoint his pack, but the garlic burned through her sinuses, drowning everything out. All she could smell was blood and spice. "Nadia?" she whispered again, her gaze locking on her sister.

The male shifted his shoulder without warning, a quick, efficient motion.

Nadia gasped, her eyes going wide, her mouth falling open as she staggered forward. Emily stilled, her heart slamming against her ribs as her gaze dropped to the knife sticking out of her sister's back. "Nadia."

The metal caught the light as Nadia fell to her knees, shock on her face. She pitched forward onto her stomach, revealing the weapon.

Silver.

Emily's pulse spiked as adrenaline surged. Her muscles tensed, and her breath hitched. She needed to move. But her body wouldn't respond, her limbs cold and heavy with exhaustion.

Panic coiled in her chest as she stared at her sister, her mind spinning.

What was happening?

Nadia coughed and sputtered on the floor, her arm stretching toward Emily.

"Take that out," Emily said urgently. "She'll die."

The massive guy shrugged. "Told her if she didn't shut the hell up on the way here, I'd stab her. Should've listened." He watched Nadia for another moment, his expression blank as she shuddered, tears streaking her cheeks.

"Who hired you?" Emily asked, her voice hoarse. Her muscles felt frozen, her body heavy and slow. What the hell was wrong with her?

"You'll know soon enough." He turned, shutting the door with a solid click.

Emily yanked at the restraints, her breath coming in short bursts. The chain holding her to the wall barely shifted. Her hands, manacled in front of her, strained as she tried to reach her sister. Pain pounded at the back of her skull, sharp and unrelenting. "Nadia, come here," she urged, voice raw.

Nadia gasped and trembled, the knife still lodged in her lower back. Blood bubbled at her lips, dripping onto the floor.

"Nadia!" Emily barked.

"What?" Nadia choked out, eyes wide and wet.

"I know it's hard, but I'm attached to the fucking wall. Move. Now."

Her sister shot her a look, half pain, half defiance. She planted her hands against the cold floor, grimacing as she dragged herself forward, each breath a loud groan.

"Good. Good. Do it again," Emily urged, pulling against the restraints, her heart hammering as she willed Nadia to reach her.

Nadia gulped and winced but did it again, inching closer.

"All right. One more time, and you'll be here. The room's not that big. You're close. Just keep coming." Emily tried to sound calm.

"Can't," Nadia gasped, her body heaving.

"I know you can." Emily softened her tone. "You're my sister. Come closer."

Nadia looked up, the pain in her black eyes so raw that Emily could almost feel it in her own back.

"All right." Nadia planted one arm against the floor and dragged herself closer.

"Good." Emily reached out. Her fingers grazed Nadia's hand, and she clutched it, pulling her sister the rest of the way.

Nadia cried out as Emily panted through her own pain. "Hold still." Emily scooted forward as far as the chain would allow, the metal biting into her wrists. Her fingers brushed the knife's hilt. She grunted and pulled with every ounce of strength she had left.

Nadia screamed, and her body bucked from the pain, but the

knife came free with a sickening slide. She collapsed onto her side, gasping, "I think that was a kidney."

"We only need one, right?" Emily gripped the bloody knife. "It's silver. Don't shift." That would propel the poison through Nadia's bloodstream too fast.

"I couldn't even if I wanted to." Nadia curled into a ball, her face wet with tears. "Thanks."

Emily looked toward the empty doorway. "Who is he?"

"I don't know." More tears spilled from Nadia's eyes. "Caidrik and I headed into town to get something for Dad to eat. There was a tree down. Caidrik got out to move it, and this truck came out of nowhere." Her eyes glassed over as if reliving the moment. "It hit him hard, and there was this crunch of bone. I've never heard anything like it. Then the guy who stabbed me jumped out and grabbed me. I fought. I really did."

"I know you did." Emily gripped the knife tighter as she examined her shackles. There had to be a way to wedge the blade into the lock.

Carefully, she pressed the blade against the shackle's hinge and winced as the edge sliced into her palm. The silver burned through her skin, its poison flowing into her bloodstream with a searing sting.

Grunting, Nadia pushed herself upright, blood soaking through her white sweater.

"I think you should stay still until that heals," Emily said through clenched teeth.

"I think I should help you get out of those so we can get out of here," Nadia shot back, her voice hoarse but determined.

Emily met her gaze. "I'm with you."

"Raya?" A male voice echoed from outside.

Emily and Nadia both stilled. Emily's breath hitched. "That was Victor."

"I think so, too," Nadia gasped.

Victor's heavy footsteps echoed outside the block windows.

Moments later, the door swung open, and he stepped inside, his gaze sweeping over them. His expression went blank.

"You fucking asshole," Emily yelled, yanking furiously at the knife, trying to wedge it against the chain.

Victor shook his head. "What the hell is going on?"

"You had him stab her," Emily barked, pulling harder against the bindings.

Victor stepped forward, his jaw going slack. "Nadia, are you bleeding?"

"Yeah," Nadia muttered, her voice rough with pain.

He looked at her, eyes narrowing. "What are you doing here?"

"Wait a minute." Emily glanced at Nadia. "Did he yell 'Raya?'"

A shadow crossed the doorway. Then Raya stepped inside.

Shock cascaded through Emily.

"Hello, ladies." Raya smiled.

Emily shook her head. "Raya?"

Victor looked from Emily to Raya. "Honey, what the hell have you done?"

Honey? Seriously? Emily tried to focus.

Raya moved beside Victor, standing close. She wore all black—jeans, boots, a sweatshirt—and had her dark hair pulled into a ponytail. "I'm doing what needed to be done, Victor."

He looked from her to Emily and back again. "Honey, we have a plan, remember? I'm going to take over the pack."

"I want both packs," Raya said flatly. "Jackson doesn't know what the hell he's doing. He's inviting outsiders in. We don't do that."

"You can join my pack," Victor said, his gaze locking on Emily. "I've been asking you to mate with me—"

Emily's thoughts spun. "Raya, what about Thane?"

Raya waved a hand in the air. "Thane will be dead in a few hours. He was a means to an end. I just had to get close enough to Jackson to learn all the pack's weaknesses, and well, get to the mines."

Heat coated Emily's throat. "You sabotaged the mines?"

"Sure." Raya shrugged. "It wasn't hard, although I would've expected more casualties. Not bad for my first couple of tries, though. The next time will be spectacular." She glanced at her watch. "After I kill him, you can take over both packs, Victor."

Victor blanched. "I don't know that I have enough soldiers to go to war."

"You do," she said. "I've sent most of their good fighters away on different educational trips." Her gaze flicked to her watch again. "There's going to be a phenomenal explosion in the mine, right between the morning and afternoon shifts. They'll lose most of their best fighters, including Thane, and then the entire territory will be ours. We can base headquarters here."

Emily's breath caught as realization dawned. "This is the Embervault Mine."

"Sure is," Raya said smoothly. "It's the new headquarters of the Granite-Slate Pack, which Victor will rule."

Victor stepped away from her. "Wait a minute. What do you plan to do with my cousins?"

"Do you really care?" Raya snarled. "You're the one who had Emily kidnapped the first time."

Victor blanched, his gaze sliding to Emily and then down. "That was just to show Philip how vulnerable she is and that she can't be the Alpha. I told them not to hurt you, Emily. Even if you hadn't escaped, they would've let you go." He glared at Raya. "I can't believe you told her. That was a secret."

Fury focused Emily. "You told Raya about the garlic?"

Raya snorted. "He did, so I made sure my guys employed the same props. But you weren't supposed to walk away the second time. Damn Jackson Tryne for finding you. I guess third time is the fucking charm." She straightened to her full and rather unimpressive height. "Now Victor, I have everything in place. All right?"

He looked from Emily to Nadia before turning back to Raya. "Sweetheart, I love you with my whole heart, and I'll give you everything you want in this life…but I don't want you to kill my cousins."

Raya planted both hands on her hips, her brown eyes sparking. "Vic, you've beaten the heck out of more than one female lover in your past. You told me all about them."

"I told you I was drinking and that I felt horrible about it whenever I sobered up," Victor snapped. "I have a bad temper. I'm trying to work on that. But that doesn't mean I want you to kill my cousins."

Raya's lips pressed into a thin line. She slowly backed away, eyes glinting dangerously. "Are you messing with me right now? I've given you everything you've ever wanted."

"I don't want this," he said, his voice rough with conviction.

Nadia groaned from the floor, drawing their attention.

Emily worked harder on the cuffs, but she couldn't find a way to loosen them with the knife. Every time she slipped, she nicked herself, exposing her skin to more silver. Pain pulsed through her wrists, sharp and relentless. "Victor, you have to get us out of here. Nadia needs a doctor," she said, her voice urgent.

Victor hesitated, looking between them and Raya. His shoulders tensed. "Yeah, I know. You're right." He took a step toward them.

"No!" Raya shrieked.

Victor muttered something, but before he could move, a gunshot echoed through the room. Emily jumped. Victor slowly turned.

Raya lowered a gun after shooting at the ceiling, her gaze hard. Pieces of plaster and dirt drifted down around her. "I can't believe you're not more appreciative," she shouted, her voice wild and cracking. "I brought them here as an offering to you. A promise of our future."

Victor shook his head slowly. "Raya, this isn't the way. I'll go to war with the other pack if that's what you want. We'll take them over and just move both territories to one spot, whether the packs like it or not. But you can't kill two defenseless females."

"You don't love me." Raya's tears streaked down her cheeks.

"I do," Victor said, stepping closer. "But I'm not going to let you do this."

Her eyes gleamed with madness, and she pointed the weapon at him. "You can't stop me. If you're not going to be the Alpha, I know who will."

"Who? Your hired muscle?" Victor spat. "The one who stabbed a defenseless female in the back? That's who you want to align yourself with?"

"Yes," Raya hissed and fired four shots center mass.

The bullets hit Victor with brutal force. His body jerked with each impact, eyes widening in shock. He dropped to his knees, gasping as silver veins crawled up his neck and across his face. His skin paled to an ashy gray as agony twisted his features.

"Oh, God," Emily whispered. "They're silver."

Victor pitched forward, landing face-first on the floor. Blood spread from beneath him, dark and thick against the stone floor. The sharp metallic scent mingled with the cold air.

Emily's heart pounded as she lifted her gaze to Raya. "You're insane."

"No," Raya snapped, her voice eerily calm. "I just know what's best for the packs. We can't keep letting outsiders in. We have to keep our bloodlines pure."

"Keeping it pure ends up with us getting sick from inbreeding," Emily spat, throwing a worried glance at Nadia, who had stopped moving.

Raya shook her head as if swatting away the words. "I don't

care. I will take over. And yes, Bulwark is the one who stabbed your sister. He's with the Ghostwind Pack and has some Slate Pack in him. I'm sure you could tell he had Alpha blood and looks like he's about to be the Alpha of the other two packs. After the mining accident, nothing will stop us."

"Jackson's going to kill you." Emily had to get free somehow.

Raya rolled her eyes, lifting the gun and checking the chamber. "Actually, as soon as the mine blows, I'm going to make sure Jackson dies. He won't see me coming."

CHAPTER 37

Jackson's computer finally stopped updating. He clicked the program open. Blood rushed through his veins, his ears pounding with each pulse.

"Jackson," Thane yelled, barreling through the front door, buck-ass naked. "I got your message. I shifted. Where is she?" He sniffed the air, his gaze dropping to the floor where blood streaked the stone floor. "Blood." He stalked through the open double-doorway into the office. "What are you doing?"

"I had a camera. I don't know if it worked," Jackson muttered, fingers flying over the keyboard. "I engaged the security system."

Thane's nostrils flared. "If you engaged the system, the cameras outside should've turned on." He leaned over Jackson's shoulder, pointing. "No. Click there."

Jackson followed his instruction. Slowly, grainy images appeared on the screen. He leaned forward, heart hammering against his ribs.

"Here." Thane grabbed the mouse and clicked several times. The images sharpened.

Jackson sat back, the wolf in him roaring. "Raya."

"What the fuck?" Thane whispered, jaw dropping open as they both watched the screen.

Raya dragged Emily from the house, a bag over his mate's head. She was limp, not fighting.

"She must've been knocked out cold," Jackson muttered, heating with fury.

They watched as Raya shoved Emily into the back of a truck and drove off.

"She had a helicopter." Jackson stood and grabbed Thane's shoulders. "Where would she go?"

Thane staggered back, shock written across his face. "I...I don't know."

"Think it through, damn it. Where would she go?" Jackson barked, adrenaline snapping and coursing through every muscle.

"This is her home," Thane said, his eyes dazed. "Would she go to Vegas?"

Jackson shook his head. "That doesn't make sense. What does she want with Emily?"

"Raya must have taken Emily for Victor," Thane said, his voice hollow.

"For Victor?" Jackson repeated, eyes narrowing.

Thane swallowed hard. "They...dated once. I thought it was over a long time ago."

What would Raya see in Victor? How had Jackson missed this? He worked with the female every day. "You didn't tell me that."

"I just found out not too long ago. We were already dating," Thane said slowly as if piecing together a puzzle in real time. "It was a summer fling with Victor. They met up at several different mining conferences that year, or so she said."

Jackson's mind raced. "Raya wouldn't take Emily to Slate Pack territory. And she's not in ours."

"No." Thane's brow furrowed, the lines deepening.

"What about the Embervault Mine?" Jackson asked, the words tasting like iron.

Thane's eyebrows shot up. "It would work. The Slate Pack's got the electricity running there. It's isolated, and nobody would hear a thing."

Jackson nodded grimly. "We'll have to fly." Already shifting before he hit the door, he bolted through the snow, feeling the percussion behind him as Thane shifted and followed. They sprinted toward his helicopter.

If Raya had planned this, it was down to the minute. She was the most efficient wolf Jackson had ever met. The betrayal burned like silver in his veins. He'd trusted her. So had Thane.

Why hadn't Jackson scented her betrayal? Why hadn't he caught the discontent beneath her practical exterior? Sure, she'd often been disapproving, but that was just her nature. He hadn't realized how deep her resentment ran. Or was it love? Were she and Victor in this together?

If so, why not just kill Emily outright?

Unless Victor wanted to make a statement.

Didn't he realize it would cost him his life? He'd seal his fate the second he touched her.

Jackson reached the helicopter and shifted back into his human form, muscles straining as he jumped into the cockpit. He yanked a pair of jeans from the emergency pack he kept in all his vehicles, sliding them on before tossing another pair to Thane. "Here. We'll have to go in fast." She had to be okay.

Thane caught the jeans and tugged them on, eyes gleaming with the same rage that burned through Jackson's blood. "We'll find her."

"We have to." Jackson turned the key, engaging the ignition. The blades began to spin, whipping the snow into a blinding vortex as the engine roared to life. He gripped the controls, heart hammering against his ribs as the helicopter lifted into the swirling snow.

She had to be alive. There was no alternative.

* * *

EMILY'S SENSES clogged with the sharp tang of blood. The coppery scent filled her nose, thick and suffocating. Nadia lay silent, unmoving, her chest barely rising and falling. Her eyelids fluttered once in a while, but the blood soaking her sweater hadn't stopped flowing.

Victor lay flat on the floor on his stomach, blood pooling beneath him and seeping into the cracks of the old wood. Four bullets. Four silver bullets to the heart would kill anybody. Even an Alpha.

Raya had left about an hour ago, and she'd taken the knife with her. So Emily just fought the chains the best she could, not getting an extra inch of freedom.

"Nice try." Raya's boots clip-clopped as she returned, her black clothing dusted with snow, her dark hair clinging to her face.

Emily tore her gaze from Victor's still form and looked up at Raya. "Your plan is insane. Neither pack will let you take over with somebody from the Ghostwind Pack."

Raya stood just inside the doorway, her arms crossed, manic eyes glinting. "I have a plan," she said, her voice disturbingly light. "My plans are the best."

"Jackson's going to kill you for this," Emily said, willing her voice to stay strong despite the trembling in her limbs. Her wrists ached from the cold metal cuffs, the chain biting into her skin with every movement.

"Jackson will never know it was me." Raya smirked. "I'll be back in my own territory just in time for the mining disaster. I'm sure Jackson will be out looking for you," she added with a tilt of her head. "He'll come running home the second he hears about the explosion. His pack is everything to him."

Emily's pulse pounded harder. "Then you think you can kill him?" Jackson wouldn't see the betrayal coming, but still. He was a fighter.

Nadia mumbled from her position on the floor, her voice weak.

"Yeah. Then I'm going to kill him," Raya said, her tone light as if they were discussing a weather forecast. "I'll probably have Bulwark with me."

"Oh, yeah. The new Alpha?" Emily managed to grit out.

"You know it'll never fly, right?" Nadia rasped.

Raya rocked back on her heels, a look of twisted delight dancing across her face. She couldn't seem to care less that her lover lay dead on the floor, blood soaking into the stone beneath him. Emily was fairly certain Victor was gone. His chest hadn't moved in minutes, and those silver veins had crawled across his skin too fast for any wolf shifter to survive.

"You don't understand." Raya's smile widened. "Bulwark has Slate Pack Alpha blood in him. He's from the McGregor family. They were kicked out years ago, and believe me, he wants revenge more than I do."

At least that explained why he'd stabbed Nadia. It hadn't just been a job. It was personal.

"So, he has a plan," Emily said, her mind racing.

"Apparently so," Raya said, her eyes gleaming. "We just worked out the details. We're going to mate and rule both packs. We'll keep them pure. No outsiders. We'll dig deep for slate, including tat his Embervault Mine, and do so efficiently and properly."

"What a lunatic," Nadia muttered, her voice rough with pain.

Unwilling amusement flickered through Emily despite her body ringing in pain. She struggled against the shackles again, but they held firm. "Where is your boy toy right now?" she asked, forcing her voice to steady. If she got free, she had to take him out after Raya.

"He had to return to his pack," Raya said, her tone almost bored. "They're preparing to attack the Granite Pack as soon as the bombs go off in Jackson's mine."

Emily had to warn Jackson somehow. Those poor miners. "You know the other two packs won't let you take over. They have a coalition."

"Oh, they will. They don't have a choice." Raya shrugged. "It'll be two packs against two packs. Erik and Seth may have great fondness for you, but they're not going to let all their soldiers die in a war. Especially since you'll be dead."

"Why aren't I already?" Emily asked. "You could've killed me. Why didn't you?"

Raya's smile vanished. Her shoulders stiffened as she stomped over to Victor's body and kicked him in the shoulder. The body barely moved.

"You were a present for him," she said, her voice quieter now, almost...wistful. "I thought we were on the same page. We agreed we'd take over all the territory. But in the end..." Her voice dropped to a murmur, tinged with something like sorrow. "He just didn't want to kill you. He wasn't strong enough."

Emily's stomach twisted. While she'd never been a Victor fan, he'd tried to do the right thing in the end. Awareness tingled along her thighs and up to her heart, sharp and sudden. Strength. Coming from outside?

Jackson?

"Well," Raya said, "I guess if you weren't a decent present for Victor, you'll be one for me." She lifted the gun, the barrel pointed straight between Emily's eyes.

"Whoa." Emily raised her shackled hands. The cold metal bit into her wrists as panic coated her throat. "You're signing your own death warrant."

"If the Slate Pack learns I've killed you, then they'll know nobody's coming to save them." Raya's tone was calm, final. "I'm sorry, but there's no other alternative but to kill you both." She angled her head, eyes gleaming with a dangerous light. "I think your sister's dead already. I'll shoot her a couple of times just to make sure. Do you want me to do you first so you don't have to watch that?"

Emily blinked once. "How about you release these," she rattled the chains, "and we fight it out? Or are you afraid?"

Raya's teeth flashed in a humorless smile. "I'm not afraid, but I'm also not stupid. You're taller and probably stronger, even with whatever problems you've got going on. I think I'll just shoot you in the head." She settled her stance, the gun steady in her hands.

Emily refused to close her eyes. She let the Alpha blood in her sing, digging deep for every ounce of strength in her body. One more time, she tried to shift, pushing past the pain, the weakness, and the doubt. This time, something broke free inside her. Freedom burned hotly through her muscles and bones. Her body shifted—

Just as a massive black wolf burst through the block windows, glass shattering in every direction, and crashed into Raya.

Raya yelled as she hit the floor, rolling several times before springing to her feet. The gun swung up, aimed at the wolf. Jackson.

He didn't give her a chance.

Leaping across the distance, his fangs slashed through her throat, and the gun clattered to the ground, useless. Her headless body followed a heartbeat later.

A second wolf bounded in. Thane.

Jackson shifted back into his human form. Emily snarled in wolf form, yanking her paws free of the shackles with a metallic clink. She stumbled, her head pounding as though nails had been driven into her skull. With a soft whimper, she shifted back to her human form, dropping to her knees.

"Emily." Jackson rushed toward her, pulling her against his

chest. "How bad are you hurt?" His hands roamed her scalp, searching for injuries.

"Ouch," she hissed, wincing. "Don't push on that."

Jackson swore under his breath as she sagged against him. Her pulse thudded weakly where his hand supported her neck.

"Nadia?" Emily called, craning her head toward her sister.

Nadia groaned from the floor. "What?"

"Are you okay?"

"Nope," Nadia gritted out. "I got stabbed. With silver. Can we go to the healer now?"

Emily dropped and clutched her sister's arm as Jackson stepped away. He crouched beside Victor, rolling him onto his back before placing two fingers to his neck.

"He's dead," Jackson confirmed grimly. "Did he kidnap you?"

"No." Emily's voice wavered. "He actually tried to help us." She sucked in air. "There are explosives at the mine. You need to get everyone out."

Jackson's head jerked.

Thane looked wildly around. "I'll find a phone." He ran out of the room.

The room tilted as Emily's vision wavered. She swayed, her knees buckling. The shift had drained her. She still had silver in her system, and her earlier attempts to cut through the shackles hadn't helped. Blood trickled sluggishly down her wrists.

"Damn it," she muttered before her legs gave out.

Jackson caught her before she hit the floor.

Again.

A week later...

EMILY ROCKED in the chair in the corner of the refined living room, her father resting on the sofa, and Nadia in a matching chair. Caidrik and Miliki flanked the doorway, standing silent and watchful. She missed Jackson. He'd been gone for a couple of days, making sure the Granite Pack was secure. They'd found all the explosives in time, and no one had been hurt.

Her gaze drifted to her father. His color had returned somewhat, though he still barely had an appetite. "How are you feeling?" she asked softly.

"I'm fine," he replied with a tired smile. "You?"

"I feel pretty good," she admitted. The first couple of days after her kidnapping had been rough, but strength now coursed through her, deeper and more solid than before. She'd sent blood samples to Dr. Gwen but hadn't heard back yet. Still, something inside her felt like she was healing. "Nadia?"

Nadia stirred in her chair and winced. "Just dandy," she muttered. The silver still lingered in her system, slowing her recovery, but she was alive, and that was what mattered. They'd spent the week trying to figure out how to protect the Slate Pack, and no good answers had arisen.

The door opened, and Emily knew who it was before she looked. Her body responded instantly, her heart picking up its pace. "Jackson." She sat up straighter, warmth spreading through her chest.

"Yeah, I'm back." He stepped inside with snow clinging to his boots. His eyes glinted a mysterious blue, like the sky before a storm. "I have good news."

She leaned forward, pulse racing. "You do?"

"Dr. Gwen gave me the results first." His smile widened. "The mating's working. Your blood shows that the genetic mutation is repairing itself. The recessive gene that caused the illness is no longer active, and your DNA markers are stabilizing. Essentially, the combination of my Alpha genetics and the mating process is correcting the mutation at a cellular level."

Emily exhaled slowly, absorbing the words. "I thought so." Relief and joy warmed her from the inside out.

Jackson glanced around at the room's other occupants. "You're all the walking wounded."

Caidrik snorted from his post. Bruises still shadowed his neck and side, and he moved stiffly from being hit by the truck, but he kept close to Nadia, his attention rarely straying from her. Apparently, when Caidrik took on a task, he took it seriously.

Emily found herself wondering who he really was and what his story might be. He didn't seem like the kind of male who stuck around for long.

A wave of energy stirred the air, sharp enough that Emily stiffened, and Jackson did the same. Power brushed against her skin, tugging at her senses.

"Philip Nightsom, come out, please," a voice called from outside.

"Ah, crap," her father muttered. He stood with a soft groan, dressed in slacks and a golf shirt instead of his usual suit. Gripping his cane, he limped toward the door. "I figured this was coming."

Emily glanced at Jackson. "We need a plan."

"My pack will contract to protect yours once I have enough members. I'm adding as we speak, and someday I can take over here if needed," Jackson said. "I don't know if your members will want that."

It was all they had.

Together, they stepped onto the porch. About thirty-five pack members stood on the snowy front lawn, mostly heads of families and soldiers. Their breath puffed white in the cold air, eyes somber with expectation.

Raul Nelson stepped forward. A sturdy man with a miner's build and weathered hands, he was both a foreman and a respected town leader. His gaze swept across the gathered pack before settling on Philip.

"We need an Alpha," Raul said firmly. "And we need a plan. What do you have?"

Philip tossed his cane back into the house. "We're going to reach an agreement with the Granite Pack for an alliance of protection. This will be just until I regain my strength."

A low rumble started in the crowd.

Raul shook his head, his jaw tight. "I'm sorry, Philip, but no. The four packs are separate for a reason."

Emily's hopes crashed. What was she going to do? "I'll step up as the Alpha." She didn't dare look at Jackson. "I'm no longer ill, and I can fight."

The crowd stirred again, their murmurs blending into a steady hum of dissent. Raul raised a hand, silencing them as his gaze settled on her. His eyes and voice were not unkind, but they held truth. "Emily, you mated the Alpha of the Granite Pack. Your allegiance has to be to him. It can't be to us. We need someone who's fully committed to our pack."

"I'm in," Philip said, though his voice trembled with fatigue.

Raul's sorrow was unmistakable. "Philip, you won't be well for quite a while—if ever. We all know the Ghostwind Pack will come rumbling. We've already been approached by Bulwark McGregor."

Nadia gasped, her breath sharp. "That asshole stabbed me in the back."

Raul ducked his chin. "I know. But he has Alpha blood in him, and he's strong. They've been adding to their pack. If he brings the Ghostwind Pack in, they'll take over and protect us."

Emily stepped forward, her pulse thudding painfully. "You know that's what they want. They don't want to be part of a pack. They want to rule."

Raul shook his head slowly, and many of the pack members dropped their gazes to the snow-covered ground.

"I'm healthy," Nadia said, her voice firm. "And I'm not mated. I'll step up as the Alpha of this pack."

Raul stared at her for several moments, his gaze serious. "Nadia, we all like you a lot, but you're not a fighter." His gaze flicked toward Jackson and the other outsiders. "You wouldn't survive the trials. You know that."

Emily stiffened. "You know about the trials?"

Raul nodded. "Yes. Every over a hundred-years-old knows about them because we were alive when Philip took over. But we're all sworn to secrecy until a new Alpha wants to take over."

"I'll still try to survive any such trials." Nadia lifted her chin.

Something inside Emily twisted and broke. She couldn't let her sister go to her death. Neither of them fully understood what the trials entailed, but she knew one thing: Nadia had spent her life farming, not fighting. Emily could not let her die trying to save the pack.

Raul shook his head, his voice heavy with resignation. "We're going to accept Bulwark's offer of the Ghostwinds protecting us if he becomes our Alpha. I don't see that we have any alternative."

"You do." A deep voice cut through the cold air with the precision of a blade. Caidrik stepped forward, standing beside Nadia. His eyes, sharp as flint, met Raul's without hesitation.

Emily looked at him, then at Jackson, who only shrugged.

"What are you talking about?" Nadia asked, her eyes narrowed.

Caidrik's low voice rumbled across the clearing. "I read the entire grimoire of this pack. A champion can step up for you to endure the trials."

Emily turned to her father. "Is that true?"

Philip's brow furrowed. "I don't know."

"Are you sure the grimoire says that?" she pressed.

"Yes," Caidrik said. "I read the whole thing. Like I told you, I like puzzles."

Raul exchanged uncertain glances with the other pack members. "I don't know. I mean, you're not an Alpha."

"To be an Alpha's champion, I don't need to have Alpha blood." Caidrik's chin lifted. "But I do have Alpha blood, thus if I survive, I become the Alpha," he said, his voice firm as he cut a glance toward Philip, then back to Raul. "My full name is Caidrik McGregor."

Emily nearly sagged against Jackson as Nadia's face paled.

"The idiot who stabbed me was your brother?" Nadia snarled.

"Half-brother," Caidrik corrected. "I'm not with the Ghost-wind Pack. Anymore."

Jackson growled. "You kept that information from me, old friend."

Caidrik shrugged. "Didn't find it important. I can mask my

scent like all Alphas, and I thought the Ghostwinds were in my past for good."

Emily's pulse hammered.

Caidrik scanned the gathered faces, his gaze unflinching. "Philip, it's up to you. If you want me gone, I'll leave. But I can survive the trials, whatever they might entail, and I can protect you from the Ghostwind Pack."

Philip's mouth flattened into a hard line. "We kicked the McGregor family out of the pack two hundred years ago."

"I'm aware," Caidrik said dryly.

Emily searched desperately for another option but found none. "Nadia?" she asked softly.

Nadia exhaled and crossed her arms. "I don't know. If you succeed, does that mean I become the Alpha?" She sounded more sad than interested in that fact.

"No," Caidrik said. "If I survive the trials, I become the Alpha. You don't want the job and would spend your entire life fighting off challengers. I'll take it."

"So, I'm not necessary." Nadia put her hands on her hips.

He turned to face her, ignoring everyone else. "Wrong. You're part of the deal. If I become the Alpha for this pack, you become my mate."

"Whoa." Emily lifted both hands. "My sister is not mating someone as a deal or contract."

Caidrik's gaze flicked from Emily to Jackson. "It worked for you."

Fire lit Nadia's eyes as she stepped forward. "If I refuse?"

"Then I walk away," Caidrik said simply. "And the Ghostwind Pack will come."

Philip stepped forward as if to reject the offer, but Nadia's voice cut through the air.

"I'll do it," she said.

Emily's chest squeezed painfully. "Nadia, are you sure?"

"Yes." Nadia's eyes blazed a deep onyx. "To save the pack and keep the Ghostwinds away? Yes."

Emily turned to Jackson, who stood beside her with his arms crossed, his eyes measuring Caidrik with the weight of an Alpha assessing a potential rival.

Finally, he nodded. "I don't think it's up to the Granite Pack, obviously, but we would accept Caidrik as the Alpha of the Slate Pack and a member of the Stope Packs Coalition—should he survive whatever the hell these trials are."

Emily took a deep breath and looked at her sister. "Are you sure?"

Nadia stared at Caidrik. "Yes. Though he just might regret this demand."

"All right." Jackson stepped forward, sliding an arm over Emily's shoulders. "We need to get going, Em. We have work to do."

The assembled group began to disperse, but not before most of the members stopped to hug Emily and offer their congratulations.

"I want to throw you a bridal shower in my new home once you set the date," Bussy told her with a wink.

Emily blushed, her cheeks heating. They hadn't talked about a wedding or even mentioned marriage, but she didn't have the heart to correct the older woman.

Finally, Emily hugged her father and sister goodbye, promising they'd meet up in a couple of weeks for dinner. Their territories might be far apart, but she had ideas. The Embervault Mine could serve as a meeting point for both packs. There was no reason they shouldn't strengthen their alliance just like Seth and Erik had.

When Jackson flew her home, snowflakes drifted softly against the helicopter's windshield, and for the first time in days, the wind kept its peace. Emily let herself relax as Jackson took her hand and held it the entire way. Her body felt stronger, her mind clearer. There was no doubt the Alpha male beside her had her heart. But they'd never talked about love.

Maybe they didn't need to. Maybe they had something more. A shared history, shared blood, and a future that stretched out as far as the mountains themselves.

Jackson landed the helicopter and hopped out, circling around to her side. He lifted her down with ease.

"You do like carrying me around," she teased.

"I truly do," he replied with a grin.

As they crossed toward the truck, snowflakes sparkled like diamonds in the air, catching the golden light filtering through the forest. Jackson paused, looking up at the sky. "The clouds are clearing and the moon will soon show."

"I know. I can feel it." Energy hummed beneath her skin, the moon's power flowing through her veins—strong and sure.

Jackson turned toward her, his eyes a thousand shades of blue. "I didn't believe in love until I met you."

Emily stilled, her breath catching in her throat. "You believe in love now?"

"I do." His voice was low and rough with truth. "The second you were taken, I knew it. I've loved you since the first time I kissed you, Emily. I've thought about you every day since. I knew you were meant to be mine."

He dropped to one knee, the snow drifting up around him as he moved. Reaching into his coat pocket, he pulled out a small velvet box and flipped it open.

"I know it's old-fashioned," he said, his voice rough with emotion, "but will you marry me?"

Emily looked down at the ring, her breath catching in her throat. The solitaire gemstone mirrored the deep black of her eyes, surrounded by platinum and jewels that shimmered in the snowy light. It was stunning. Perfect in every way. Her heart swelled, the world narrowing to the man kneeling before her.

"Yes," she whispered.

Jackson slipped the ring onto her finger, and it fit perfectly, as if it had been waiting for her all along. She blinked against the rush of tears that threatened to fall.

"I love you, Jackson," she said softly.

"I know." His lips curved into a smile just before he pulled her into his arms and kissed her, deep and claiming. Heat rushed through her, grounding her as much as it set her soul free.

When he finally pulled back, she was breathless. "You know?"

"Well, I hoped." Jackson flashed his teeth in a grin. A reminder of the predator beneath his skin. But all she saw was the love in his eyes.

"Come on, Em." He took her hand in his. "Let's go home."

* * *

READY FOR THE conclusion to the Stope Packs series? Preorder Enforcer and get the special preorder price of $4.99. Prices will revert to regular price on release week:

Loyalty is fragile. Blood is currency. And the biggest threat comes from within.

Caidrik McGregor has spent his life as a mercenary, fighting for those who could afford his blade and walking away before the dust settled. Now, he's been offered something far more dangerous—a chance to claim the Alpha seat of the Slate Pack, the same pack that cast out his family generations ago. To take it, he must survive the brutal trials, silence the doubters, and crush the rivals waiting for him to fail. The prize isn't just power. It's Nadia Hodge, the newly discovered daughter of the current Alpha, bound to him if he survives.

Nadia never needed a pack, let alone an Alpha deciding her fate. She didn't grow up with their rules, wasn't raised to play their games, and has no intention of letting a hardened outsider control her future. But war is coming, led by Caidrik's half-brother, and someone inside their own ranks is leaving bodies behind. If she wants to protect the people who now call her family, she may have no choice but to stand at Caidrik's side.

With enemies circling and trust in short supply, Caidrik and Nadia must decide what matters most—vengeance, power, or the unexpected pull of a bond neither of them saw coming.

* * *

CHECK out the newest Dark Romance, One Dark Kiss , a sexy retelling of Snow White! Here's a quick excerpt:

Rosalie

Alone, I cross my legs again beneath the intimidating metal table secured to the floor, feeling as out of place as a raven in a nursery rhyme. The heat clunks and whispers from a grate in the ceiling but fails to warm the interview room, and when the door finally opens, the heavy frame scrapes against the grimy cement floor.

My spine naturally straightens, and my chin lifts as my client stalks inside, his hands cuffed to a chain secured around his narrow waist. He doesn't shuffle. Or walk. Or saunter.

No. This man…stalks.

His gaze rakes me, and I mean, *rakes* me. Black eyes—deep and dark—glint with more than one threat of violence in their depths. He kicks back the lone metal chair opposite me and sits in one fluid motion. The scent of motor oil in fresh rain, something all male, wafts toward me.

I swallow.

The guard, a burly man with gray hair, stares at me, concern in his eyes.

"Please remove his cuffs," I say, my focus not leaving my client.

My client. I don't practice criminal law. Never have and don't want to.

The guard hesitates. "Miss, I—"

"I appreciate it." I make my voice as authoritative as possible, considering I'm about to crap my pants. Or rather, my best navy-blue pencil skirt bought on clearance at the Women's Center Thrift Store. I don't live there, but I'm happy to shop there. Rich people give away good items.

In a jangle of metal, the guard hitches toward us, releases the cuffs, and turns on his scuffed boot toward the door. "Want me to stay inside?"

"No, thank you." I wait until he shrugs, exits, and shuts the door. "Mr. Sokolov? I'm Rosalie Mooncrest, your new attorney from Cage and Lion."

"What happened to my old attorney?" His voice is the rasp of a blade on a sharpening stone.

I clear my throat and focus only on his eyes and not the tattoo of a panther prowling across the side of his neck, amethyst eyes glittering. "Mr. Molasses died in a car accident a month ago." Molasses was a partner in the firm, and he represented Alexei in the criminal trial that had led to a guilty verdict. "I take it he wasn't in touch with you often?"

"No." Alexei leans back and finishes removing the cuffs from his wrists to slap onto the table. "You're responsible for my being brought to this minimum-security section of this prison?"

Actually, my firm has juice and a named partner had made this happen. "Yes, and it's temporary. You're back to your normal cell block after this meeting."

His chin lifts. "So this plush locale for our conference is for you, princess? The prestigious law firm doesn't want you dirtied by the bowels of this place?"

Probably true. "I'm here to help you, Mr. Sokolov."

His eyes glitter sharper than the panther's on his neck. "Don't call me that name again."

I frown. "Sokolov?"

"Yes. It's Alexei. No mister."

Fair enough. I can't help but study him. Unruly black hair, unfathomable dark eyes, golden-brown skin, and bone structure chipped out of a mountain with a finely sharpened tool. Brutally rugged, the angles of his face reveal a primal strength that's ominously beautiful. The deadliest predators in life usually are.

Awareness filters through me. I don't like it.

Worse yet, he's studying me right back, as if he has Superman's x-ray vision and no problem using it. He lingers inappropriately on my breasts beneath my crisp white blouse before sliding to my face, his gaze a rough scrape I can feel. "You fuck your way through law school?"

My mouth drops open for the smallest of seconds. "Are you insane?"

"Insanity is relative. It depends on who has who locked in what cage," he drawls.

Did he just quote Ray Bradbury? "You might want to remember that I'm here to help you."

"Hence my question. Not that I'm judging. If you want to do the entire parole board to get me out, then don't hold back. If that isn't your plan, then I'd like to know that you understand the law."

It's official. Alexei Sokolov is an asshole. "Listen, Mr. Sokolov—"

"That name. You don't want me to tell you again." His threat is softly spoken.

A shiver tries to take me, so I shift my weight, hiding my reaction. I stare him directly in the eyes, as one does with any bully. "Why? What are you going to do?" I jerk my head toward the door, where no doubt the guard awaits on the other side.

Alexei leans toward me and metal clangs. "Peaflower? I can have you over this table, your skirt hiked up, and spank your ass raw before the dumbass guard can find his keys, much less gather the backup he'd need to get you free. You won't sit for a week. Maybe two." His gaze warms. "Now that's a very pretty blush."

"That's my planning a murder expression," I retort instantly, my cheeks flaming hot.

His lip curls for the briefest of moments in almost a smile. "Women who look like you don't usually have a brain."

My eyebrows shoot up so quickly it's a shock a migraine doesn't follow. He did not just say that. "You are one backass-ward son of a bitch," I blurt out, completely forgetting any sense of professionalism.

That smile tries to take hold and almost makes it. Not quite, though. "Fuck, you're a contradiction." He flattens a hand on the table. A large, tattooed, dangerous looking hand. "As a rule, a beautiful woman is a terrible disappointment."

Now he's quoting freakin Carl Jung? "You must've had a lot of time to read here in prison…the last seven years."

"I have." A hardness invades his eyes. "You any good at your job?"

The most inappropriate humor takes me, and I look around the room. "Does it matter? I don't see a plenitude of counselors in here trying to help you."

"Big word. Plenitude. I would've gone with cornucopia. Has a better sound to it."

I need to regain control of this situation. "Listen, Mr.—"

He stiffens and I stop. Cold.

We look at each other, and I swear, the room itself has a heartbeat that rebounds around us. I don't want to back down. But also, I know in every cell of my being, he isn't issuing idle threats. A man like him never bluffs.

Surprisingly, triumph that I refrained from using his last name doesn't light his eyes. Instead, contemplation and approval?

I *really* don't like that.

My legs tremble like I've run ten miles, and my lungs are failing to catch up. I suppose anybody would feel like this if trapped with a hell beast in a small cage. There's more than fear to my reaction. Adrenaline has that effect on people. That must be it. I reach into my briefcase and retrieve several pieces of paper. "If you want me as your attorney, you need to sign this retainer agreement so I can file a Notice of Appearance with the court."

"And if I don't?"

I place the papers on the cold table. "Then have a nice life." I meet his stare evenly.

"My funds are low. I don't suppose you'll take cigarettes or sex in trade?"

Is that amusement in his eyes? That had better not be amusement. I examine his broad shoulders and, no doubt, impressive chest beneath the orange jumpsuit. How can he look sexy in orange? Plus, the man hasn't been with a woman in seven years—he'd be on fire. A little part of me, one I'll never admit to, considers the offer just for the, no doubt, multiple and wild orgasms. "I don't smoke and you're not my type. But no worries. My firm is taking your case pro bono until we unbind your trust fund."

He latches onto the wrong part of the statement. "What's your type?"

I inhale through my nose, trying to keep a handle on my temper.

"Don't tell me," he continues, his gaze probing deep. "Three-piece suit, Armani, luxury vehicles?"

"Actually, that's my best friend's type," I drawl. Well, if you add in guns, the Irish mafia, and a frightening willingness to kill.

Alexei scratches the whiskers across his cut jaw. "Right. When was the last time you were with an actual man? You know, somebody who doesn't ask for guidance every step of the way?"

That fact that I don't remember is not one I'll share. My thighs heat, and my temper sparks. "Was this approach charming seven years ago?"

"Not really. Though I didn't need to be charming back then."

True. He was the heir to one of the four most powerful social media companies in the world before he went to prison. Apparently, his family had deserted him immediately. "You might want to give it a try now."

His eyes warm to dark embers, rendering me temporarily speechless. "You don't think I can charm the panties off you?"

"All right. You need to dial it down." I hold out a hand and press down on imaginary air. "A lot."

Heat swells from him. Somehow. "Dial what down?"

"You," I hiss. "All of this. The obnoxious, rudely sexist, prowling panther routine. Use your brain, if you have one. It's our first meeting, and you're driving me crazy. You want me on your side."

"I'd rather have you under me."

I shut my eyes and slam both index fingers to the corners, pressing in. This is unbelievable.

"Getting a headache? I know a remedy for that."

I make the sound of a strangled cat.

His laugh is warm. Rich. Deep.

Jolting, I open my eyes. The laugh doesn't fit with the criminal vibe. It's enthralling.

He stops.

I miss the sound immediately. Maybe I need a vacation.

Using one finger, he draws the paper across the table. "Pen."

I fumble in my briefcase for a blue pen and hand it over.

He signs the retainer quickly and shoves it back at me. "What's the plan?"

The switch in topics gives me whiplash. Even so, I step on

firm ground again. "The prosecuting attorney in your case was just arrested for blackmail, peddling influence, and extortion… along with the judge, his co-conspirator, who presided over your trial and sentenced you."

His expression doesn't alter. "You can secure my freedom?"

That's my plan, but I don't want to raise his hopes. "I don't know. My best guess is that I can secure you a new trial."

"Will I be free for the duration?"

"I'll make a motion to the court the second I leave here but can't guarantee the outcome." I tilt my head. "Your family's influence would be helpful."

His chin lowers in an intimidating move. "I don't have a family. Don't mention them again."

I blink. "One more comment."

"Go ahead."

"I'm sorry about your brother's death." His younger brother, rather his half brother, was killed a month ago, possibly by my friend's boyfriend, if one could call Thorn Beathach a boyfriend.

Alexei just stares at me.

I feel like a puzzle being solved. "There's a chance his death was part of some sort of social media turf war against Thorn Beathach, who owns Malice Media." Alexei's family owns a rival social media platform, and from what I understand, it's war between them all.

"So?"

This is a mite awkward. "Thorn is currently dating my best friend, so if there's a conflict of interest, I want you to know about it." Not that anybody would ever catch Thorn, if he had killed Alexei's brother after the man had injured Alana. I'm still not sure he was the killer, anyway.

"Are you finished mentioning my family?" Alexei's tone strongly suggests that I am.

"Yes," I whisper.

He cocks his head. "How many criminal trials have you won?"

"None," I say instantly. It's crucial to be honest with clients. "I haven't lost any, either."

His head tips up and he watches me from half-closed lids. "You're in charge of the pro bono arm of the firm?"

"No."

"Why you, then?"

It's a fair question as well as a smart one. "I've never lost in a civil trial, so the partners assigned me your case, even though this is criminal procedure."

"Why?"

"Because I'm good and they want you free." I shrug. "This is positive exposure for the firm." Which is what my boss, Jacqueline Lion, told me when assigning me to the docket. "We have several verdicts being overturned because of the judge's corruption, and yours came up, being the most high profile. Losing your case harmed the firm seven years ago."

His nostrils flare. "The firm? The loss hurt *the firm*?"

"Yes." Damn, he's intimidating. Do I want him free to roam the streets? "This is a chance to fix the damage caused."

"And promote you to partner?" he guesses.

My life is none of his business. "I'm good at my job, Alexei." Yeah, I don't use his last name. "You can go with outside counsel. I'll rip up your retainer agreement if you want."

"I want you."

I hear the double entendre and ignore it. "Then it's my way and you'll follow my directives."

Now he smiles. Full on, straight teeth, shocking dimple in his right cheek.

Everything inside me short circuits and flashes electricity into places sparks don't belong.

He taps his fingers on the table. "I signed the agreement, and this means you work for me. Correct?"

"Yes." But I call the shots.

He moves so suddenly to plant his hand over mine, that I freeze. "You need to learn now that I'm in charge of every situation. Do you understand?"

I try to free myself and fail. His large palm is warm, heavy, and scarred over my skin, with the hard metal table beneath it a shockingly cold contrast. My lungs stutter and hot air fills them. "Whatever game you're playing, stop it right now."

His hand easily covers mine, and his fingers keep me trapped in sizzling heat. "I don't play games, Peaflower. Learn that now."

"Peaflower?" I choke out, leaving my hand beneath his because I have no choice.

"Your eyes," he murmurs. "The blue dissolves into violet like the Butterfly Pea flower. A man could find solace from everlasting torment just staring into those velvety depths."

I have no words for him. Are there words? Scarred, barely uncuffed, and intense, he just whispered the most romantic words imaginable. And he's a killer. Just because the judge was corrupt doesn't mean Alexei hadn't committed cold-blooded murder. Two things can be true at once. "We need to keep this professional, if you want me to help you."

He releases me and stands. "Guard," he calls out.

My hand feels chilled and lonely.

Keys jangle on the other side of the door.

"Rosalie, this is your out. If you tear up the retainer, I'll find another lawyer. If you stay, if you decide to represent me, there's no quitting. You're in this for the duration. Tell me you get me." Fire burns in his eyes now.

I stand, even though my knees are knocking together. "I'm doing my job."

"Just so we understand each other."

The door opens, and the same guard from before moves inside, pauses, and visibly finds his balls before securing the cuffs on Alexei, who watches me the entire time. He allows the guard to lead him to the door.

Once there, he looks over his shoulder. "I hope you stick with me in this. Also, you might want to conduct a background check on Miles Molasses from your firm. He was a co-conspirator to the judge and prosecutor." His teeth flash. "How convenient that he just died in an accident. Right?"

ACKNOWLEDGMENTS

Every author, much like a wolf, needs a strong pack. I'm beyond grateful for mine—not only for cheering me on with enthusiastic howls but also for tolerating my truly questionable sense of humor. I owe you all one. Or several.

Big Tone, my own grumpy-sunshine hero. Your patience, strength, and ability to put up with my writing marathons (and the inevitable snack shortages that come with them) make you nothing short of legendary. I'm incredibly lucky to have you in my corner—especially since yo

Gabe, who channels the essence of the wolf and the heart of a warrior every time he steps onto the football field. Watching you play is a thrill, and I have no doubt you'll dominate every pack you're part of—just don't start howling during team huddles.

Karlina, an artistic powerhouse whose creative vision is as striking as the most vivid shifter tale. Your talent knows no bounds, and I can't wait to see the magic you unleash on the world. Just don't let Hollywood tame you.

Asha Hossain of Asha Hossain Designs, for a cover so mesmerizing it practically compels readers to pick up this book —no hypnotic Alpha stare needed.

Chelle Olson of Literally Addicted to Detail, whose edits illuminate the story like moonlight through the trees. Without you, some scenes might have wandered off into the woods, never to return.

Stella Bloom, who brings this world to life with a voice as

smooth and captivating as a wolf's midnight prowl. If story-telling were a supernatural ability, you'd have a gift straight from the fates.

Caitlin Blasdell, my incredible agent, whose guidance has kept me from getting lost in the wilderness of publishing. Without you, I'd probably still be circling the same plot points, wondering how I got there.

Anissa Beatty, my assistant and the fearless leader of Rebecca's Rebels, whose organizational skills rival the sharp instincts of an Alpha tracking their prey. If deadlines were a rogue threat, I know you'd have them handled.

Rebecca's Rebels—Joan Lai, Gabi Brockelsby, Heather Frost, Kimberly Frost, Madison Fairbanks, Karen Clementi, Leanna Feazel, and Asmaa Qayyum—your keen eyes and sharp feedback are the reason this book stands strong. Without you, some chapters might have ended up as total train wrecks.

Book Brush and Writer Space, for spreading the word about my books far and wide, making sure they find their perfect readers.

To my unwavering support pack, who always have my back and make sure I don't lose my mind: Gail and Jim English, Kathy and Herbie Zanetti, Debbie and Travis Smith, Stephanie and Don West, Jessica and Jonah Namson, and Chelli and Jason Younker—you all mean the world to me.

And last but never least, to you, the reader—because without you, this book would just be words howling into the void. I apologize for the puns... but let's be honest, I was never going to resist them.

Keep running wild!

READING ORDER

I know a lot of you like the exact reading order for a series, so here's the exact reading order as of the release of this book, although if you read most novels out of order, it's okay.

<u>GRIMM BARGAINS</u>

1. One Cursed Rose
2. One Dark Kiss
3. One Shattered Crown

<u>KNIFE'S EDGE, ALASKA SERIES</u>

1. Dead of Winter
2. Thaw of Spring

<u>DARK PROTECTORS</u>

1. Fated
2. Claimed
3. Tempted Novella

4. Hunted
5. Consumed
6. Provoked
7. Twisted Novella
8. Shadowed
9. Tamed Novella
10. Marked
11. Wicked Ride
12. Wicked Edge
13. Wicked Burn
14. Talen Novella
15. Wicked Kiss
16. Wicked Bite
17. Teased novella
18. Tricked novella
19. Tangled novella
20. Vampire's Faith (**A great entry point for series.**)
21. Demon's Mercy
22. Vengeance novella
23. Alpha's Promise
24. Hero's Haven
25. Vixen novella
26. Guardian's Grace
27. Vampire novella
28. Rebel's Karma
29. Immortal's Honor
30. A Vampire's Kiss novella
31. Garrett's Destiny
32. Warrior's Hope
33. A Vampire's Mate novella
34. Prince of Darkness
35. Eye of the Cat
36. Heart of the Hunter

STOPE PACKS (wolf shifters)

1. Wolf
2. Alpha
3. Shifter
4. Predator
5. Enforcer

LAUREL SNOW SERIES

1. You Can Run
2. You Can Hide
3. You Can Die
4. You Can Kill
5. You Can Scream

DEEP OPS SERIES

1. Hidden
2. Taken Novella
3. Fallen
4. Shaken (in Pivot Anthology)
5. Broken
6. Driven
7. Unforgiven
8. Frostbitten
9. Unforgotten

THE ANNA ALBERTINI FILES

1. Disorderly Conduct
2. Bailed Out
3. Adverse Possession
4. Holiday Rescue novella

   5. Santa's Subpoena
   6. Holiday Rogue novella
   7. Tessa's Trust
   8. Holiday Rebel novella
   9. Habeas Corpus
  10. Celtic Justice

SIN BROTHERS/BLOOD BROTHERS

1. Forgotten Sins
2. Sweet Revenge
3. Blind Faith
4. Total Surrender
5. Deadly Silence
6. Lethal Lies
7. Twisted Truths

SCORPIUS SYNDROME SERIES

Scorpius Syndrome/The Brigade Novellas

1. Scorpius Rising
2. Blaze Erupting
3. Power Surging - TBA
4. Hunter Advancing - TBA

Scorpius Syndrome NOVELS

1. Mercury Striking
2. Shadow Falling
3. Justice Ascending
4. Storm Gathering
5. Winter Igniting
6. Knight Awakening

MONTANA MAVERICK SERIES

1. Against the Wall
2. Under the Covers
3. Rising Assets
4. Over the Top
5. Holding the Reins

Redemption, WY

1. Rescue Cowboy Style (Novella in the Lone Wolf Anthology)
2. Rescue Hero Style (Novella in the Peril Anthology)
3. Rescue Rancher Style (Novella in the Cowboy Anthology)
4. Book # 1 launch - subscribe to my newsletter for more information about the new series.

ABOUT THE AUTHOR

New York Times, USA Today, Publisher's Weekly and Wall Street Journal and Amazon #1 bestselling author Rebecca Zanetti has published more than eighty novels and novellas, which have been translated into several languages, with millions of copies sold world-wide. Her books have received Publisher's Weekly, Library Journal, and Kirkus starred reviews, favorable Washington Post and New York Times Book Reviews, and have been included in Amazon best books of the year.

Rebecca has ridden in a locked Chevy trunk, has asked the unfortunate delivery guy to release her from a set of handcuffs, and has discovered the best silver mine shafts in which to bury a body...all in the name of research. Honest. Find Rebecca at: RebeccaZanetti.com

Made in United States
Troutdale, OR
11/05/2025

41274824R10204